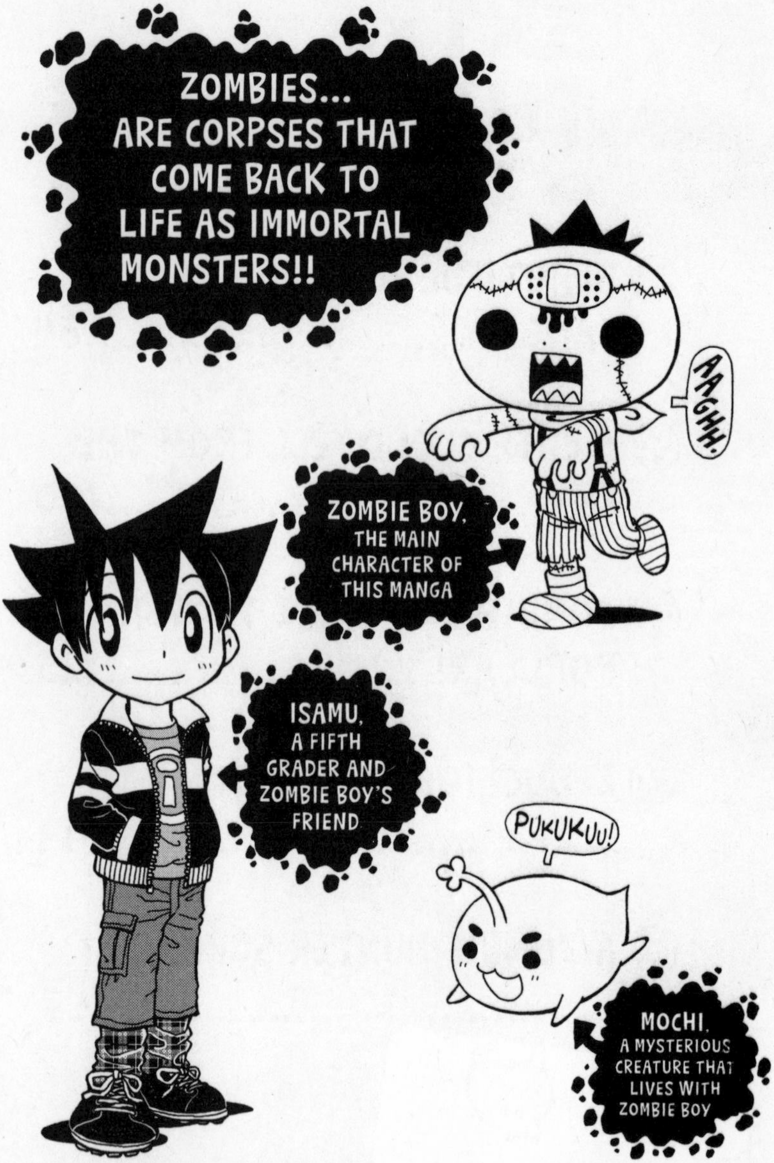
ZOMBIES... ARE CORPSES THAT COME BACK TO LIFE AS IMMORTAL MONSTERS!!
AAGHH.
ZOMBIE BOY, THE MAIN CHARACTER OF THIS MANGA
ISAMU, A FIFTH GRADER AND ZOMBIE BOY'S FRIEND
PUKUKUU!
MOCHI, A MYSTERIOUS CREATURE THAT LIVES WITH ZOMBIE BOY

ZOMBiE BOY'S METAMORPHOSiS COLLECTiON

URCHIN ZOMBIE BOY

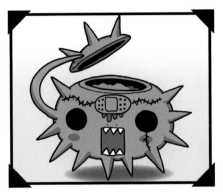

Just like actual urchins, this zombie lives in the ocean. He's always wanted to be as premium an item as real urchins, so he works hard at it every day. His goal is to grow more spines. If you catch one, he'll feed you his insides himself, but it doesn't taste anywhere near as good as genuine urchin roe. If he gets angry, he starts hurling himself around, so be careful.

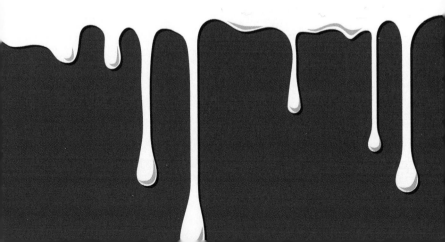

YASUNARI NAGATOSHI

Thank you for buying the fifth volume
of *Zo Zo Zombie*!! We're now into my
least favorite season again. Every year,
the cold sinks deeper into my bones
and I dislike going out more and more.
Spring, come soooon!!

ZO ZO ZOMBIE
VOL. 5

SHOPPING ON THE WAY HOME

CROSSING

SHIKABANE MARKET

YASUNARI NAGATOSHI

TABLE OF CONTENTS

MANGA

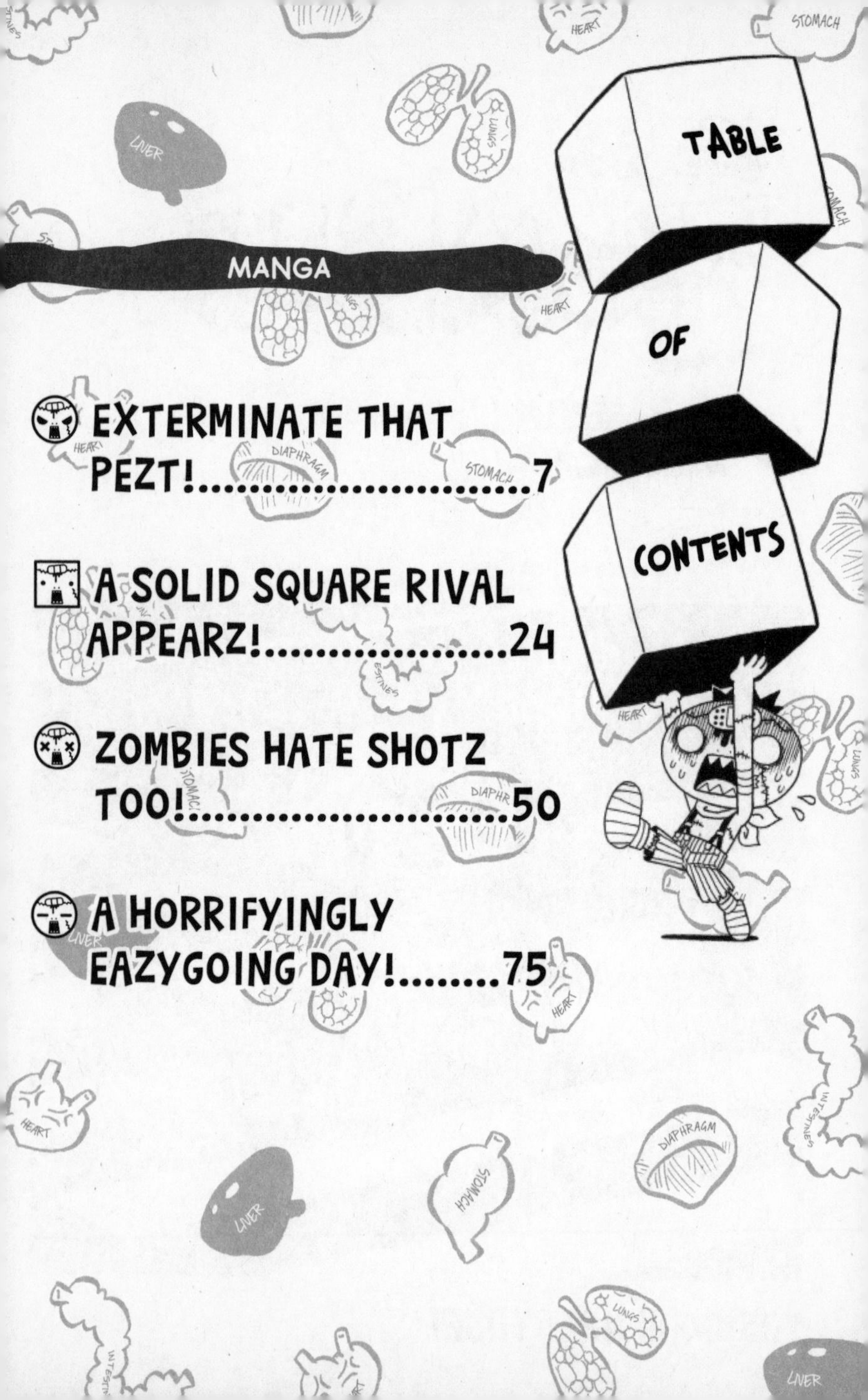

EXTERMINATE THAT PEZT!

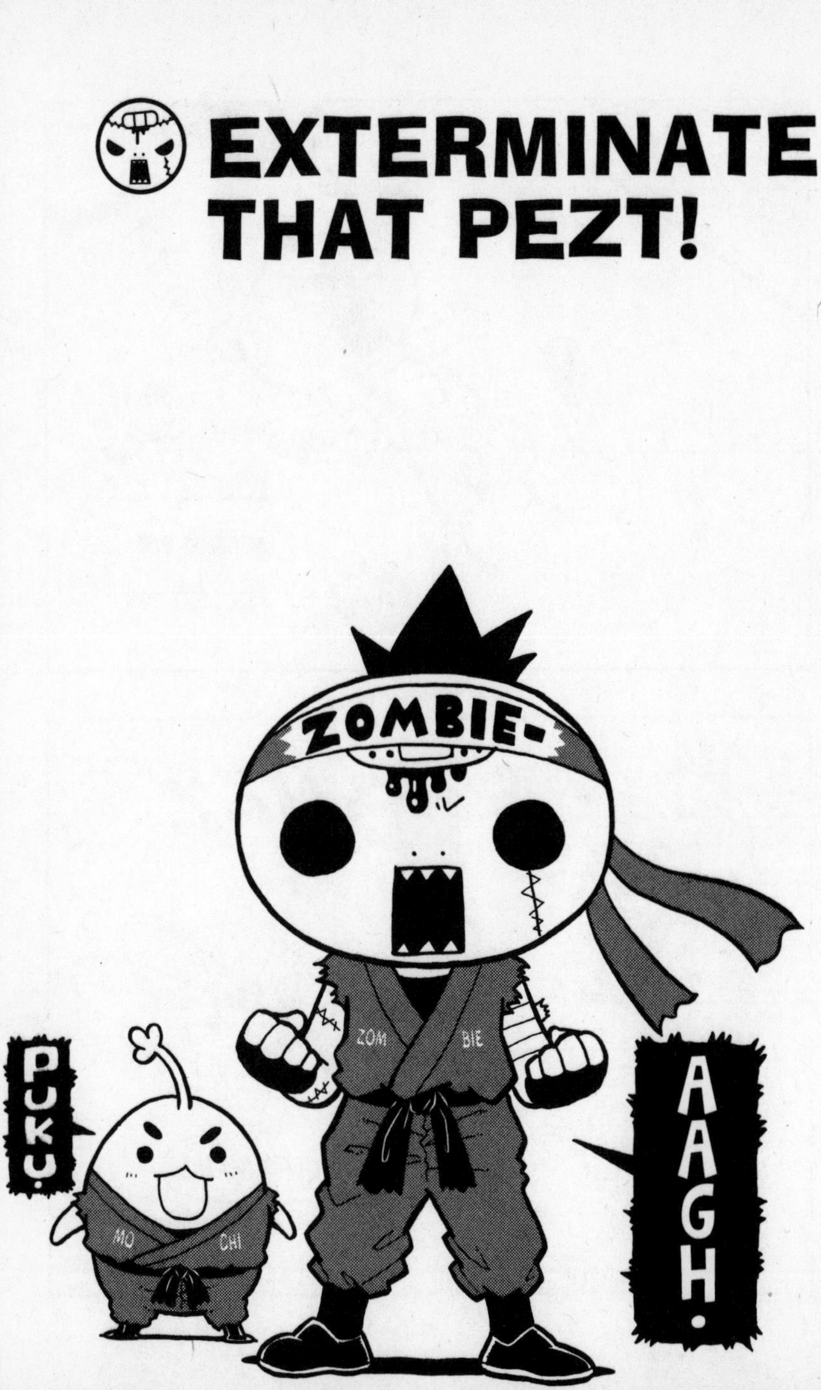
ZOMBIE-
ZOM BIE
AAGH!
PUKU!
MO CHI

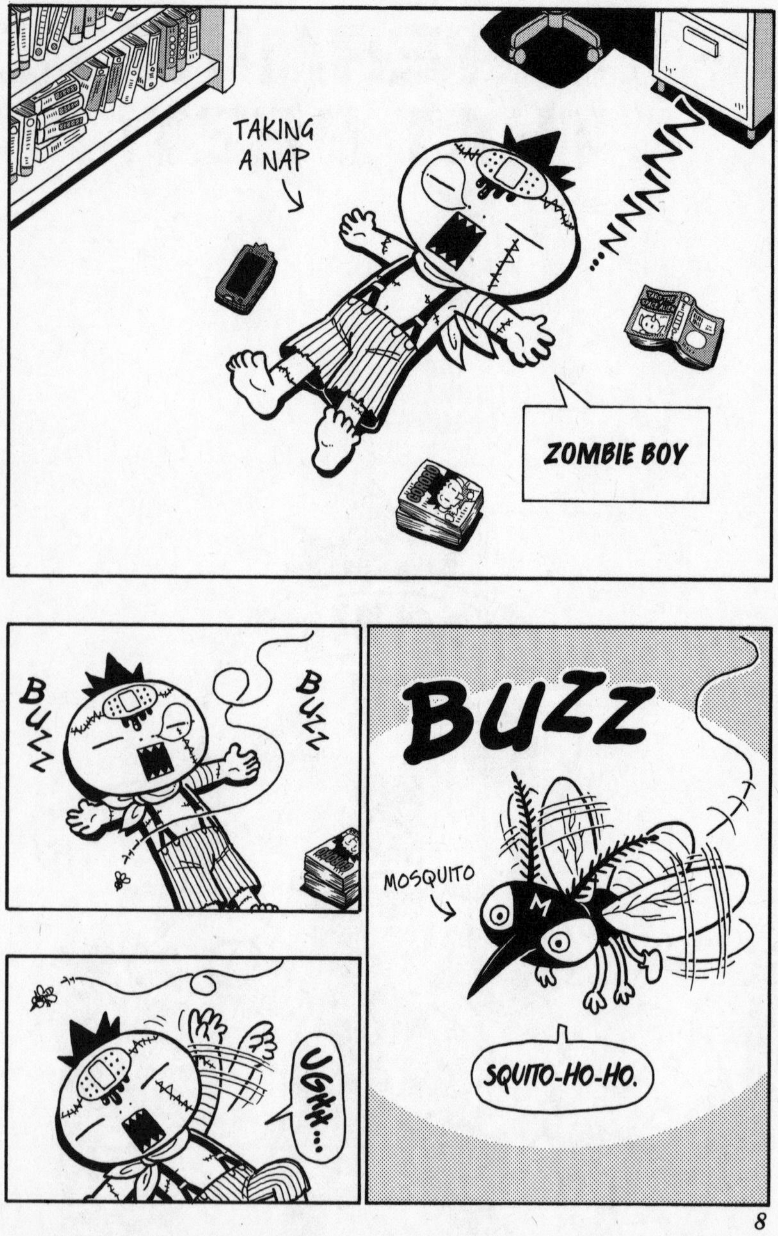
...NNNNNN
TAKING A NAP
ZOMBIE BOY
BUZZ
MOSQUITO
SQUITO-HO-HO.
BUZZ
BUZZ
UGHH...

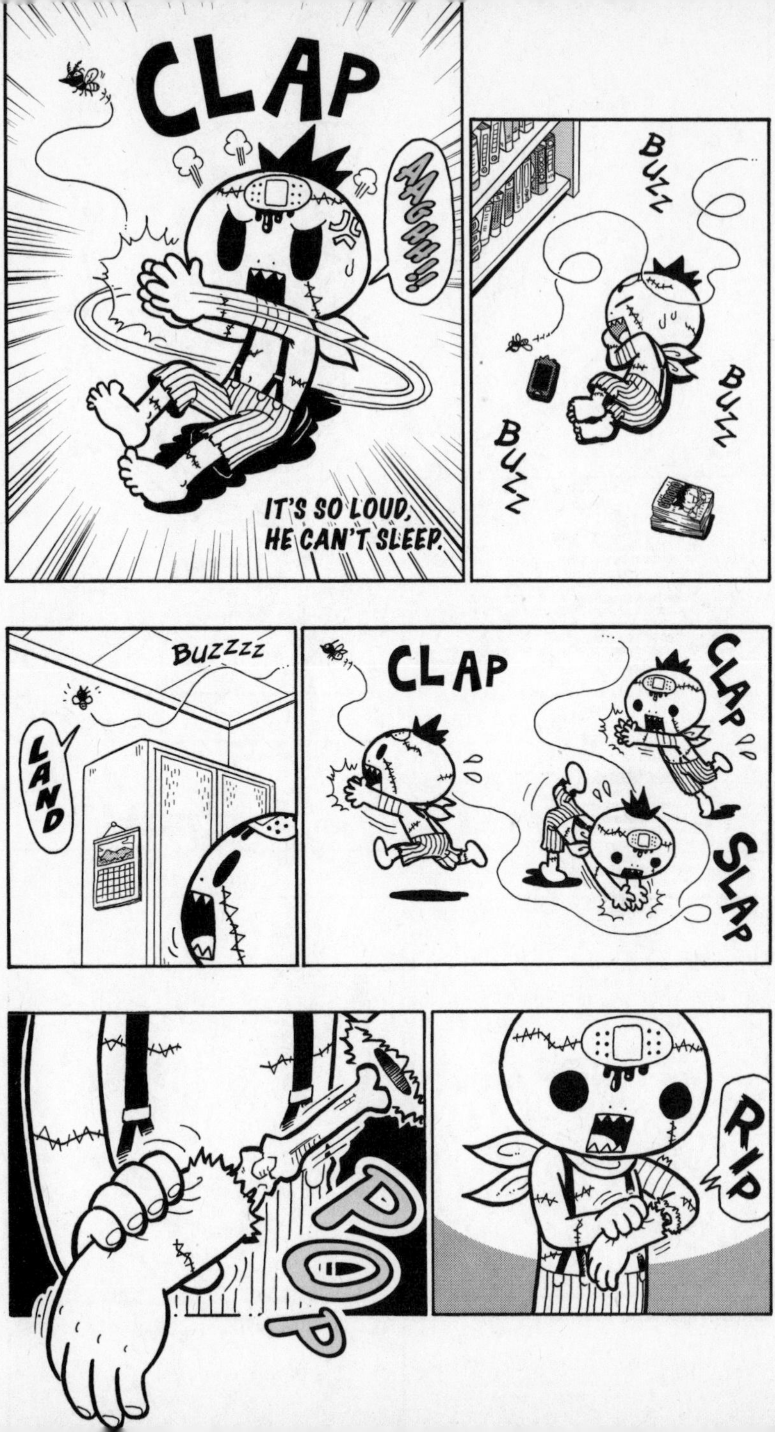
BUZZ
BUZZ
BUZZ
CLAP
AAGHH!!
IT'S SO LOUD, HE CAN'T SLEEP.
CLAP
CLAP
SLAP
BUZZZZ
LAND
RIP
POP

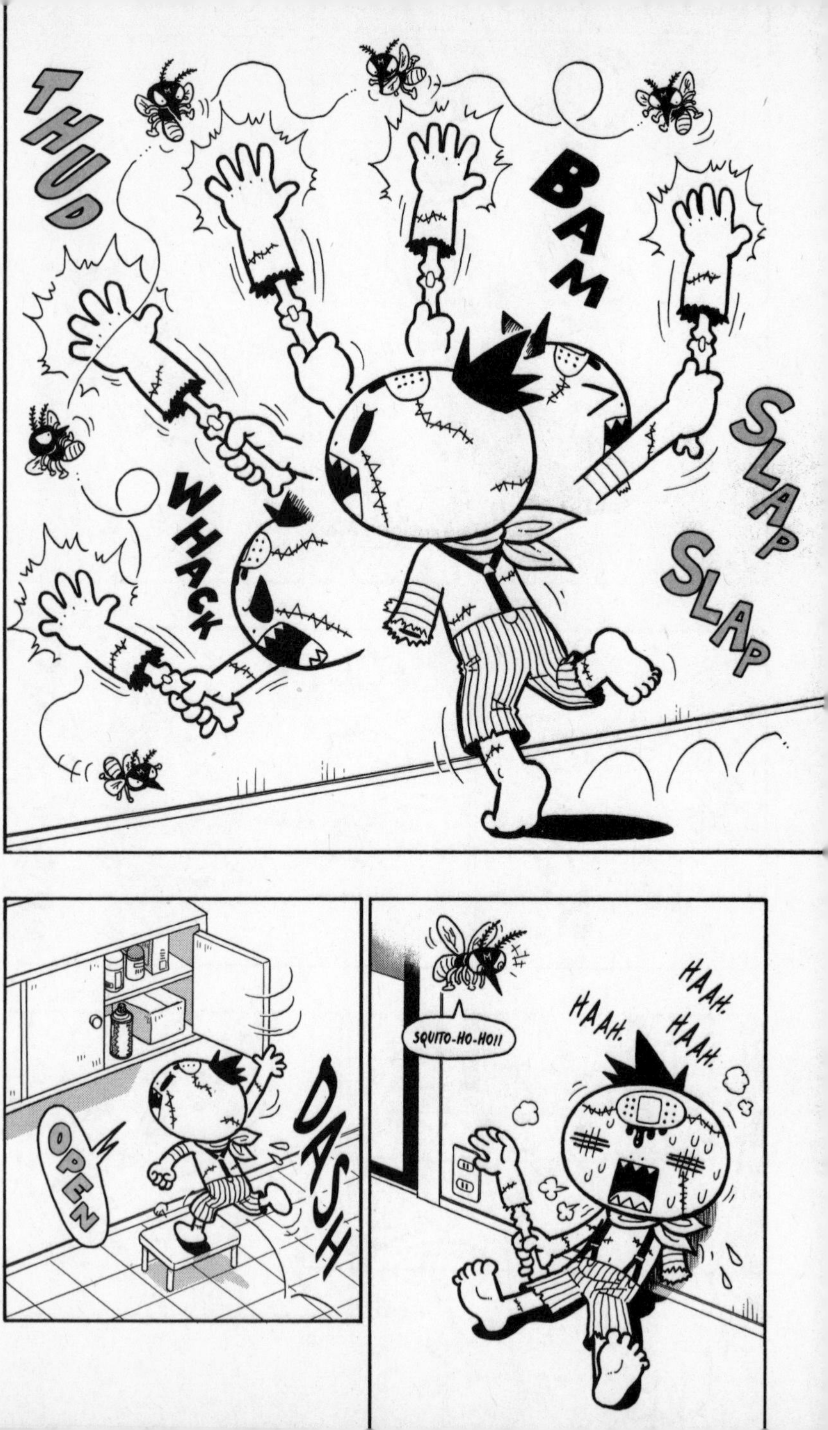
BAM
SLAP
SLAP
THUD
WHACK
HAAH.
HAAH.
HAAH.
SQUITO-HO-HO!!
DASH
OPEN

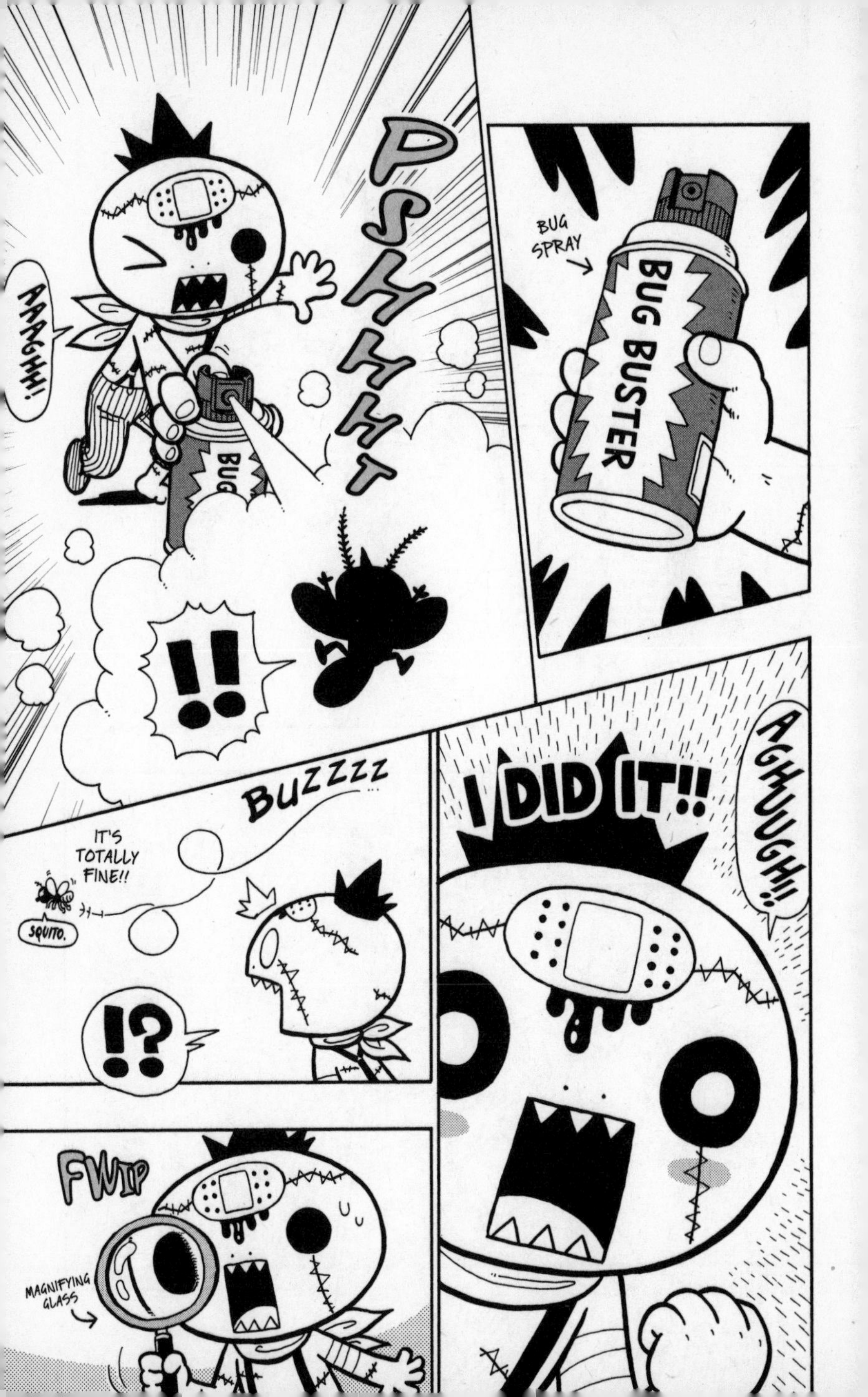
BUG SPRAY
BUG BUSTER
PSHHHT
AAAGHH!
BUG
!!
AGHUUUGH!!!
I DID IT!!
BUZZZZ...
IT'S TOTALLY FINE!!
SQUITO.
!?
FWIP
MAGNIFYING GLASS

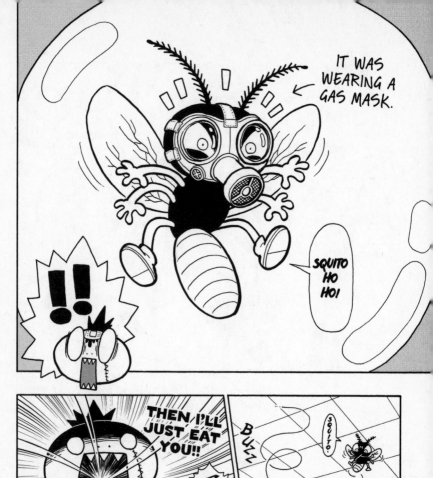

IT WAS WEARING A GAS MASK.

SQUITO HO HO!

THEN I'LL JUST EAT YOU!!

AGHUUGHH!!

VOOOOOMOOOOO

BUZZ BUZZ BUZZ

SQUITO.

UGHUUGHH..

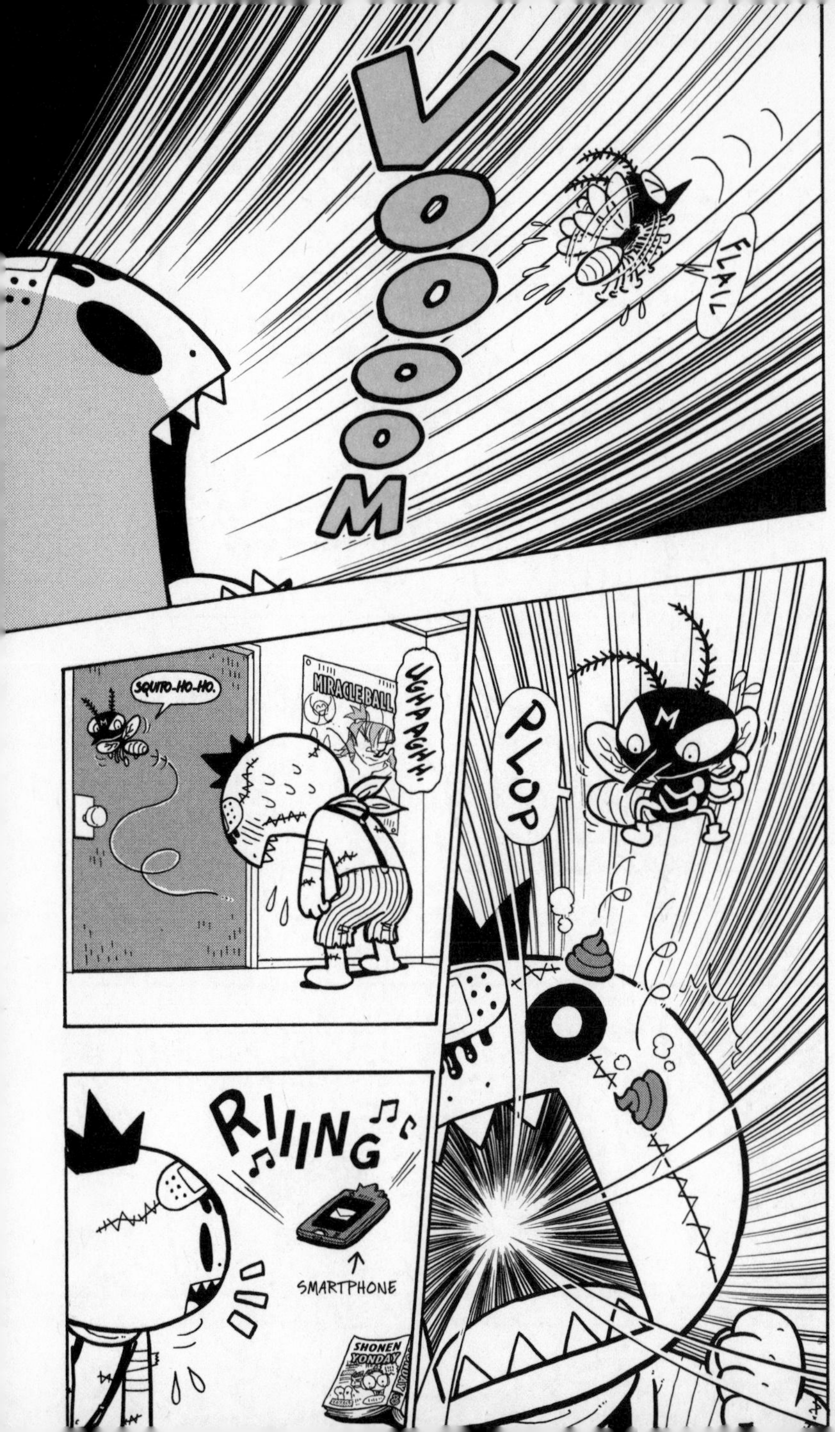
VOOOOOOM
FLAIL
PLOP
UGHPPAGHH.
SQUITO-HO-HO.
MIRACLE BALL
RIIING
SMARTPHONE
SHONEN YONDAY

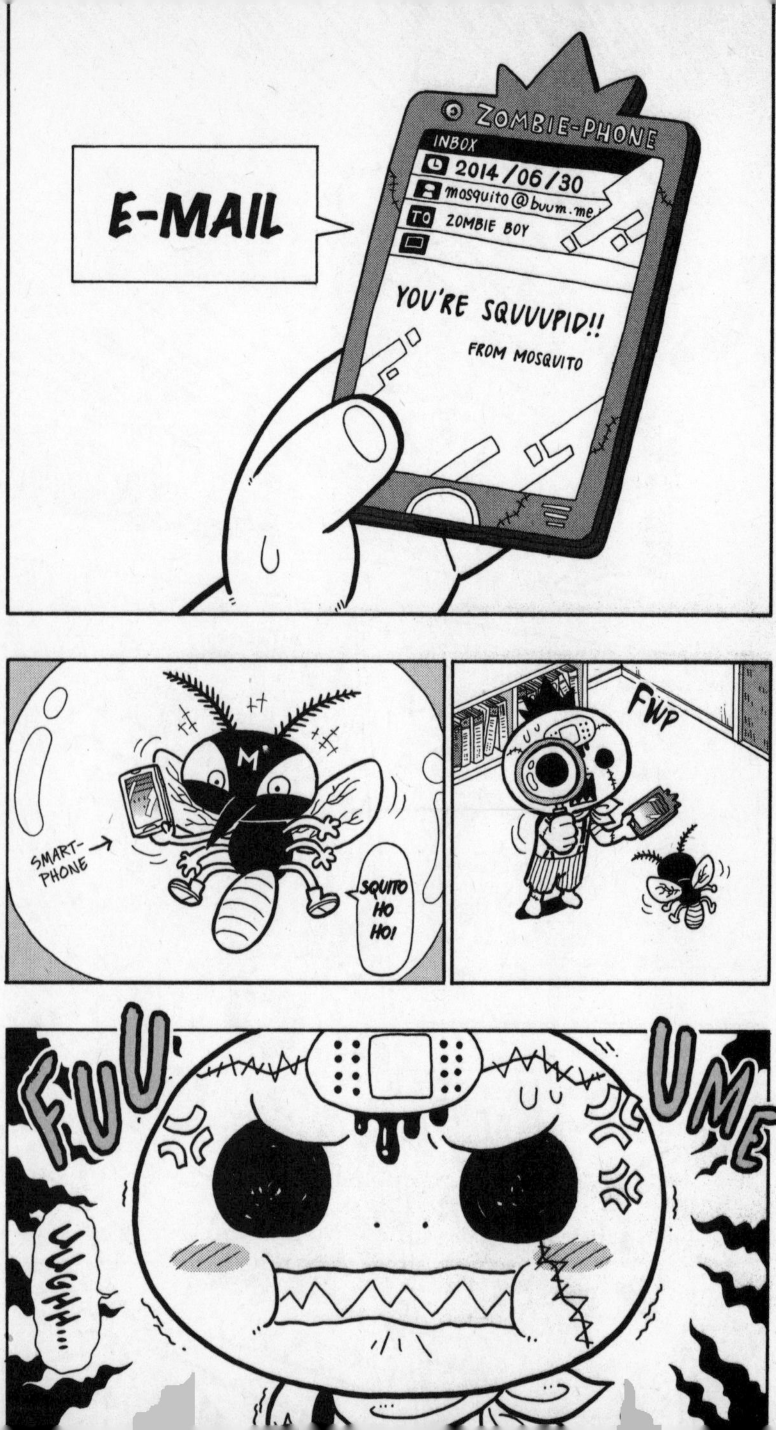
E-MAIL
ZOMBIE-PHONE
INBOX
2014/06/30
mosquito@buum.me
TO ZOMBIE BOY
YOU'RE SQUUUPID!!
FROM MOSQUITO
FWP
SMART-PHONE
SQUITO HO HO!
FUU UME
UGHHH...

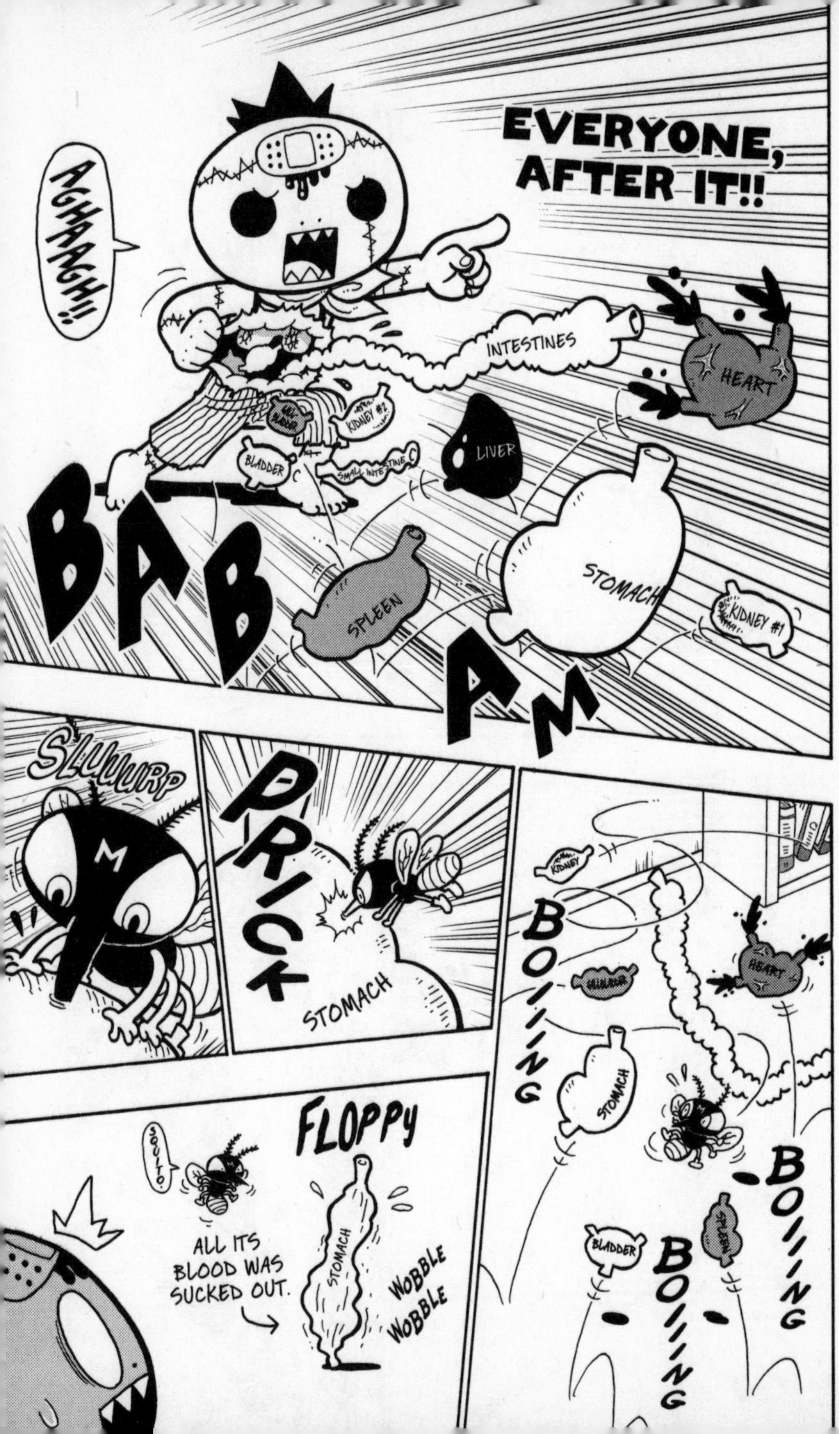
EVERYONE, AFTER IT!!
AGHAAGH!!
INTESTINES
HEART
LIVER
KIDNEY #2
BLADDER
SMALL INTESTINE
STOMACH
SPLEEN
KIDNEY #1
BABBAM
KIDNEY
HEART
BOIIING
STOMACH
BOIIING
BLADDER
BOIIING
PRICK
STOMACH
SLUUURP
SQUITO.
FLOPPY
ALL ITS BLOOD WAS SUCKED OUT.
STOMACH
WOBBLE WOBBLE

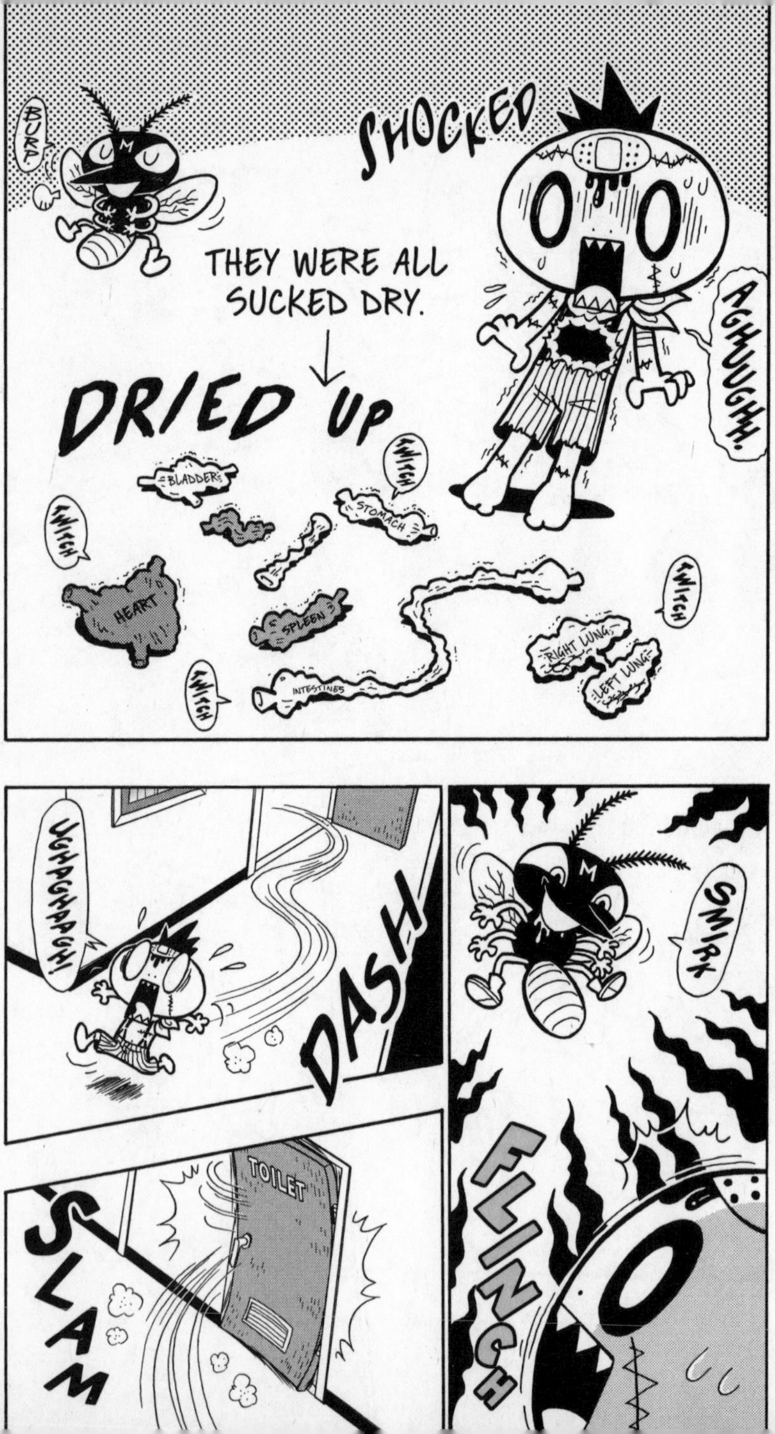
SHOCKED
AGHUUGHH.
BURP.
THEY WERE ALL SUCKED DRY.
DRIED UP
TWITCH
BLADDER
STOMACH
TWITCH
HEART
TWITCH
SPLEEN
RIGHT LUNG
LEFT LUNG
INTESTINES
TWITCH
SMIRK
FLINCH
UGHAGHAAGH!
DASH
TOILET
SLAM

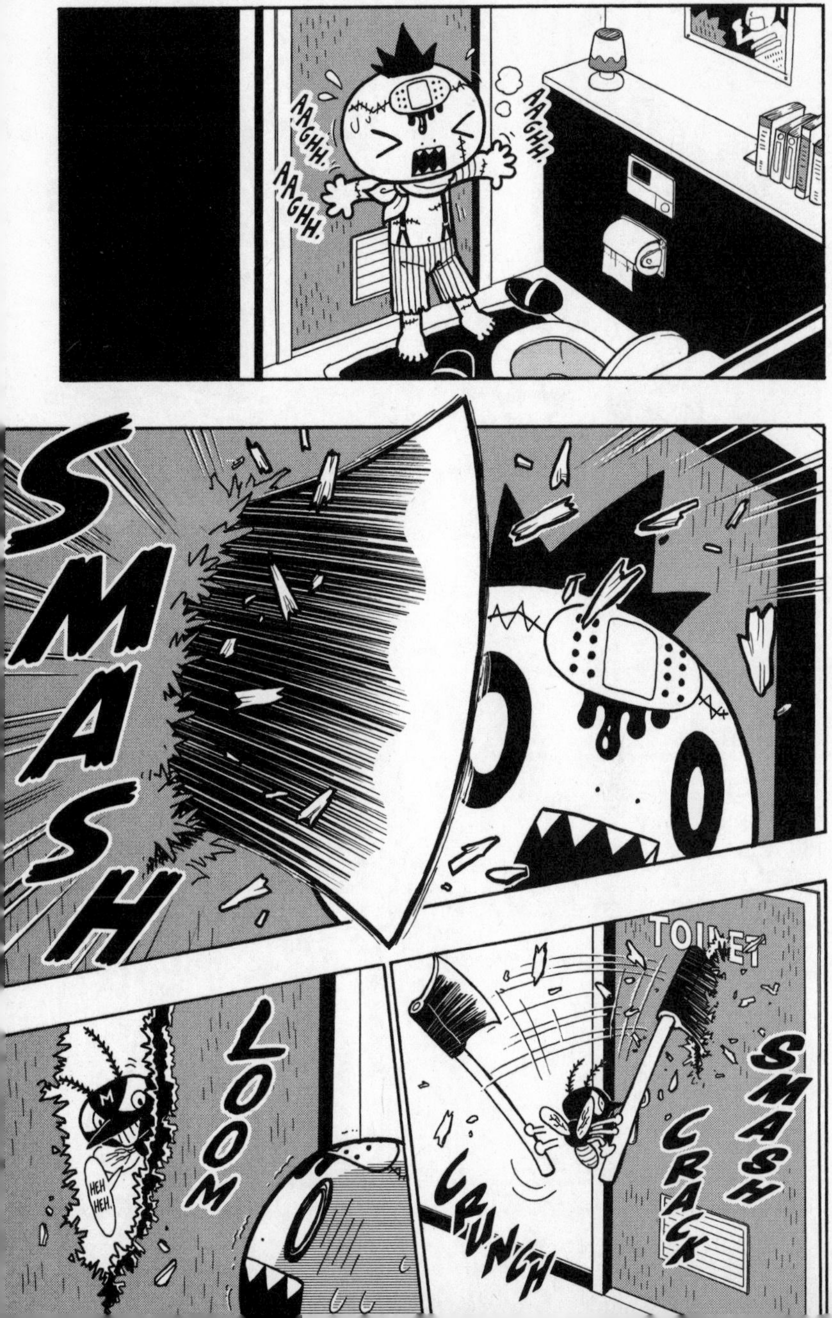
AAGHH.
AAGHH.
AAGHH.
SMASH
TOILET
SMASH
CRACK
CRUNCH
LOOOM
HEH HEH.

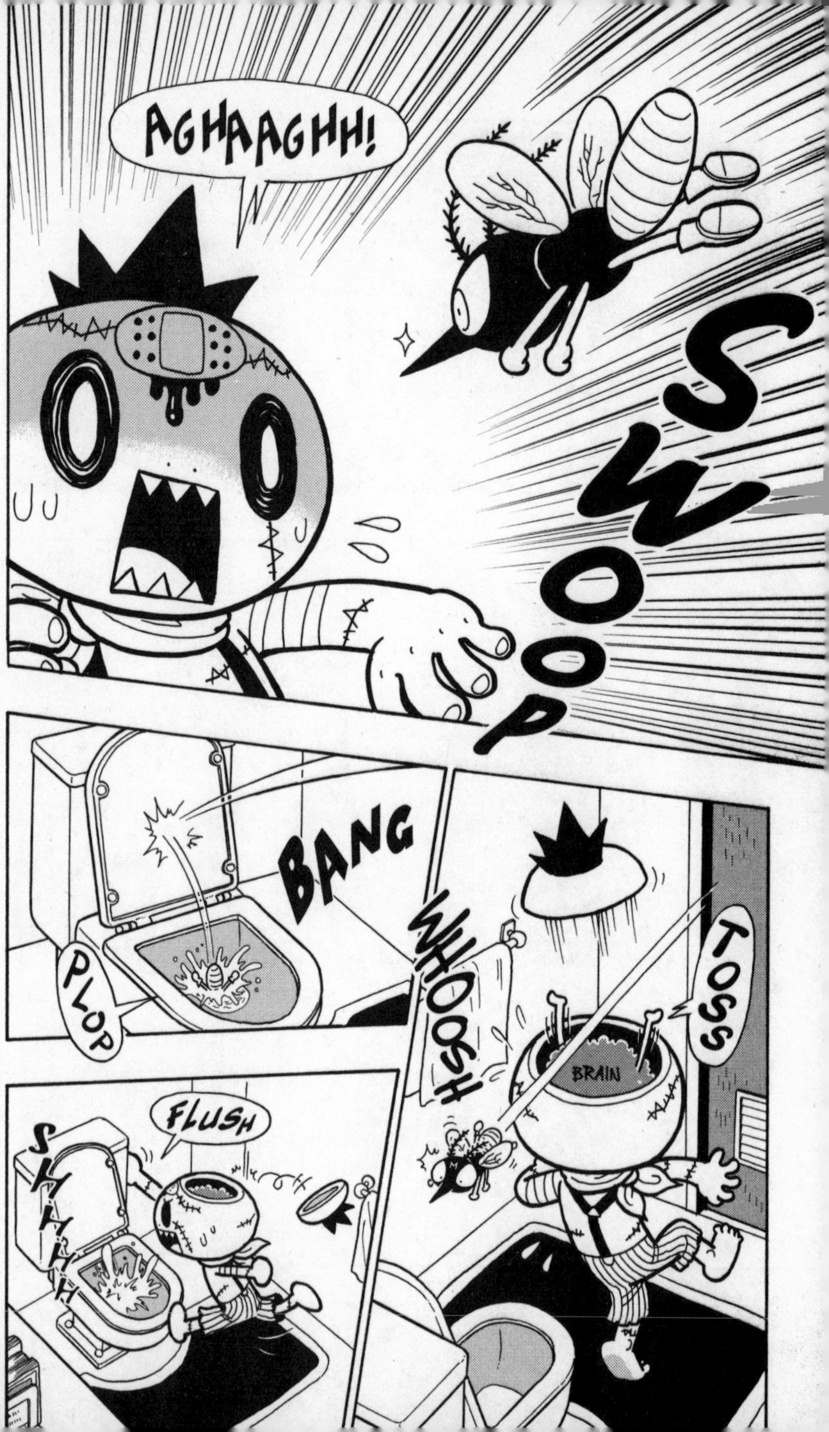
AGHAAGHH!
SWOOP
WHOOSH
TOSS
BRAIN
BANG
PLOP
FLUSH
SHHHHH

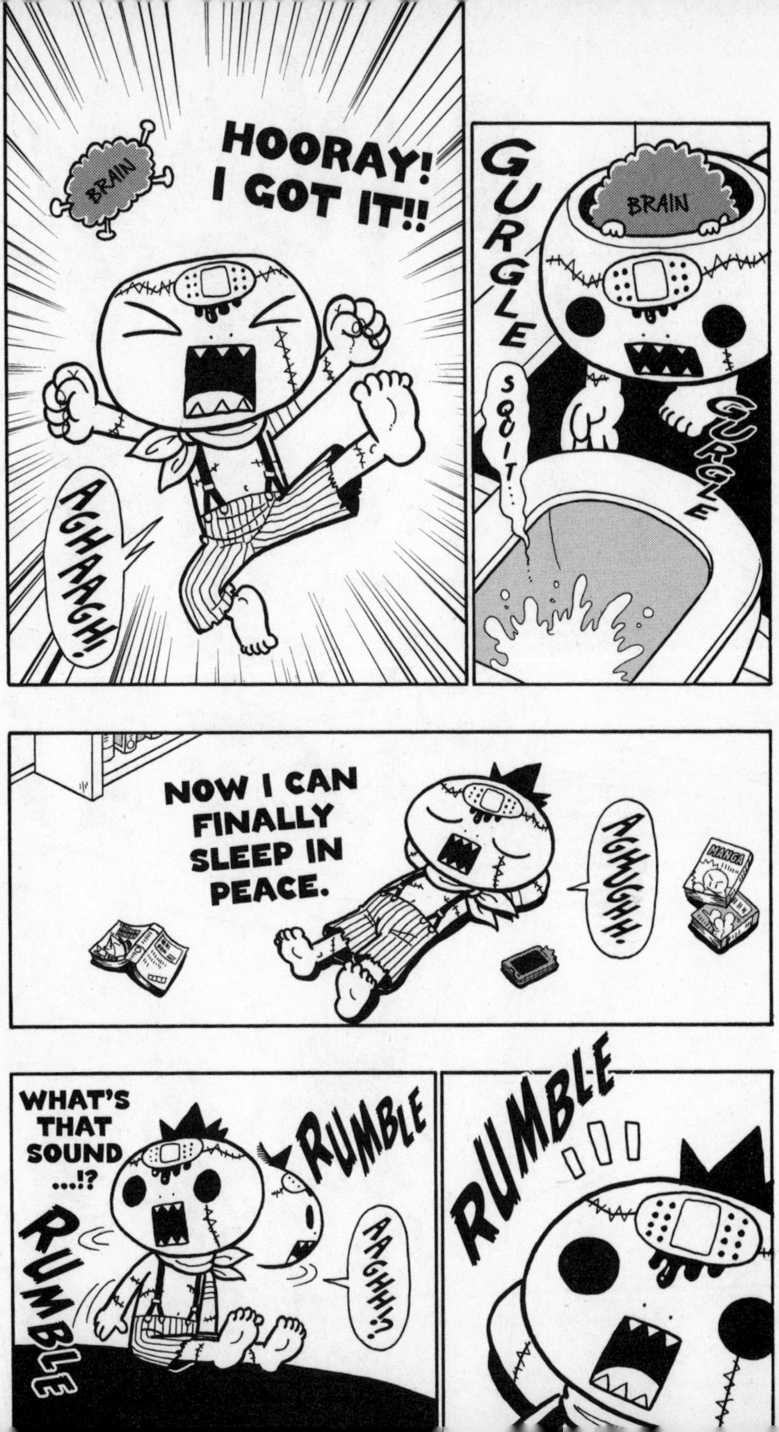
BRAIN
GURGLE
SQUIT...
GURGLE
BRAIN
HOORAY! I GOT IT!!
AGHAAAGH!!
NOW I CAN FINALLY SLEEP IN PEACE.
AGHUGHH.
MANGA
RUMBLE
WHAT'S THAT SOUND ...!?
RUMBLE
RUMBLE
AAGHH!?

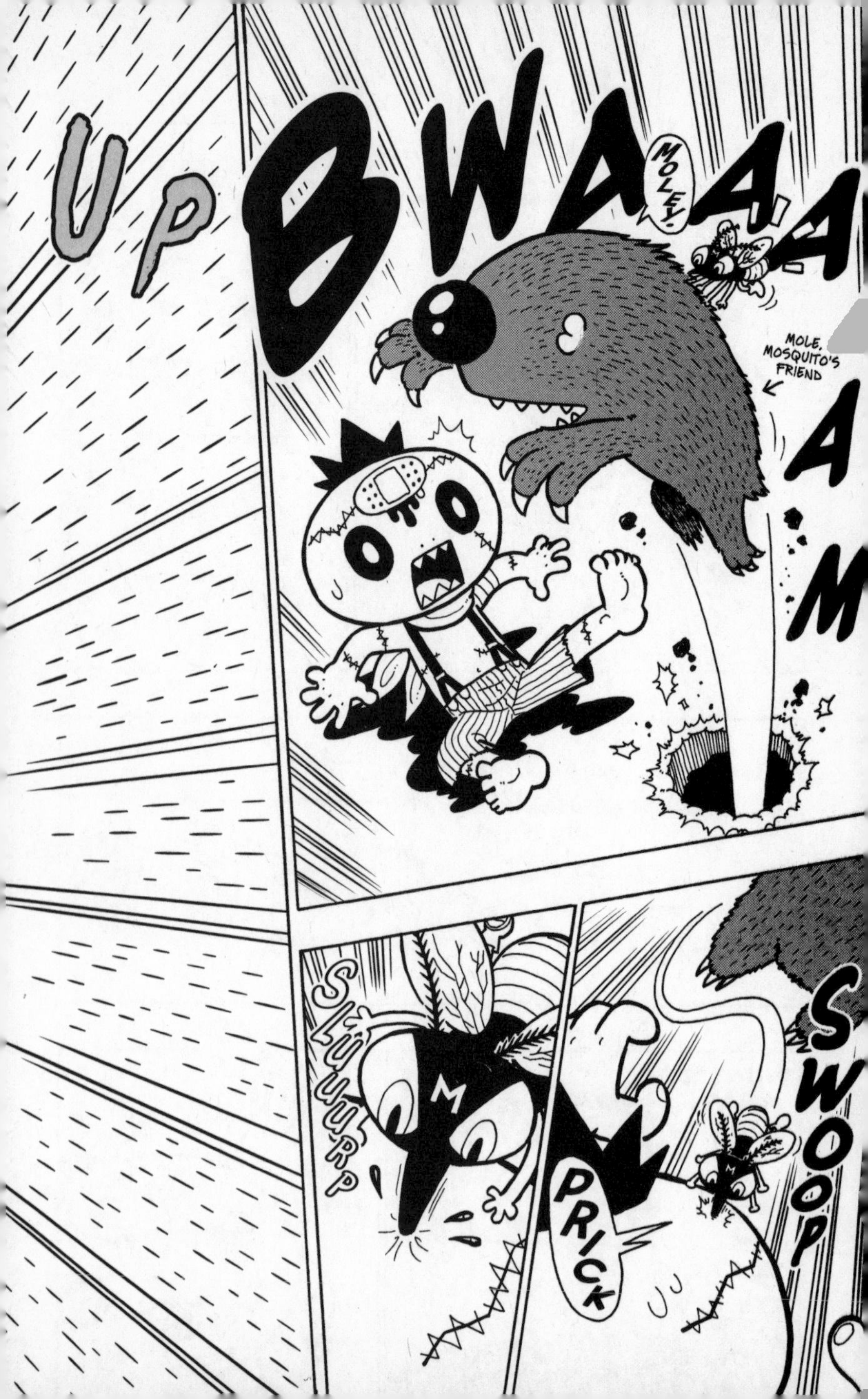
BWAAAAAM
MOLEY!
MOLE, MOSQUITO'S FRIEND
SWOOP
PRICK
SLUUURP
UP

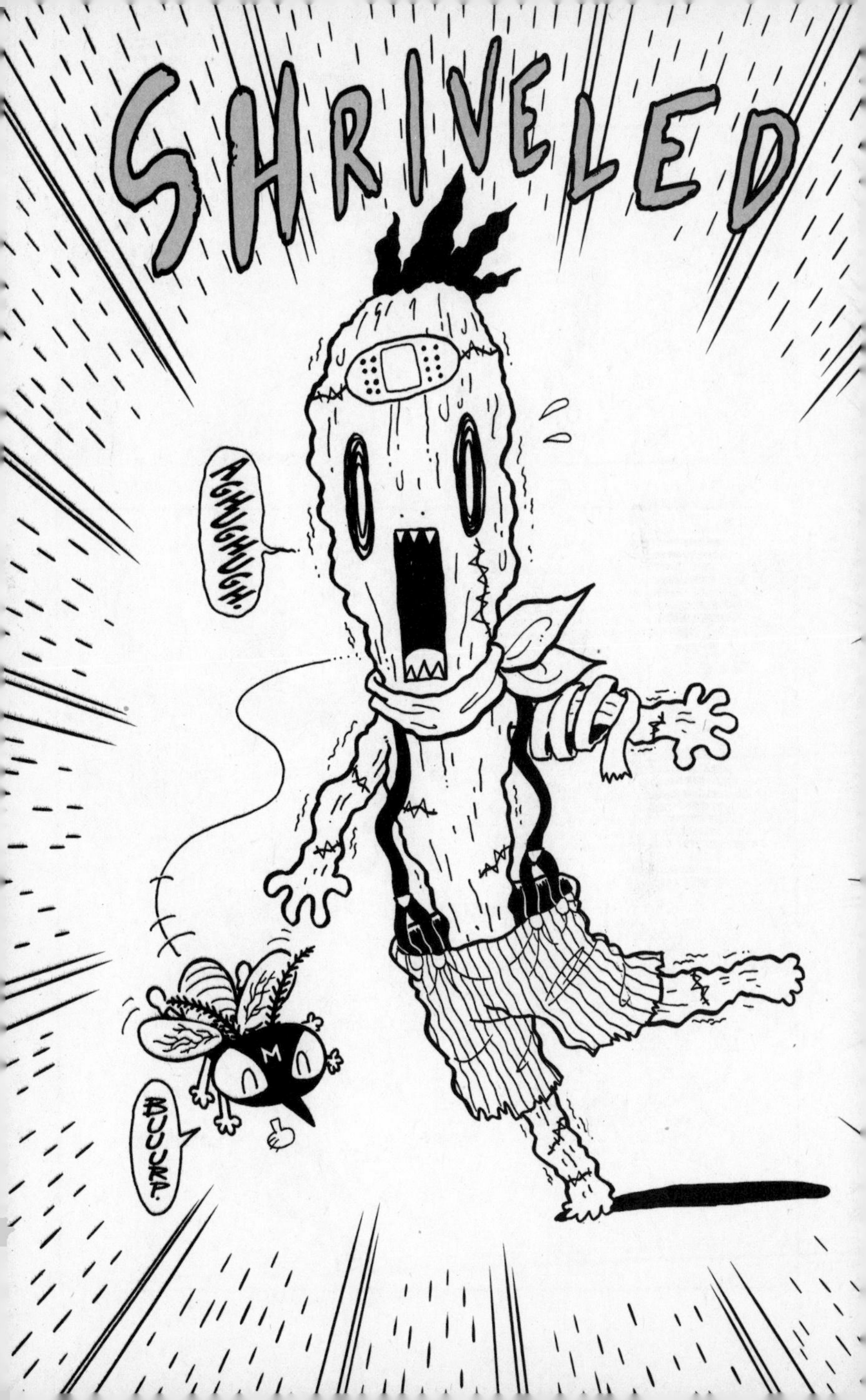
SHRIVELED
AGHUGHUGH.
BUUURP.

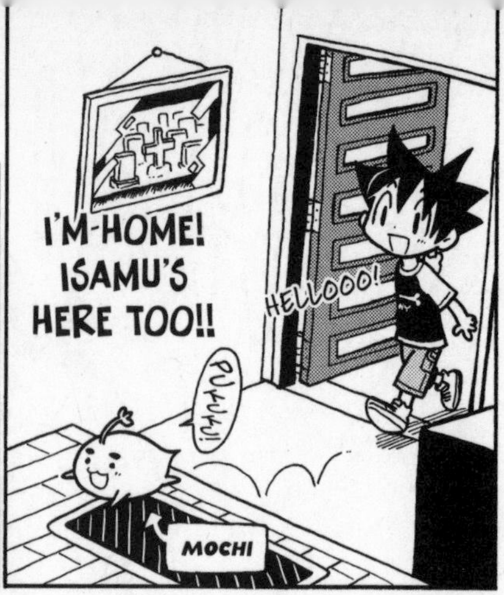
HELLOOO!
I'M HOME! ISAMU'S HERE TOO!!
PUKUKU!!
MOCHI

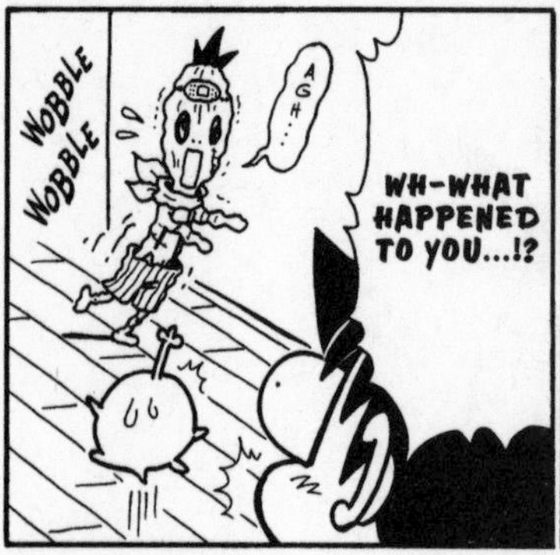
WH-WHAT HAPPENED TO YOU...!?
AGH...
WOBBLE WOBBLE

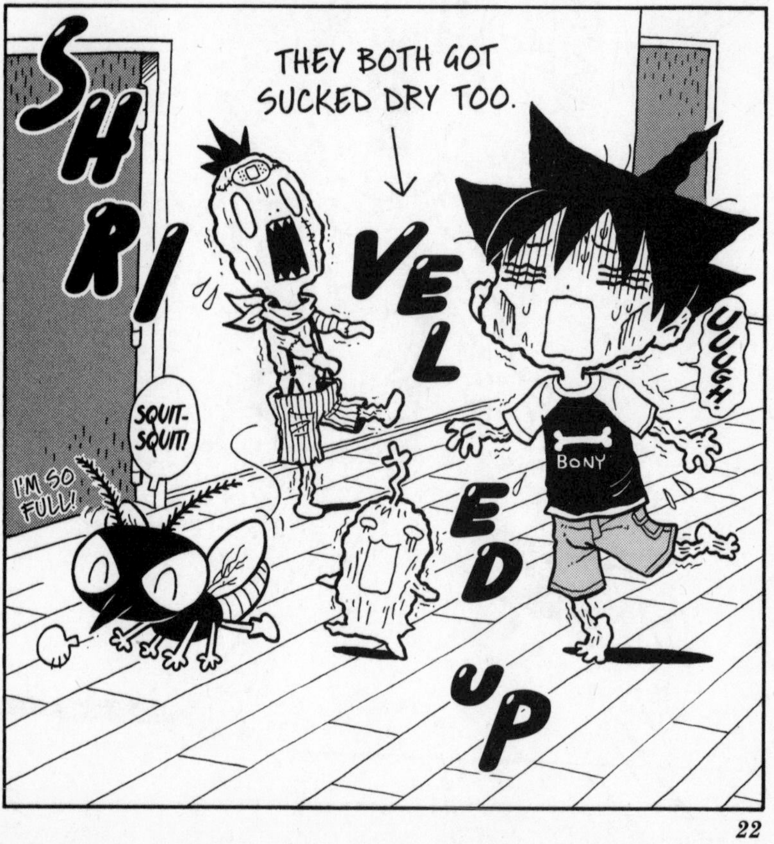
UUUGH.
THEY BOTH GOT SUCKED DRY TOO.
SHRIVELED UP
SQUIT-SQUIT!
I'M SO FULL!

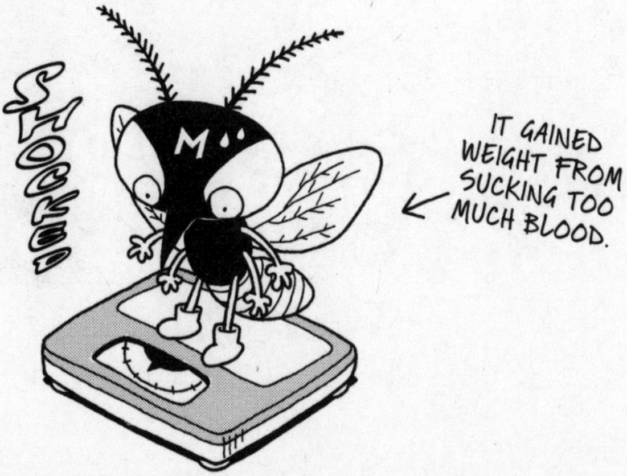
SHOCKED
IT GAINED WEIGHT FROM SUCKING TOO MUCH BLOOD.

A SOLID SQUARE RIVAL APPEARZ!

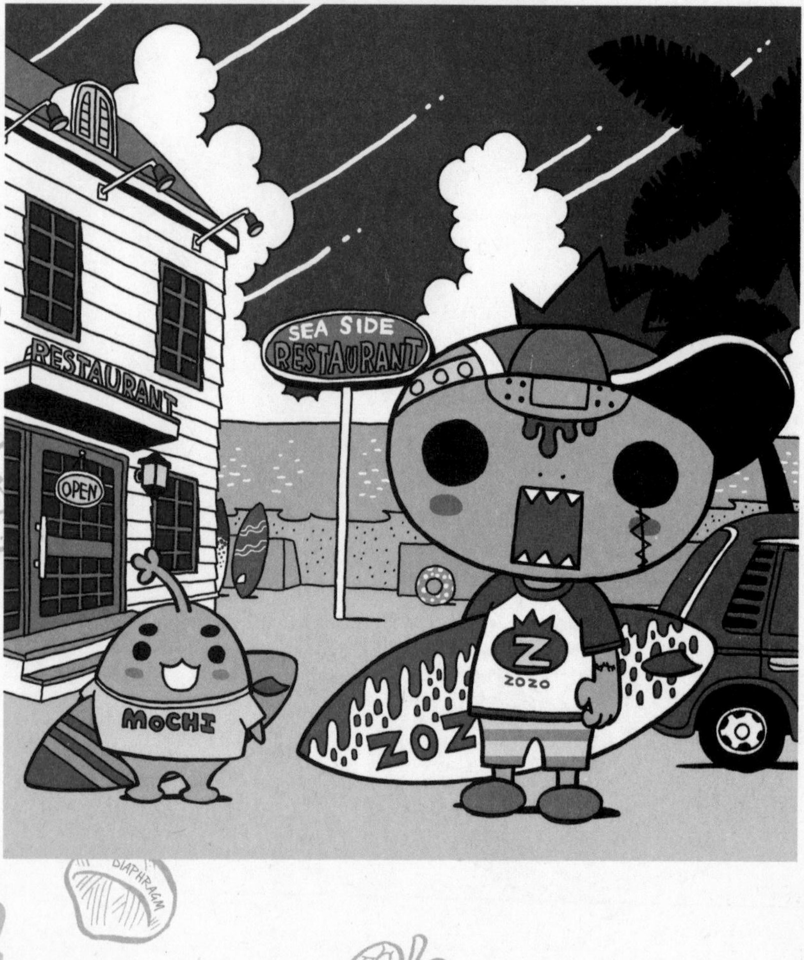

SEA SIDE
RESTAURANT
RESTAURANT
OPEN
MOCHI
ZOZO
ZOZ

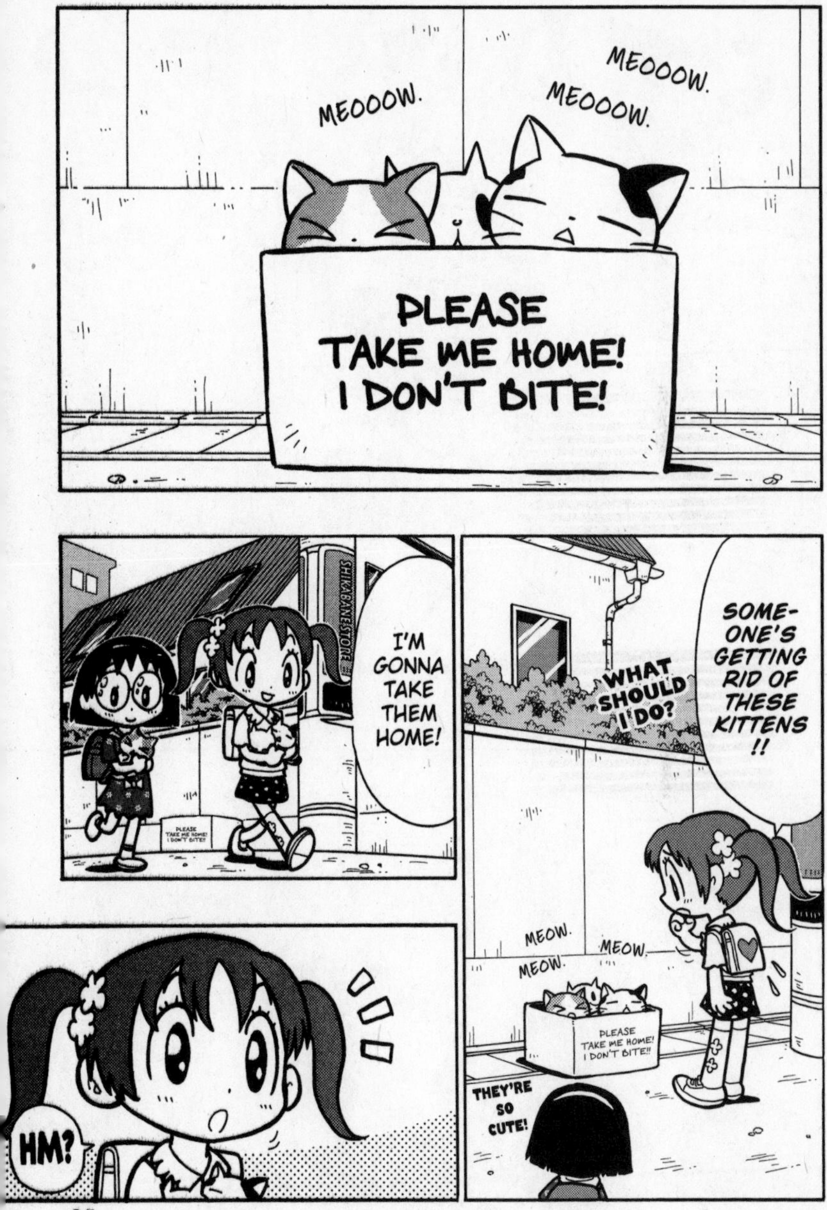
MEOOOW.
MEOOOW.
MEOOOW.
PLEASE TAKE ME HOME! I DON'T BITE!
SOME-ONE'S GETTING RID OF THESE KITTENS !!
WHAT SHOULD I DO?
MEOW.
MEOW.
MEOW.
PLEASE TAKE ME HOME! I DON'T BITE!!
THEY'RE SO CUTE!
SHIKABANE STORE
I'M GONNA TAKE THEM HOME!
PLEASE TAKE ME HOME! I DON'T BITE!
HM?

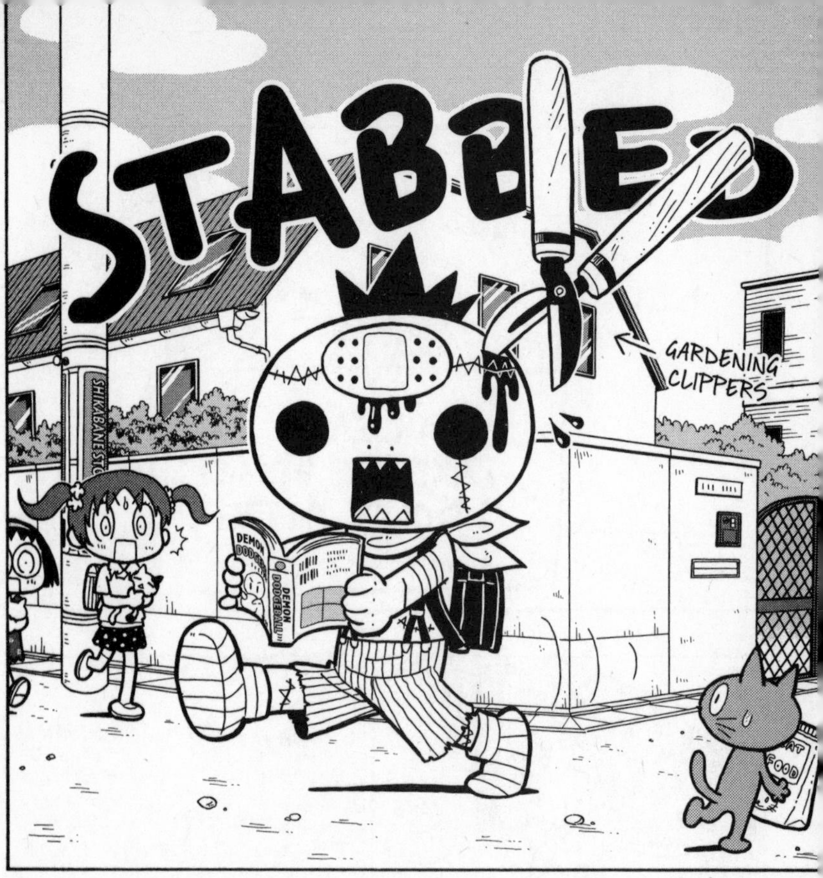
STABBED
GARDENING CLIPPERS
DEMON DODGEBALL

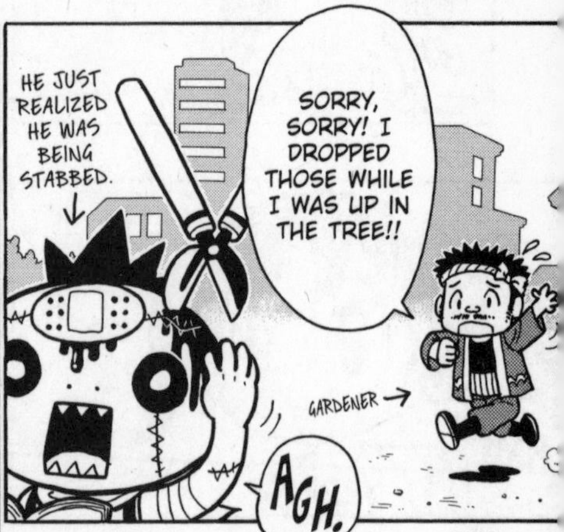
SORRY, SORRY! I DROPPED THOSE WHILE I WAS UP IN THE TREE!!
HE JUST REALIZED HE WAS BEING STABBED.
GARDENER
AGH.

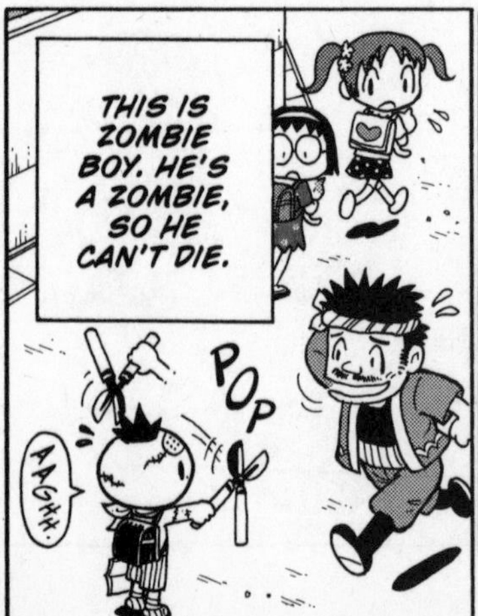
THIS IS ZOMBIE BOY. HE'S A ZOMBIE, SO HE CAN'T DIE.
POP
AAGHH.

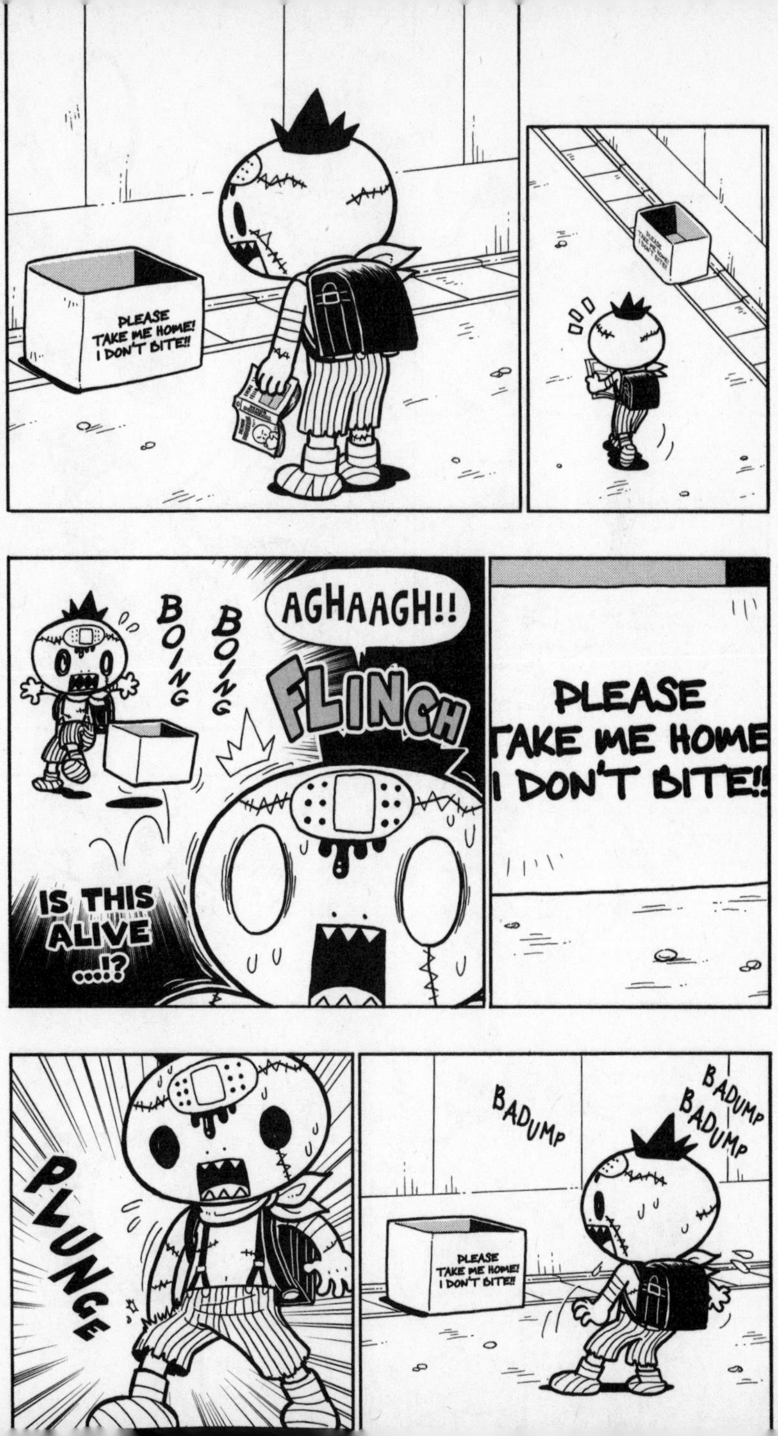
PLEASE
TAKE ME HOME!
I DON'T BITE!!
PLEASE
TAKE ME HOME
I DON'T BITE!!
AGHAAGH!!
FLINCH
BOING
BOING
IS THIS ALIVE ...!?
BADUMP
BADUMP
BADUMP
PLEASE
TAKE ME HOME!
I DON'T BITE!!
PLUNGE

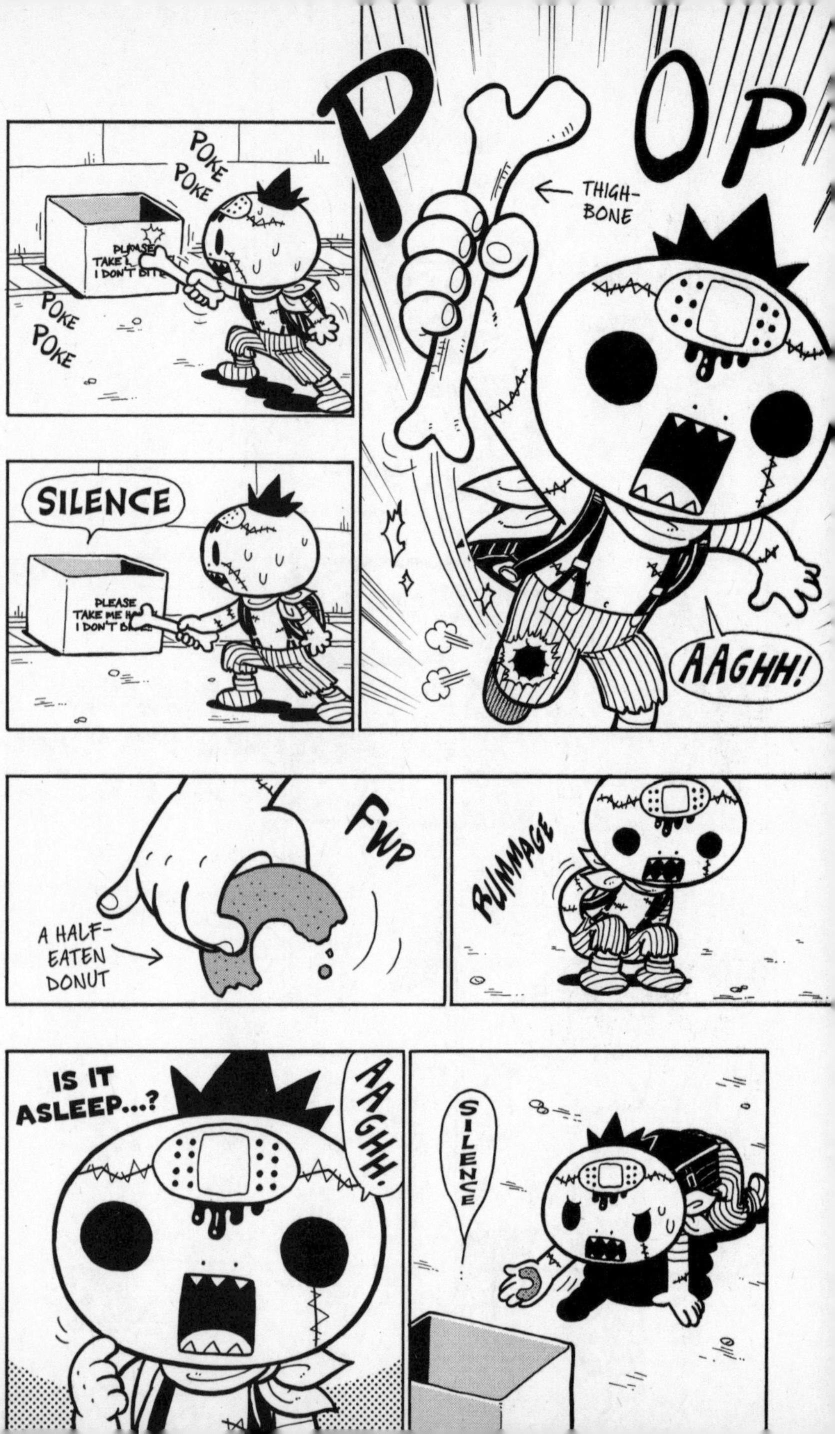
POP
THIGH-BONE
AAGHH!
POKE POKE
POKE POKE
SILENCE
RUMMAGE
FWP
A HALF-EATEN DONUT
SILENCE
IS IT ASLEEP...?
AAGHH.

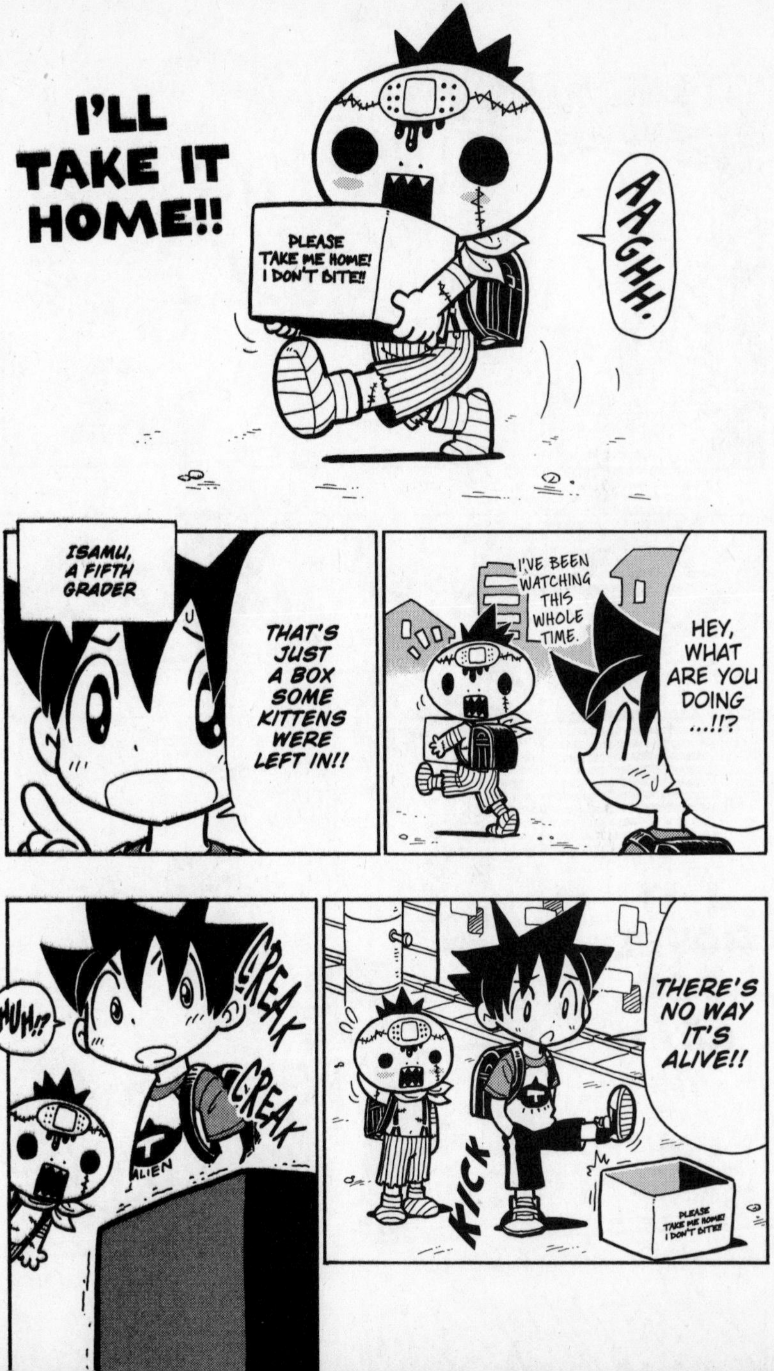
AAGHH.
PLEASE TAKE ME HOME! I DON'T BITE!!
I'LL TAKE IT HOME!!
HEY, WHAT ARE YOU DOING ...!!?
I'VE BEEN WATCHING THIS WHOLE TIME.
ISAMU, A FIFTH GRADER
THAT'S JUST A BOX SOME KITTENS WERE LEFT IN!!
THERE'S NO WAY IT'S ALIVE!!
KICK
PLEASE TAKE ME HOME! I DON'T BITE!!
CREAK
CREAK
HUH!?
ALIEN

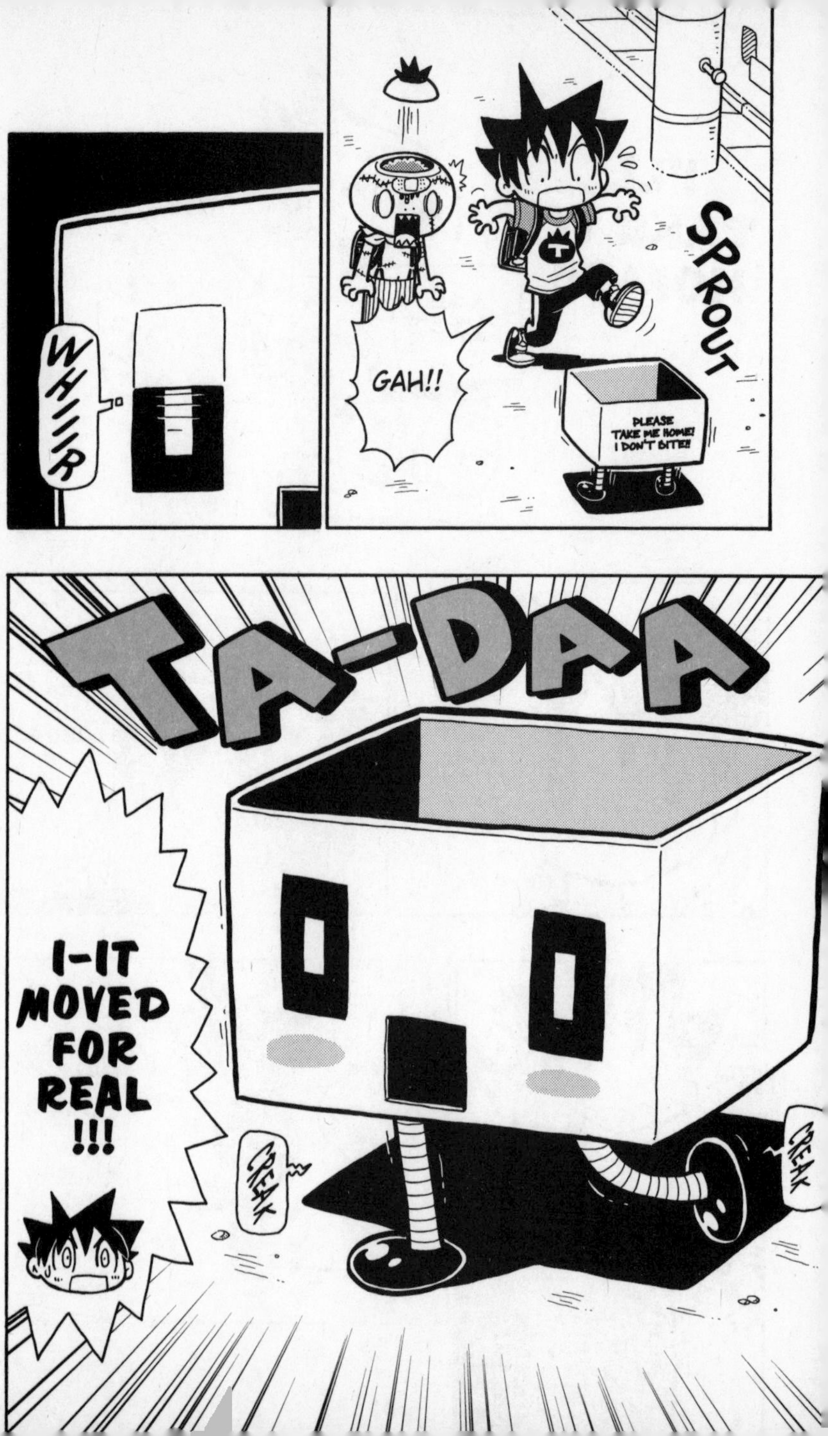
SPROUT
GAH!!
PLEASE TAKE ME HOME! I DON'T BITE!!
WHIIR
TA-DAA
I-IT MOVED FOR REAL!!!
CREAK
CREAK

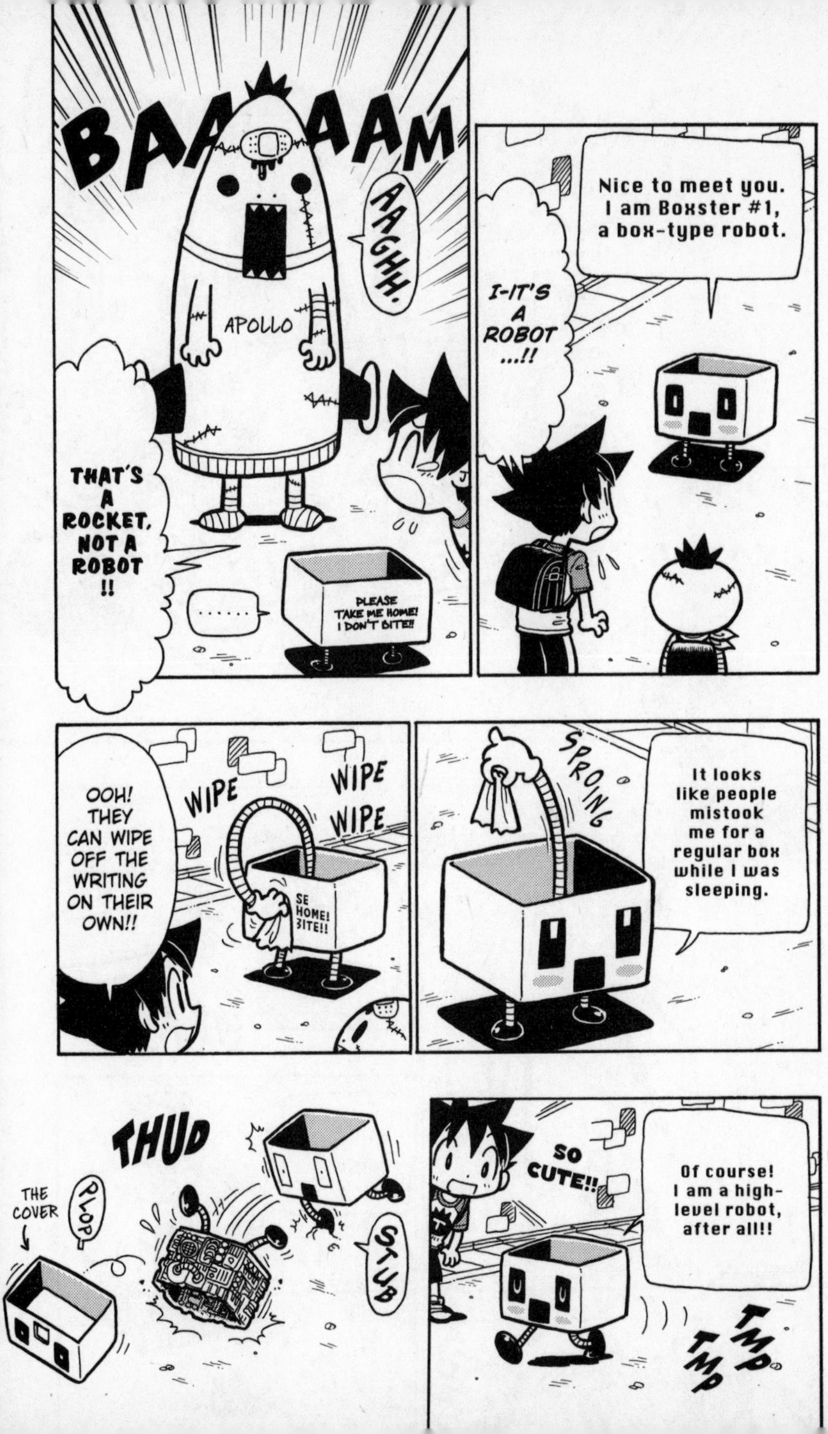
Nice to meet you. I am Boxster #1, a box-type robot.
I-IT'S A ROBOT ...!!
BAAAAM
AAGHH.
APOLLO
THAT'S A ROCKET, NOT A ROBOT!!
......
PLEASE TAKE ME HOME! I DON'T BITE!!
SPROING
It looks like people mistook me for a regular box while I was sleeping.
WIPE WIPE WIPE
OOH! THEY CAN WIPE OFF THE WRITING ON THEIR OWN!!
SE HOME! BITE!!
Of course! I am a high-level robot, after all!!
SO CUTE!!
TMP TMP
THUD
STUB
PLOP
THE COVER

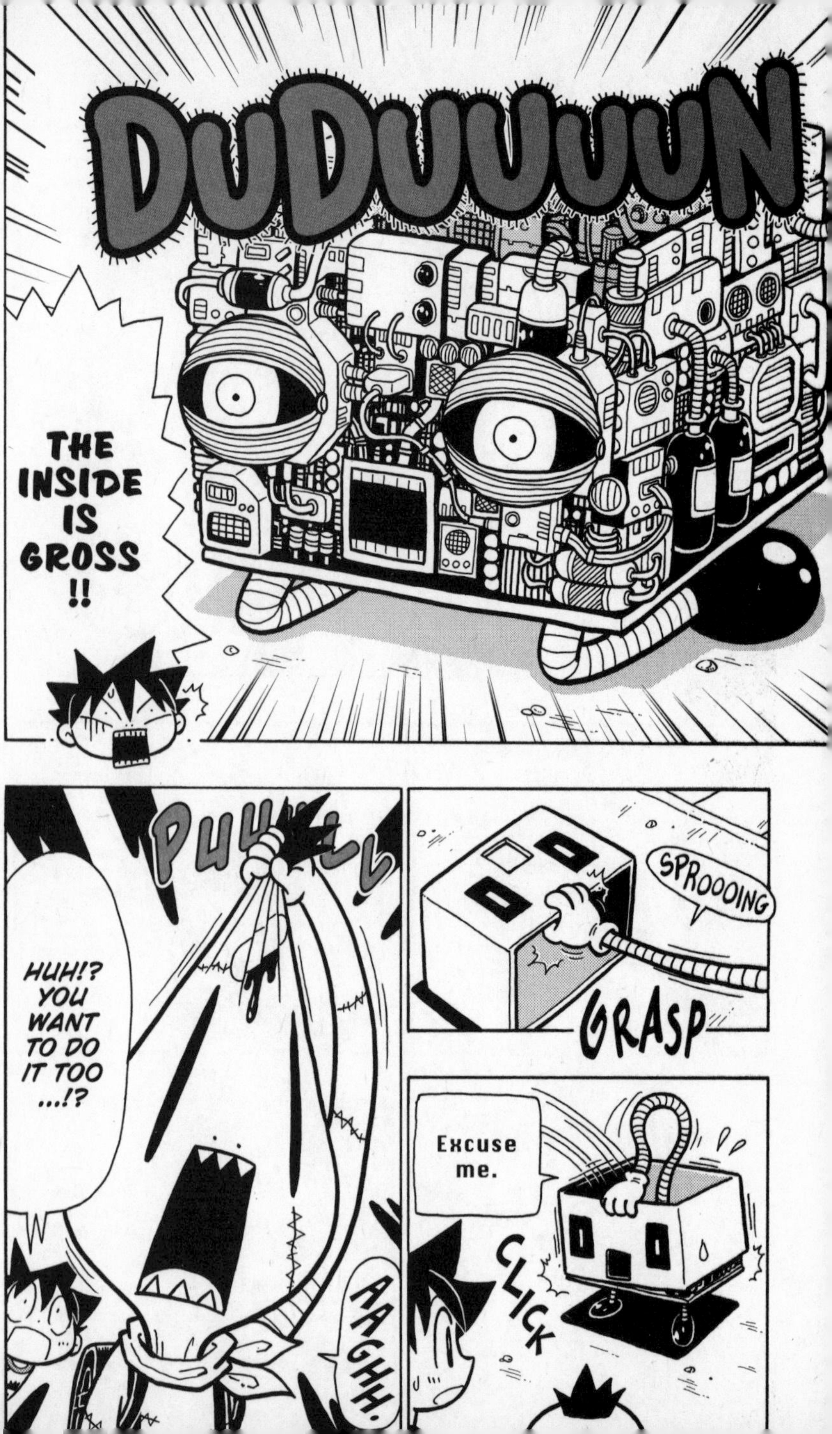
DUDUUUUN
THE INSIDE IS GROSS !!
SPROOOING
GRASP
Excuse me.
CLICK
PUUULL
HUH!? YOU WANT TO DO IT TOO ...!?
AAGHH.

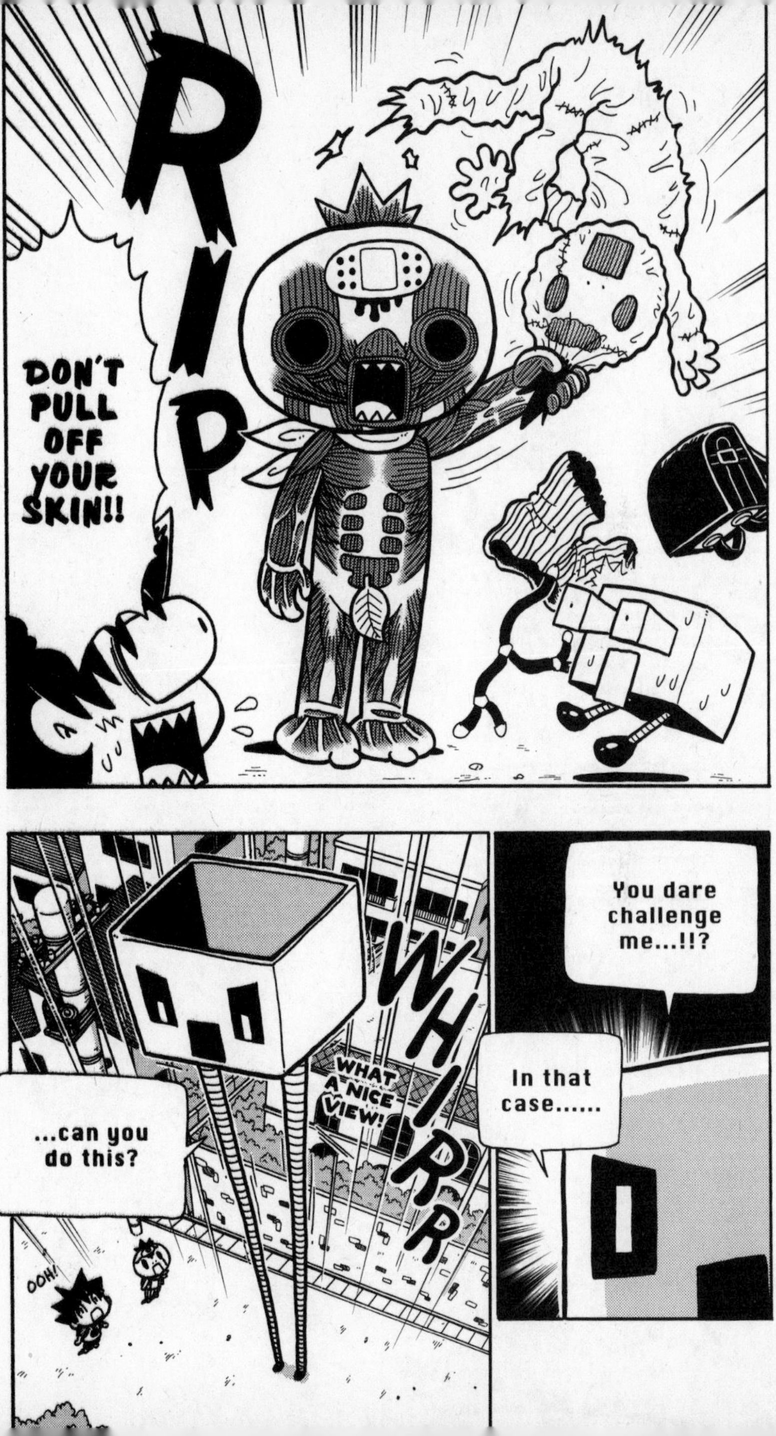
RIP
DON'T PULL OFF YOUR SKIN!!
You dare challenge me...!!?
In that case......
WHIRRR
WHAT A NICE VIEW!
...can you do this?
OOH!

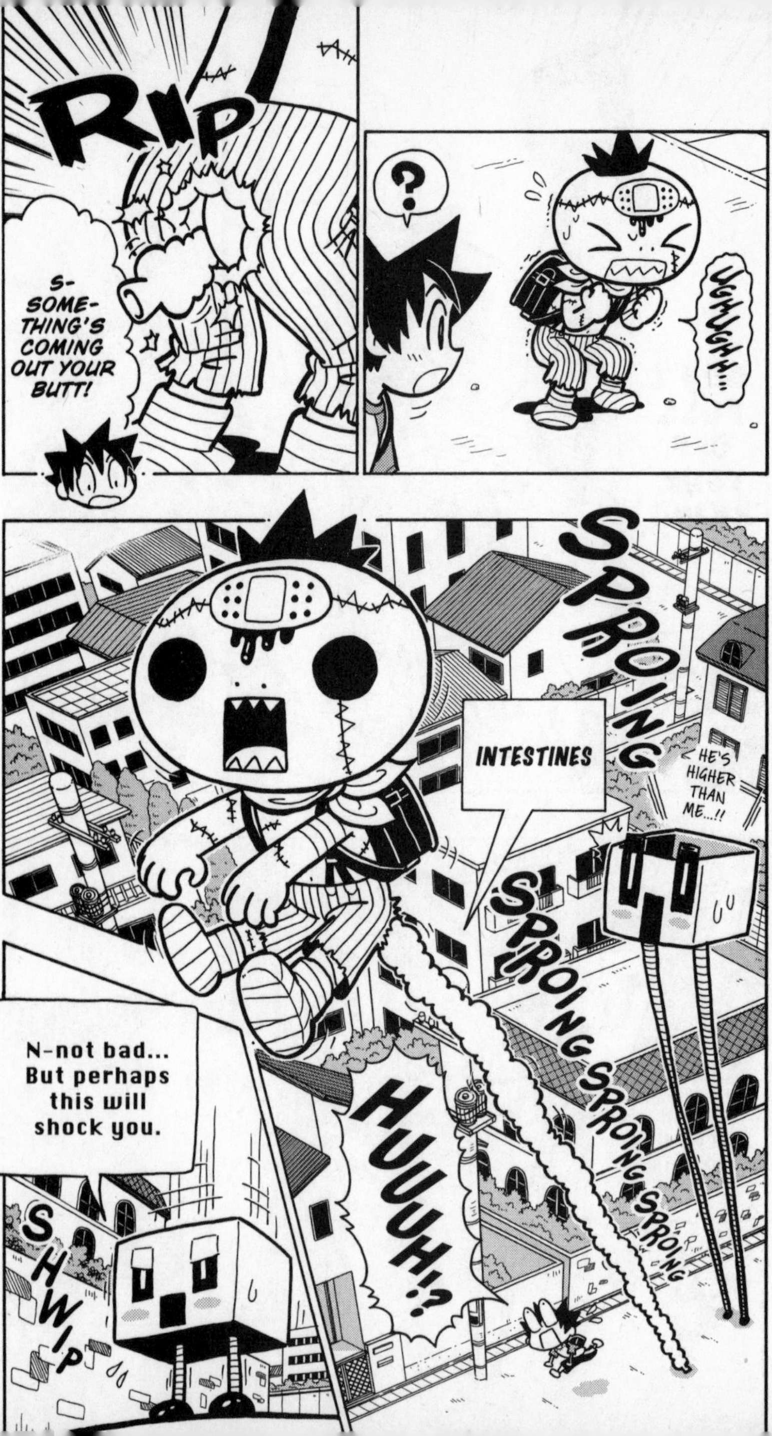
?
UGHUGHH...
RIP
S-SOMETHING'S COMING OUT YOUR BUTT!
SPROING
INTESTINES
HE'S HIGHER THAN ME...!!
SPROING SPROING SPROING SPROING
HUUUH!?
N-not bad... But perhaps this will shock you.
SHWIP

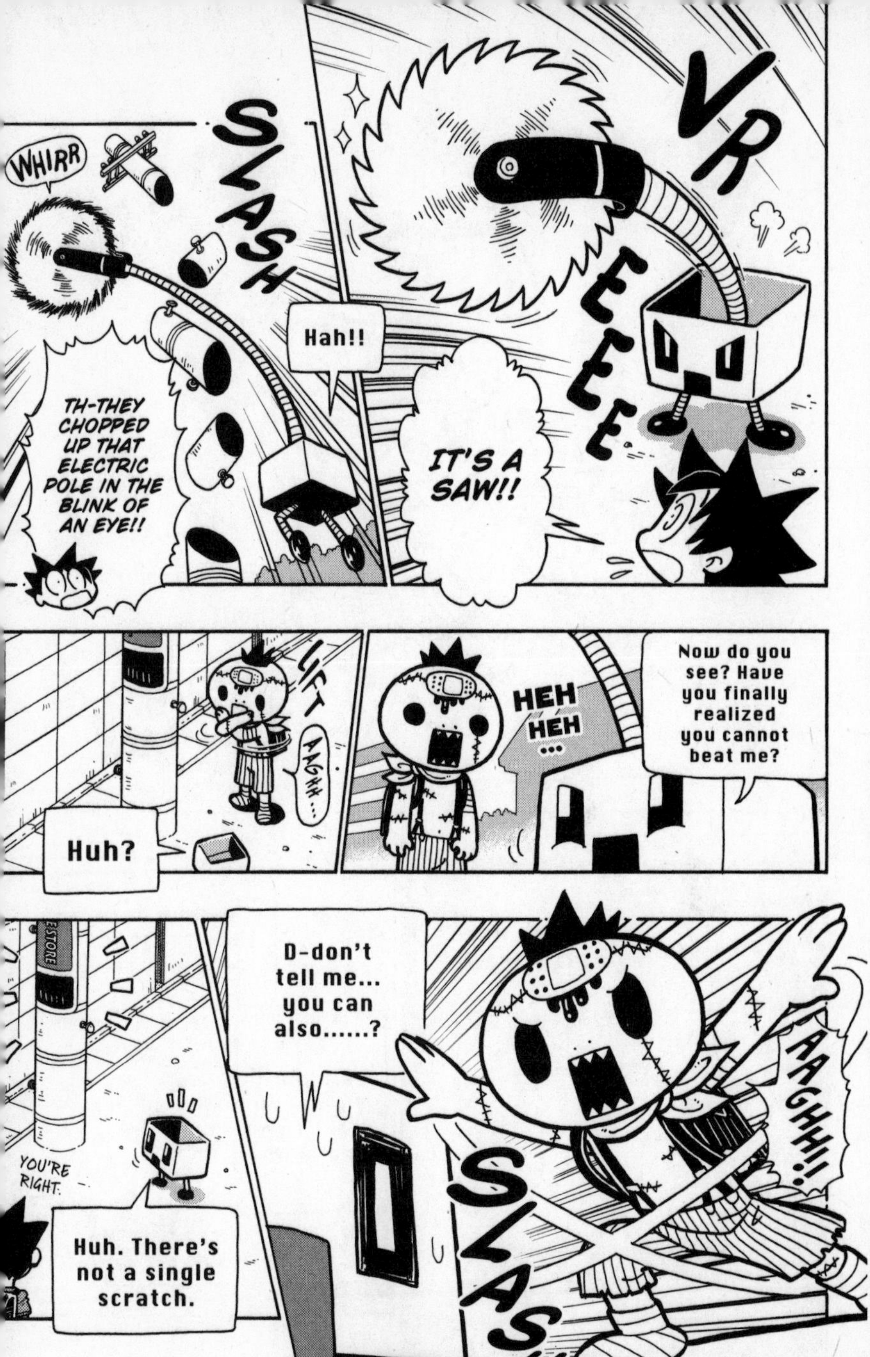

VREEEE
Hah!!
IT'S A SAW!!
SLASH
WHIRR
TH-THEY CHOPPED UP THAT ELECTRIC POLE IN THE BLINK OF AN EYE!!
Now do you see? Have you finally realized you cannot beat me?
HEH HEH ...
LIFT
AAGHH...
Huh?
D-don't tell me... you can also......?
AAGHH!!
SLASH
Huh. There's not a single scratch.
YOU'RE RIGHT.

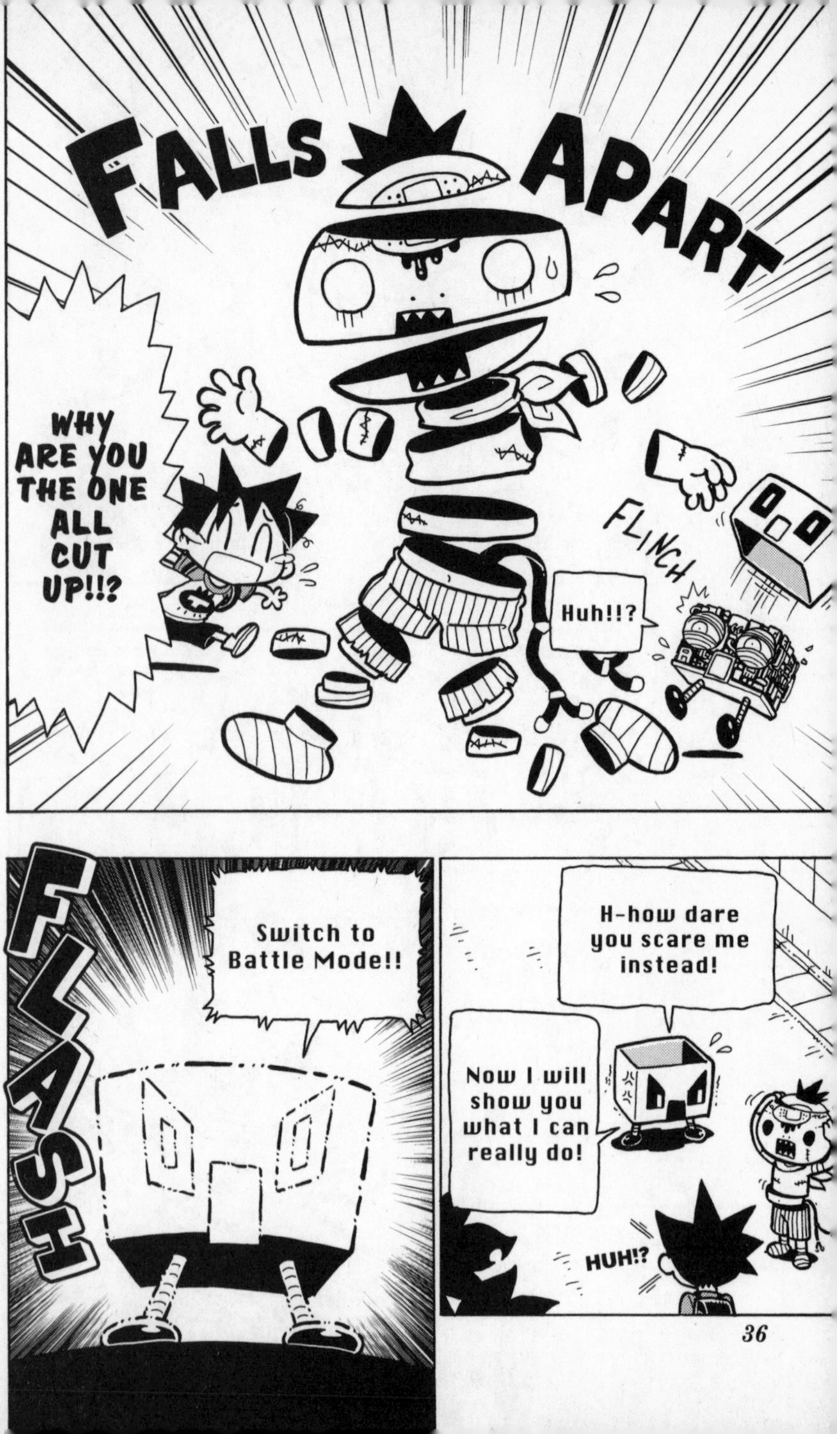
FALLS APART
FLINCH
Huh!!?
WHY ARE YOU THE ONE ALL CUT UP!!?
H-how dare you scare me instead!
Now I will show you what I can really do!
HUH!?
FLASH
Switch to Battle Mode!!

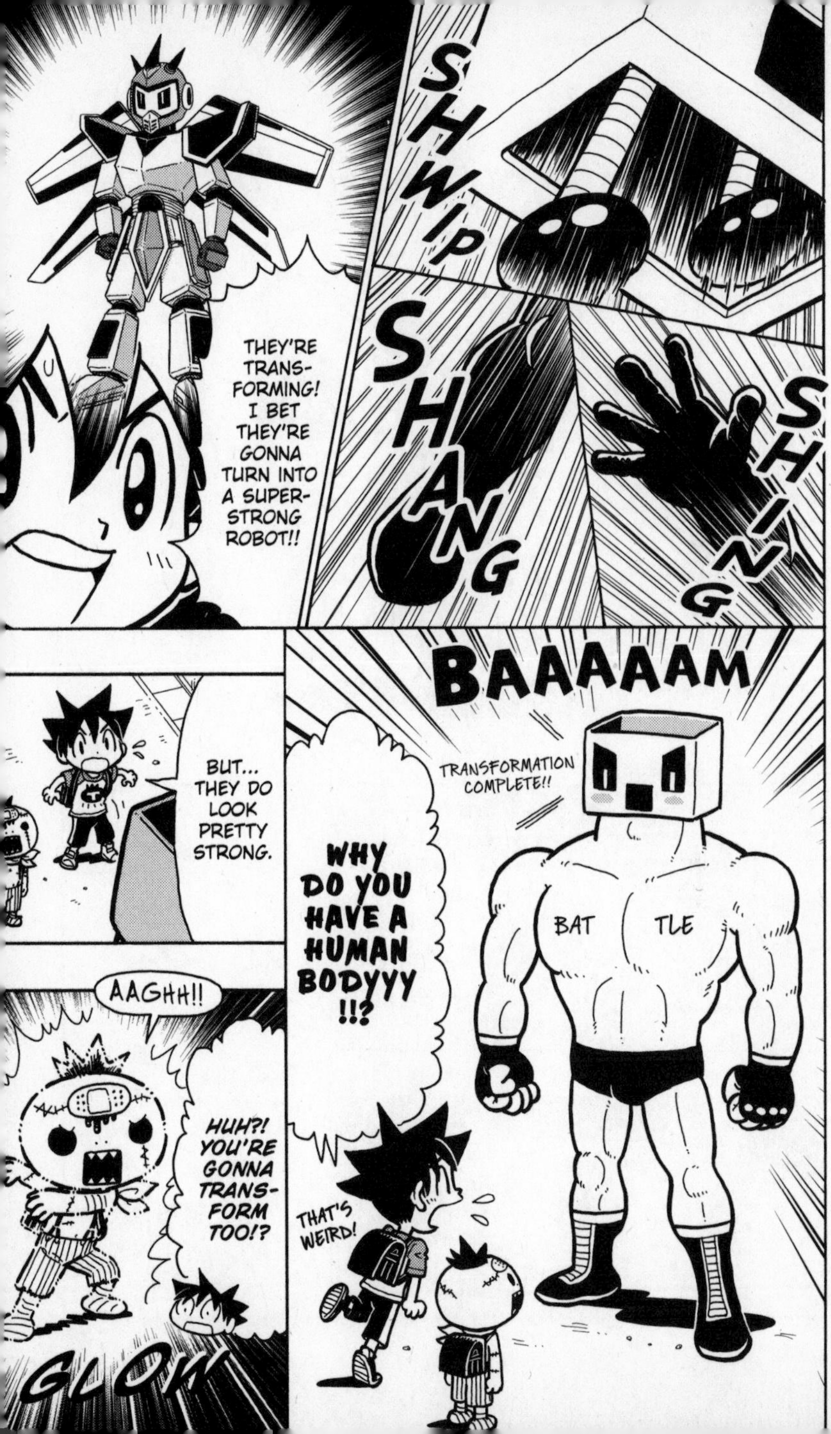
SHWIP
SHING
SHANG
THEY'RE TRANS-FORMING! I BET THEY'RE GONNA TURN INTO A SUPER-STRONG ROBOT!!
BAAAAAM
TRANSFORMATION COMPLETE!!
BAT TLE
WHY DO YOU HAVE A HUMAN BODYYY!!?
THAT'S WEIRD!
BUT... THEY DO LOOK PRETTY STRONG.
AAGHH!!
HUH?! YOU'RE GONNA TRANS-FORM TOO!?
GLOW

......
I CAN TELL BY LOOKING THAT YOU'RE WAY WEAKER!!
WHAT'S THE POINT IN THAT!?
SLIDE

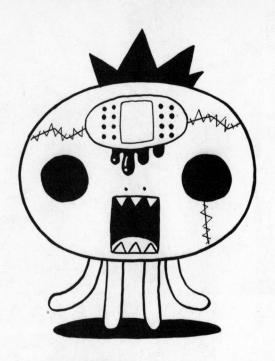

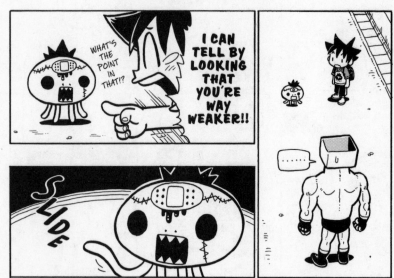

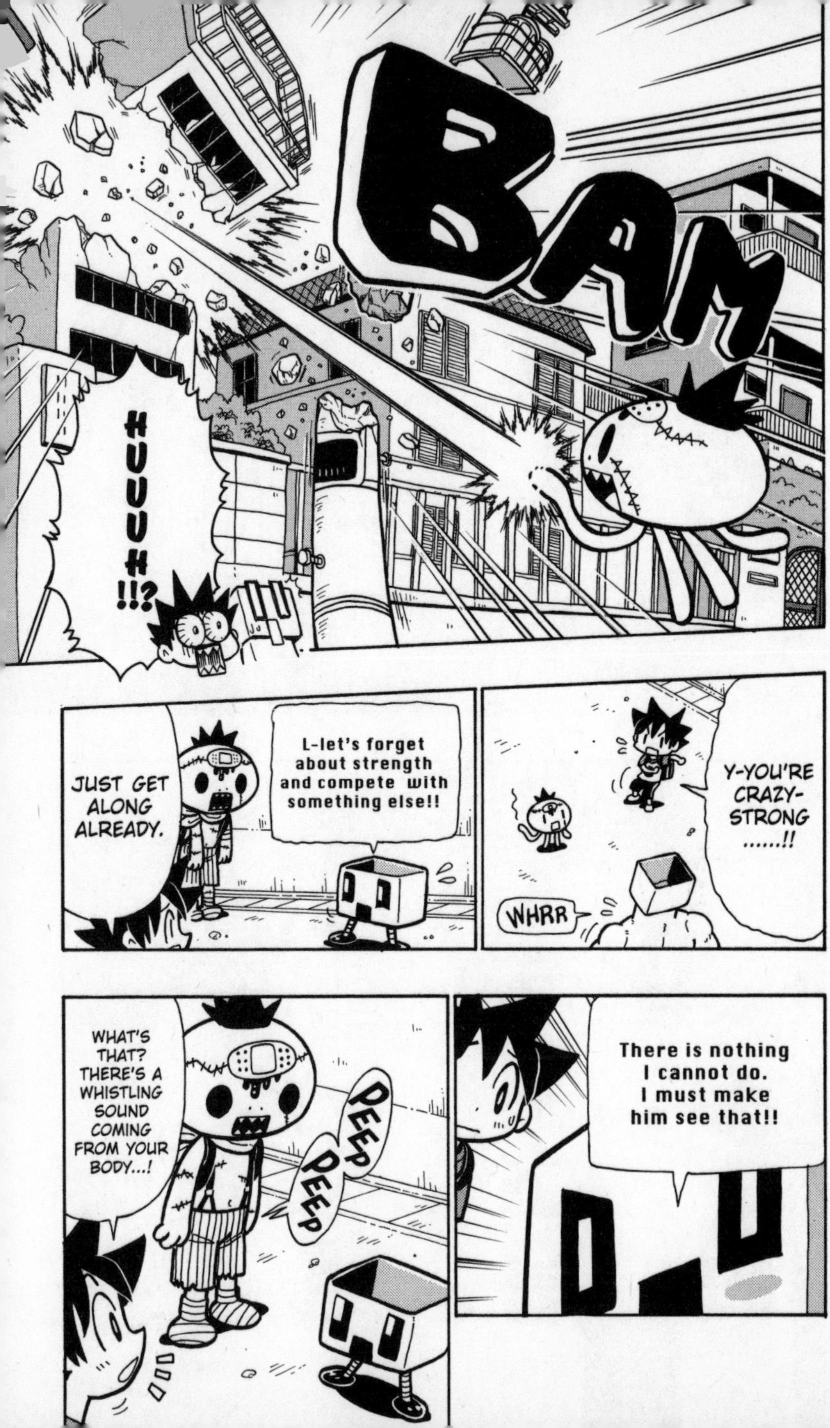
BAM
HUUUUH!!?
Y-YOU'RE CRAZY-STRONG ......!!
WHRR
L-let's forget about strength and compete with something else!!
JUST GET ALONG ALREADY.
There is nothing I cannot do. I must make him see that!!
PEEP PEEP
WHAT'S THAT? THERE'S A WHISTLING SOUND COMING FROM YOUR BODY...!

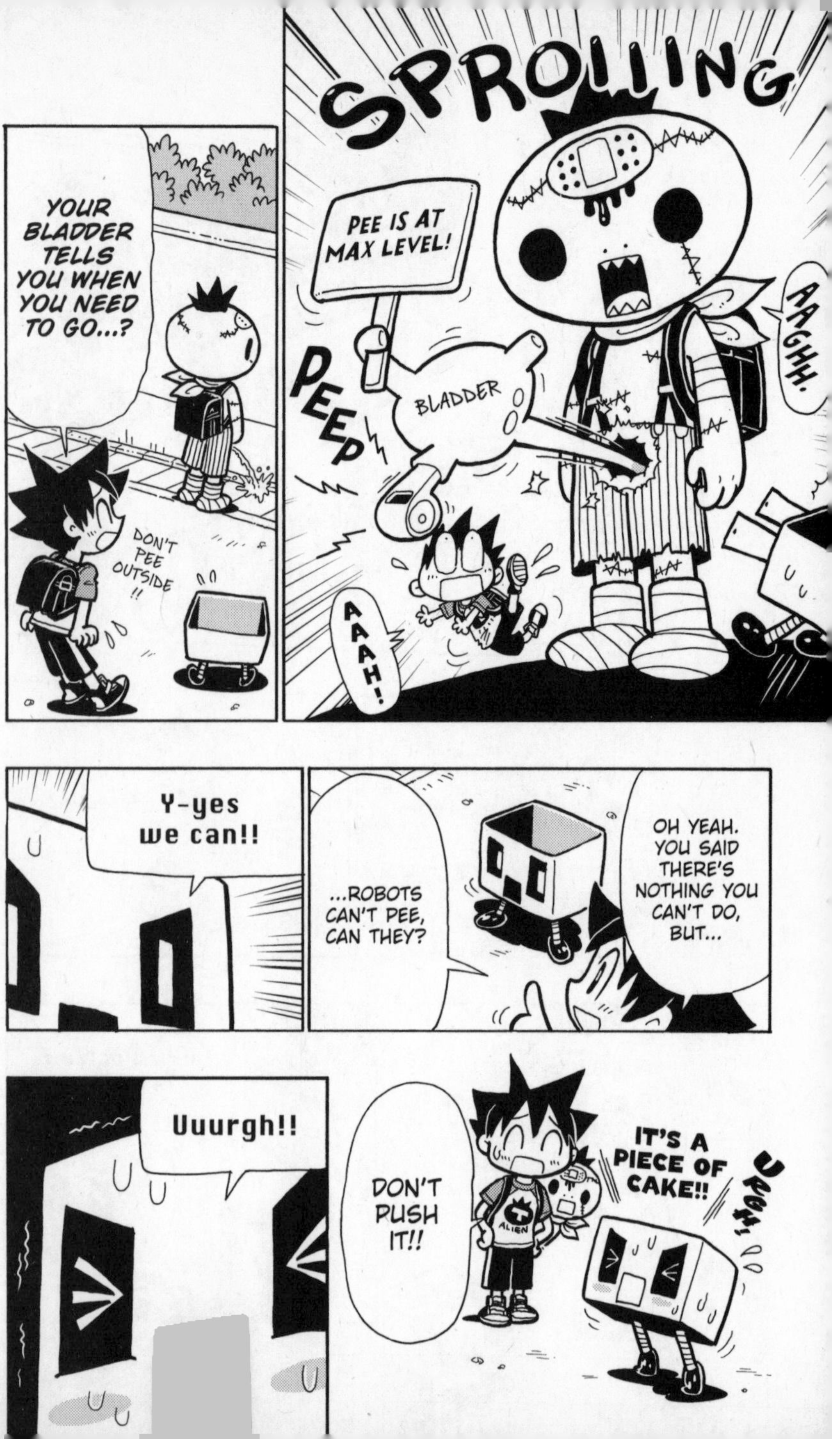
SPROIIING
PEE IS AT MAX LEVEL!
AAGHH.
BLADDER
PEEP
AAAH!
YOUR BLADDER TELLS YOU WHEN YOU NEED TO GO...?
DON'T PEE OUTSIDE !!
OH YEAH. YOU SAID THERE'S NOTHING YOU CAN'T DO, BUT...
...ROBOTS CAN'T PEE, CAN THEY?
Y-yes we can!!
IT'S A PIECE OF CAKE!!
DON'T PUSH IT!!
Uuurgh!!

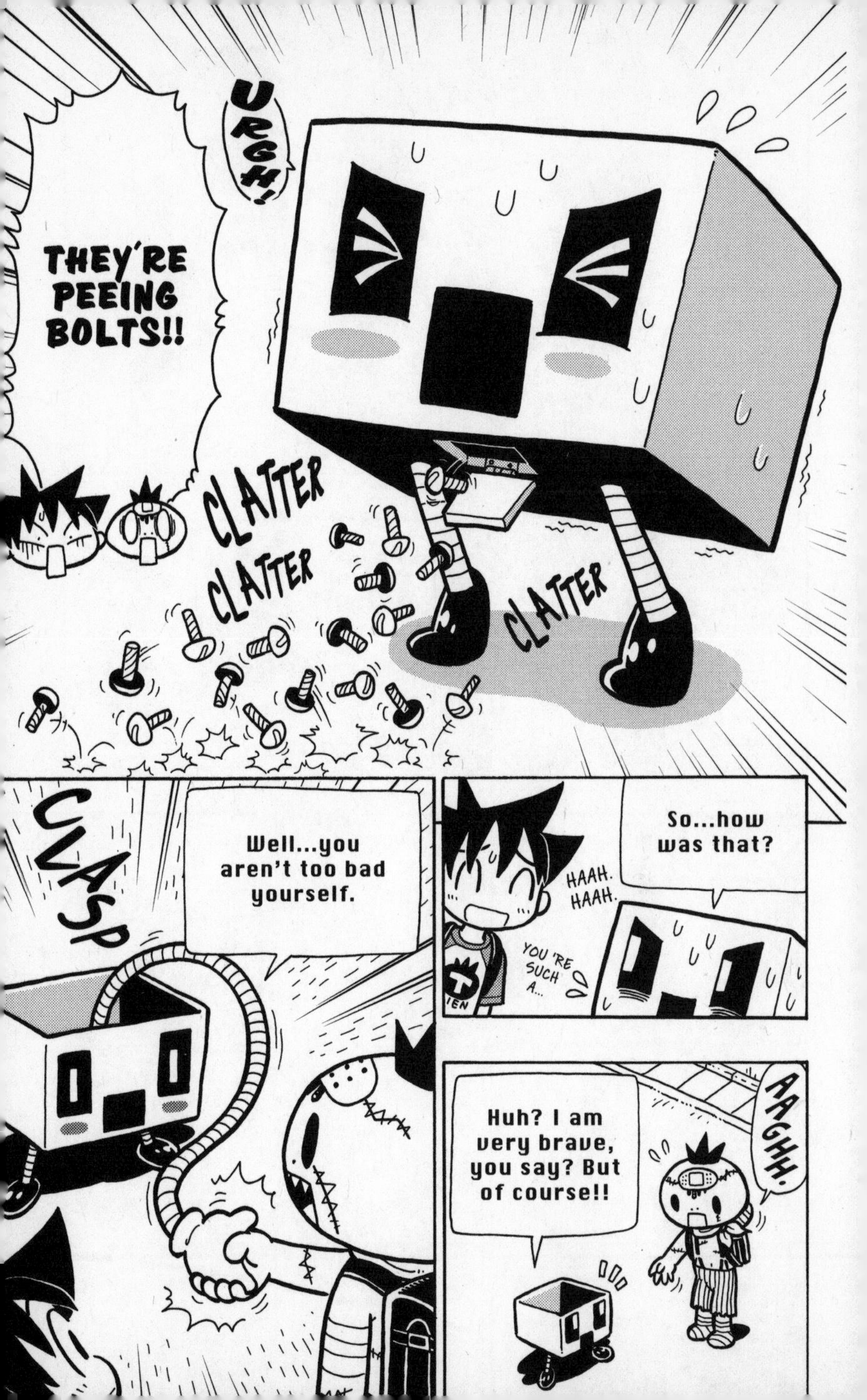
URGH!
THEY'RE PEEING BOLTS!!
CLATTER
CLATTER
CLATTER
So...how was that?
HAAH. HAAH.
YOU'RE SUCH A...
Huh? I am very brave, you say? But of course!!
AAGHH.
CLASP
Well...you aren't too bad yourself.

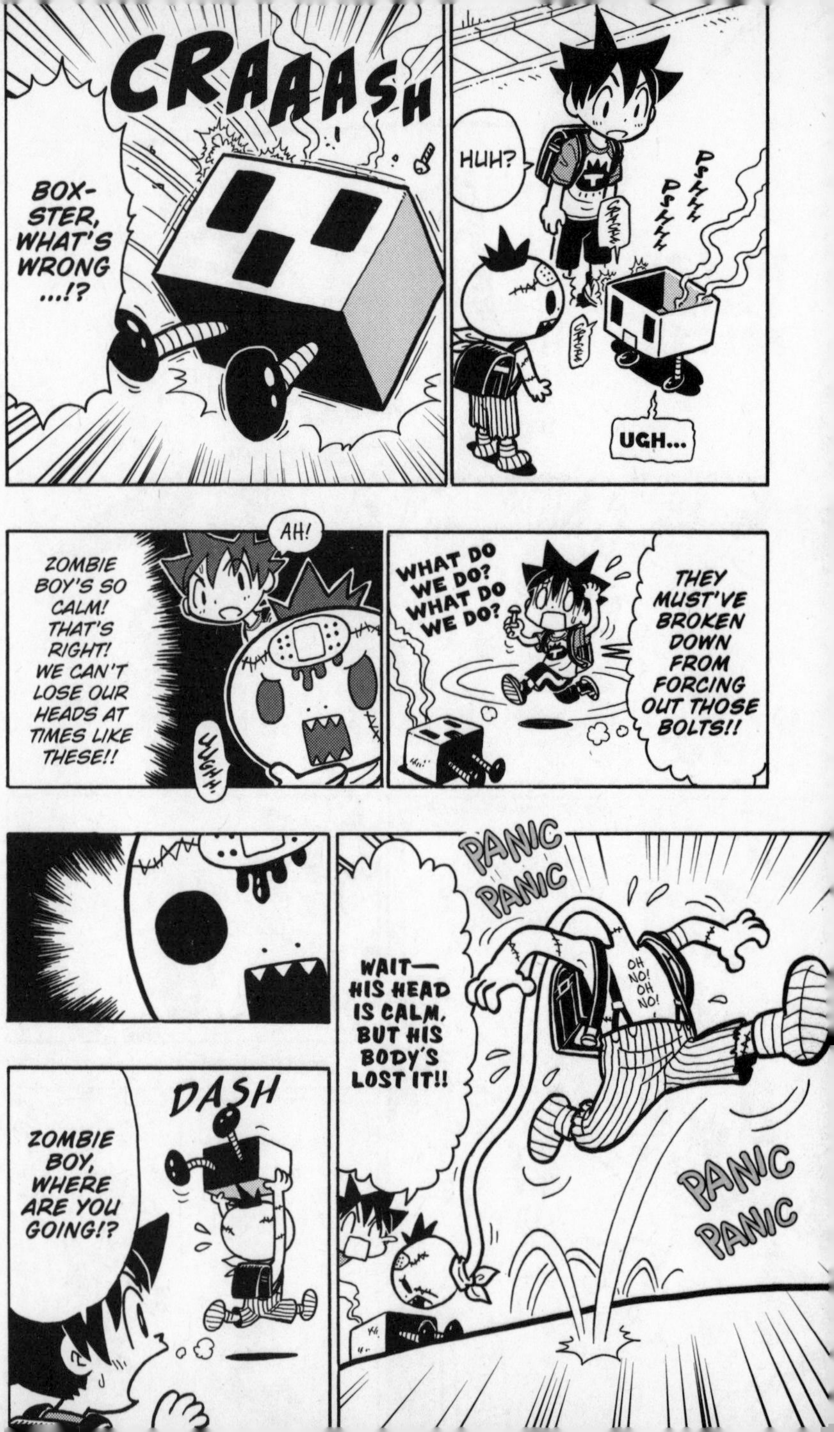
HUH?
PSHHH PSHHH
UGH...
CRAAASH
BOX-STER, WHAT'S WRONG ...!?
THEY MUST'VE BROKEN DOWN FROM FORCING OUT THOSE BOLTS!!
WHAT DO WE DO? WHAT DO WE DO?
AH!
ZOMBIE BOY'S SO CALM! THAT'S RIGHT! WE CAN'T LOSE OUR HEADS AT TIMES LIKE THESE!!
PANIC PANIC
WAIT— HIS HEAD IS CALM, BUT HIS BODY'S LOST IT!!
OH NO! OH NO!
PANIC PANIC
DASH
ZOMBIE BOY, WHERE ARE YOU GOING!?

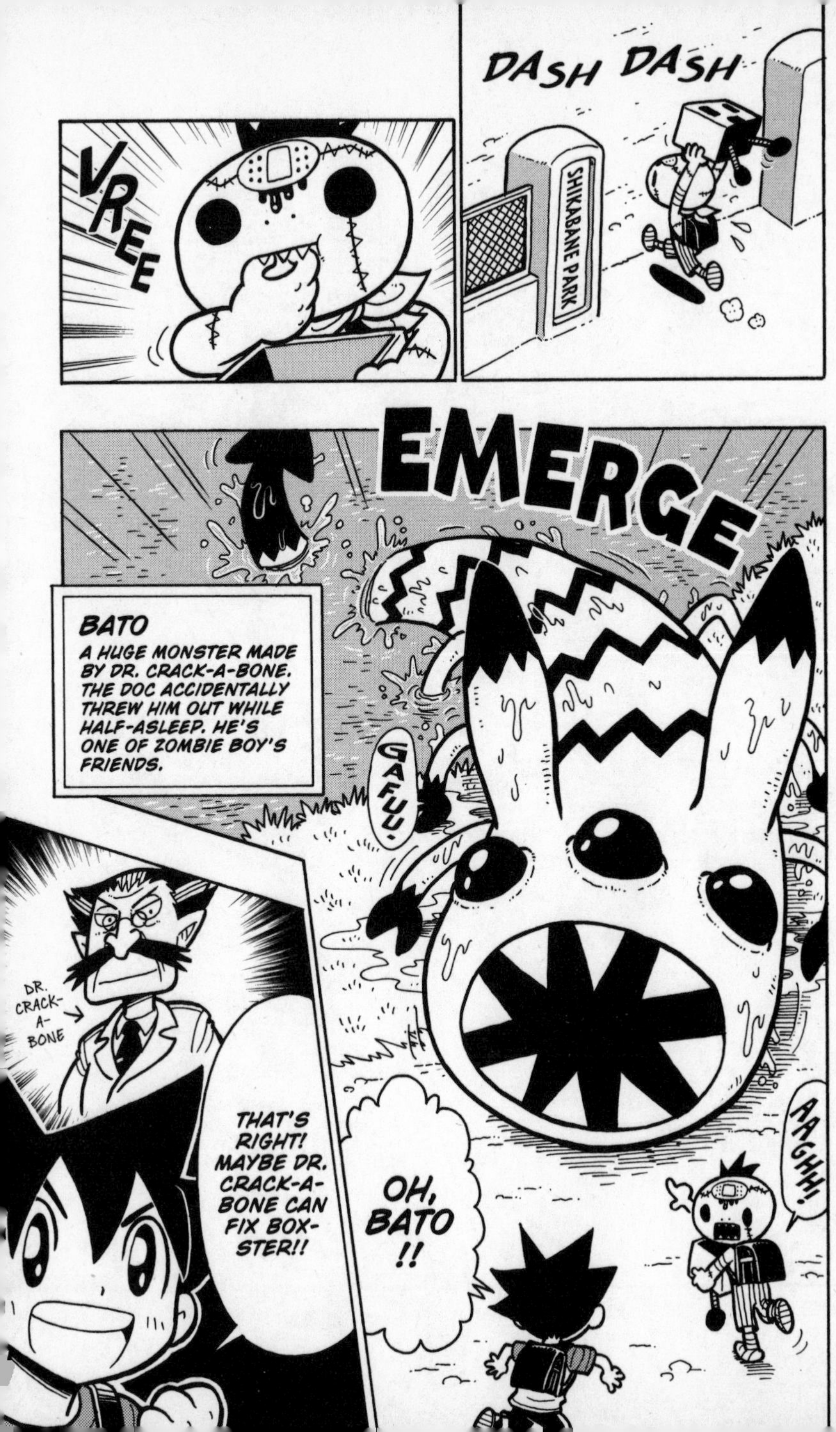
DASH DASH
SHIKABANE PARK
VREE
EMERGE
BATO
A HUGE MONSTER MADE BY DR. CRACK-A-BONE. THE DOC ACCIDENTALLY THREW HIM OUT WHILE HALF-ASLEEP. HE'S ONE OF ZOMBIE BOY'S FRIENDS.
GAFUU.
AAGHH!
OH, BATO!!
DR. CRACK-A-BONE
THAT'S RIGHT! MAYBE DR. CRACK-A-BONE CAN FIX BOX-STER!!

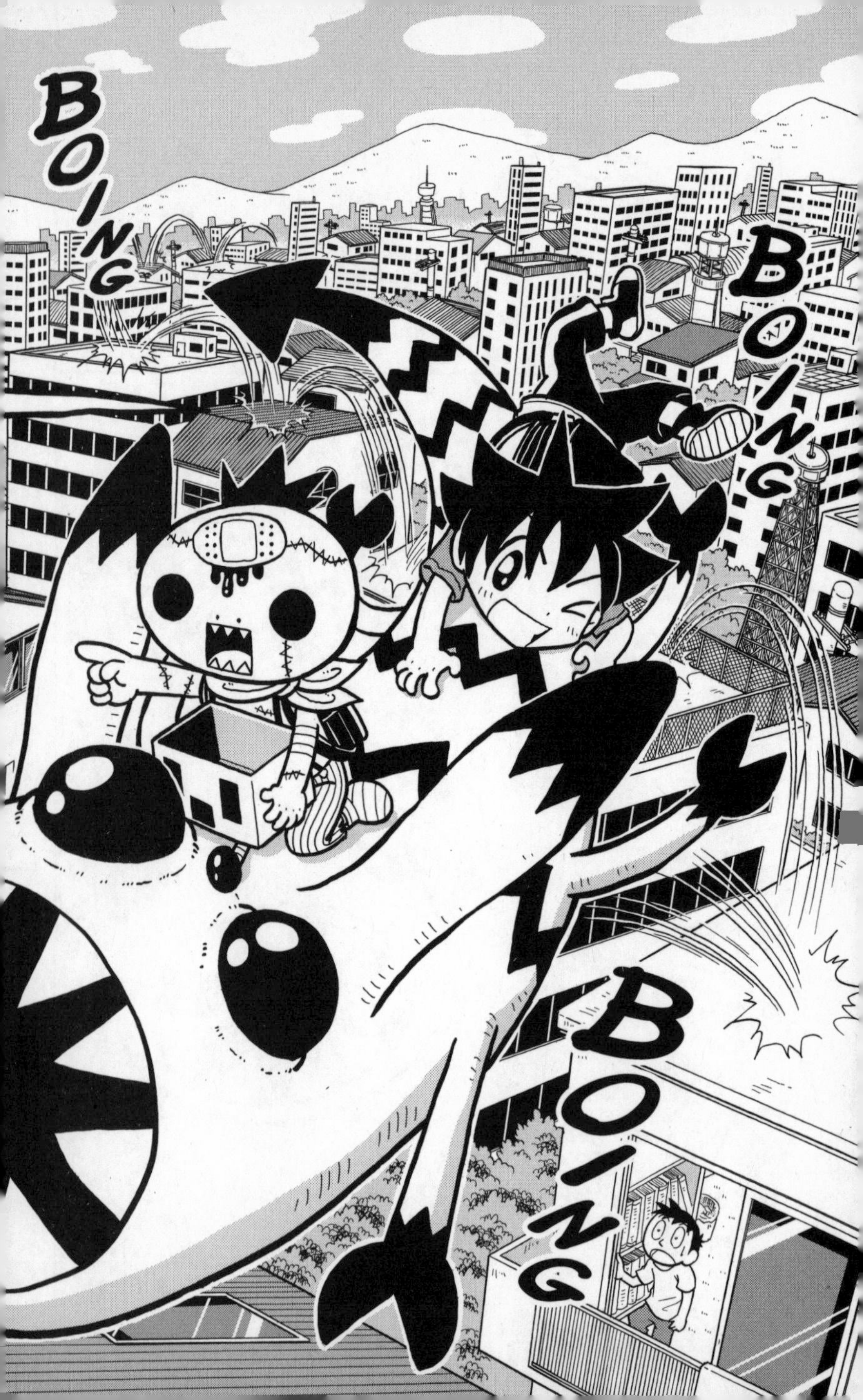
BOING
BOING
BOING

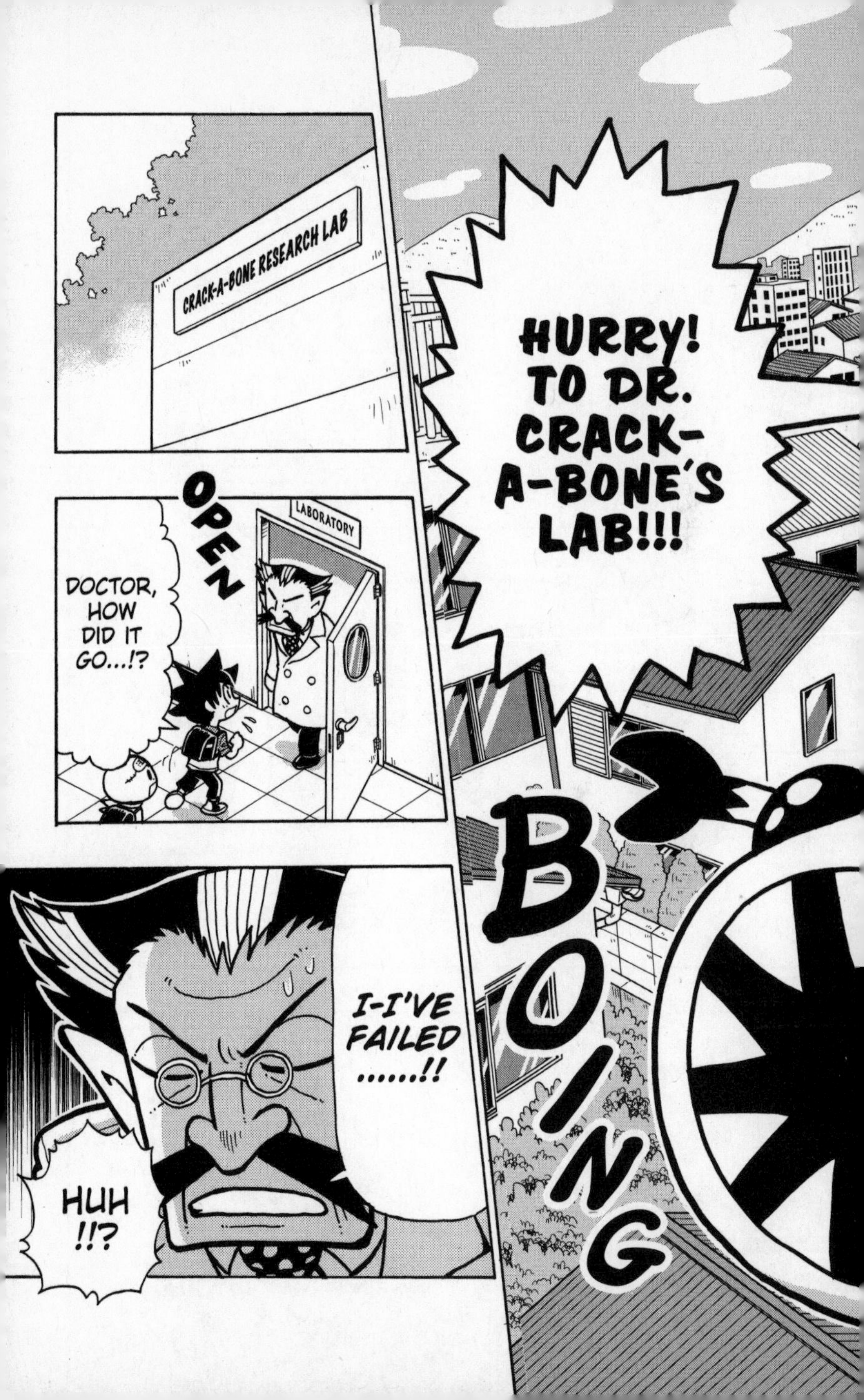
HURRY! TO DR. CRACK-A-BONE'S LAB!!!
BOING
CRACK-A-BONE RESEARCH LAB
LABORATORY
OPEN
DOCTOR, HOW DID IT GO...!?
I-I'VE FAILED ......!!
HUH !!?

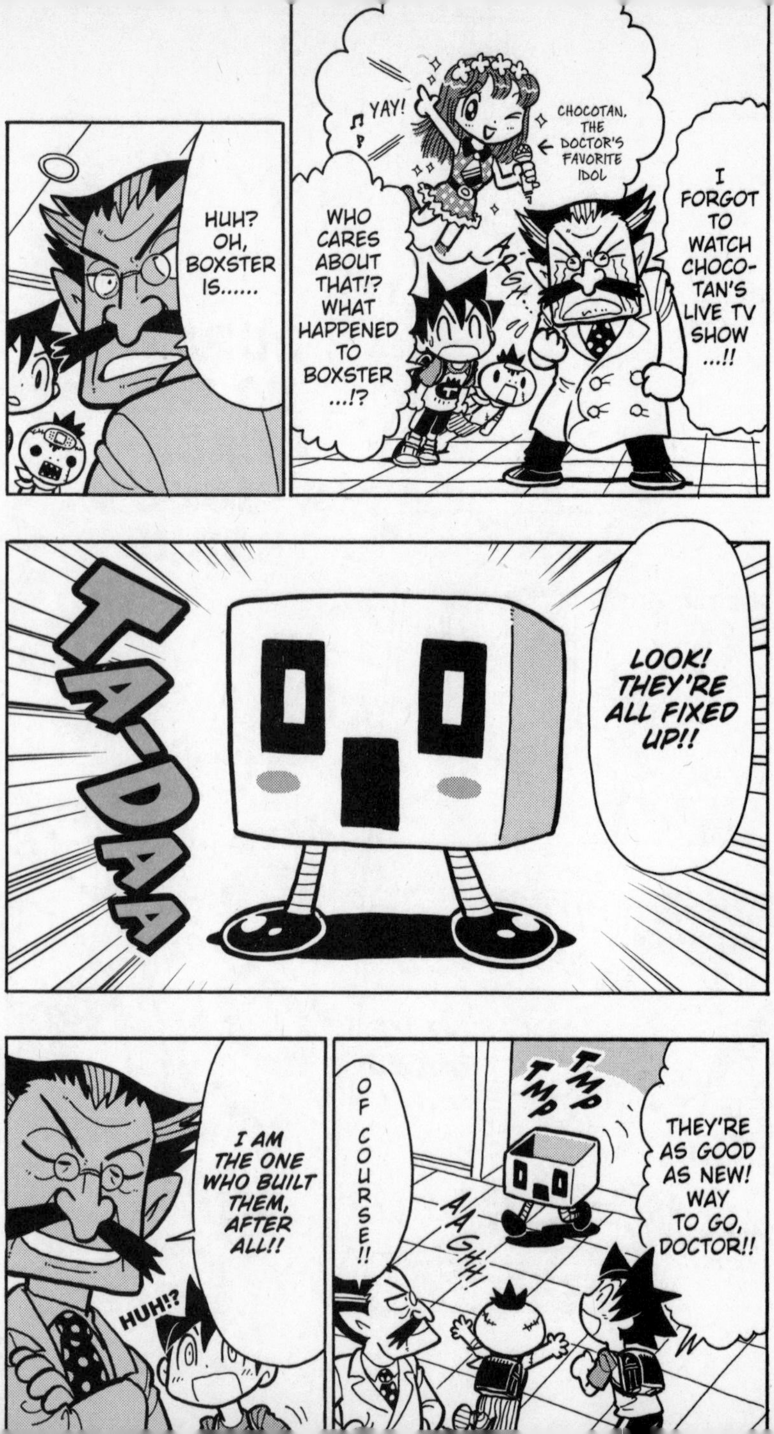
I FORGOT TO WATCH CHOCO-TAN'S LIVE TV SHOW ...!!
CHOCOTAN, THE DOCTOR'S FAVORITE IDOL
YAY!
ARGH...
WHO CARES ABOUT THAT!? WHAT HAPPENED TO BOXSTER ...!?
HUH? OH, BOXSTER IS......
LOOK! THEY'RE ALL FIXED UP!!
TA-DAA
THEY'RE AS GOOD AS NEW! WAY TO GO, DOCTOR!!
TMP TMP
AAGHH!
OF COURSE!!
I AM THE ONE WHO BUILT THEM, AFTER ALL!!
HUH!?

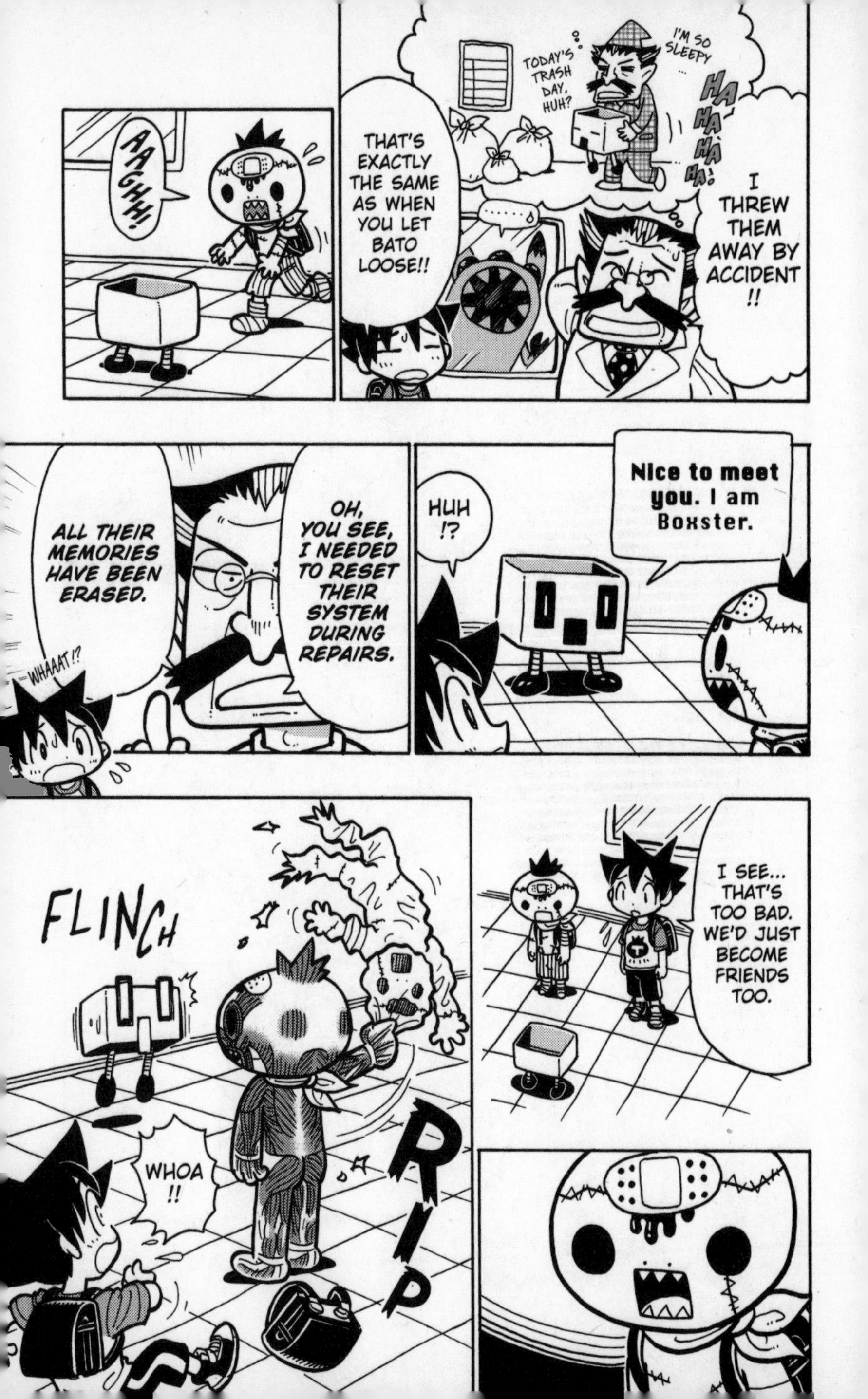
I'M SO SLEEPY...
TODAY'S TRASH DAY, HUH?
HA HA HA HA!
I THREW THEM AWAY BY ACCIDENT!!
......
THAT'S EXACTLY THE SAME AS WHEN YOU LET BATO LOOSE!!
AAGHH!!
Nice to meet you. I am Boxster.
HUH!?
OH, YOU SEE, I NEEDED TO RESET THEIR SYSTEM DURING REPAIRS.
ALL THEIR MEMORIES HAVE BEEN ERASED.
WHAAAT!?
I SEE... THAT'S TOO BAD. WE'D JUST BECOME FRIENDS TOO.
FLINCH
RIP
WHOA!!

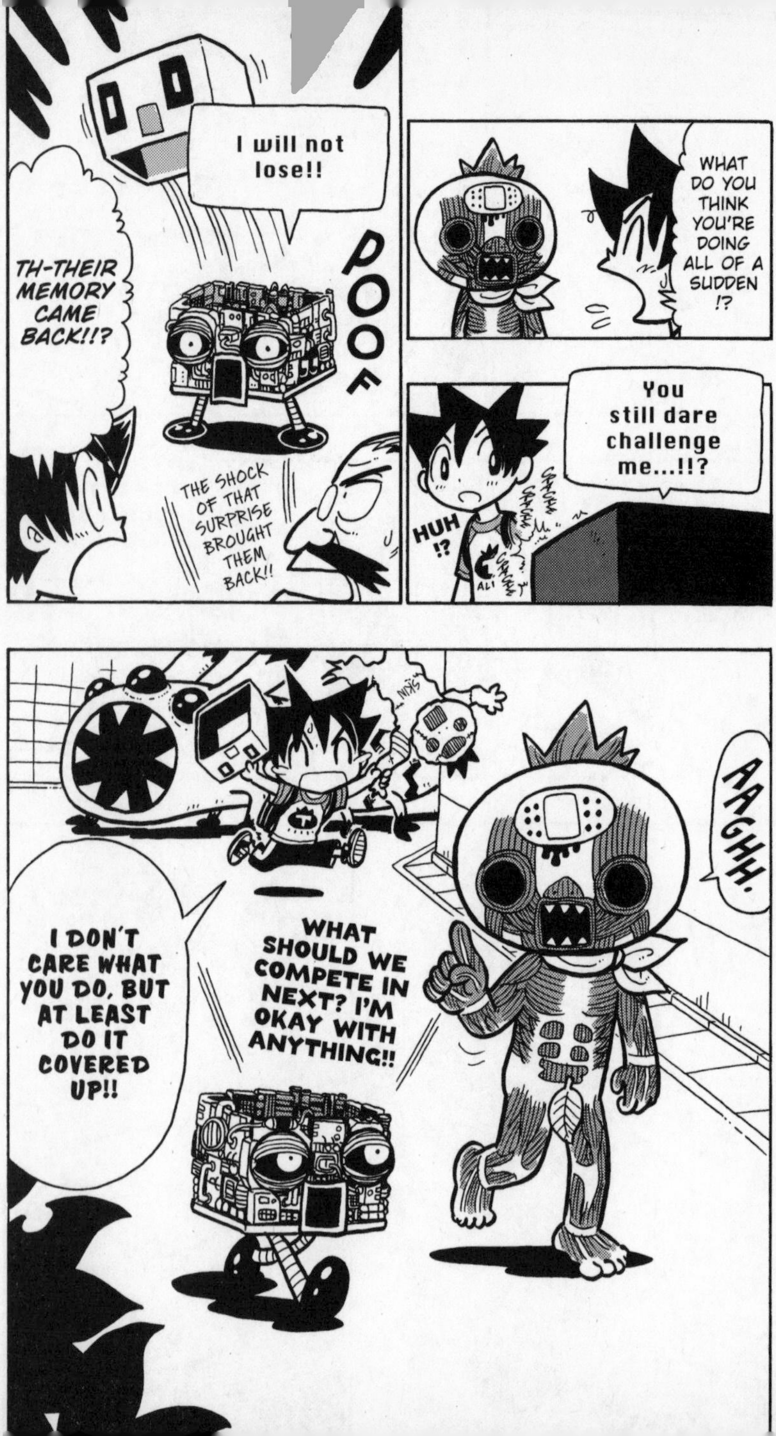
WHAT DO YOU THINK YOU'RE DOING ALL OF A SUDDEN !?
You still dare challenge me...!!?
HUH !?
I will not lose!!
POOF
TH-THEIR MEMORY CAME BACK!!?
THE SHOCK OF THAT SURPRISE BROUGHT THEM BACK!!
AAGHH.
WHAT SHOULD WE COMPETE IN NEXT? I'M OKAY WITH ANYTHING!!
I DON'T CARE WHAT YOU DO, BUT AT LEAST DO IT COVERED UP!!

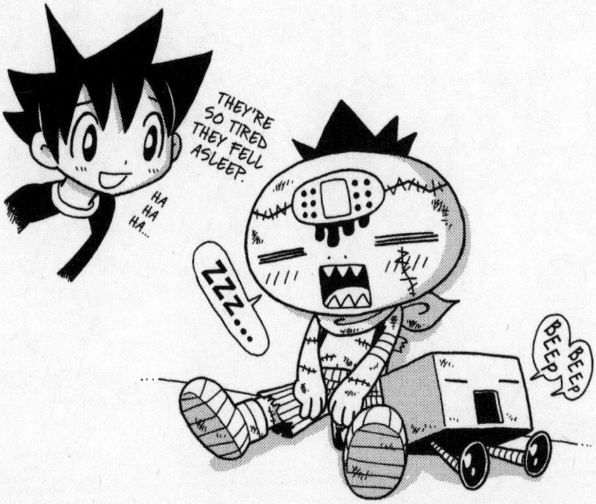
THEY'RE SO TIRED THEY FELL ASLEEP.
HA HA HA...
ZZZ...
BEEP BEEP
...
...

ZOMBIES HATE SHOTZ TOO!

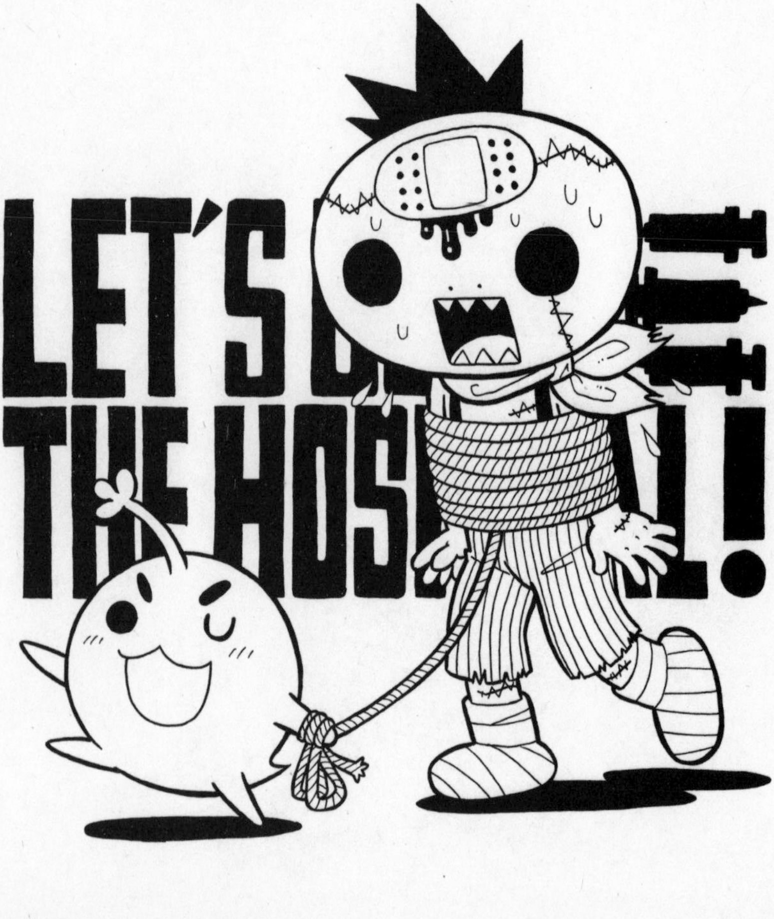
LET'S
THE

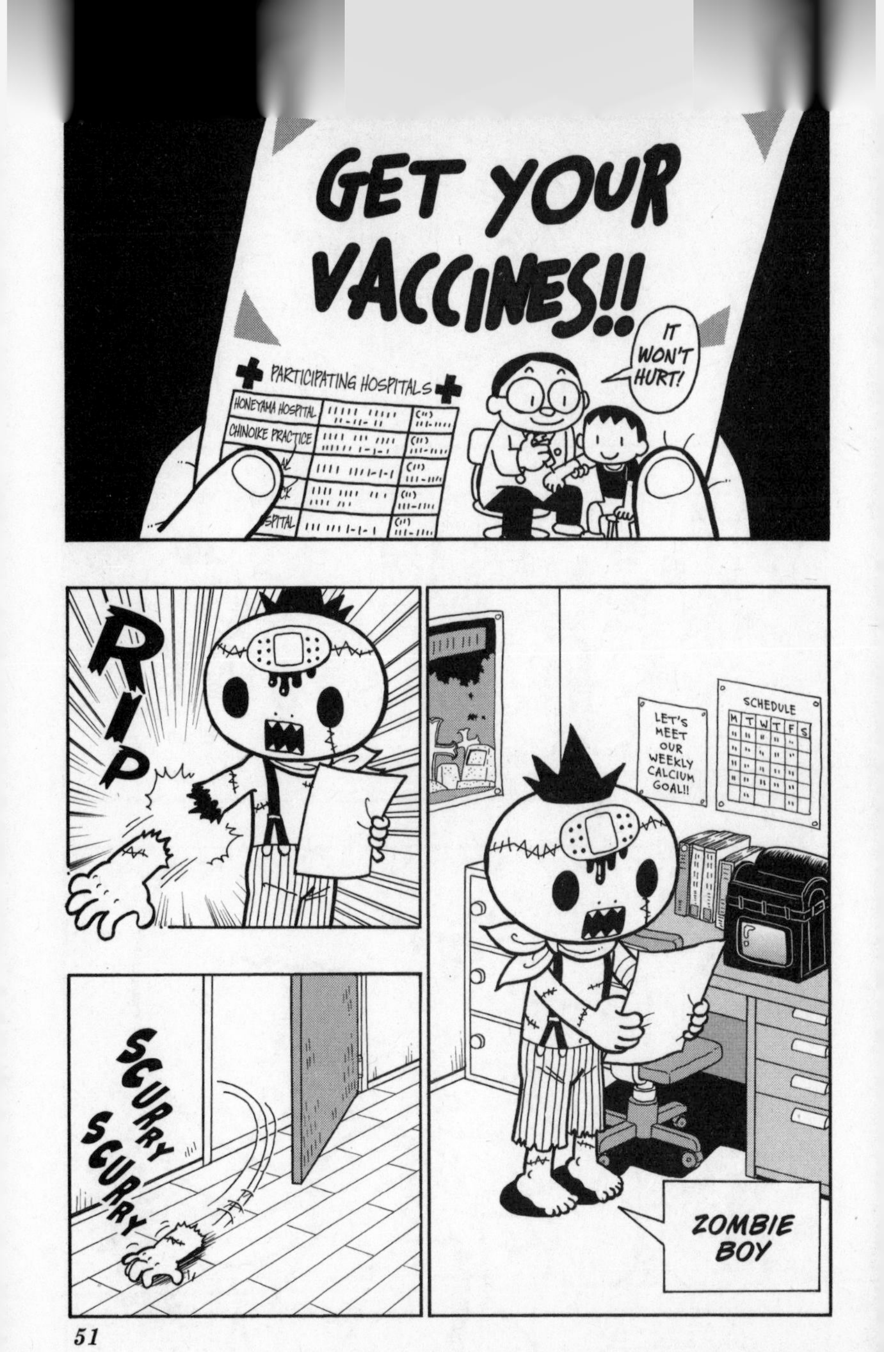
GET YOUR VACCINES!!
PARTICIPATING HOSPITALS
HONEYAMA HOSPITAL
CHINOIKE PRACTICE
IT WON'T HURT!
SCHEDULE
LET'S MEET OUR WEEKLY CALCIUM GOAL!!
ZOMBIE BOY
RIP
SCURRY SCURRY

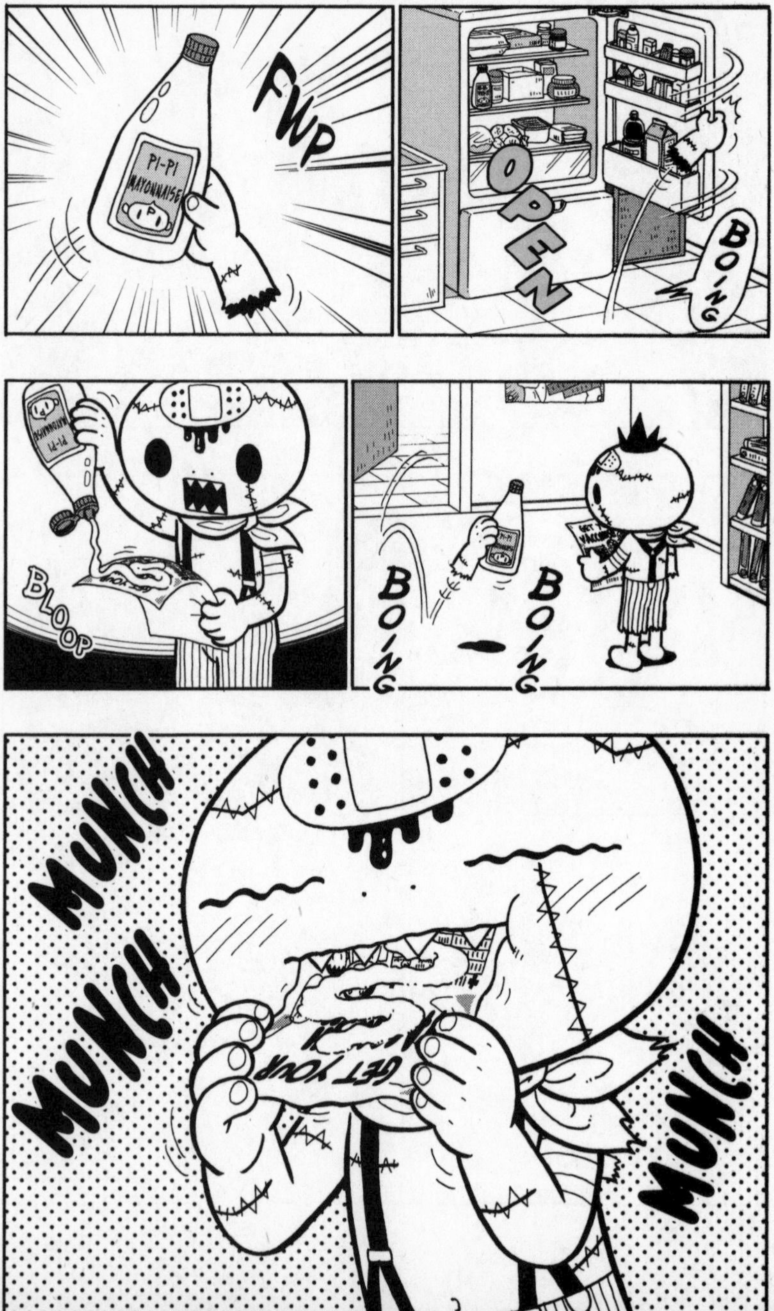
OPEN
BOING
PI-PI MAYONNAISE
PI
FWP
BOING
BOING
PI-PI
BLOOP
PI-PI MAYONNAISE
GET YOUR
MUNCH
MUNCH
MUNCH
GET YOUR

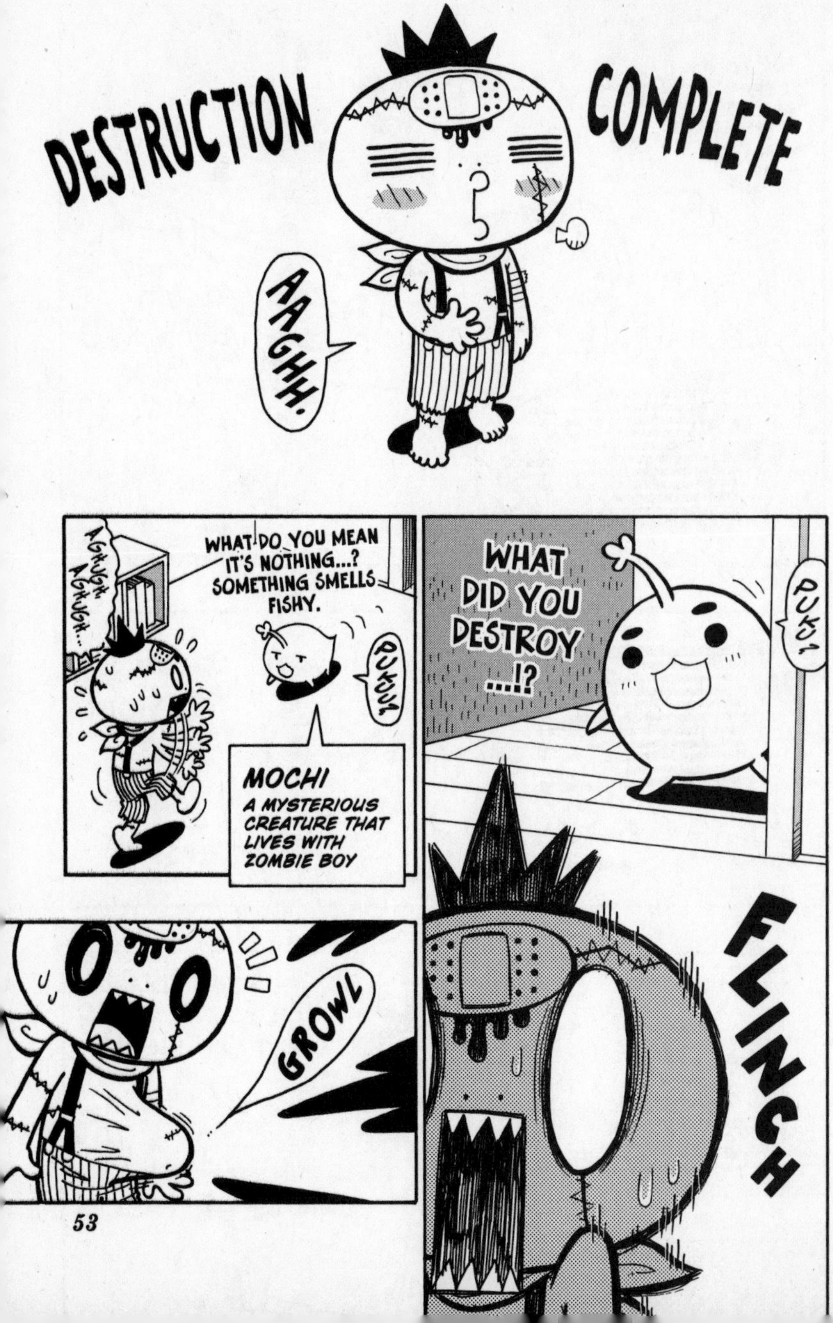
DESTRUCTION COMPLETE
AAGHH.
WHAT DID YOU DESTROY ...!?
PUKU!
AGHUGH AGHUGH...
WHAT DO YOU MEAN IT'S NOTHING...? SOMETHING SMELLS FISHY.
PUKU!
MOCHI
A MYSTERIOUS CREATURE THAT LIVES WITH ZOMBIE BOY
FLINCH
GROWL

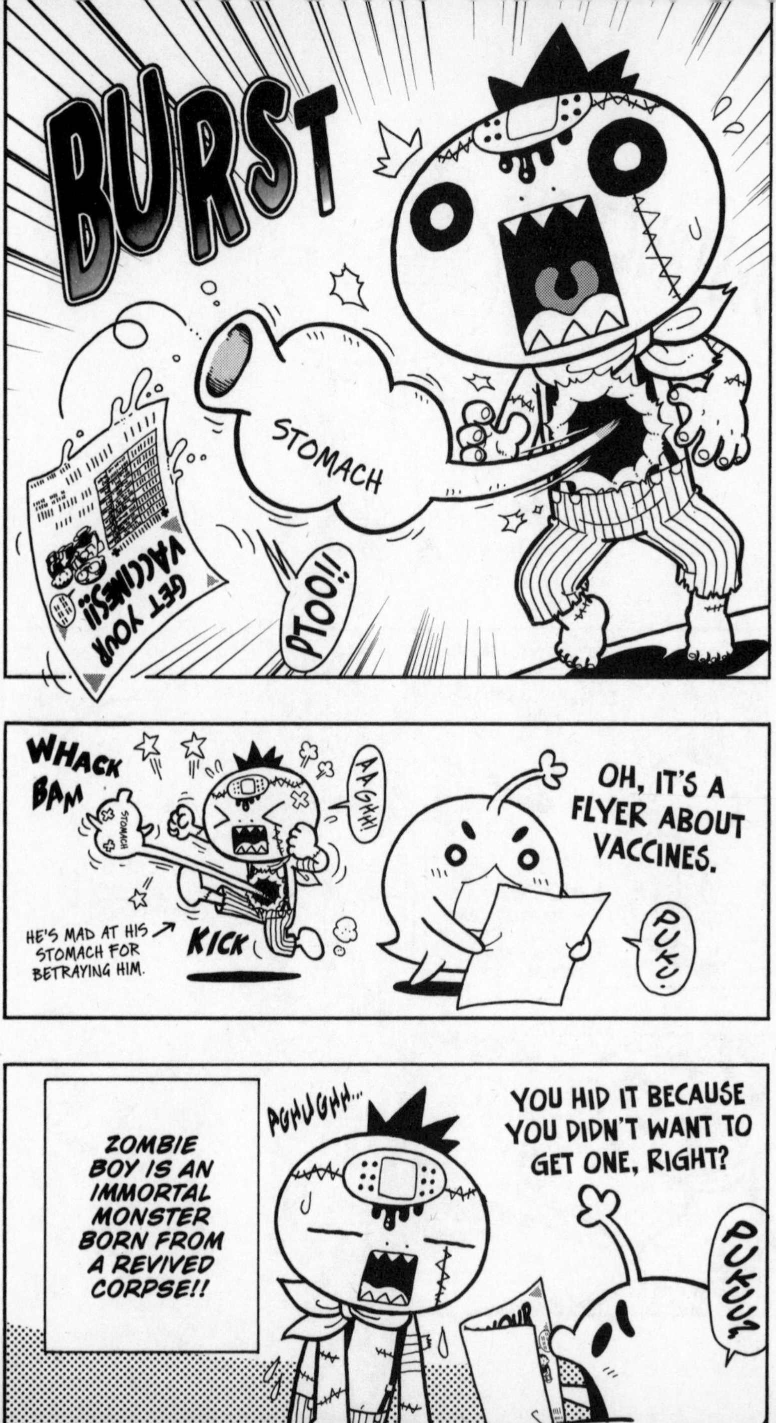
BURST
STOMACH
GET YOUR VACCINES!!
PTOO!!
OH, IT'S A FLYER ABOUT VACCINES.
PUKU.
AAGHH!
WHACK
BAM
STOMACH
KICK
HE'S MAD AT HIS STOMACH FOR BETRAYING HIM.
YOU HID IT BECAUSE YOU DIDN'T WANT TO GET ONE, RIGHT?
PUKUU?
PGHUGHH...
ZOMBIE BOY IS AN IMMORTAL MONSTER BORN FROM A REVIVED CORPSE!!

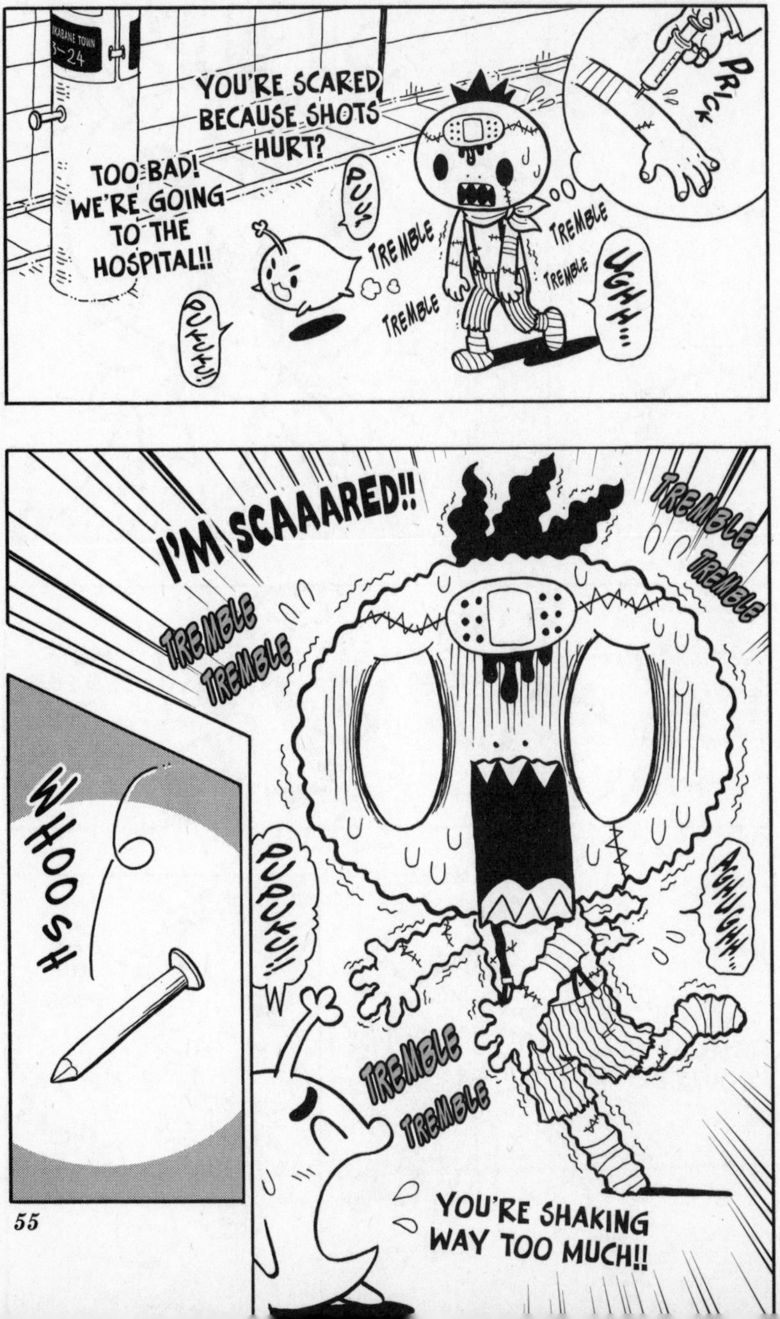
PRICK
IKABANE TOWN
3-24
UGHH...
TREMBLE
TREMBLE
TREMBLE
TREMBLE
YOU'RE SCARED BECAUSE SHOTS HURT?
PUU
TOO BAD! WE'RE GOING TO THE HOSPITAL!!
PUFUFU!
I'M SCAAARED!!
TREMBLE TREMBLE
TREMBLE TREMBLE
AGHUGHH...
PUPUFUFU!!
TREMBLE TREMBLE
YOU'RE SHAKING WAY TOO MUCH!!
WHOOSH

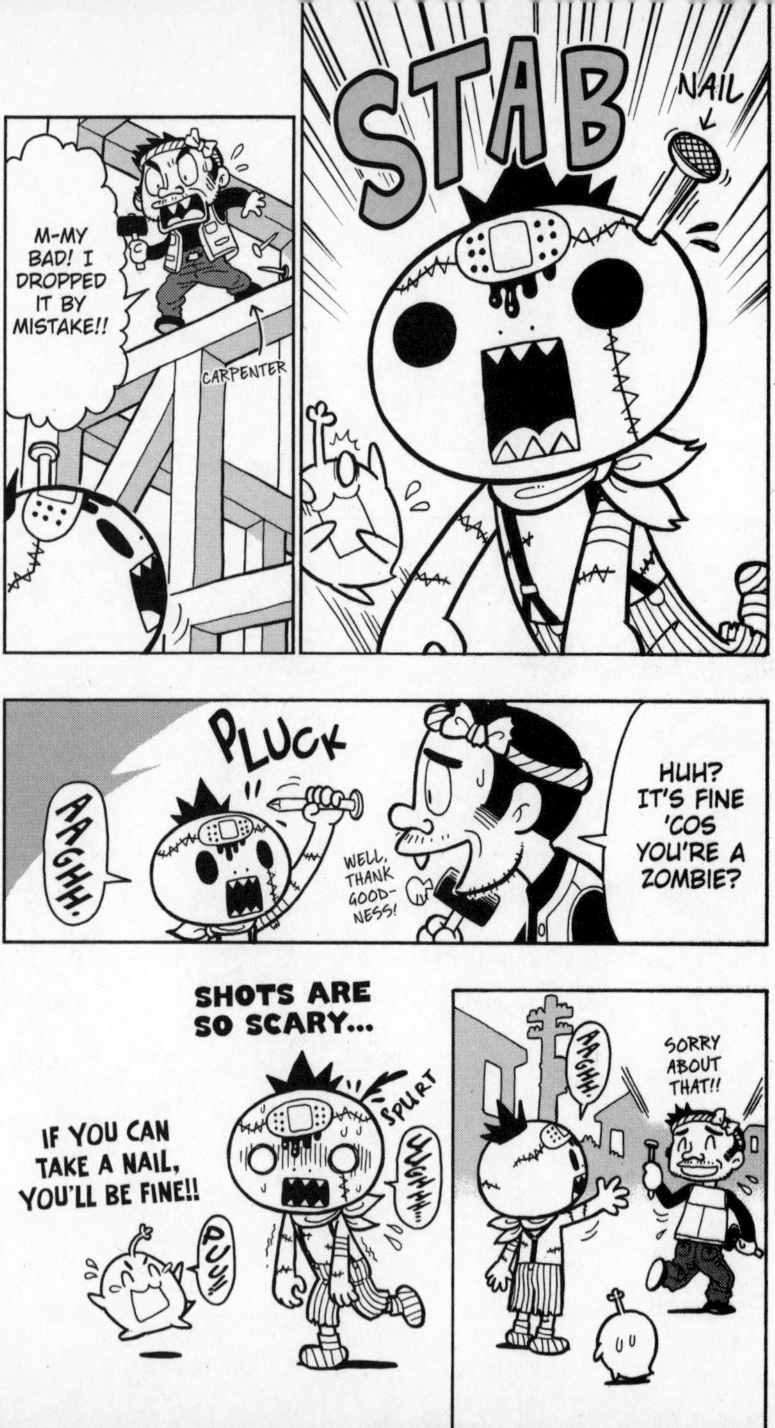
STAB
NAIL
M-MY BAD! I DROPPED IT BY MISTAKE!!
CARPENTER
HUH? IT'S FINE 'COS YOU'RE A ZOMBIE?
WELL, THANK GOOD-NESS!
PLUCK
AAGHH.
SORRY ABOUT THAT!!
AAGHH.
SHOTS ARE SO SCARY...
SPURT
UGGHH...
IF YOU CAN TAKE A NAIL, YOU'LL BE FINE!!
PUU

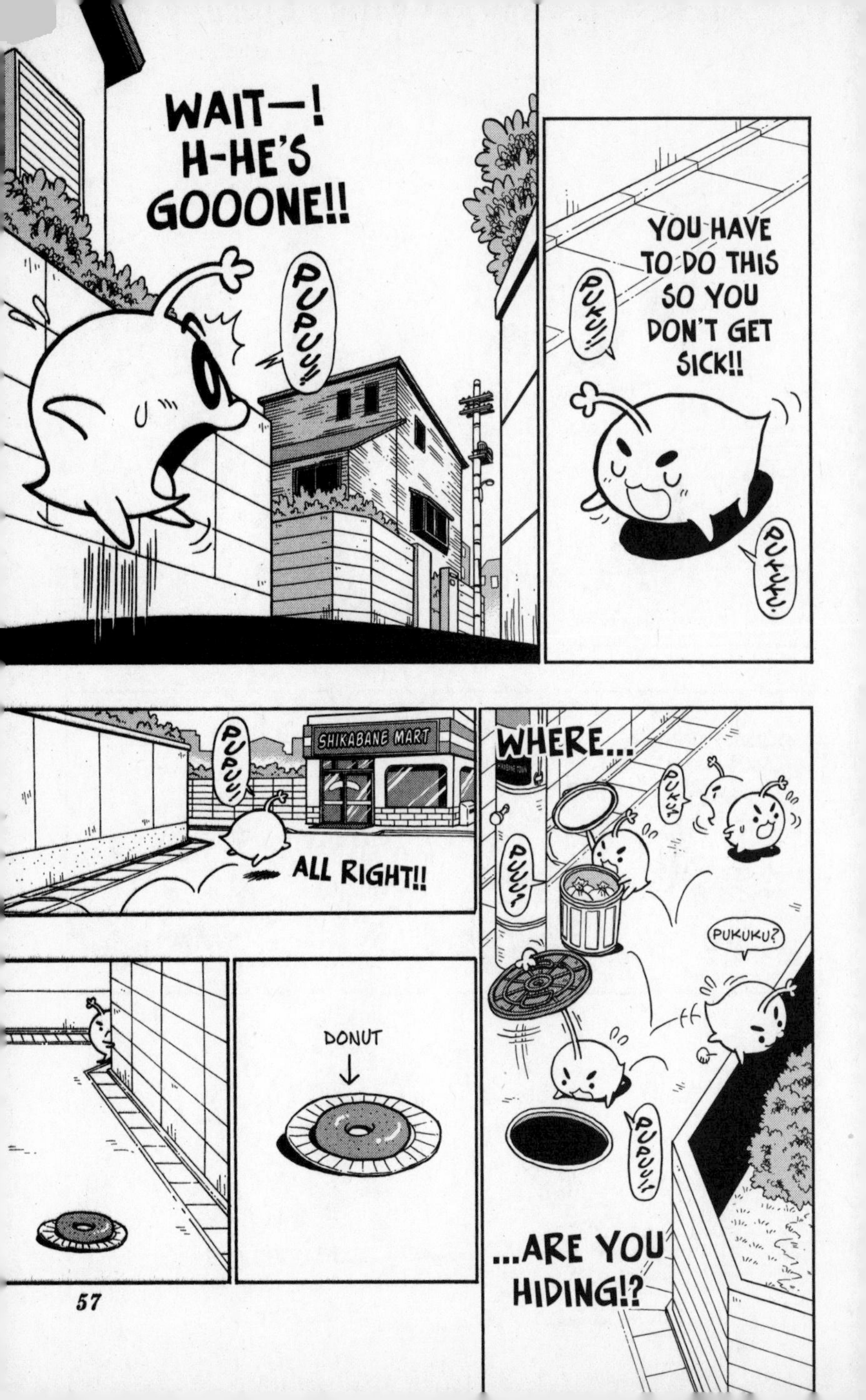

YOU HAVE TO DO THIS SO YOU DON'T GET SICK!!
PUKU!!
PUKUKU.
WAIT—! H-HE'S GOOONE!!
PUPUU!!
WHERE...
PUKU!
PUPUU?
PUKUKU?
PUPUU!?
...ARE YOU HIDING!?
SHIKABANE MART
PUPUU!
ALL RIGHT!!
DONUT

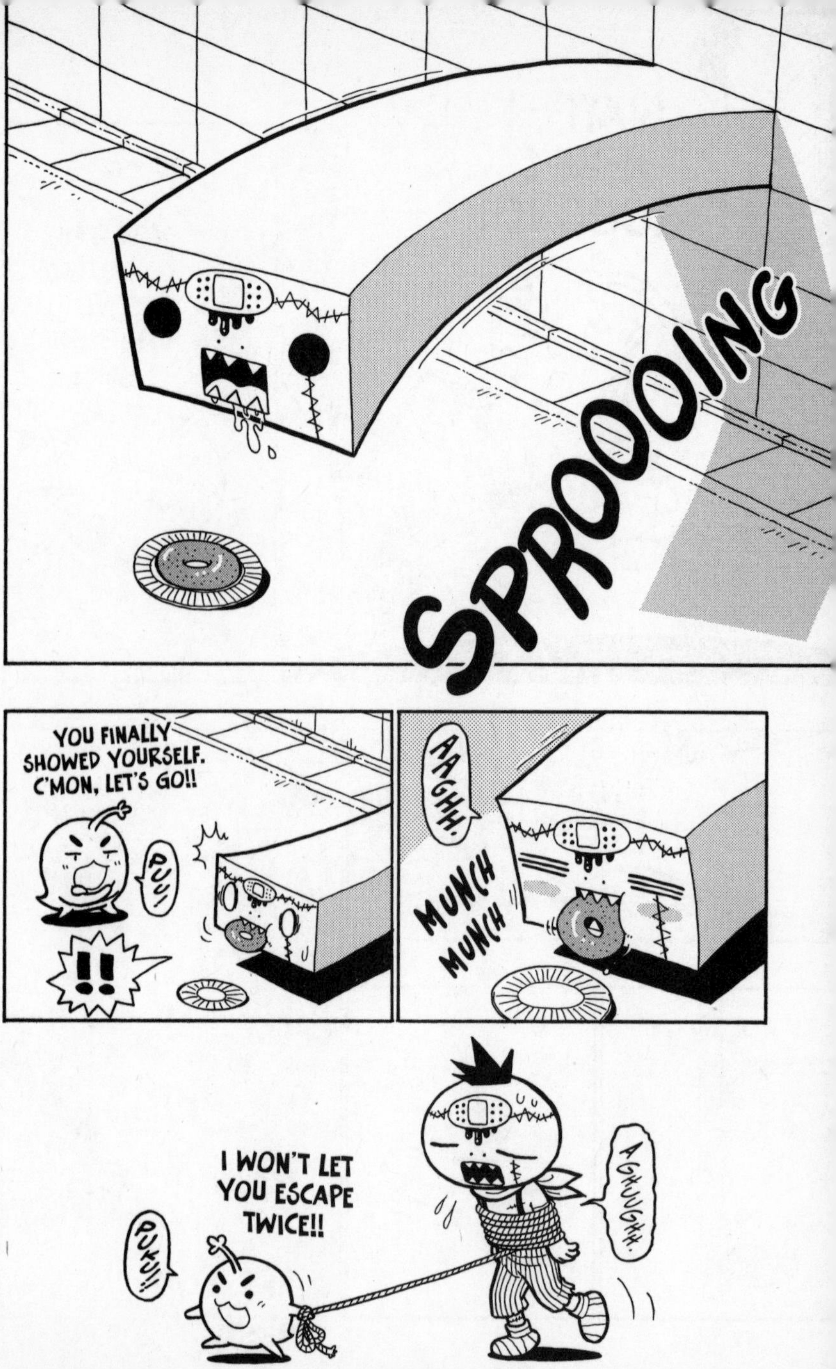
SPROOOING
AAGHH.
MUNCH MUNCH
YOU FINALLY SHOWED YOURSELF. C'MON, LET'S GO!!
PUU!
!!
AGHUUGHH.
I WON'T LET YOU ESCAPE TWICE!!
PUKU!!

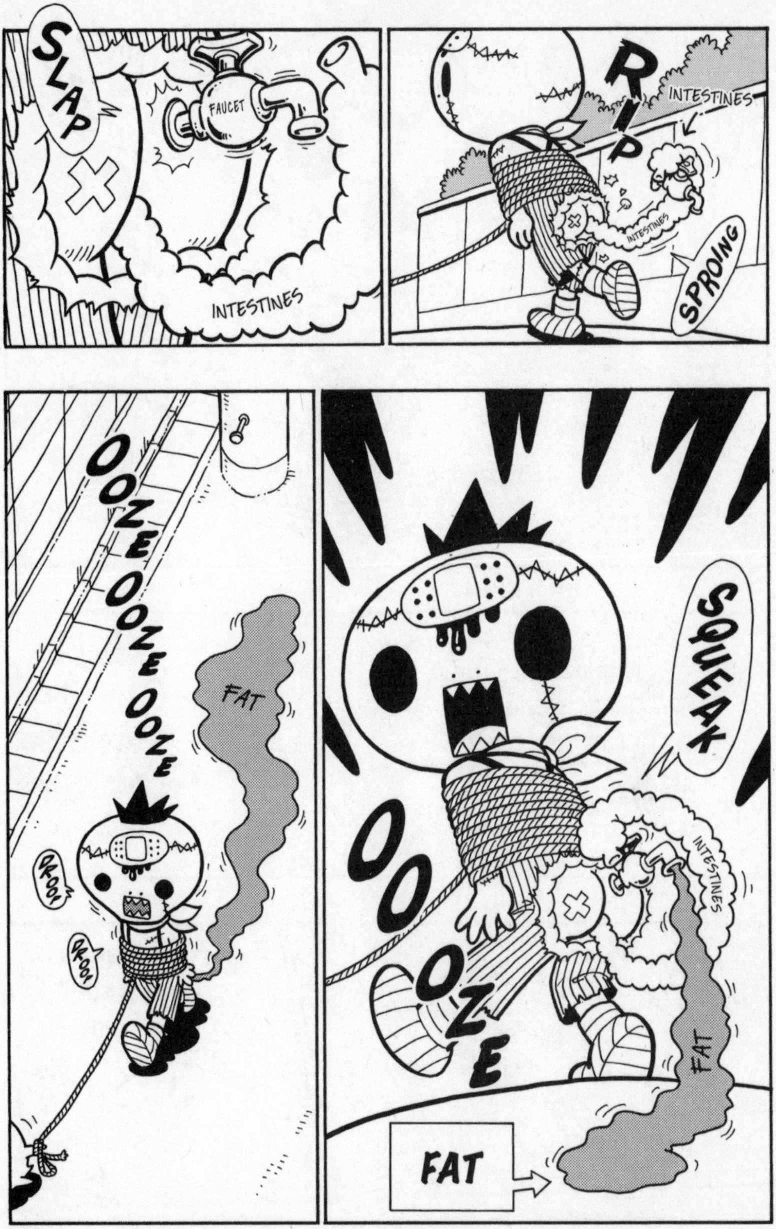
RIP
INTESTINES
INTESTINES
SPROING
SLAP
FAUCET
INTESTINES
SQUEAK
INTESTINES
OOOOZE
FAT
FAT
OOZE OOZE OOZE
FAT
DROOL
DROOL

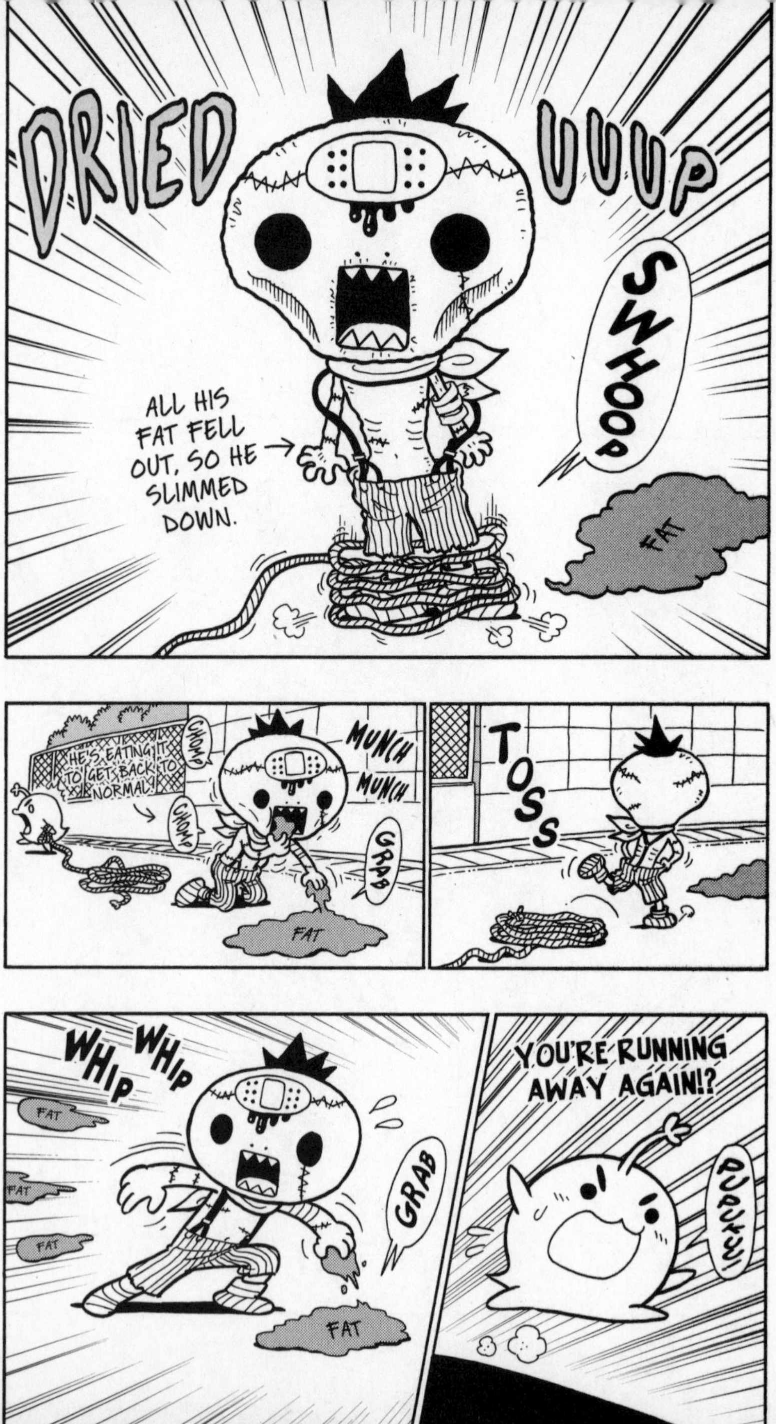
DRIED UUUP
SWHOOP
ALL HIS FAT FELL OUT, SO HE SLIMMED DOWN.
FAT
TOSS
MUNCH
MUNCH
CHOMP
HE'S EATING IT TO GET BACK TO NORMAL.
CHOMP
GRAB
FAT
YOU'RE RUNNING AWAY AGAIN!?
WHIP WHIP
FAT
FAT
FAT
GRAB
FAT

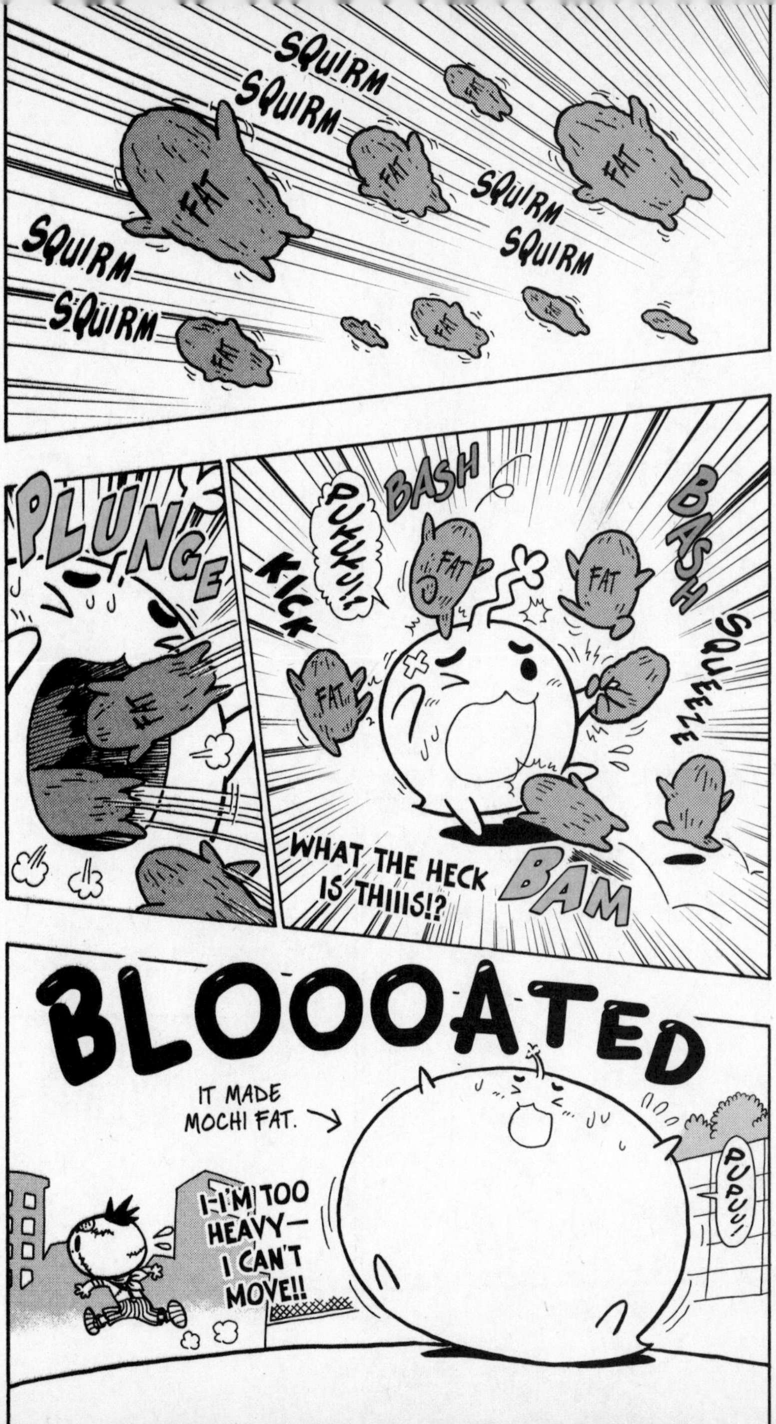
SQUIRM
SQUIRM
SQUIRM
SQUIRM
SQUIRM
SQUIRM
FAT
FAT
FAT
FAT
FAT
PUKUKUU!!
BASH
BASH
KICK
FAT
FAT
FAT
SQUEEEZE
WHAT THE HECK IS THIIIS!?
BAM
PLUNGE
FAT
BLOOOATED
IT MADE MOCHI FAT.
PUPUU
I-I'M TOO HEAVY—I CAN'T MOVE!!

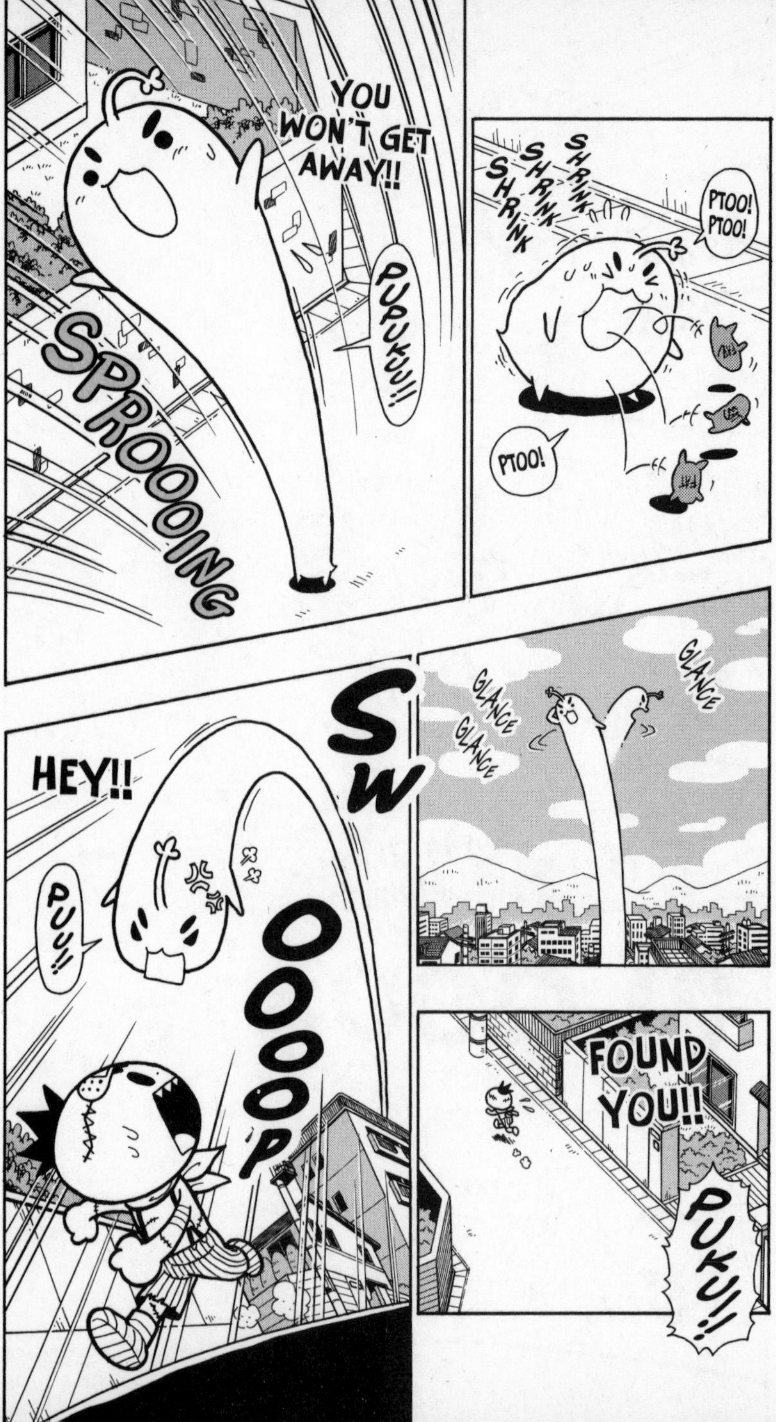
SHRINK SHRINK SHRINK
PTOO! PTOO!
PTOO!
YOU WON'T GET AWAY!!
PUPUKUU!!
SPROOOING
GLANCE
GLANCE GLANCE
FOUND YOU!!
PUKU!!
SWOOOOOP
HEY!!
PUU!!

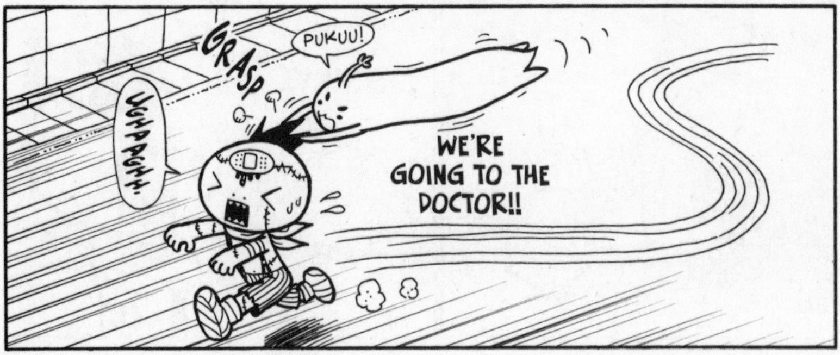
PUKUU!
GRASP
WE'RE GOING TO THE DOCTOR!!
UGHHHUHH.

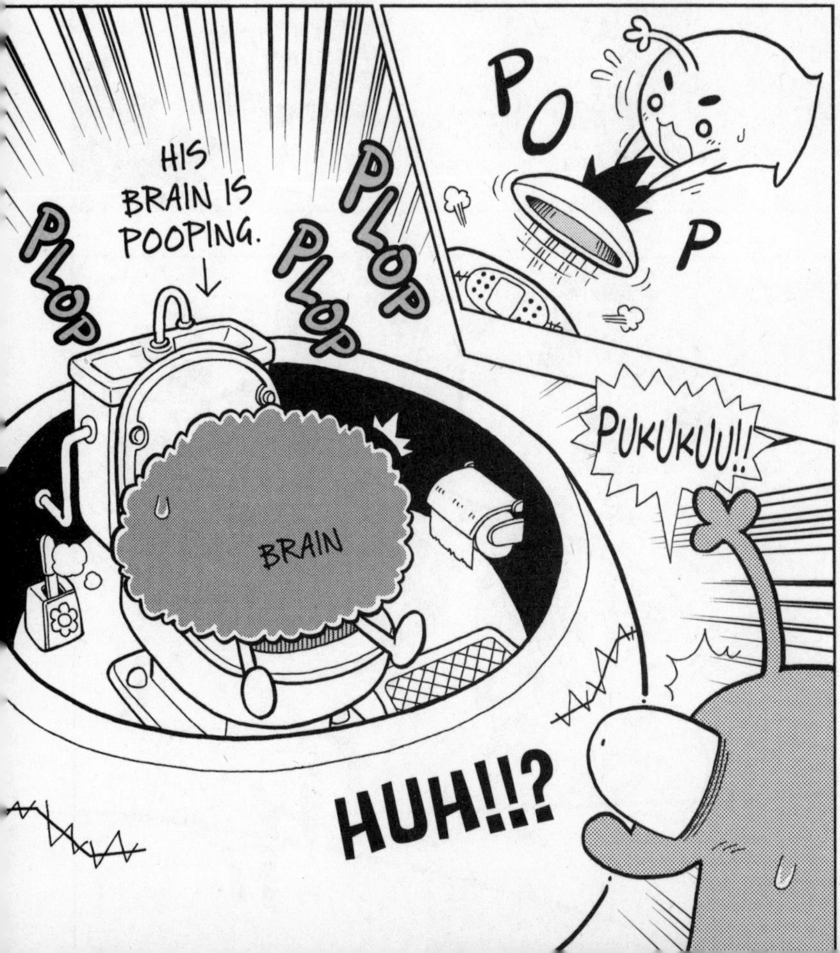
POP
PLOP
PLOP
HIS BRAIN IS POOPING.
PLOP
PUKUKUU!!
BRAIN
HUH!!?

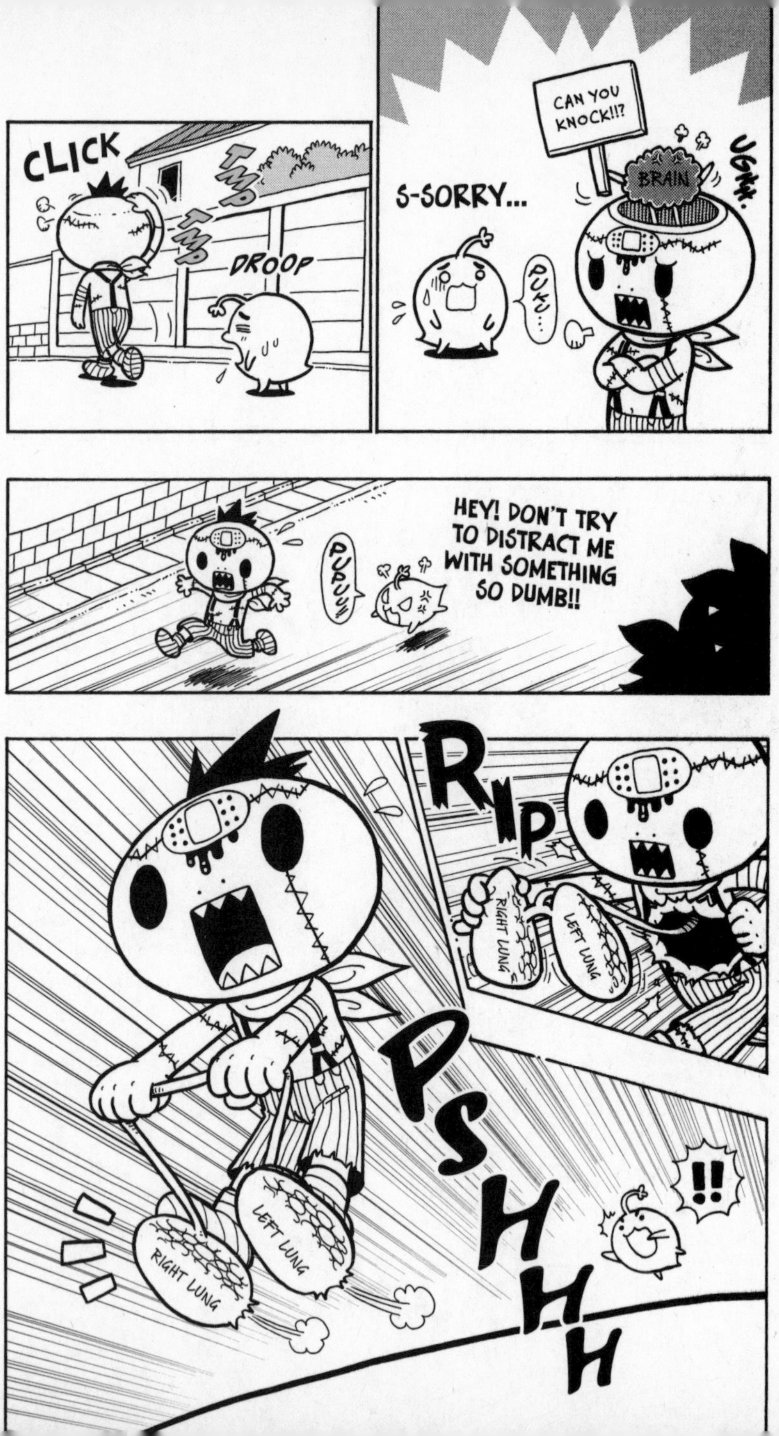
CAN YOU KNOCK!!?
BRAIN
UGHH.
S-SORRY...
PUKU...
CLICK
TMP
TMP
DROOP
HEY! DON'T TRY TO DISTRACT ME WITH SOMETHING SO DUMB!!
PUPUU!!
RIP
RIGHT LUNG
LEFT LUNG
PSHHHH
!!
LEFT LUNG
RIGHT LUNG

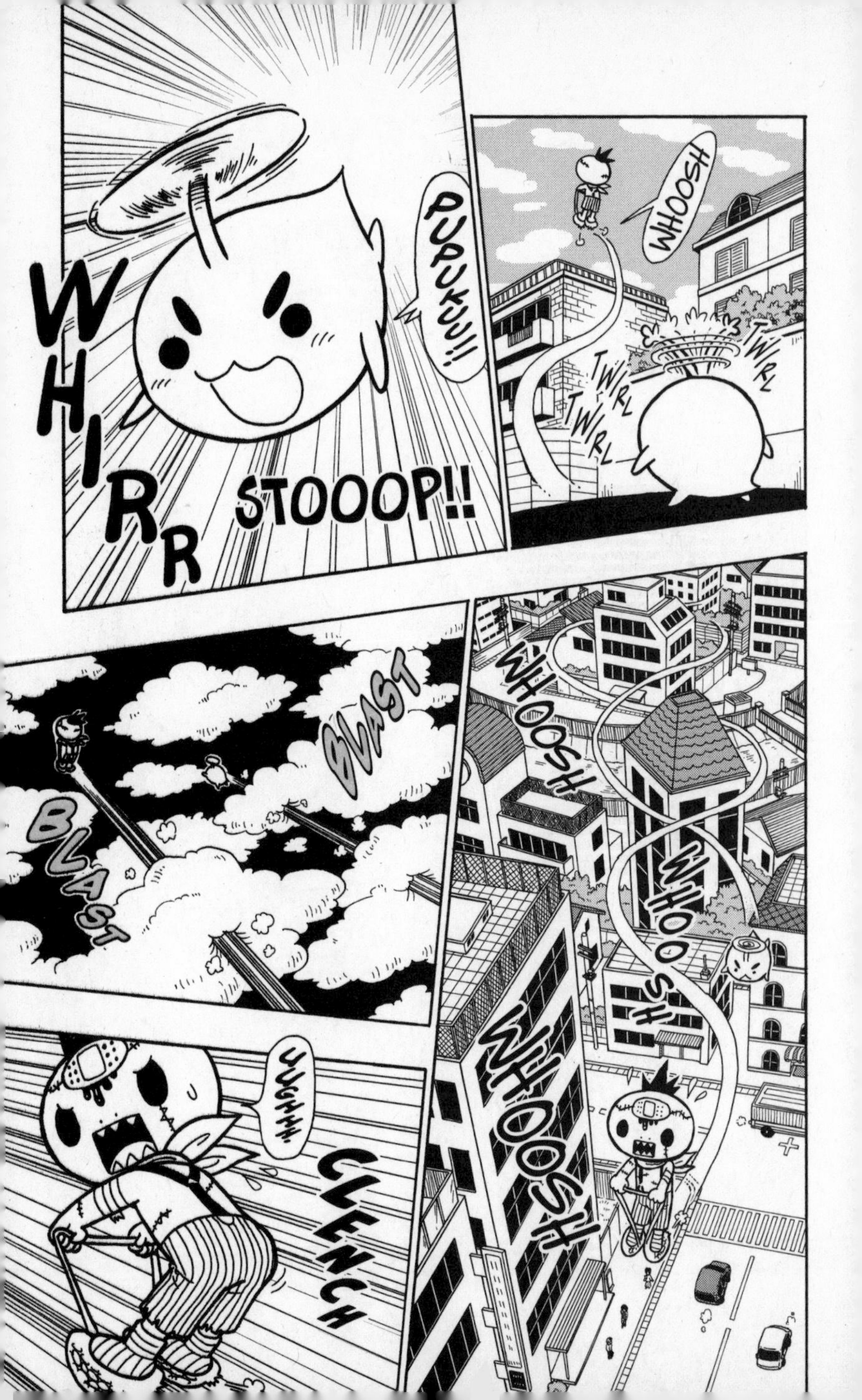
WHOOSH
TWIRL
TWIRL
TWIRL
PUPUKUU!!
WHIRRR
STOOOP!!
WHOOSH
WHOOSH
WHOOSH
WHOOSH
BLAST
BLAST
UUGHHH
CLENCH

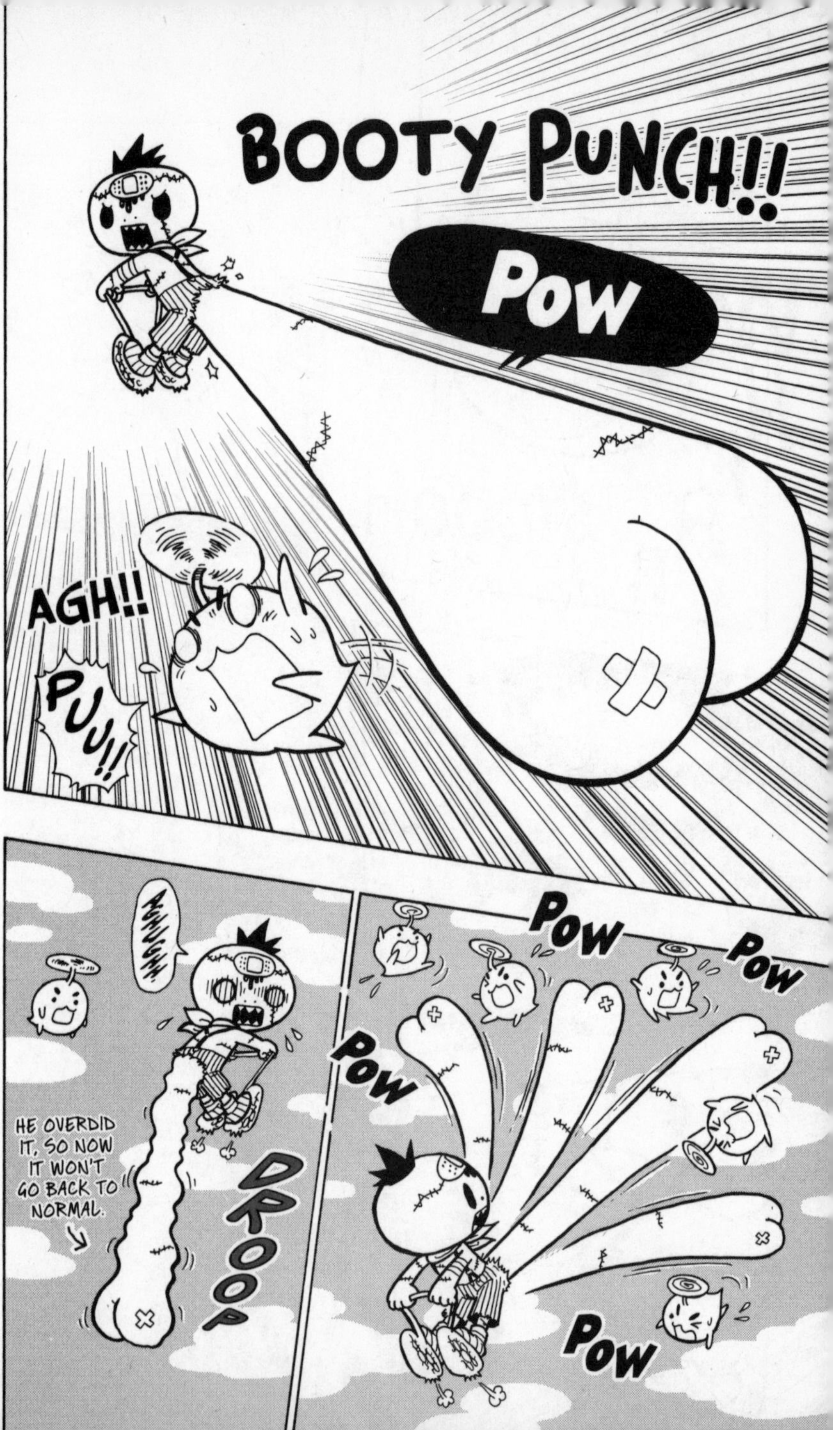

BOOTY PUNCH!!
POW
AGH!!
PUUU!!
POW
POW
POW
POW
AGHUGHH.
HE OVERDID IT, SO NOW IT WON'T GO BACK TO NORMAL.
DROOOP

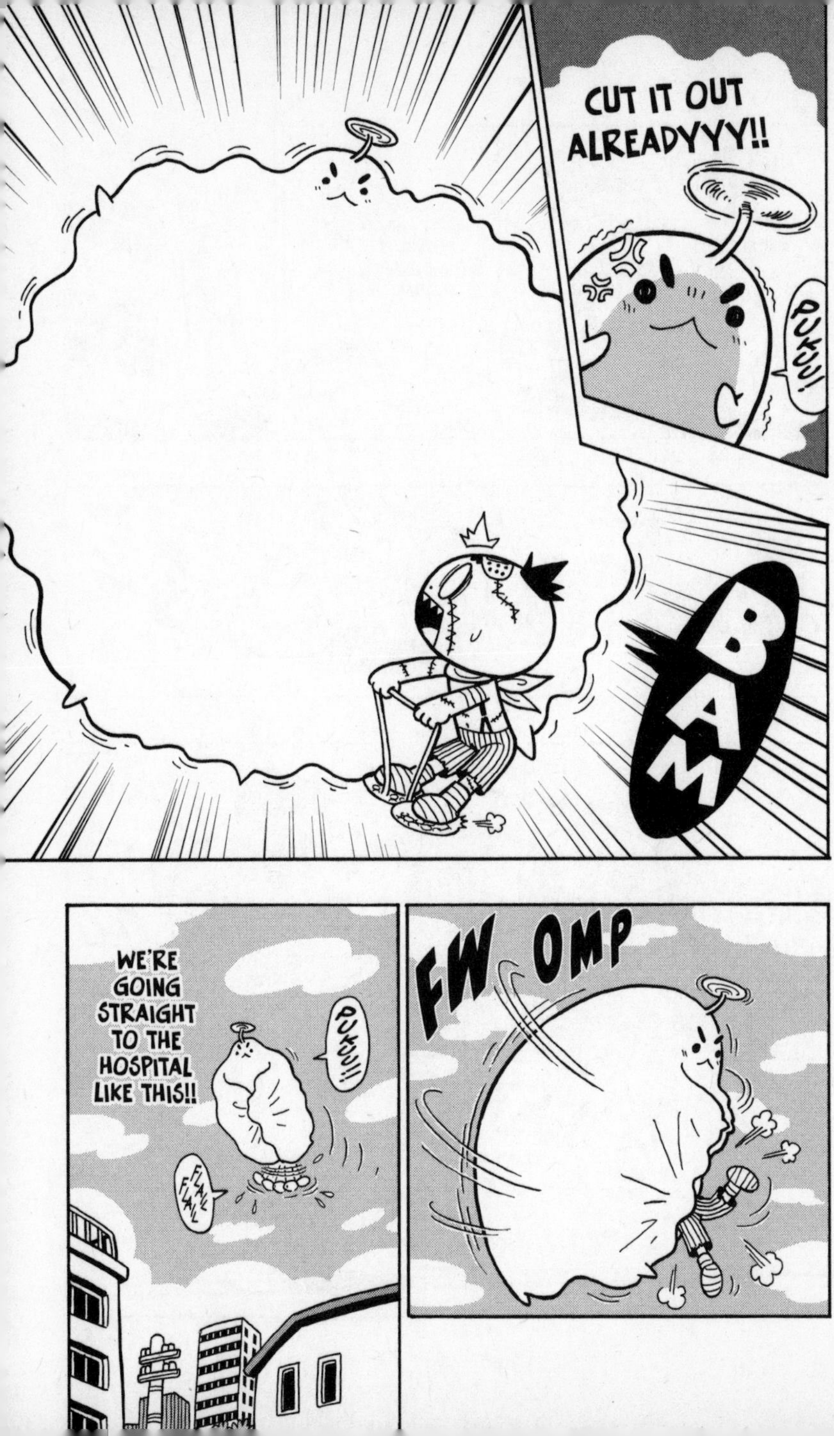
CUT IT OUT ALREADYYY!!
PUKUU!
BAM
FW OMP
WE'RE GOING STRAIGHT TO THE HOSPITAL LIKE THIS!!
PUKUU!!
FLAIL FLAIL

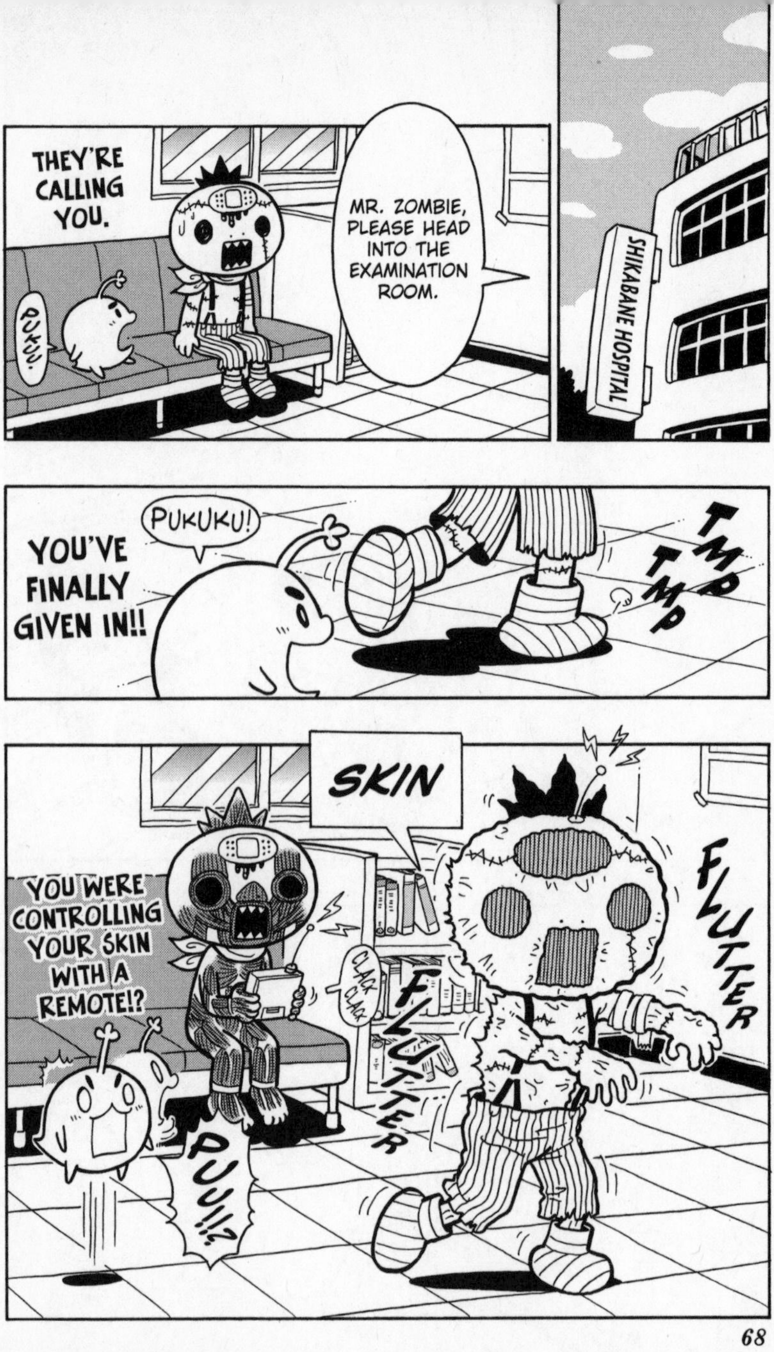
SHIKABANE HOSPITAL
MR. ZOMBIE, PLEASE HEAD INTO THE EXAMINATION ROOM.
THEY'RE CALLING YOU.
PUKUKU.
TMP TMP
PUKUKU!
YOU'VE FINALLY GIVEN IN!!
FLUTTER
SKIN
FLUTTER
CLACK CLACK
YOU WERE CONTROLLING YOUR SKIN WITH A REMOTE!?
PUU!!?

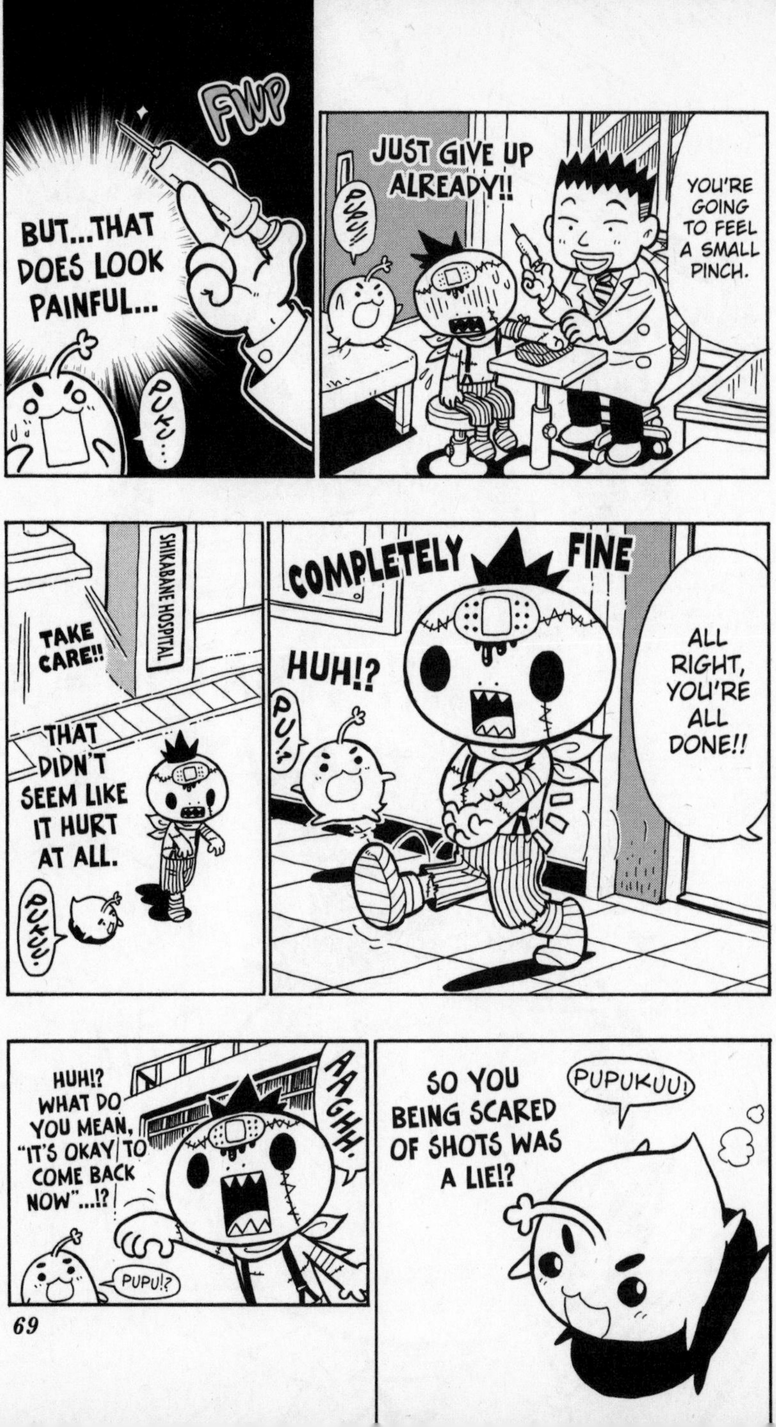
YOU'RE GOING TO FEEL A SMALL PINCH.
JUST GIVE UP ALREADY!!
PUPU!!
FWP
BUT...THAT DOES LOOK PAINFUL...
PUKU...
ALL RIGHT, YOU'RE ALL DONE!!
COMPLETELY FINE
HUH!?
PU!?
SHIKABANE HOSPITAL
TAKE CARE!!
THAT DIDN'T SEEM LIKE IT HURT AT ALL.
PUKUU.
PUPUKUU!
SO YOU BEING SCARED OF SHOTS WAS A LIE!?
AAGHH.
HUH!? WHAT DO YOU MEAN, "IT'S OKAY TO COME BACK NOW"...!?
PUPU!?

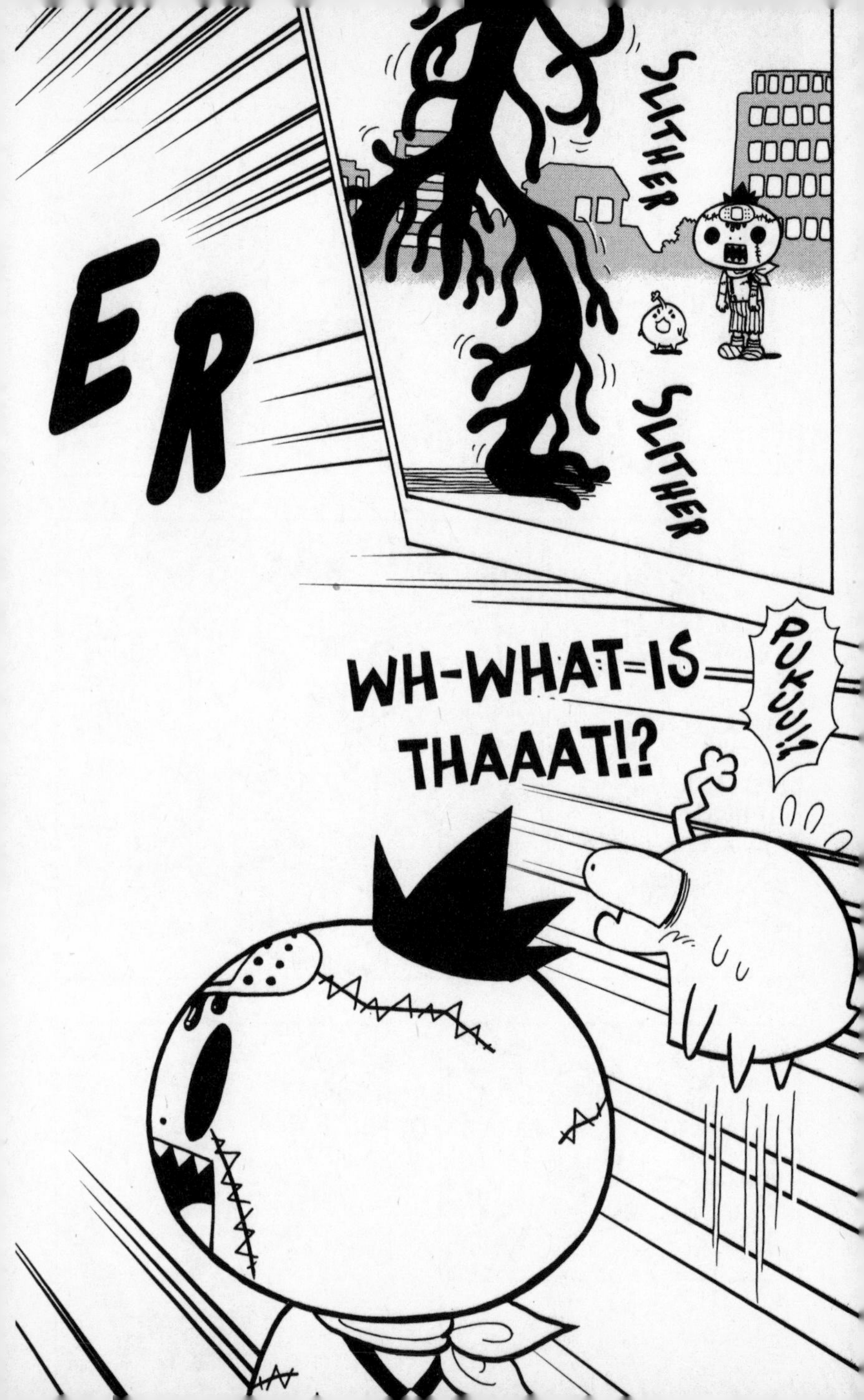
SLITHER
SLITHER
ER
PUKUU!!
WH-WHAT IS THAAAT!?

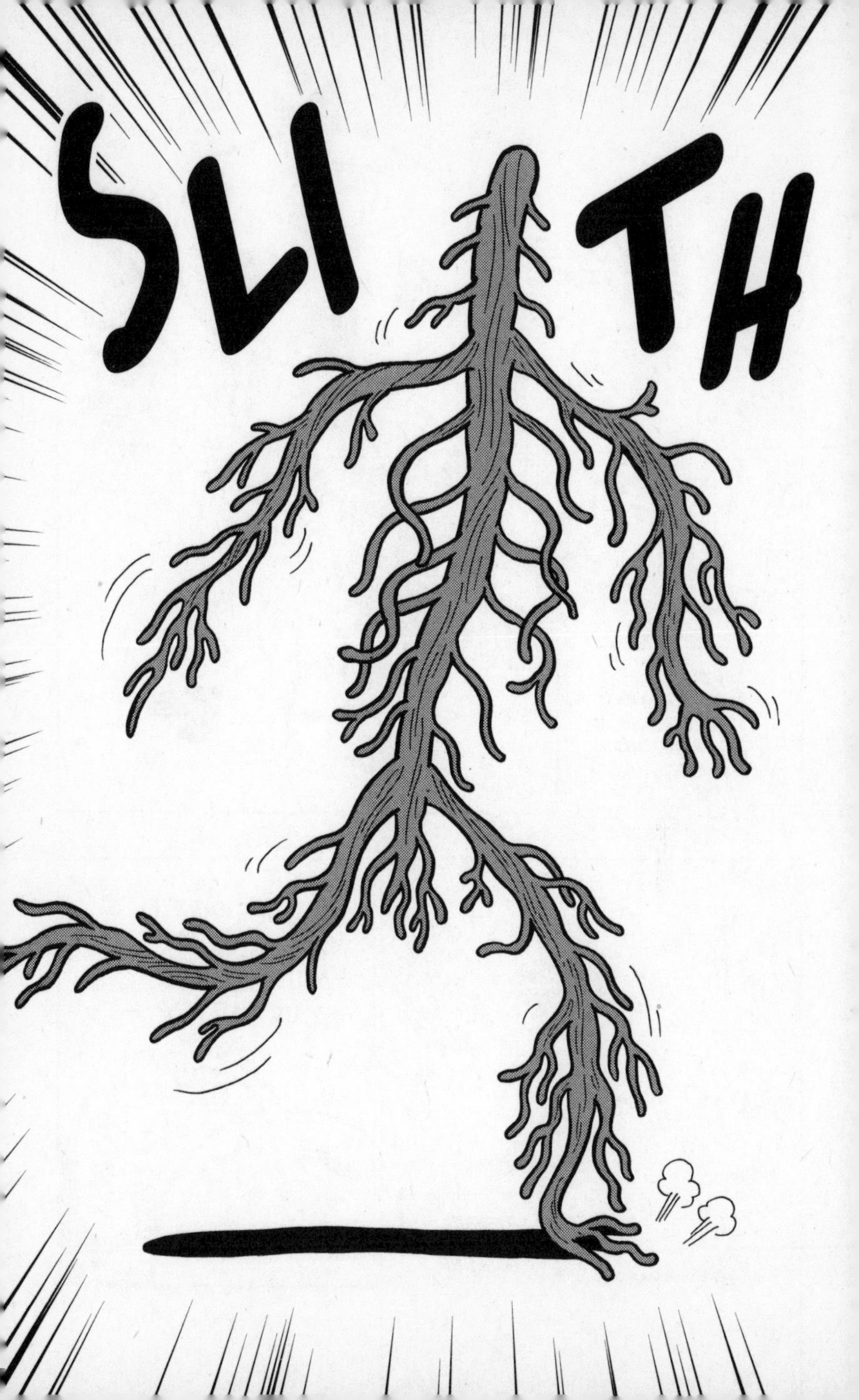
SLI TH

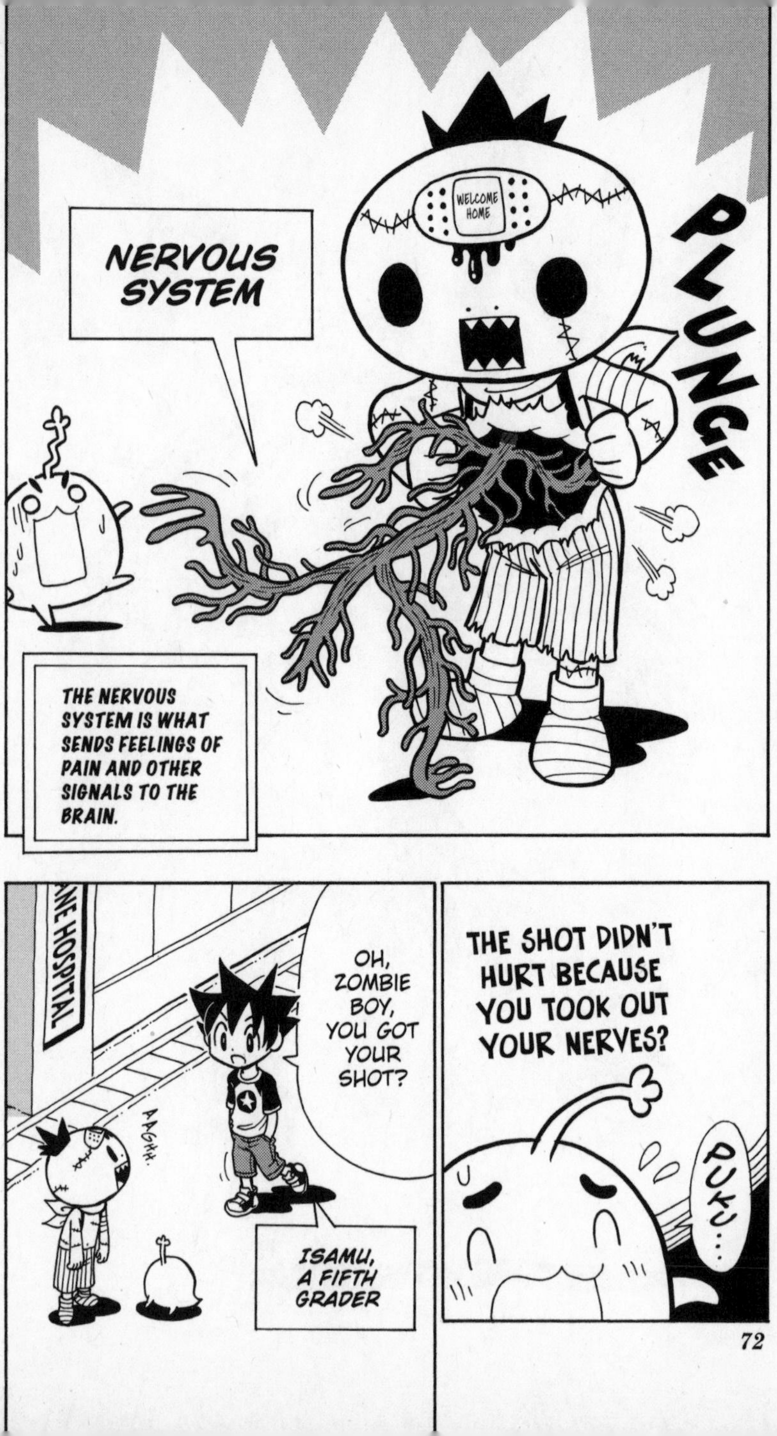
PLUNGE
WELCOME HOME
NERVOUS SYSTEM
THE NERVOUS SYSTEM IS WHAT SENDS FEELINGS OF PAIN AND OTHER SIGNALS TO THE BRAIN.
THE SHOT DIDN'T HURT BECAUSE YOU TOOK OUT YOUR NERVES?
PUKU...
OH, ZOMBIE BOY, YOU GOT YOUR SHOT?
ANE HOSPITAL
AAGHH.
ISAMU, A FIFTH GRADER

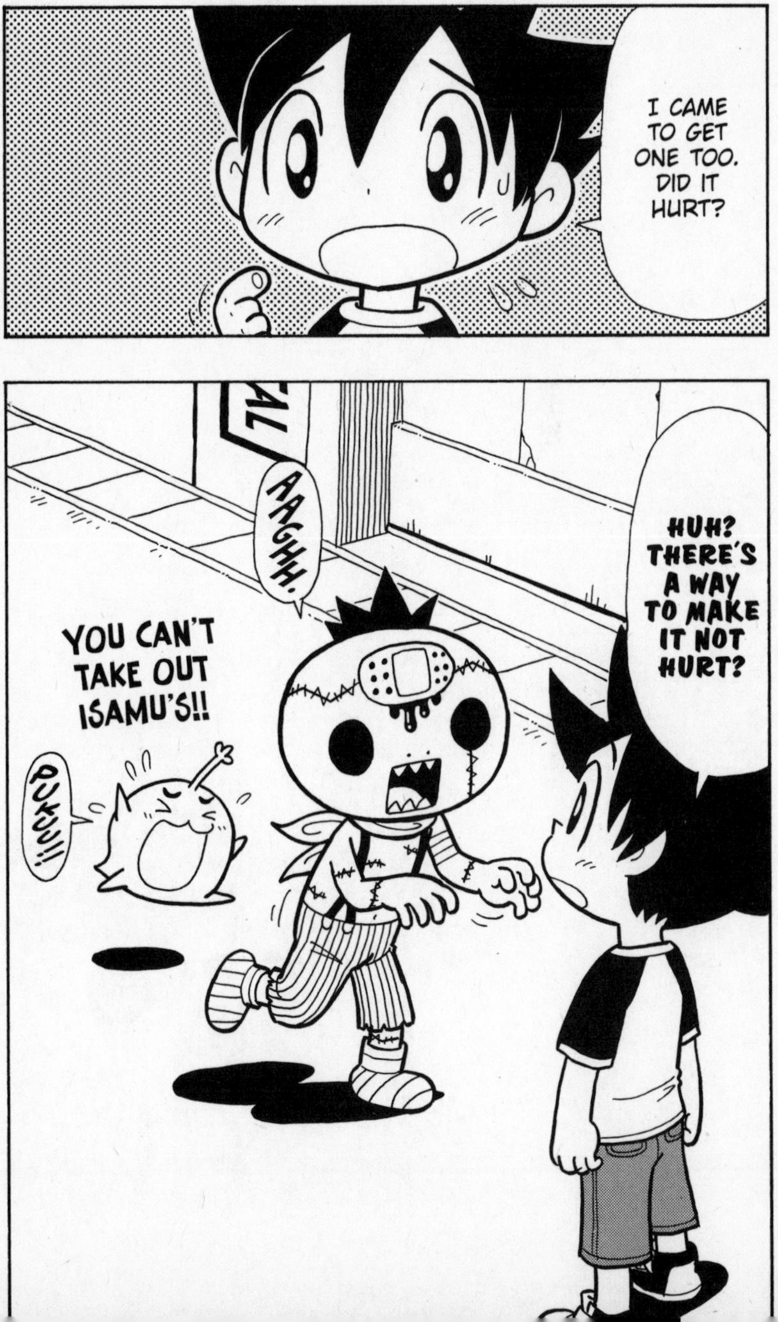
I CAME TO GET ONE TOO. DID IT HURT?
HUH? THERE'S A WAY TO MAKE IT NOT HURT?
AAGHH.
YOU CAN'T TAKE OUT ISAMU'S!!
PUKUU!!

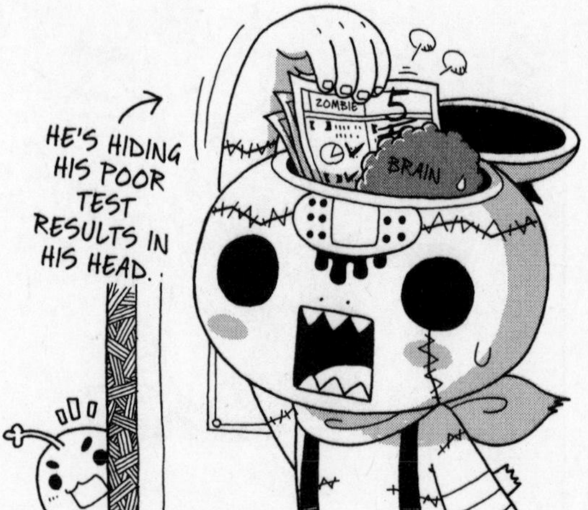
HE'S HIDING HIS POOR TEST RESULTS IN HIS HEAD...
ZOMBIE
5
BRAIN

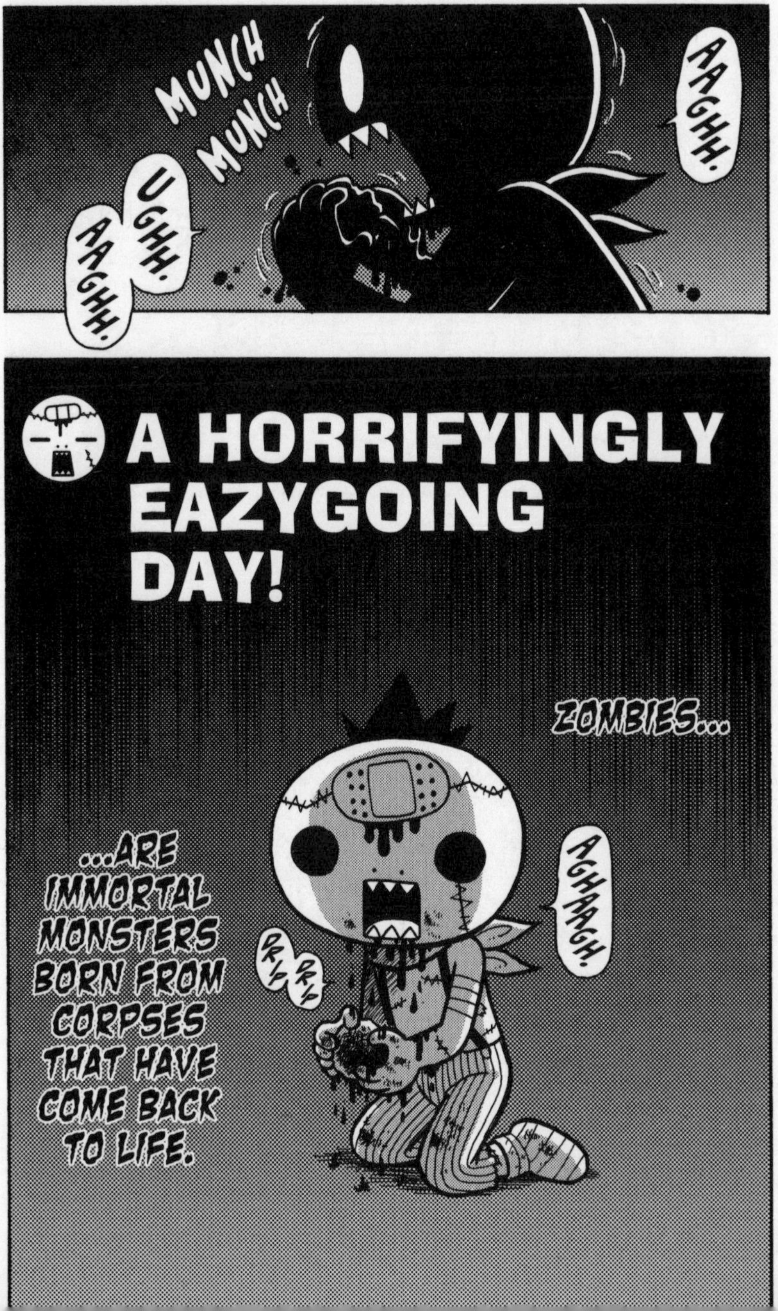
AAGHH.
MUNCH MUNCH
UGHH. AAGHH.
A HORRIFYINGLY EAZYGOING DAY!
ZOMBIES...
AGHAAGH.
DRIP DRIP
...ARE IMMORTAL MONSTERS BORN FROM CORPSES THAT HAVE COME BACK TO LIFE.

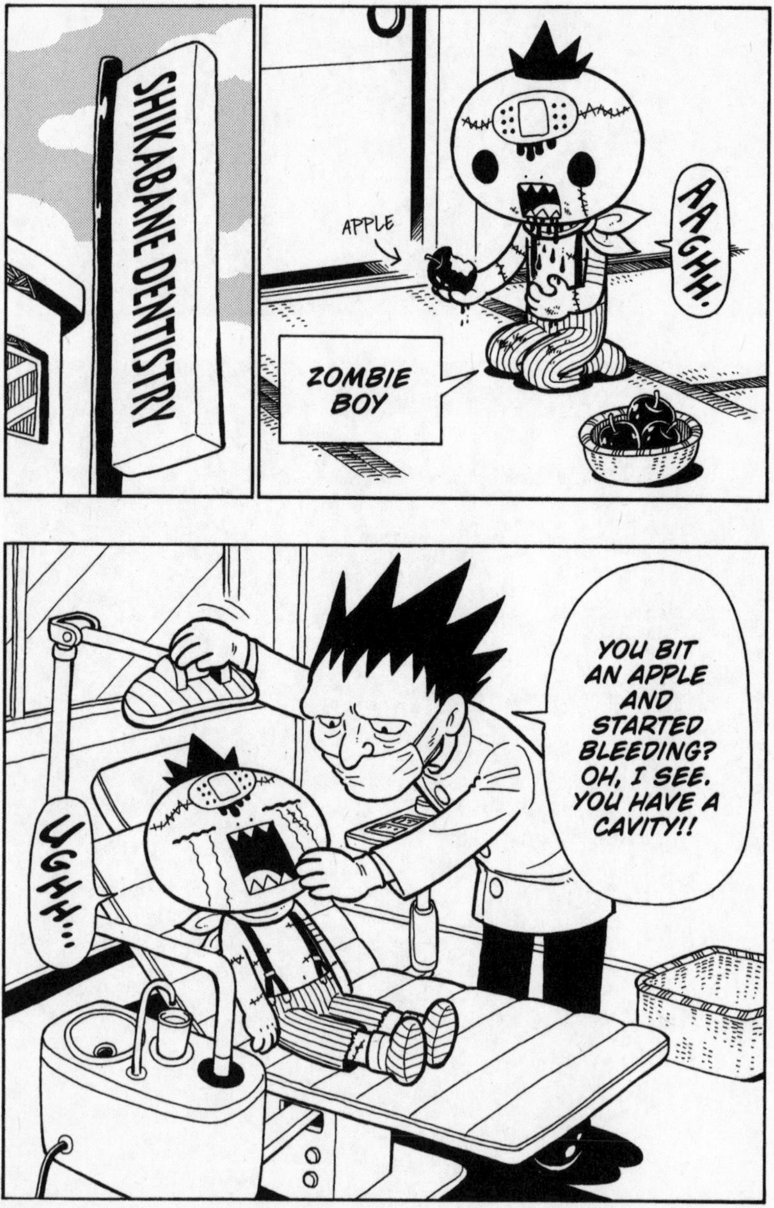
AAGHH.
APPLE
ZOMBIE BOY
SHIKABANE DENTISTRY
YOU BIT AN APPLE AND STARTED BLEEDING? OH, I SEE. YOU HAVE A CAVITY!!
UGHH...

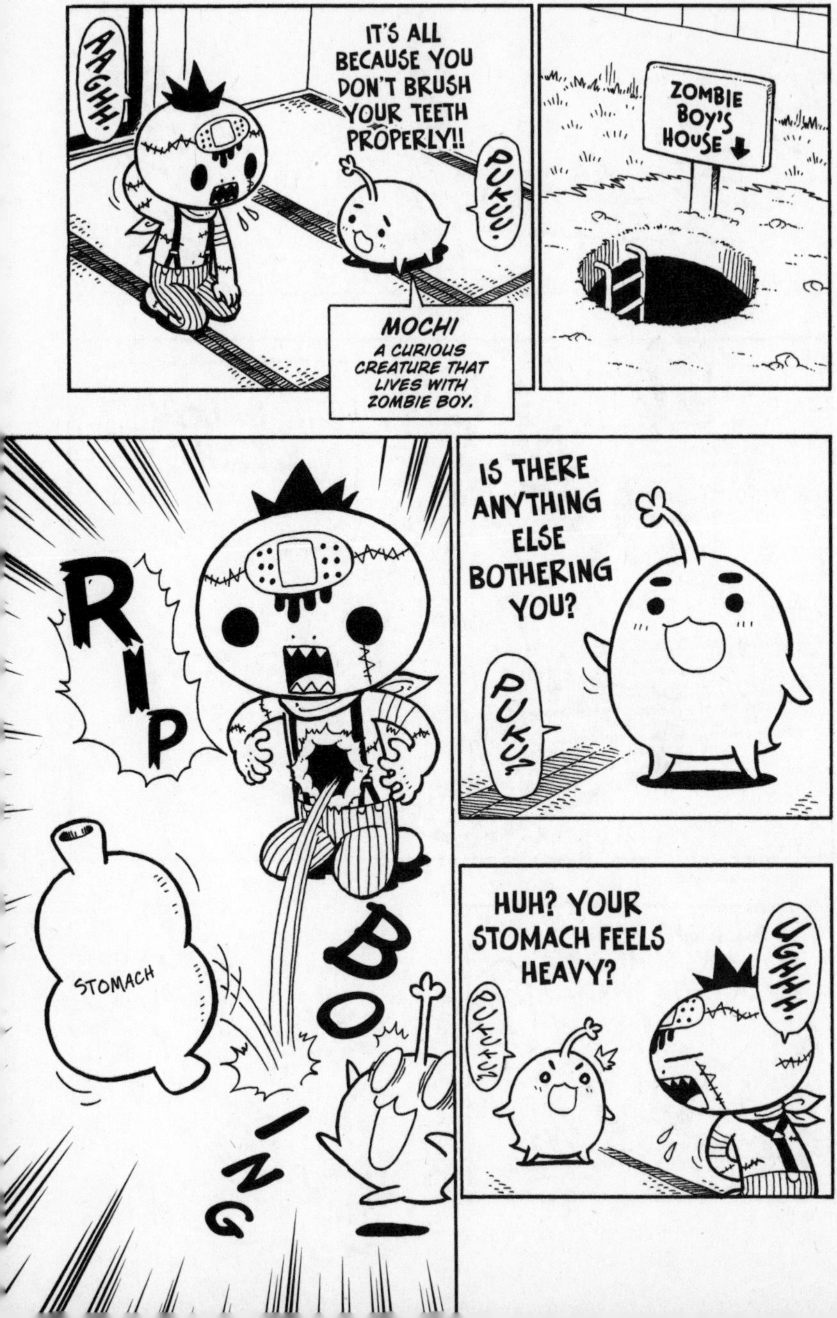
ZOMBIE BOY'S HOUSE
IT'S ALL BECAUSE YOU DON'T BRUSH YOUR TEETH PROPERLY!!
PUKUU.
AAGHH.
MOCHI
A CURIOUS CREATURE THAT LIVES WITH ZOMBIE BOY.
IS THERE ANYTHING ELSE BOTHERING YOU?
PUKU?
UGHHH.
HUH? YOUR STOMACH FEELS HEAVY?
PUKUKU?
RIP
BOING!
STOMACH

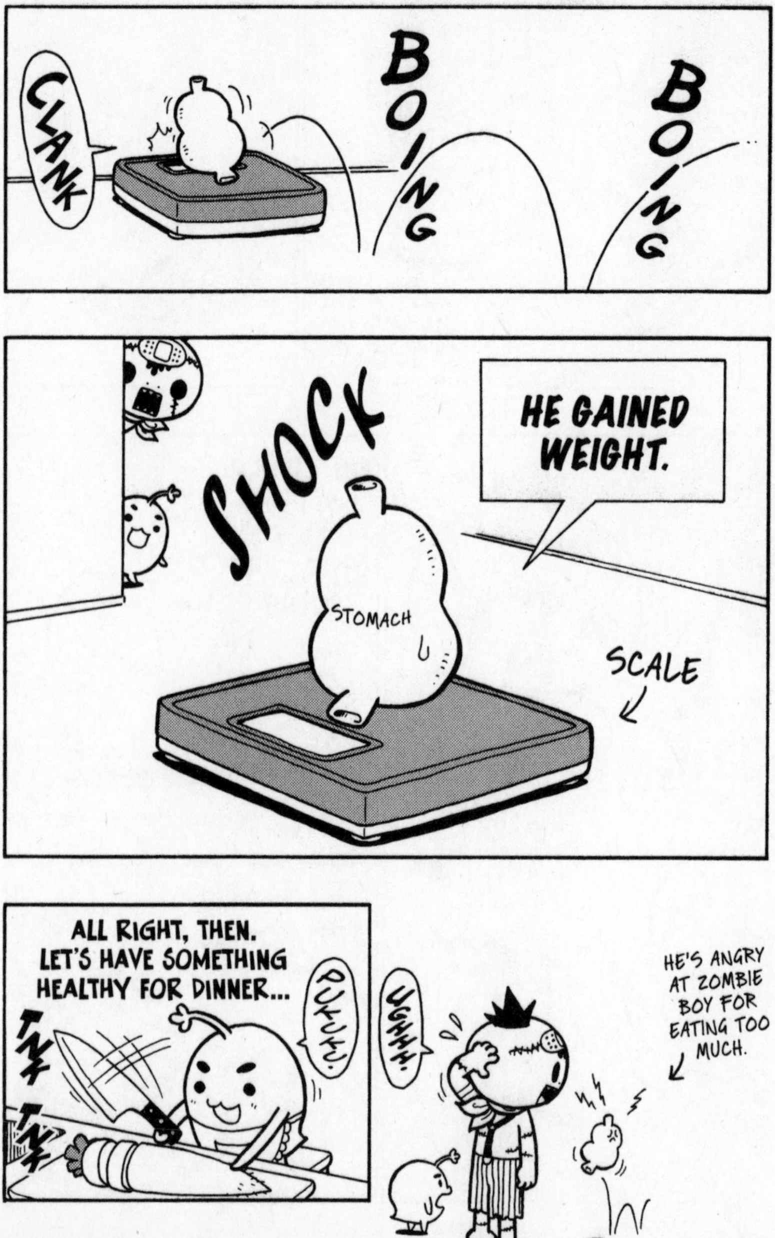

BOING
BOING
CLANK
HE GAINED WEIGHT.
SHOCK
STOMACH
SCALE
HE'S ANGRY AT ZOMBIE BOY FOR EATING TOO MUCH.
UGHHH.
ALL RIGHT, THEN. LET'S HAVE SOMETHING HEALTHY FOR DINNER...
PUKUKU.
TNK
TNK

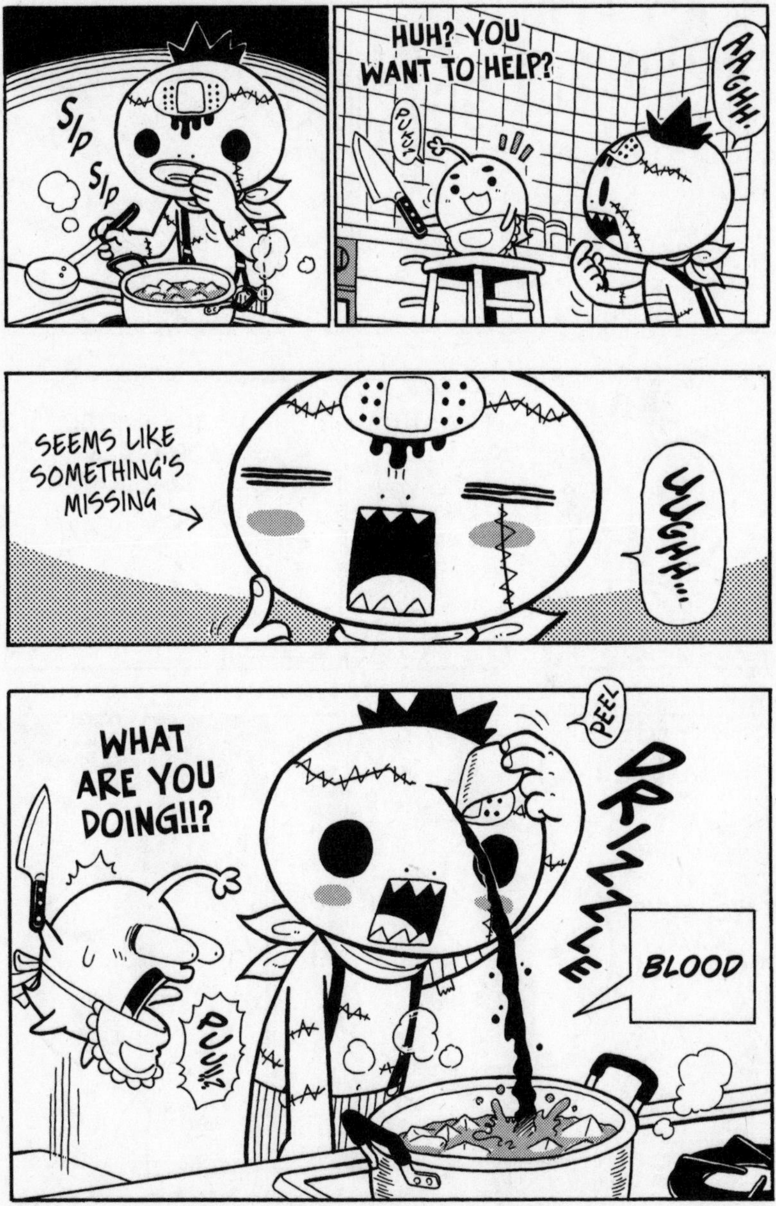
AAGHH.
HUH? YOU WANT TO HELP?
PUKU!
SIP SIP
UUGHH...
SEEMS LIKE SOMETHING'S MISSING
PEEL
DRIZZLE
BLOOD
WHAT ARE YOU DOING!!?
PUU!!?

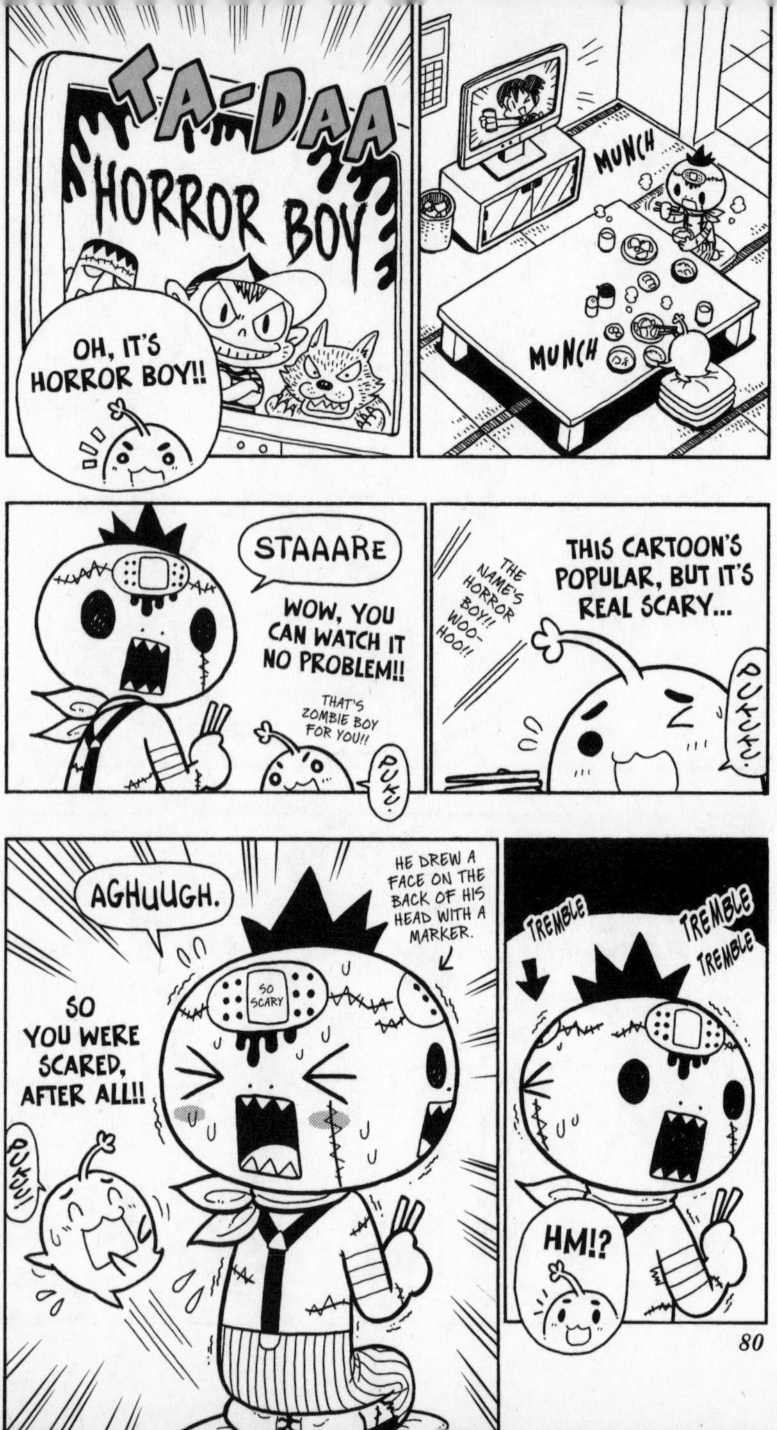
MUNCH
MUNCH
TA-DAA
HORROR BOY
OH, IT'S HORROR BOY!!
THE NAME'S HORROR BOY!! WOO-HOO!!
THIS CARTOON'S POPULAR, BUT IT'S REAL SCARY...
PUKUKU.
STAAARE
WOW, YOU CAN WATCH IT NO PROBLEM!!
THAT'S ZOMBIE BOY FOR YOU!!
PUKU.
TREMBLE
TREMBLE
TREMBLE
HM!?
AGHUUGH.
HE DREW A FACE ON THE BACK OF HIS HEAD WITH A MARKER.
SO SCARY
SO YOU WERE SCARED, AFTER ALL!!
PUKUU!

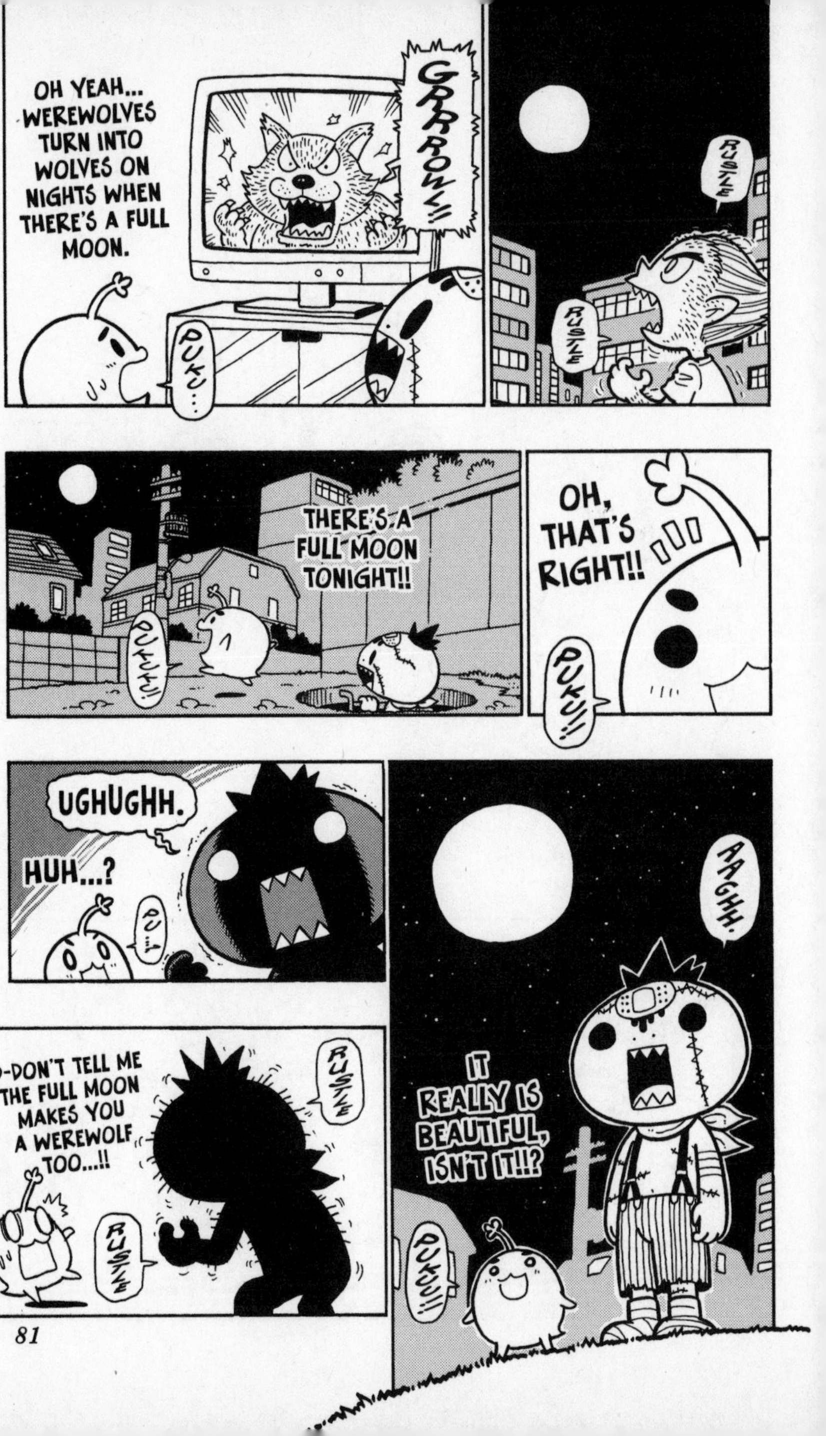
RUSTLE
RUSTLE
GRRROWL!!
OH YEAH... WEREWOLVES TURN INTO WOLVES ON NIGHTS WHEN THERE'S A FULL MOON.
PUKU...
OH, THAT'S RIGHT!!
PUKU!!
THERE'S A FULL MOON TONIGHT!!
PUKUKU!
AAGHH.
IT REALLY IS BEAUTIFUL, ISN'T IT!!?
PUKU!!
UGHUGHH.
HUH...?
PU...!
RUSTLE
D-DON'T TELL ME THE FULL MOON MAKES YOU A WEREWOLF TOO...!!
PU!!
RUSTLE

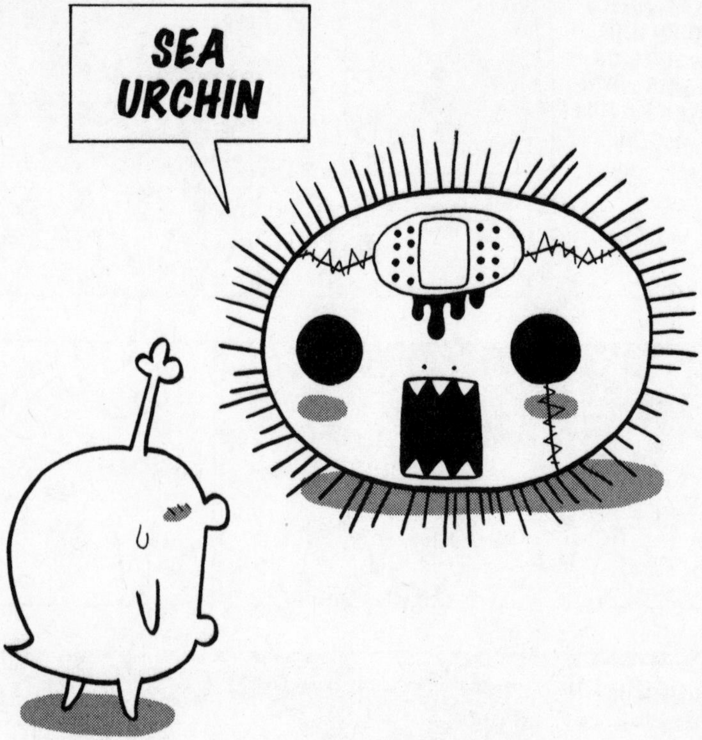
SEA URCHIN

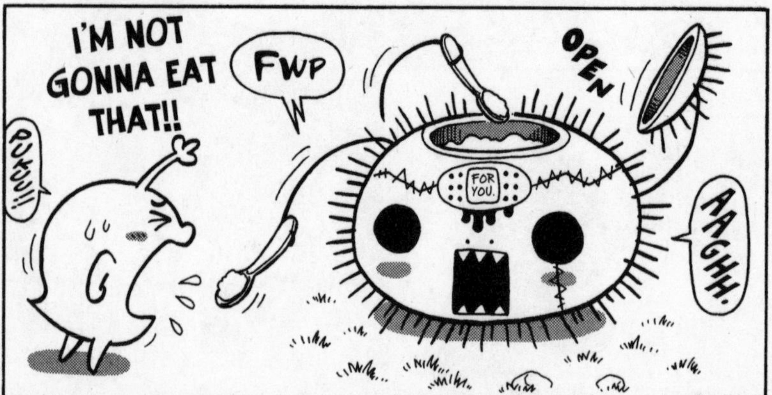
AAGHH.
OPEN
FOR YOU.
FWP
I'M NOT GONNA EAT THAT!!
PUKUU!!

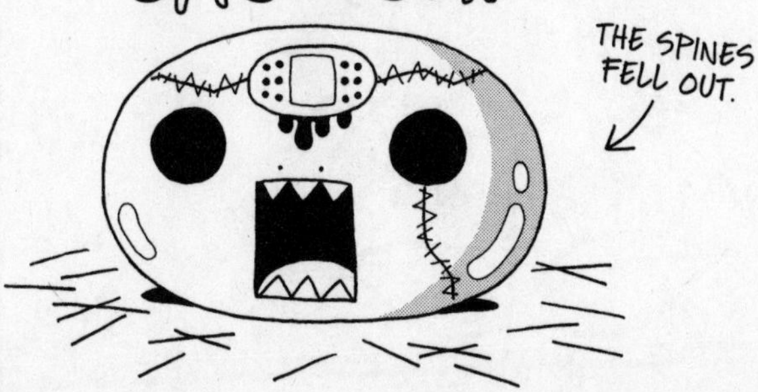
SMOOOOTH
THE SPINES FELL OUT.

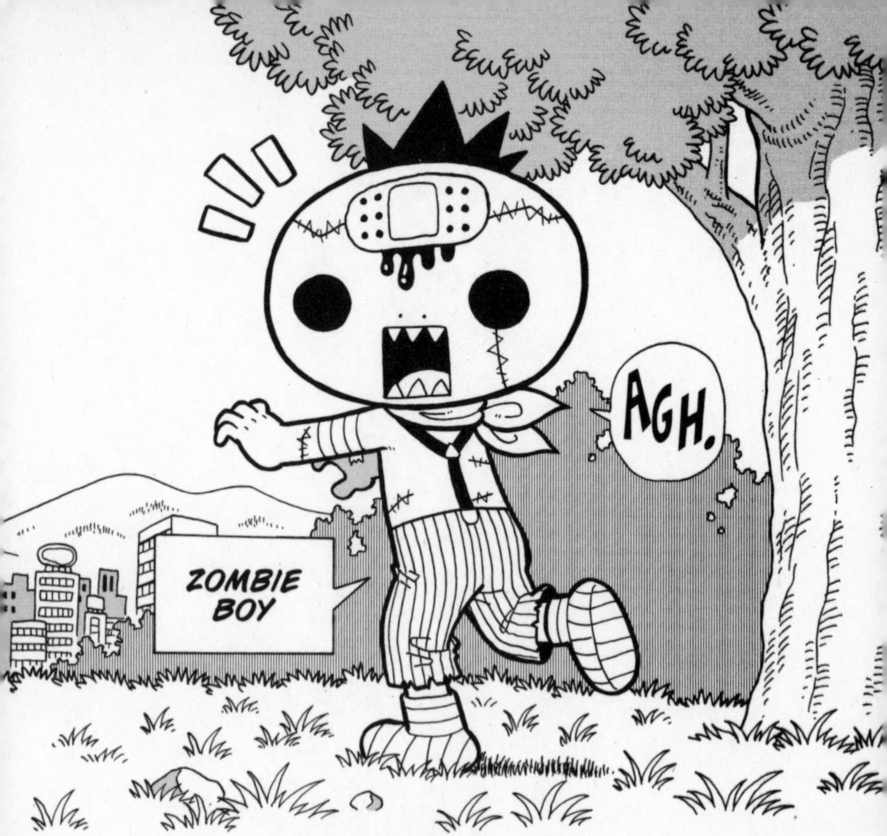
AGH.
ZOMBIE BOY

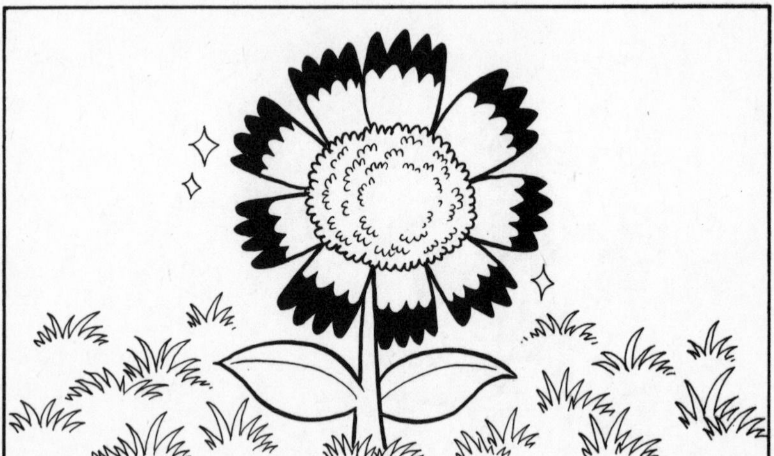

BEAUTIFUL FLOWERZ HAVE FANGZ!

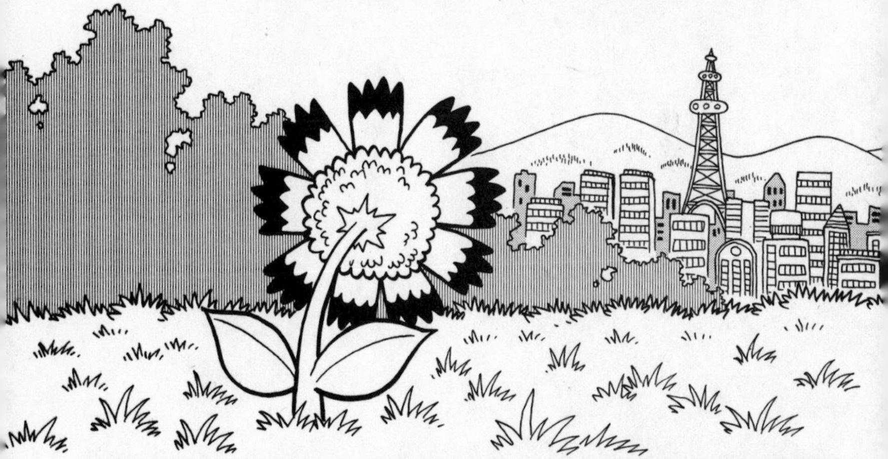

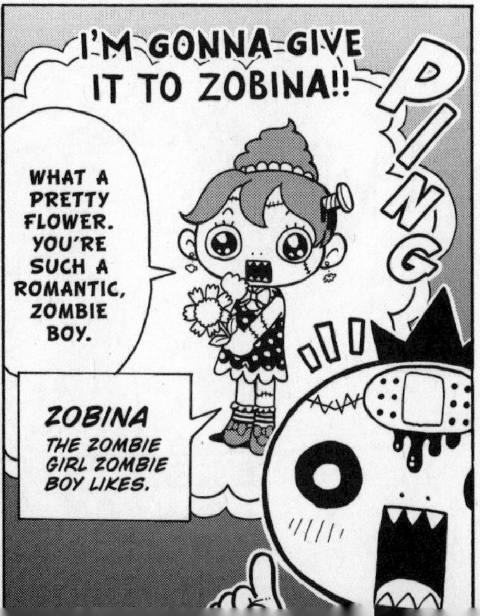
I'M GONNA GIVE IT TO ZOBINA!!
PING
WHAT A PRETTY FLOWER. YOU'RE SUCH A ROMANTIC, ZOMBIE BOY.
ZOBINA
THE ZOMBIE GIRL ZOMBIE BOY LIKES.

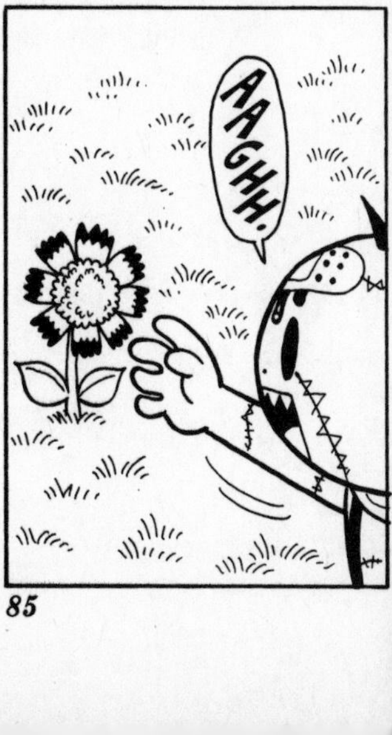
AAGHH.

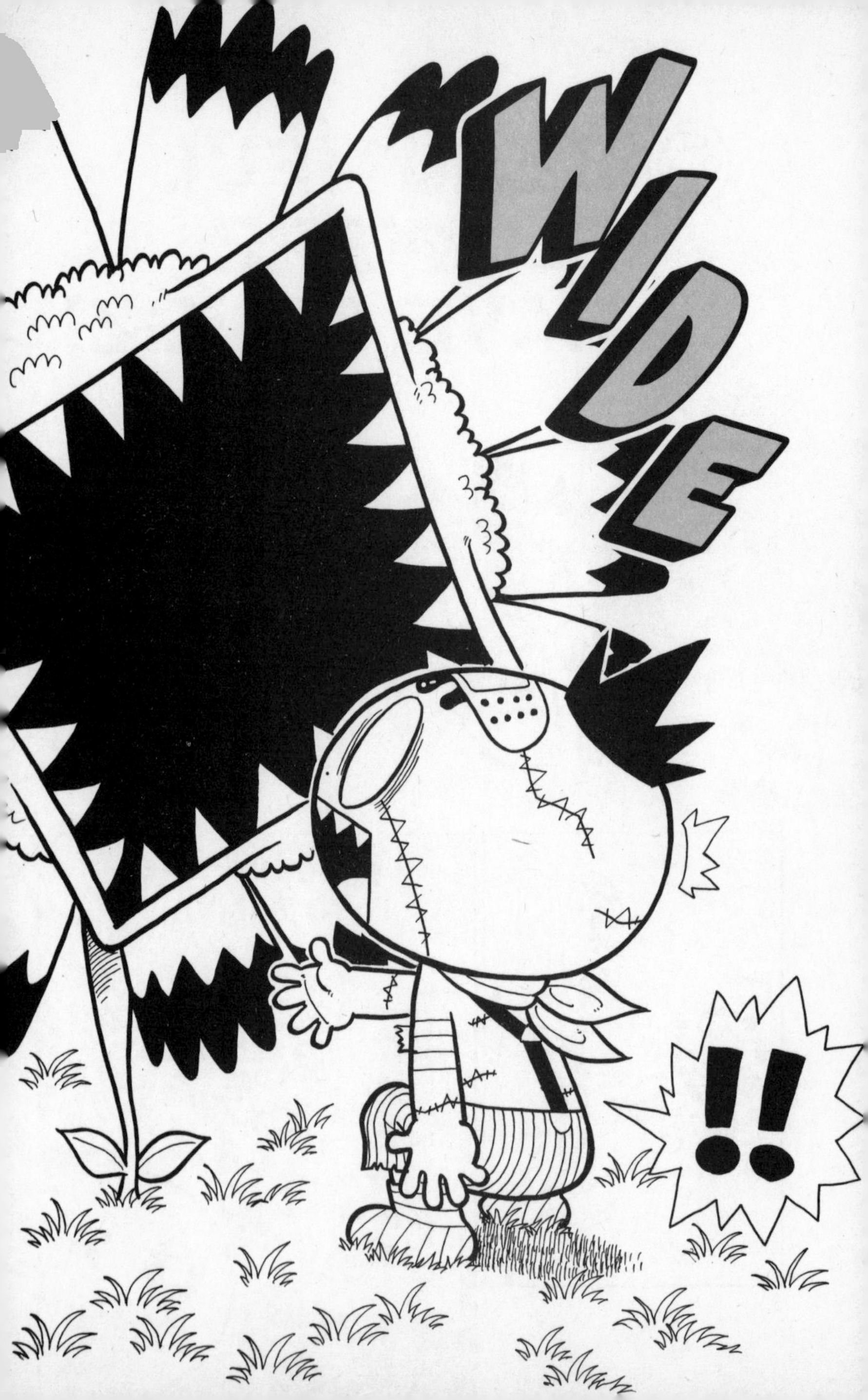
WIDE
!!

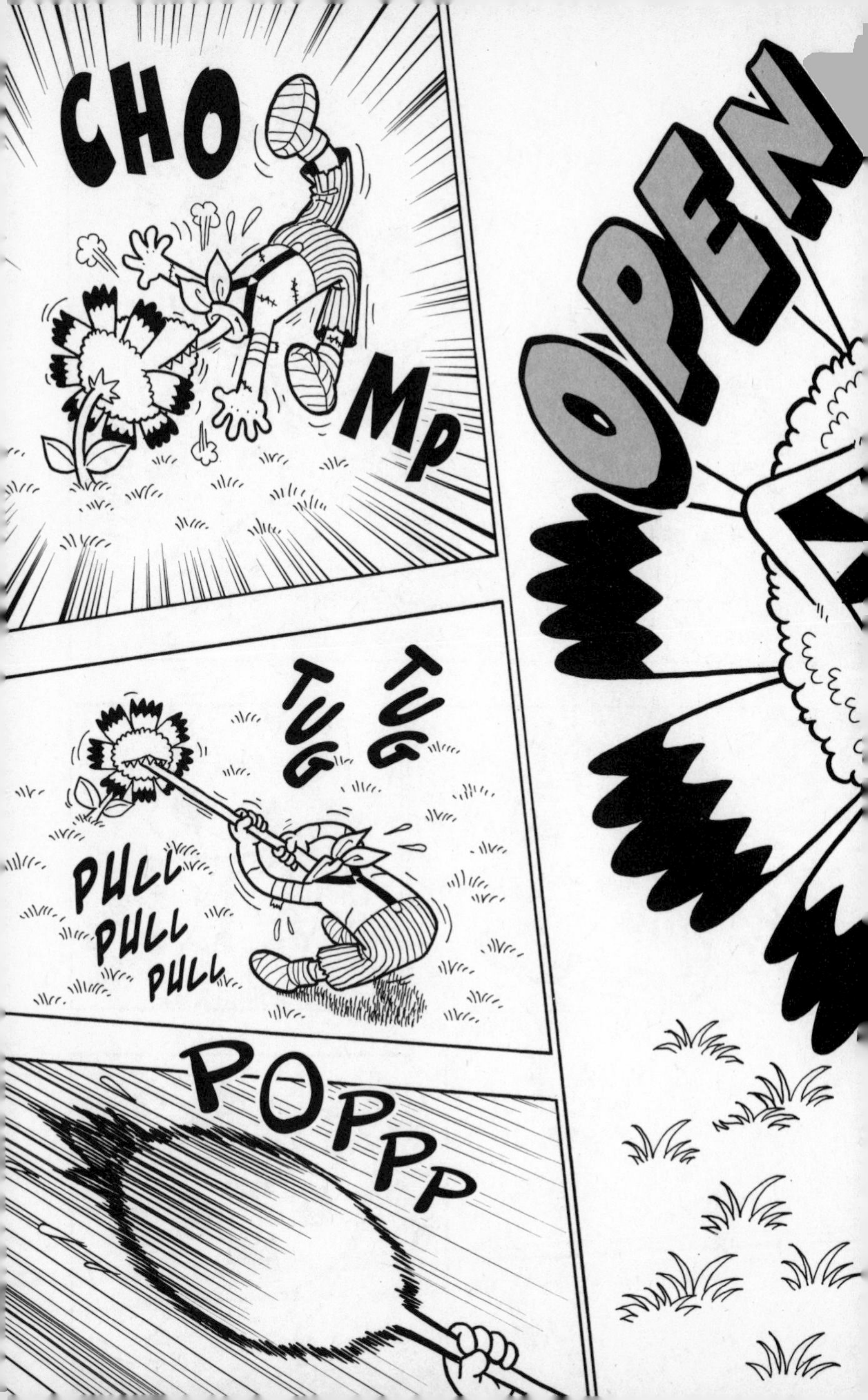
OPEN
CHOMp
TUG TUG
PULL PULL PULL
POPPP

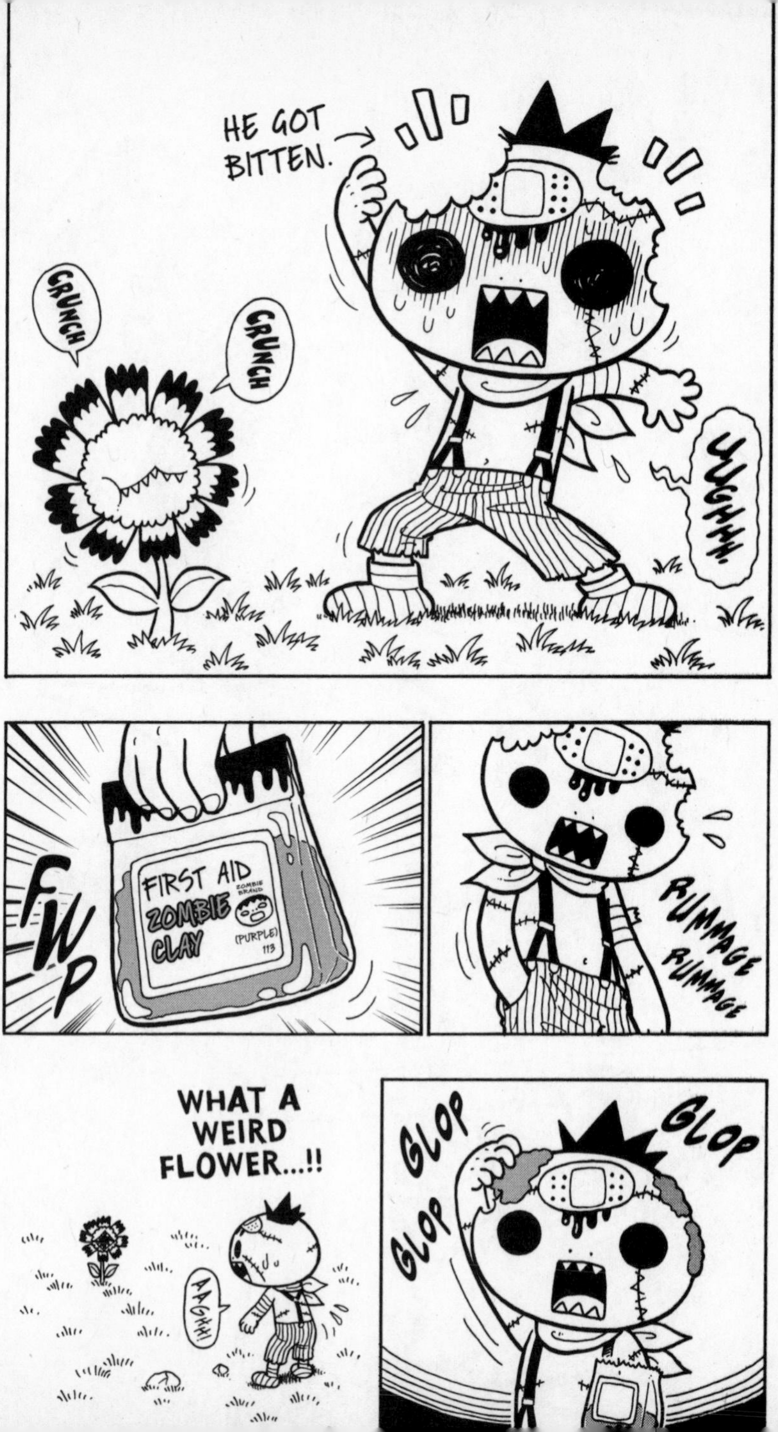
HE GOT BITTEN.
CRUNCH
CRUNCH
UUGHHH.
RUMMAGE RUMMAGE
FWP
FIRST AID
ZOMBIE BRAND
ZOMBIE CLAY
(PURPLE)
113
GLOP GLOP GLOP
WHAT A WEIRD FLOWER...!!
AAGHH!

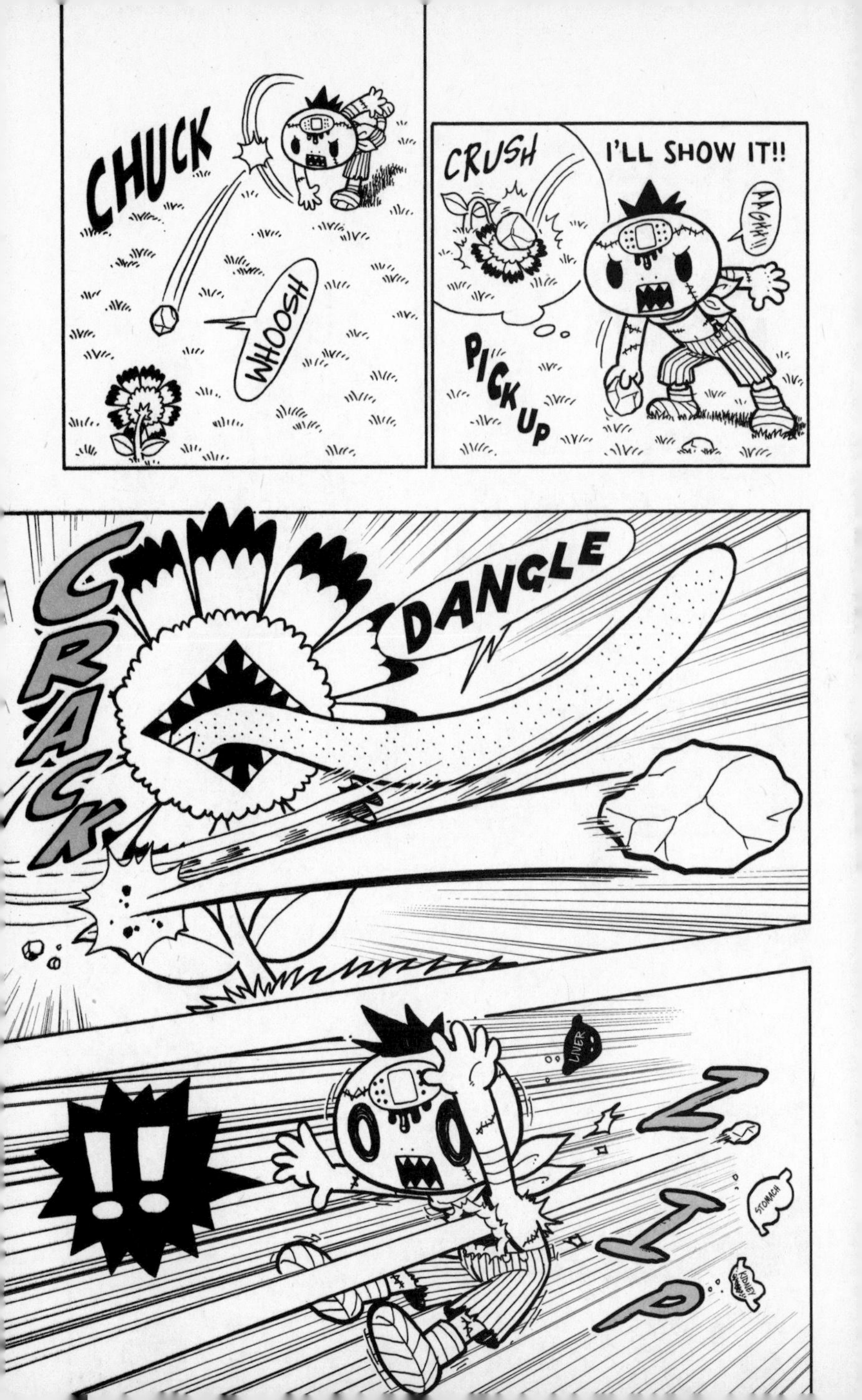
I'LL SHOW IT!!
AAGHH!!
CRUSH
PICK UP
CHUCK
WHOOSH
DANGLE
CRACK
LIVER
ZIP
STOMACH
KIDNEY
!!

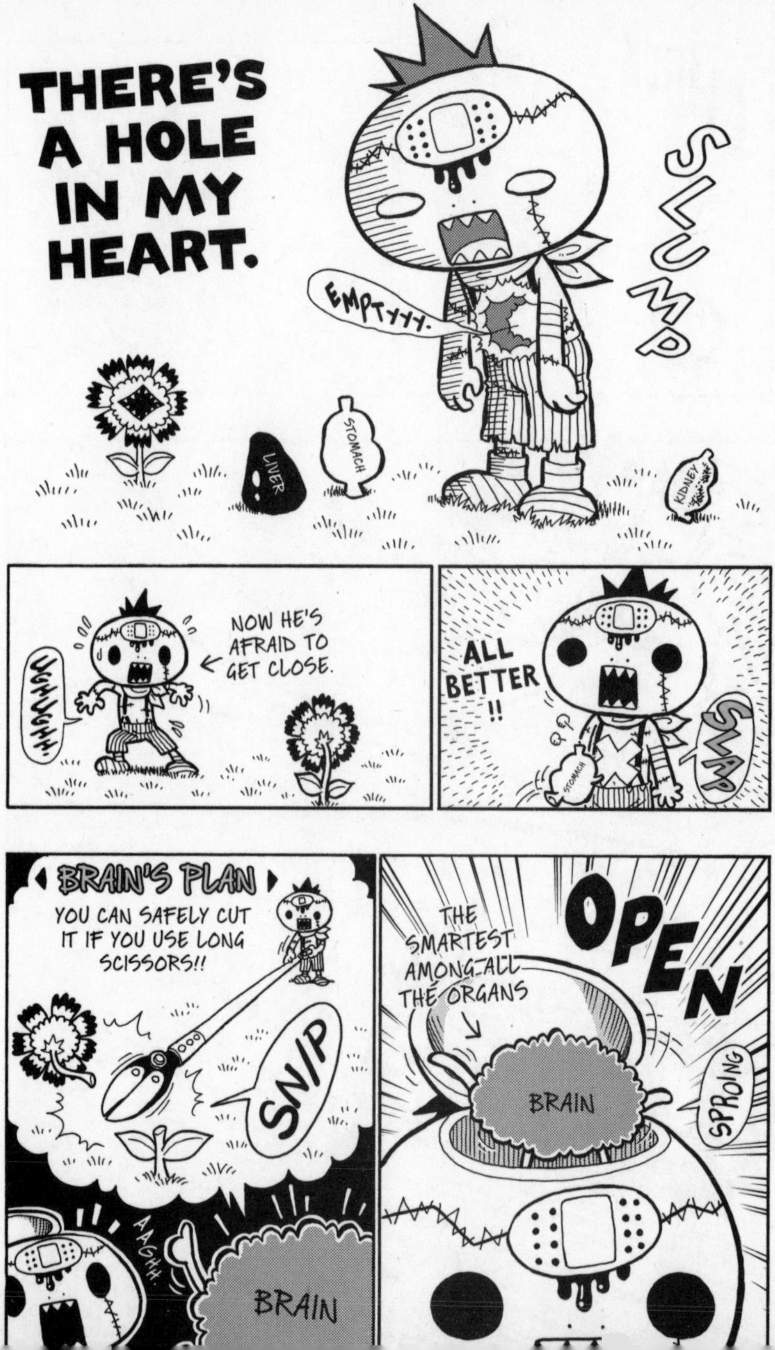
SLUMP
EMPTYYY.
THERE'S A HOLE IN MY HEART.
STOMACH
LIVER
KIDNEY
SLAP
ALL BETTER!!
STOMACH
NOW HE'S AFRAID TO GET CLOSE.
UGHUGHH.
OPEN
THE SMARTEST AMONG ALL THE ORGANS
SPROING
BRAIN
BRAIN'S PLAN
YOU CAN SAFELY CUT IT IF YOU USE LONG SCISSORS!!
SNIP
AAGHH
BRAIN

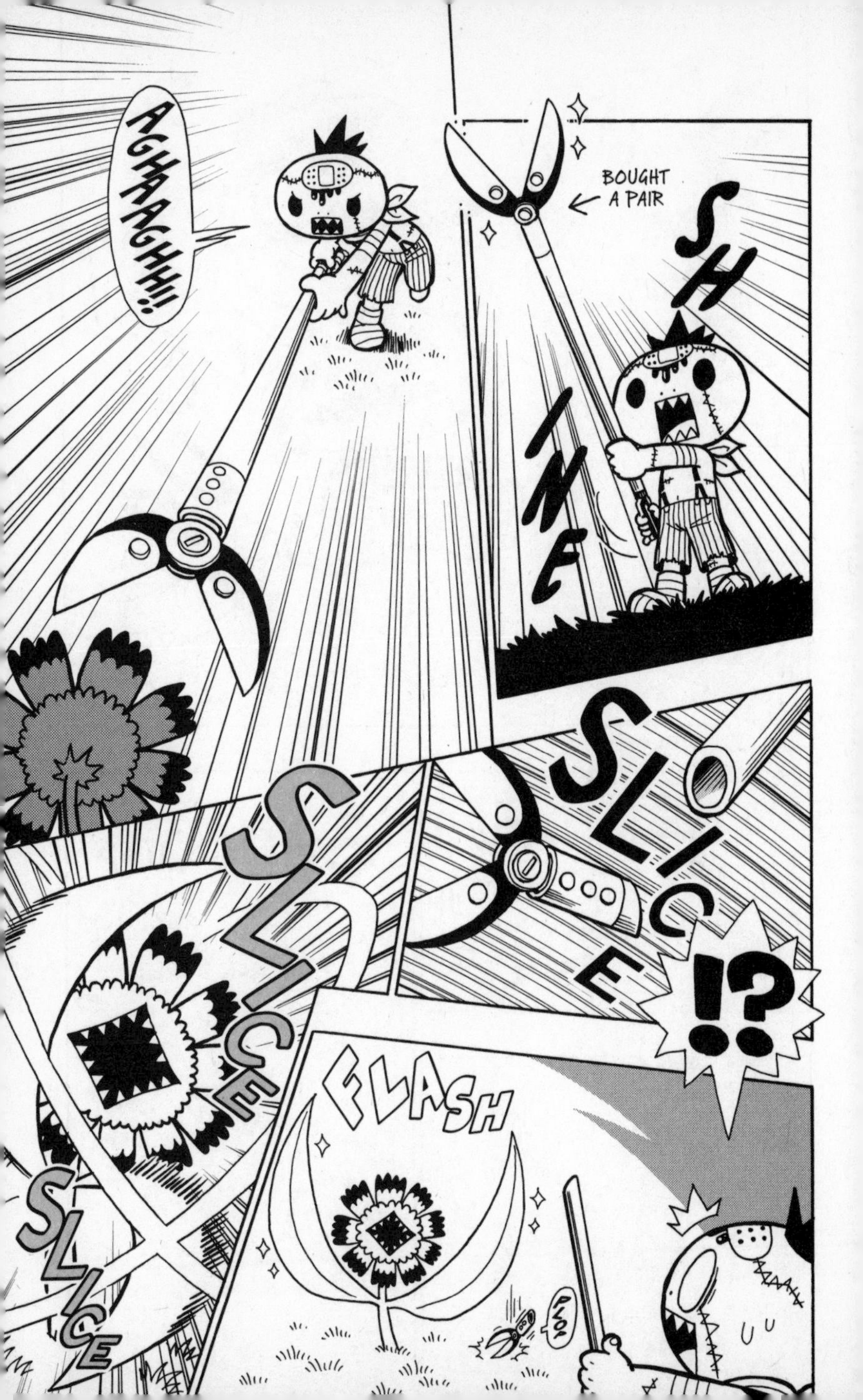
BOUGHT A PAIR
SHINE
AGHAAGHH!!
SLICE
!?
SLICE
SLICE
FLASH
PLOP

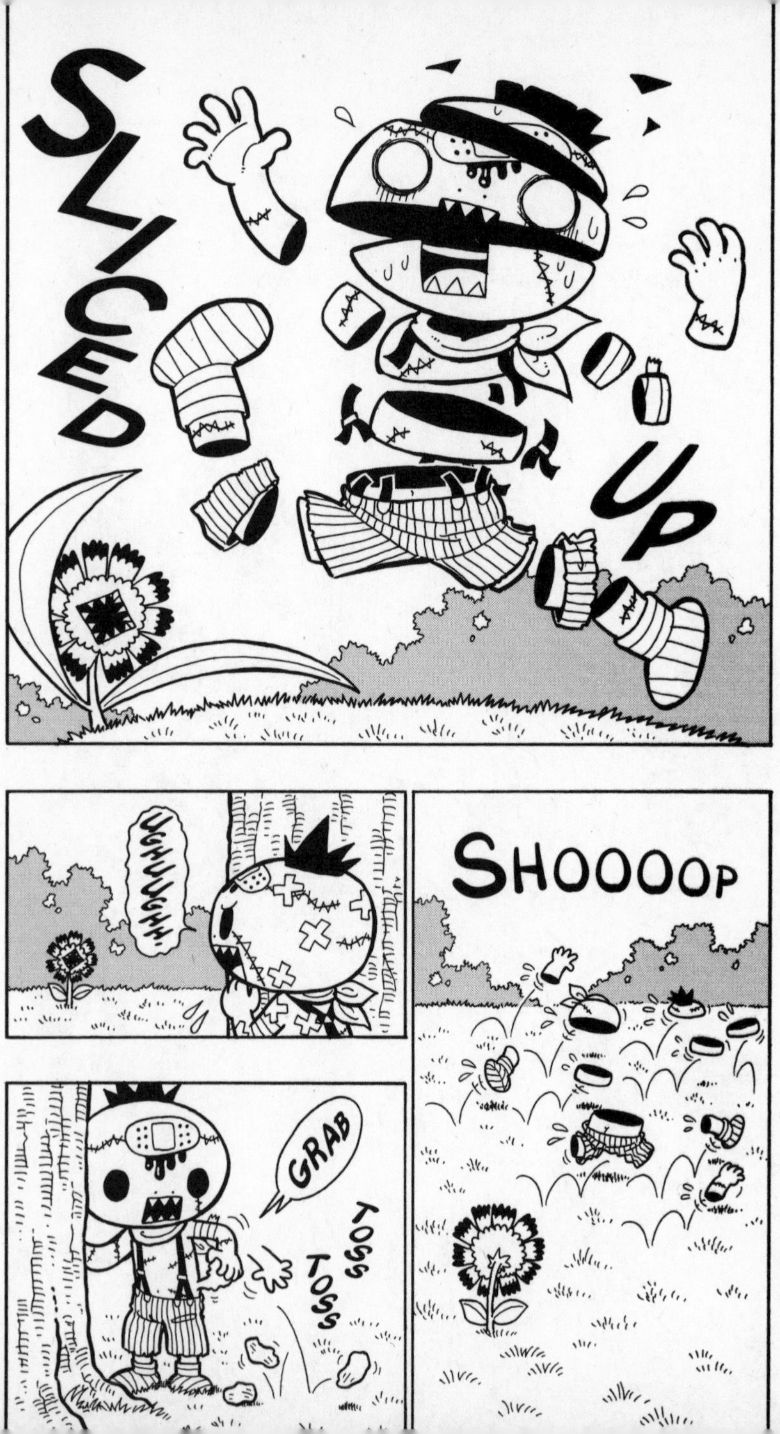
SLICED
UP
SHOOOOP
UGHUUGHH.
GRAB
TOSS
TOSS

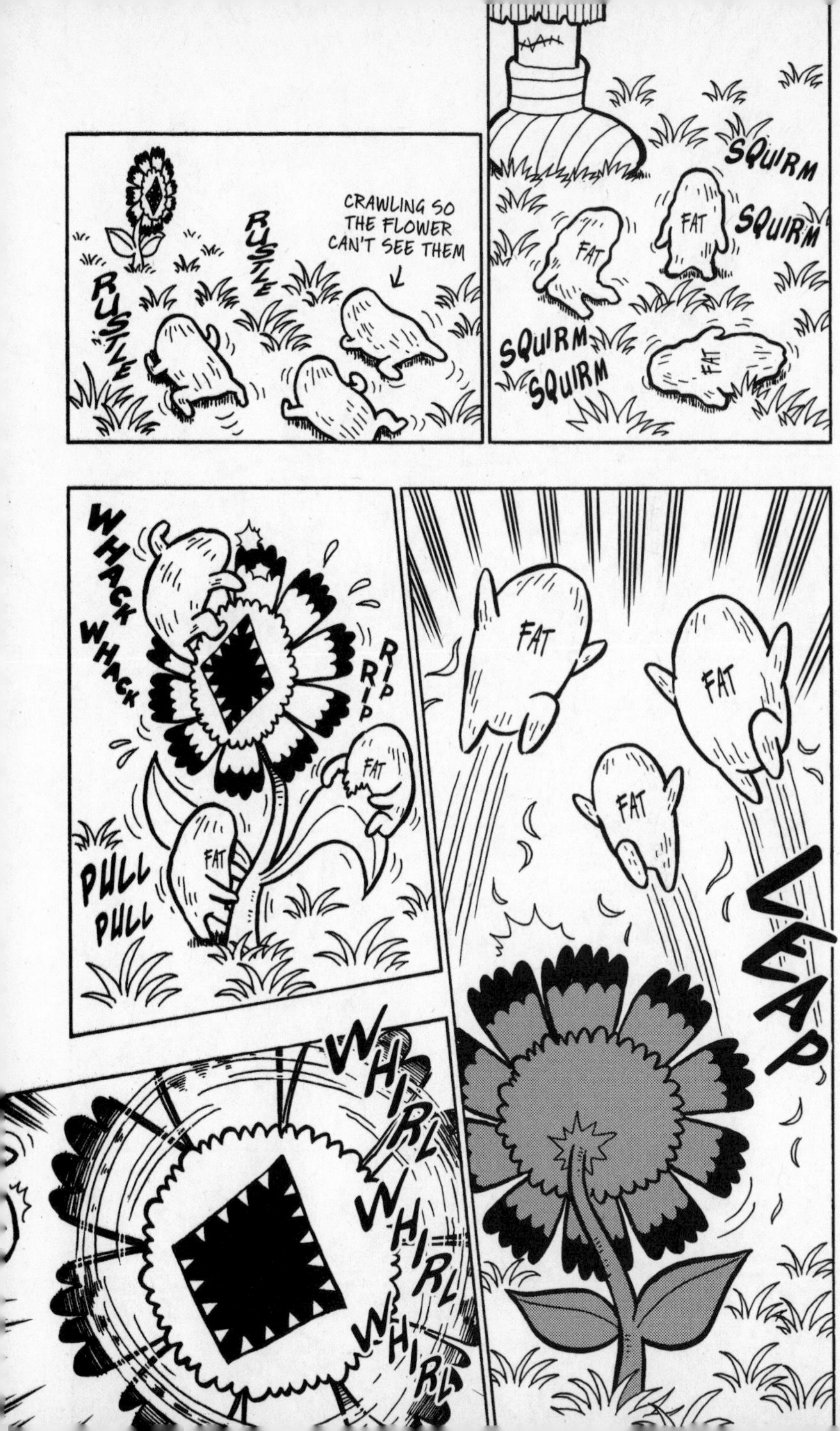
SQUIRM
SQUIRM
FAT
FAT
SQUIRM
SQUIRM
FAT
CRAWLING SO THE FLOWER CAN'T SEE THEM
RUSTLE
RUSTLE
FAT
FAT
FAT
LEAP
WHACK
WHACK
RIP
RIP
FAT
FAT
PULL
PULL
WHIRL
WHIRL
WHIRL

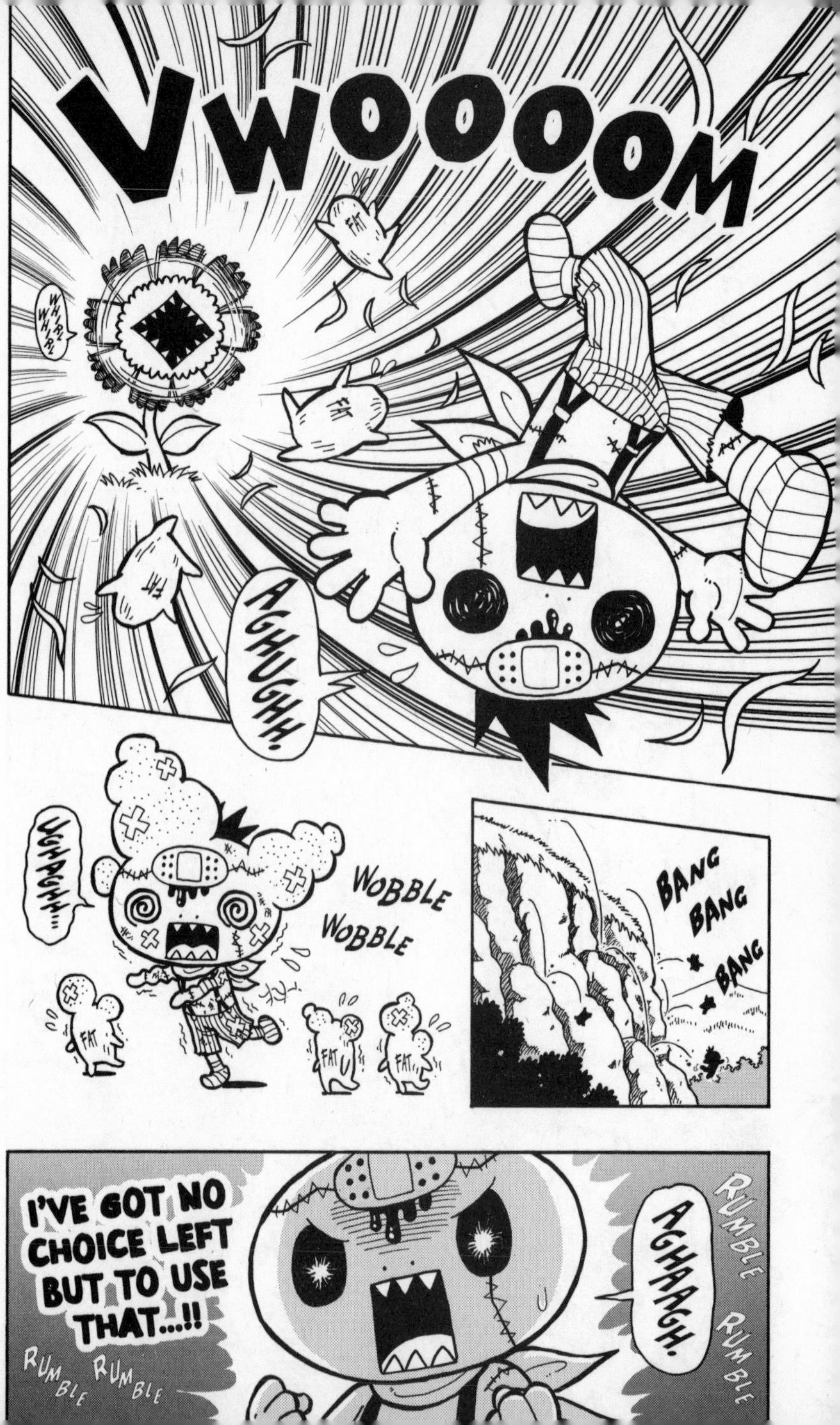
VWOOOOM
WHIRL WHIRL
FAT
FAT
FAT
AGHUGHH.
BANG
BANG
BANG
UGHAGHH...
WOBBLE
WOBBLE
FAT
FAT
FAT
RUMBLE
AGHAAGH.
I'VE GOT NO CHOICE LEFT BUT TO USE THAT...!!
RUMBLE
RUMBLE
RUMBLE
RUMBLE

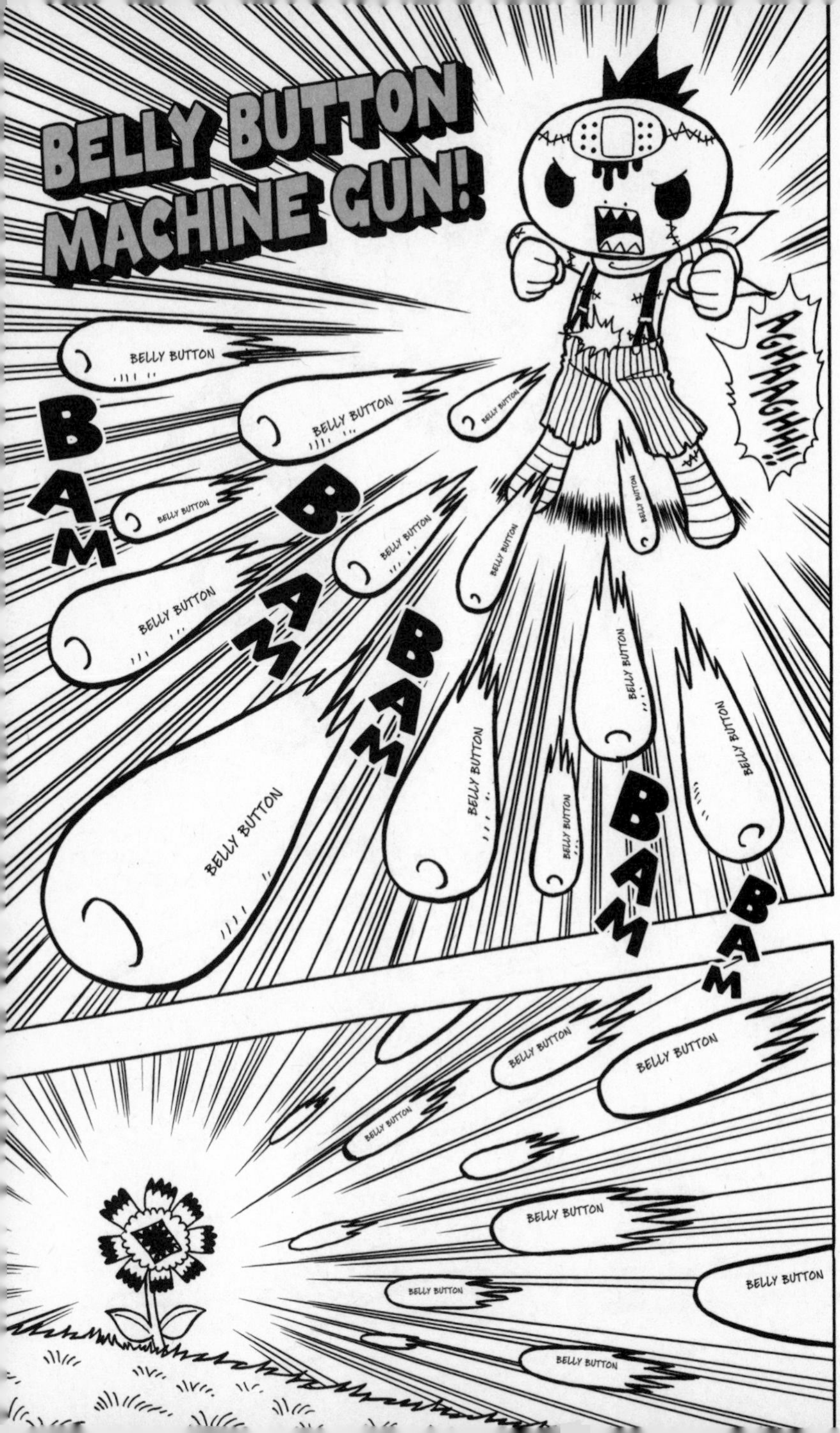
BELLY BUTTON MACHINE GUN!
AGHAAGHH!!
BELLY BUTTON
BELLY BUTTON
BELLY BUTTON
BAM
BAM
BAM
BAM
BAM
BELLY BUTTON
BELLY BUTTON
BELLY BUTTON
BELLY BUTTON
BELLY BUTTON
BELLY BUTTON
BELLY BUTTON
BELLY BUTTON
BELLY BUTTON
BELLY BUTTON
BELLY BUTTON
BELLY BUTTON
BELLY BUTTON
BELLY BUTTON
BELLY BUTTON
BELLY BUTTON
BELLY BUTTON
BELLY BUTTON

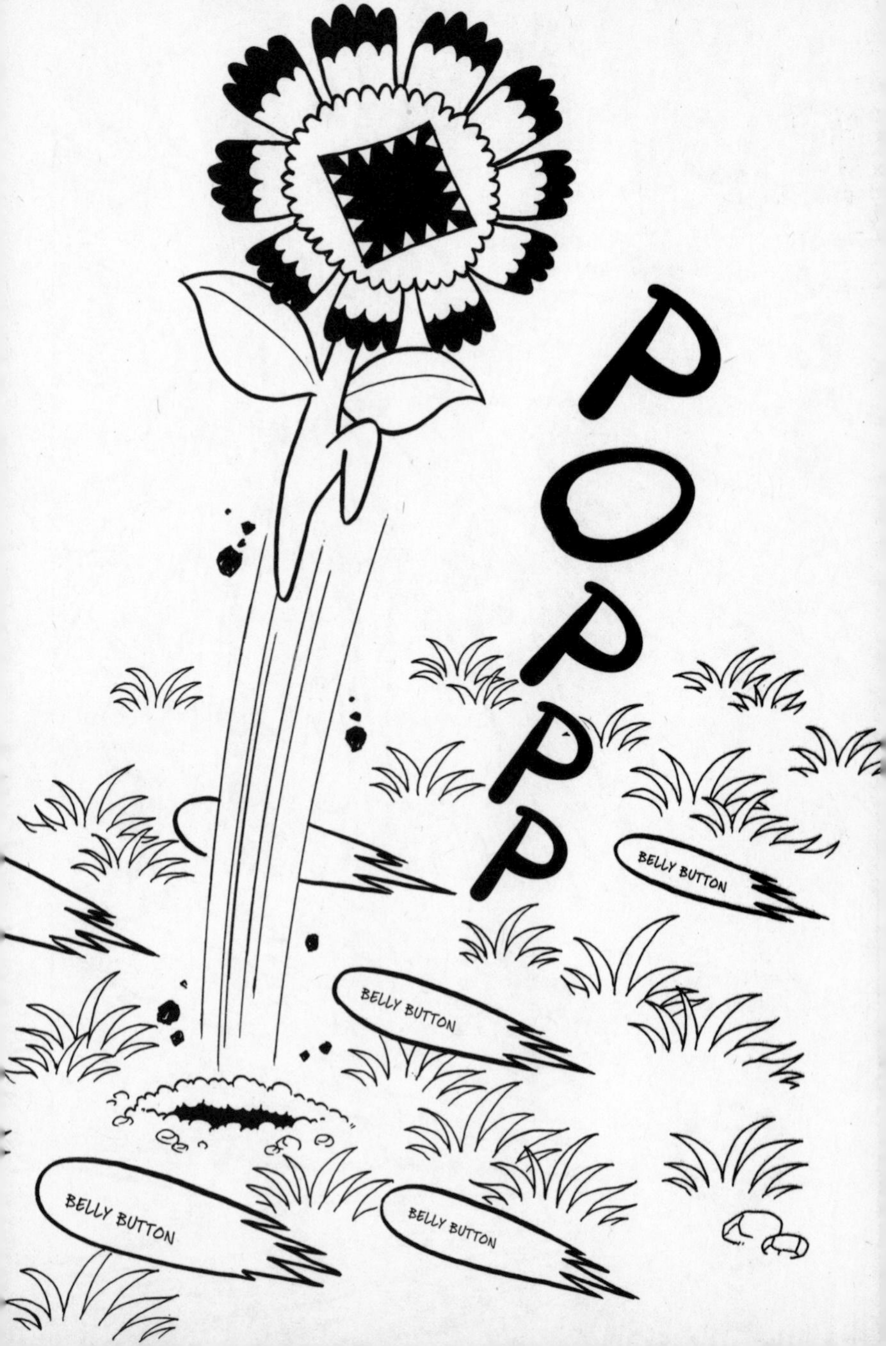
POPPP
BELLY BUTTON
BELLY BUTTON
BELLY BUTTON
BELLY BUTTON

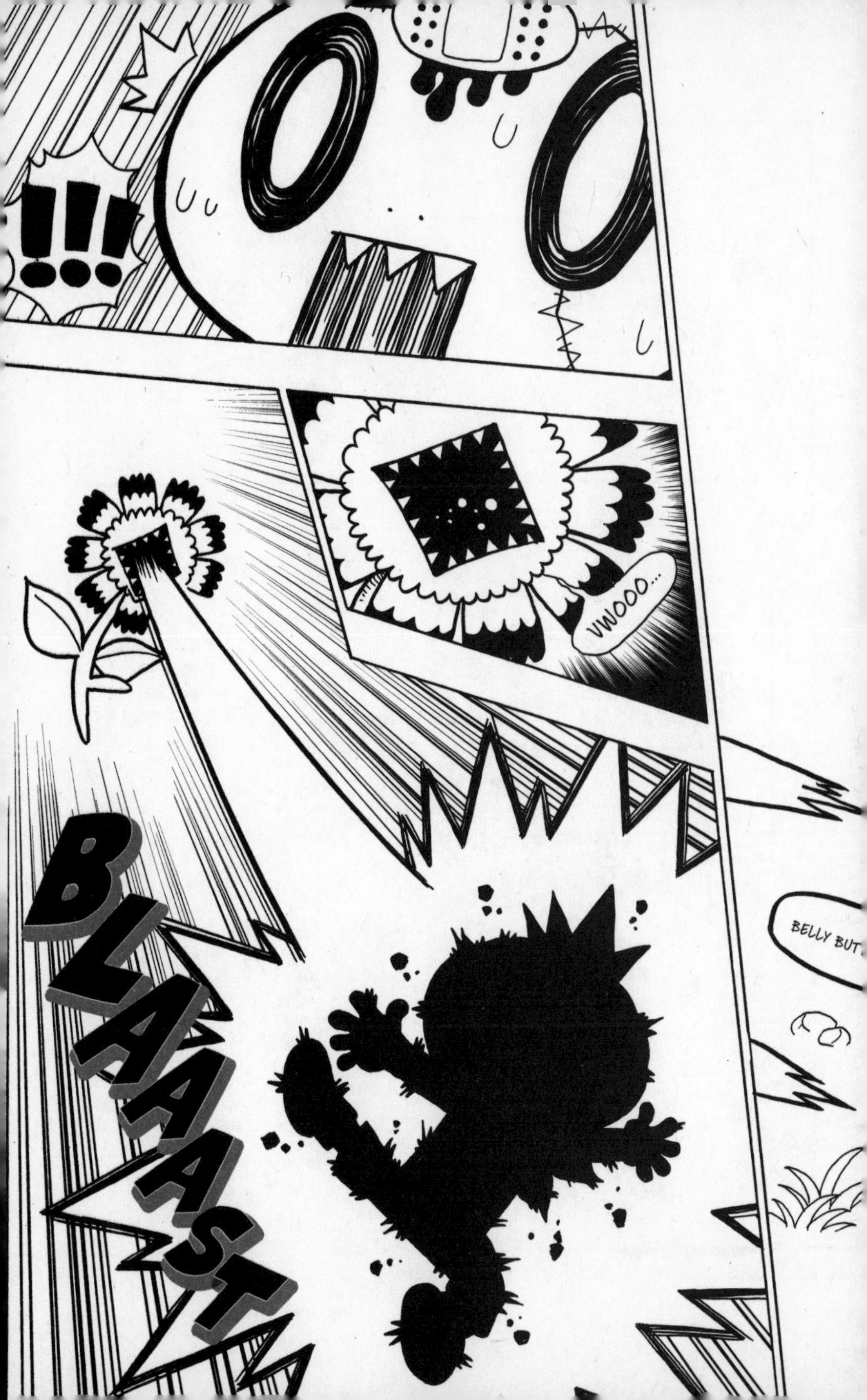
!!!
VWOOO...
BELLY BUT
BLAAAST

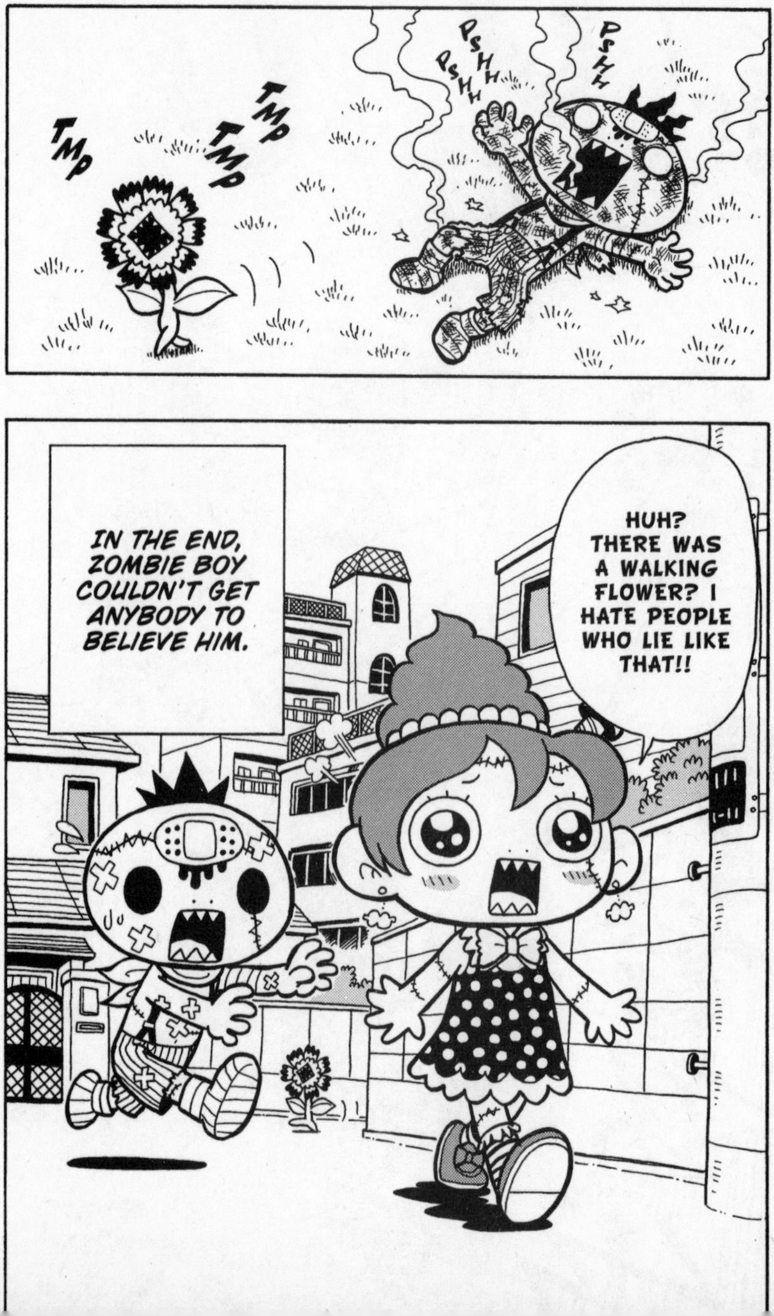
PSHH
PSHH
PSHH
TMP
TMP
TMP
HUH? THERE WAS A WALKING FLOWER? I HATE PEOPLE WHO LIE LIKE THAT!!
IN THE END, ZOMBIE BOY COULDN'T GET ANYBODY TO BELIEVE HIM.

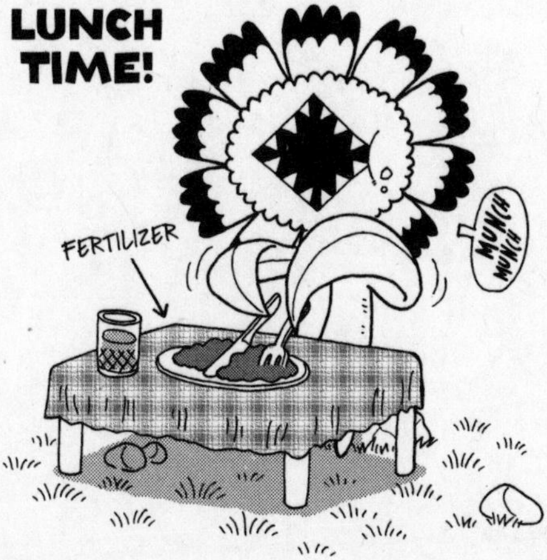
LUNCH TIME!
FERTILIZER
MUNCH MUNCH

A CUTE CLOUD FELL FROM THE ZKY!

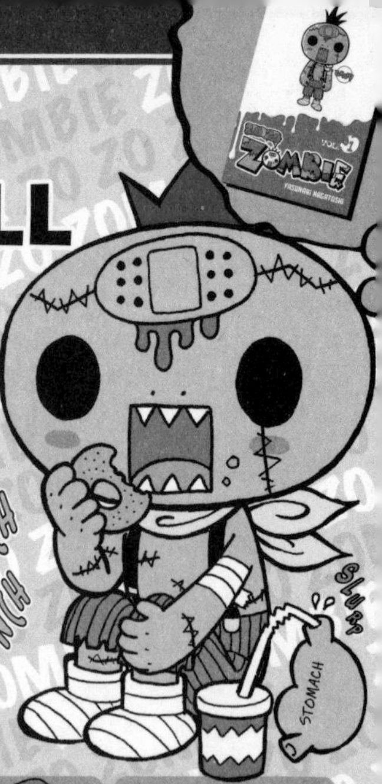
MUNCH
MUNCH
SLURP
STOMACH

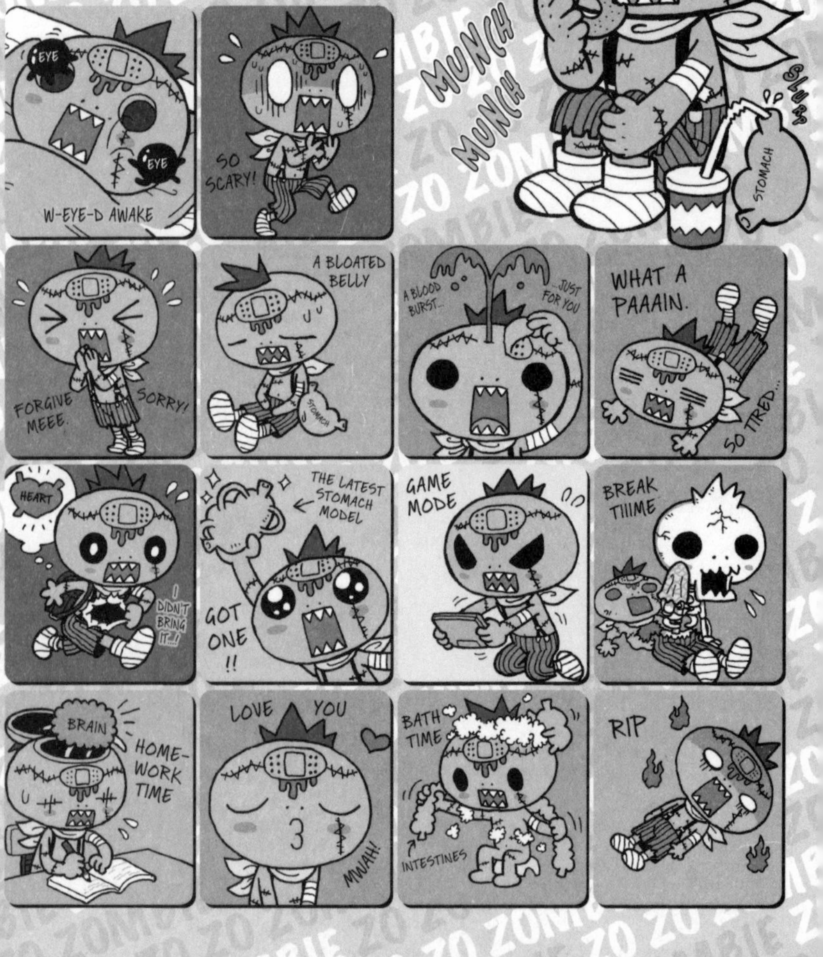
SO SCARY!
EYE
EYE
W-EYE-D AWAKE
WHAT A PAAAIN.
SO TIRED...
A BLOOD BURST...
...JUST FOR YOU
A BLOATED BELLY
STOMACH
SORRY!
FORGIVE MEEE.
BREAK TIIIME
GAME MODE
THE LATEST STOMACH MODEL
GOT ONE !!
HEART
I DIDN'T BRING IT...!
RIP
BATH TIME
INTESTINES
LOVE YOU
MWAH!
BRAIN
HOME-WORK TIME

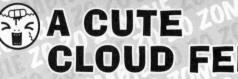

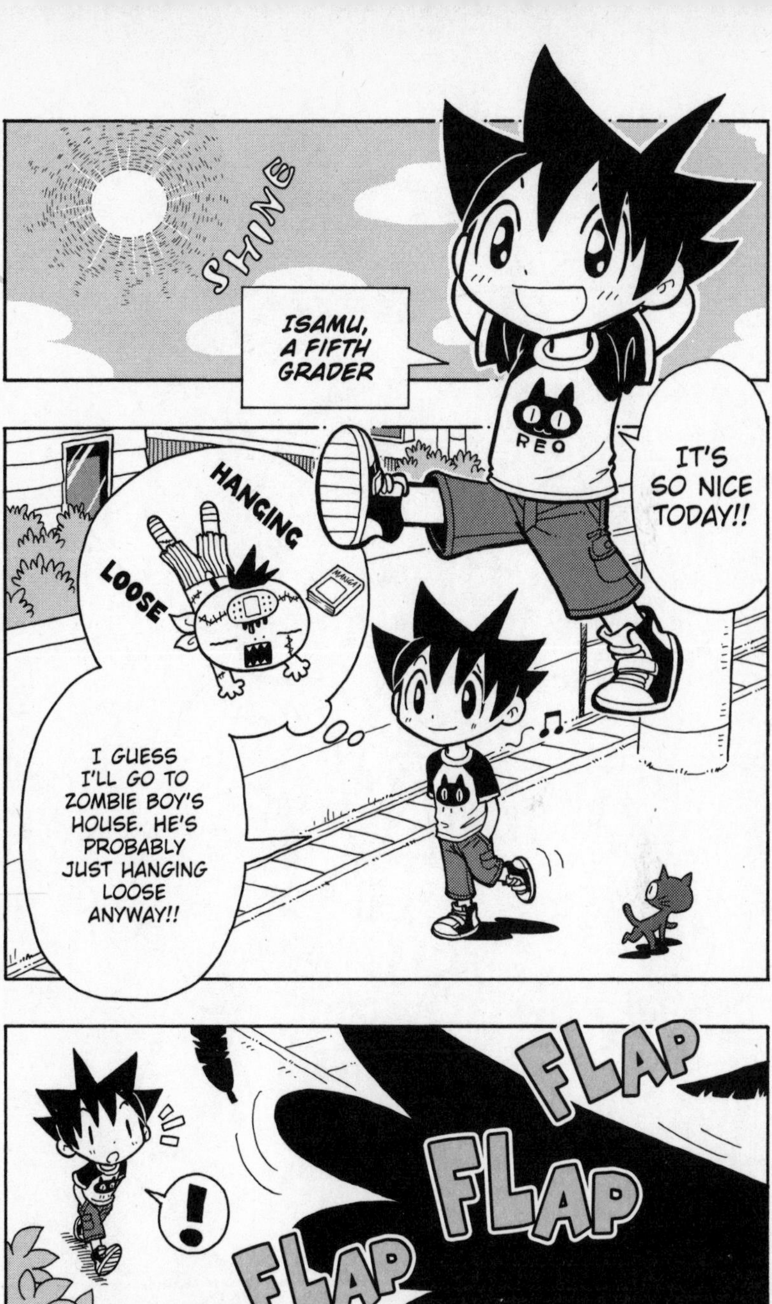
SHINE
ISAMU, A FIFTH GRADER
IT'S SO NICE TODAY!!
HANGING
LOOSE
MANGA
REO
I GUESS I'LL GO TO ZOMBIE BOY'S HOUSE. HE'S PROBABLY JUST HANGING LOOSE ANYWAY!!
FLAP
FLAP
FLAP
!

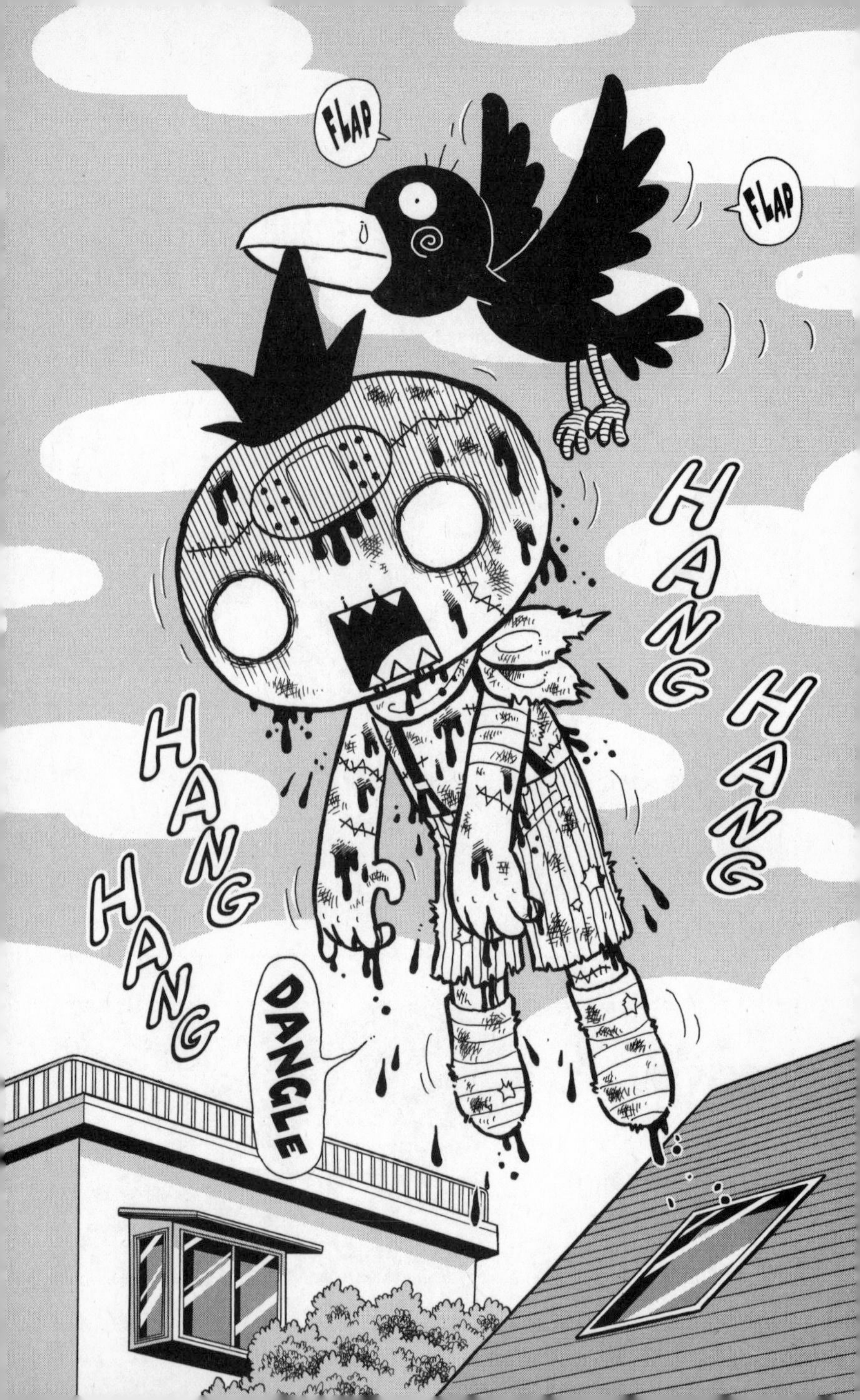
FLAP
FLAP
HANG HANG
HANG HANG
DANGLE

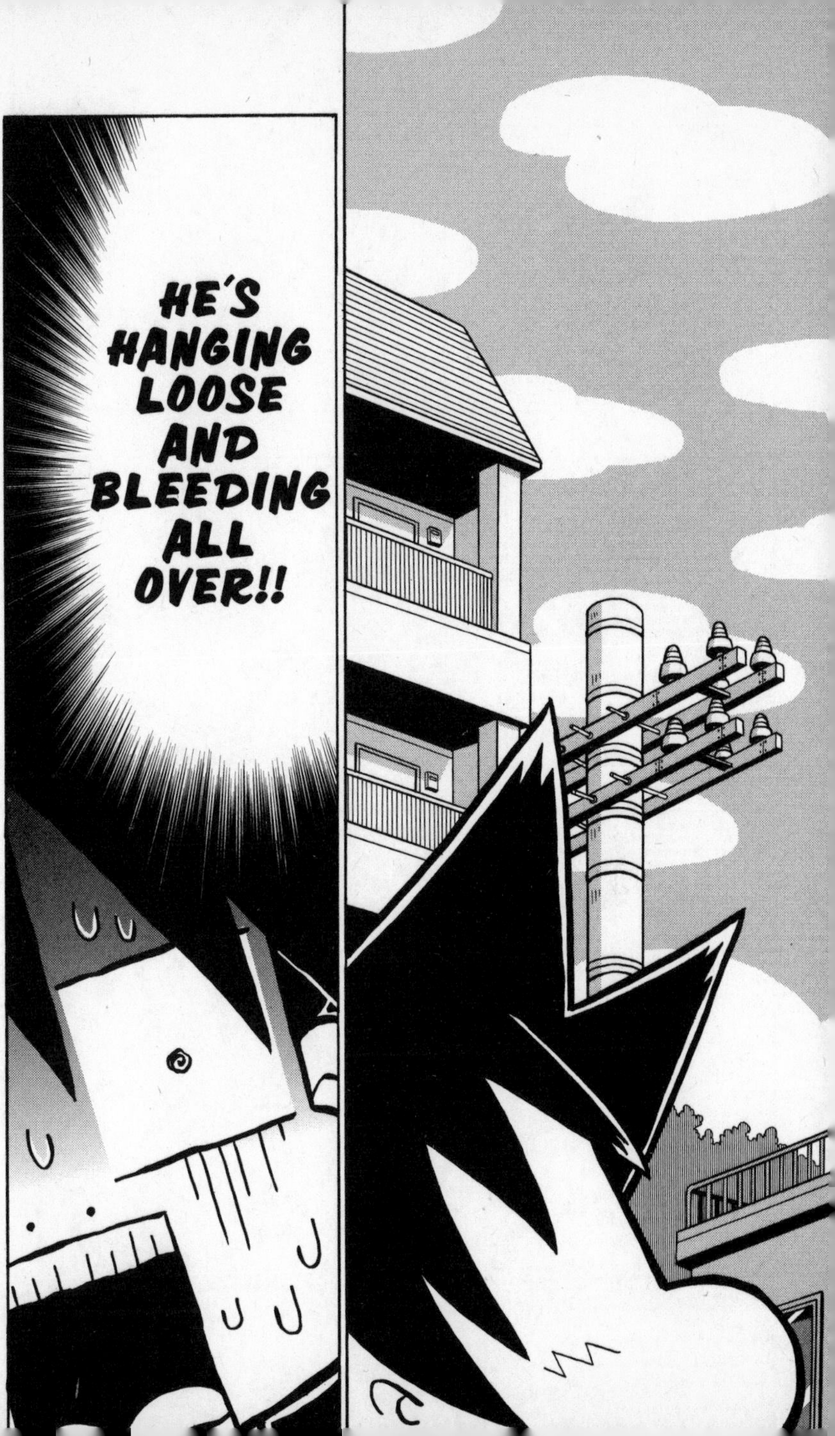
HE'S HANGING LOOSE AND BLEEDING ALL OVER!!

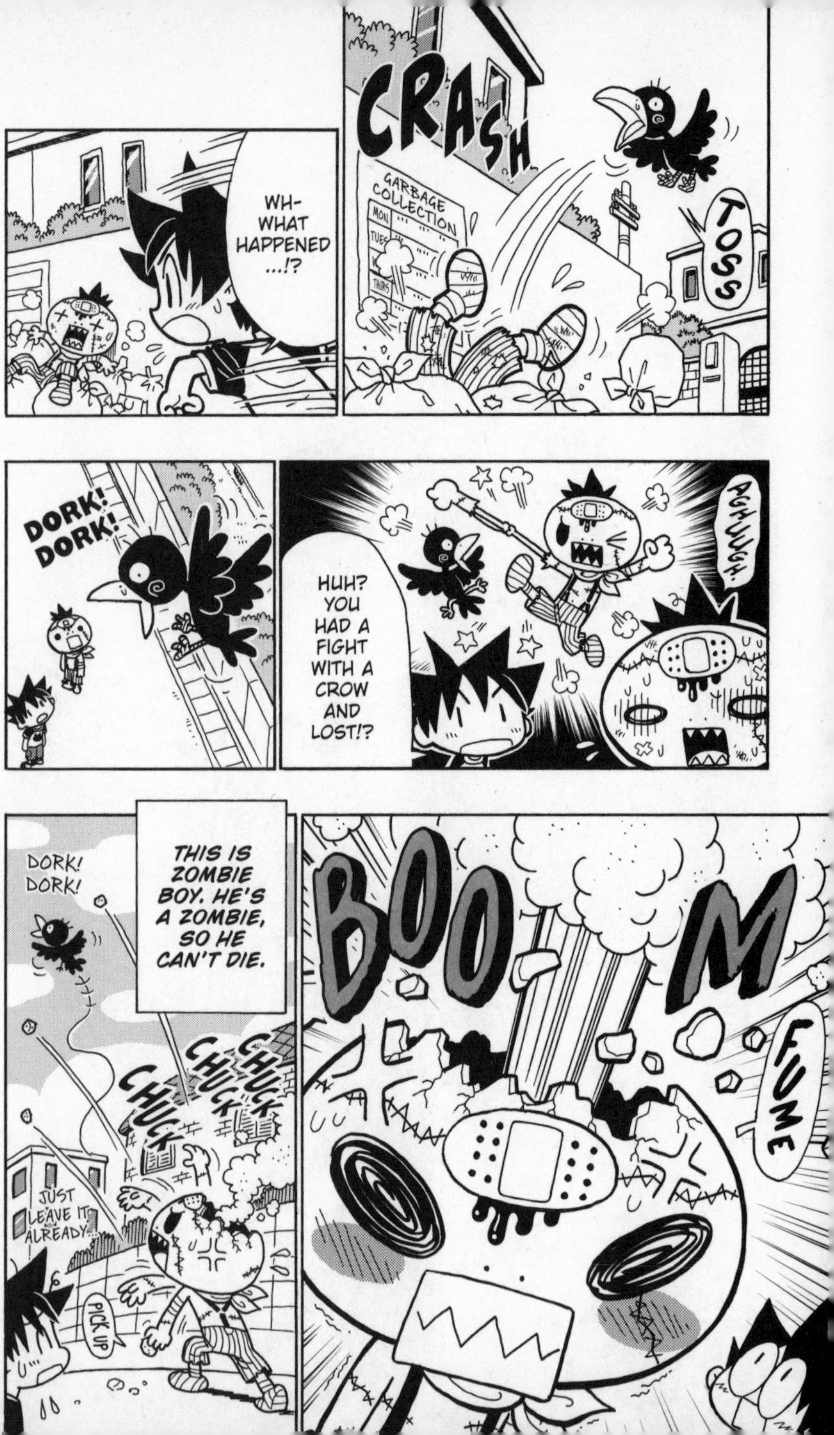
CRASH
GARBAGE COLLECTION
MON
TUES
THURS
TOSS
WH-WHAT HAPPENED ...!?
AGHUUGH.
HUH? YOU HAD A FIGHT WITH A CROW AND LOST!?
DORK! DORK!
BOO-M
FUME
THIS IS ZOMBIE BOY. HE'S A ZOMBIE, SO HE CAN'T DIE.
DORK! DORK!
CHUCK CHUCK CHUCK
JUST LEAVE IT ALREADY...
PICK UP

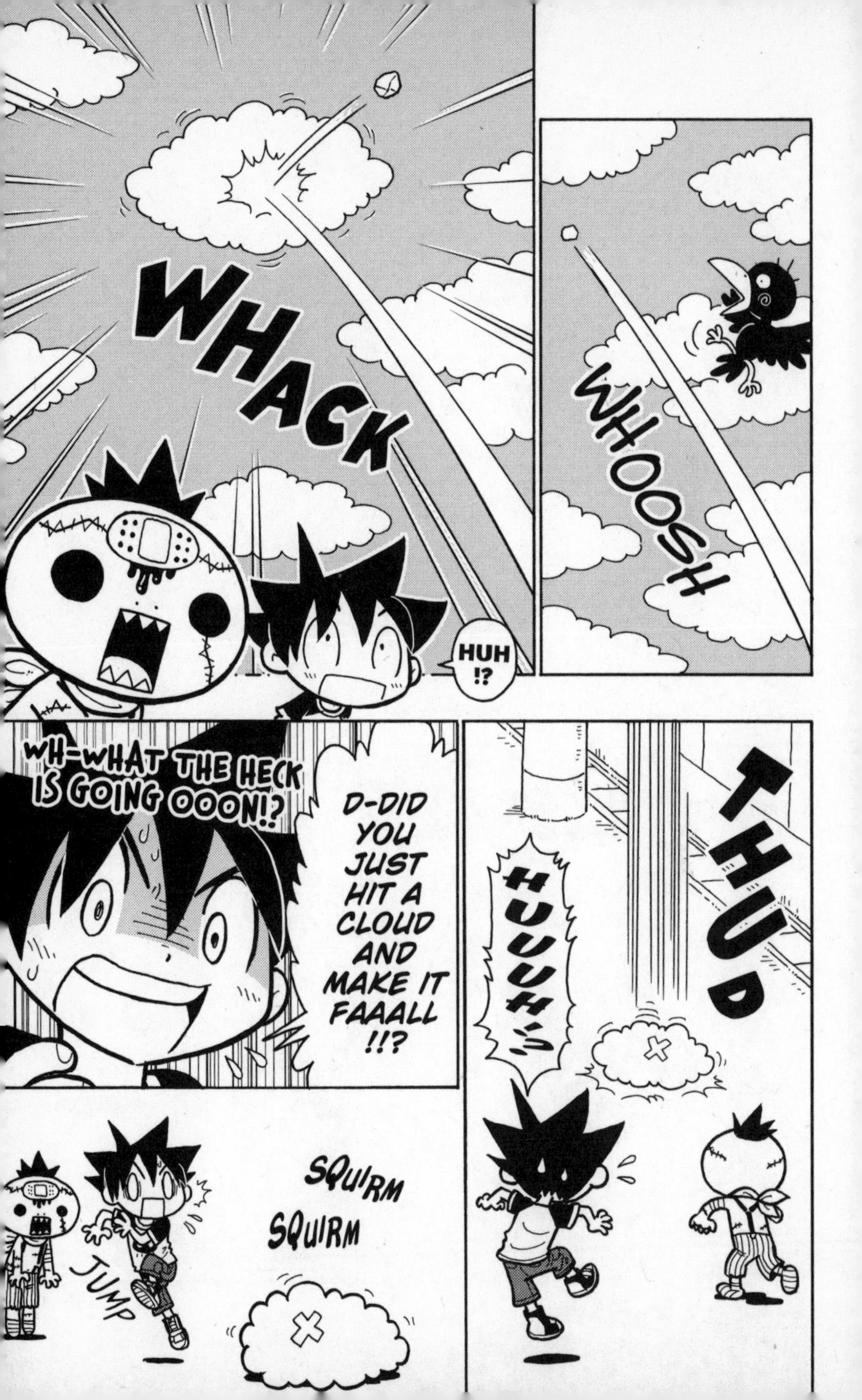
WHOOSH
WHACK
HUH !?
THUD
HUUUUH!?
D-DID YOU JUST HIT A CLOUD AND MAKE IT FAAALL !!?
WH-WHAT THE HECK IS GOING OOON!?
SQUIRM
SQUIRM
JUMP

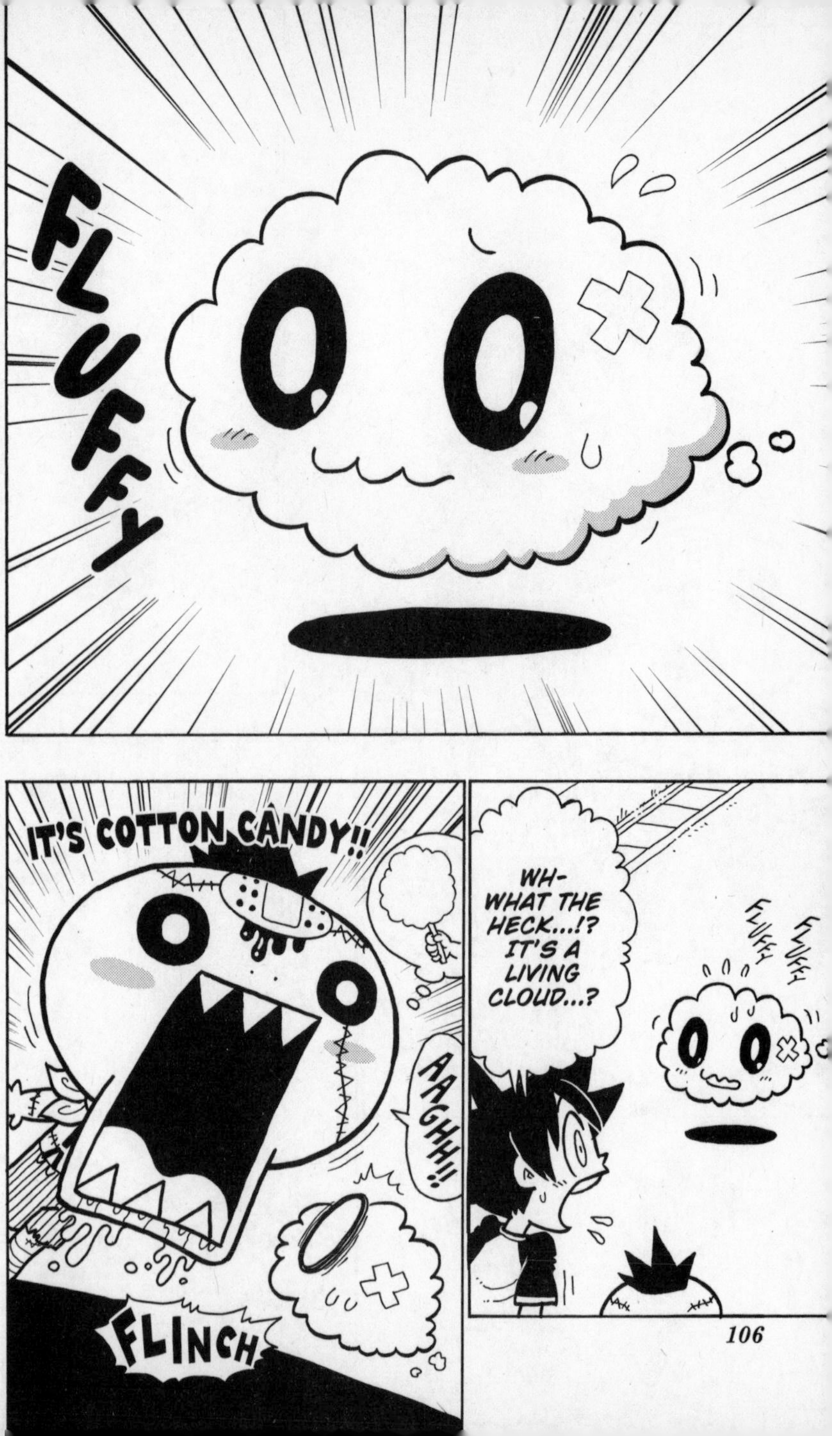
FLUFFY
WH- WHAT THE HECK...!? IT'S A LIVING CLOUD...?
FLUFFY
FLUFFY
IT'S COTTON CANDY!!
AAGHH!!
FLINCH

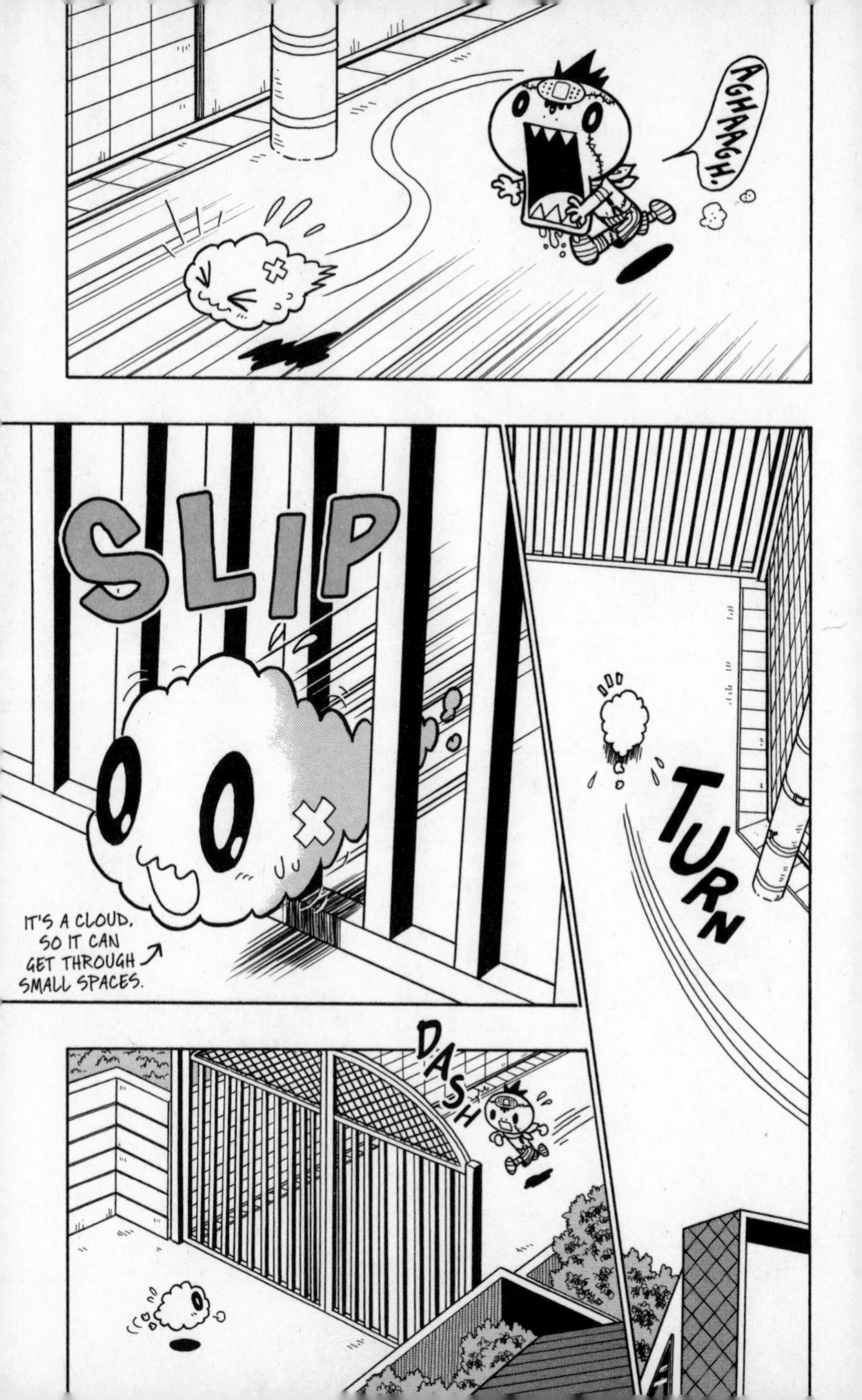
AGHAAGH.
TURN
SLIP
IT'S A CLOUD, SO IT CAN GET THROUGH SMALL SPACES.
DASH

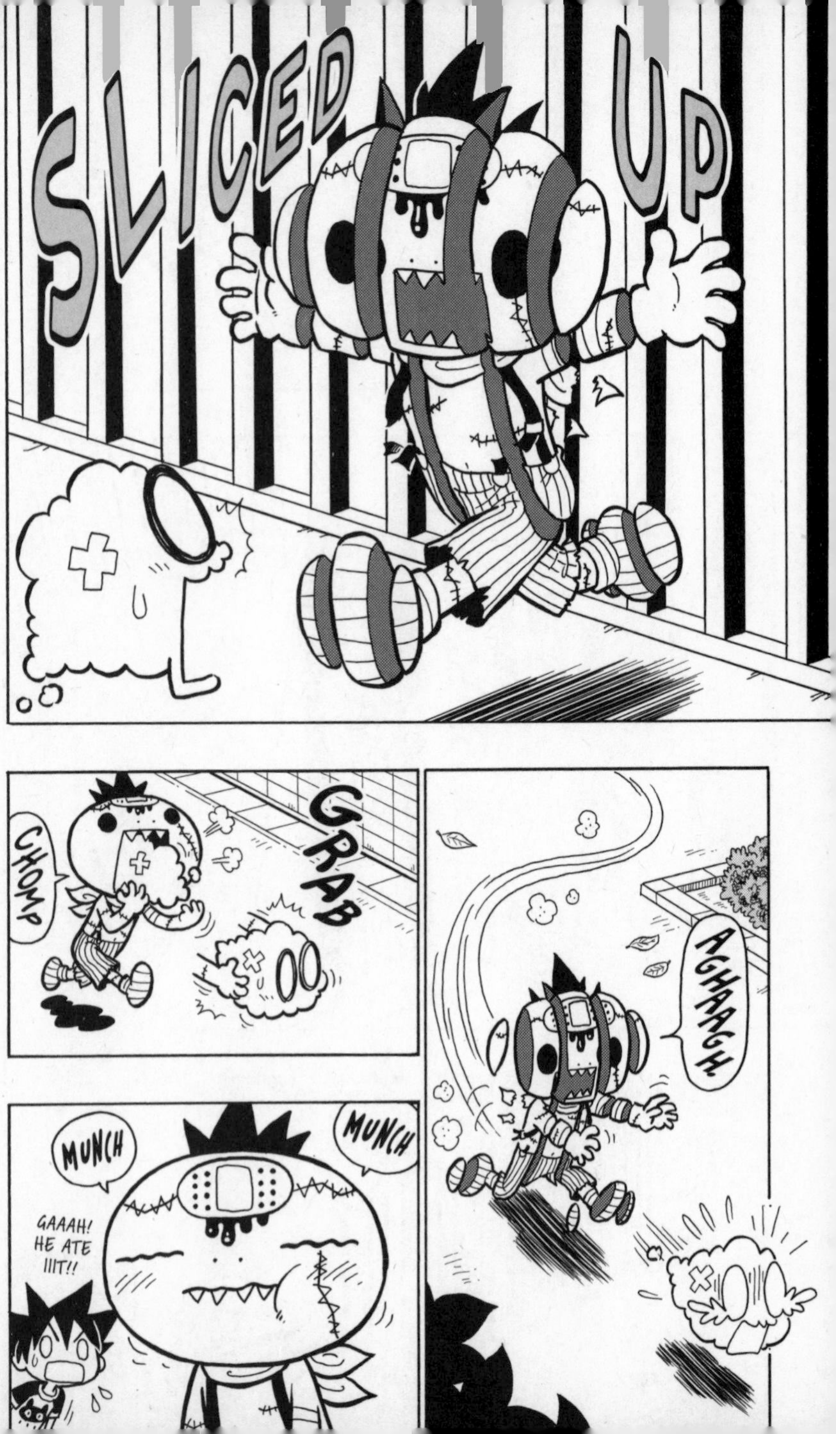
SLICED UP
AGHAAAGH
GRAB
CHOMP
MUNCH
MUNCH
GAAAH! HE ATE IIIT!!

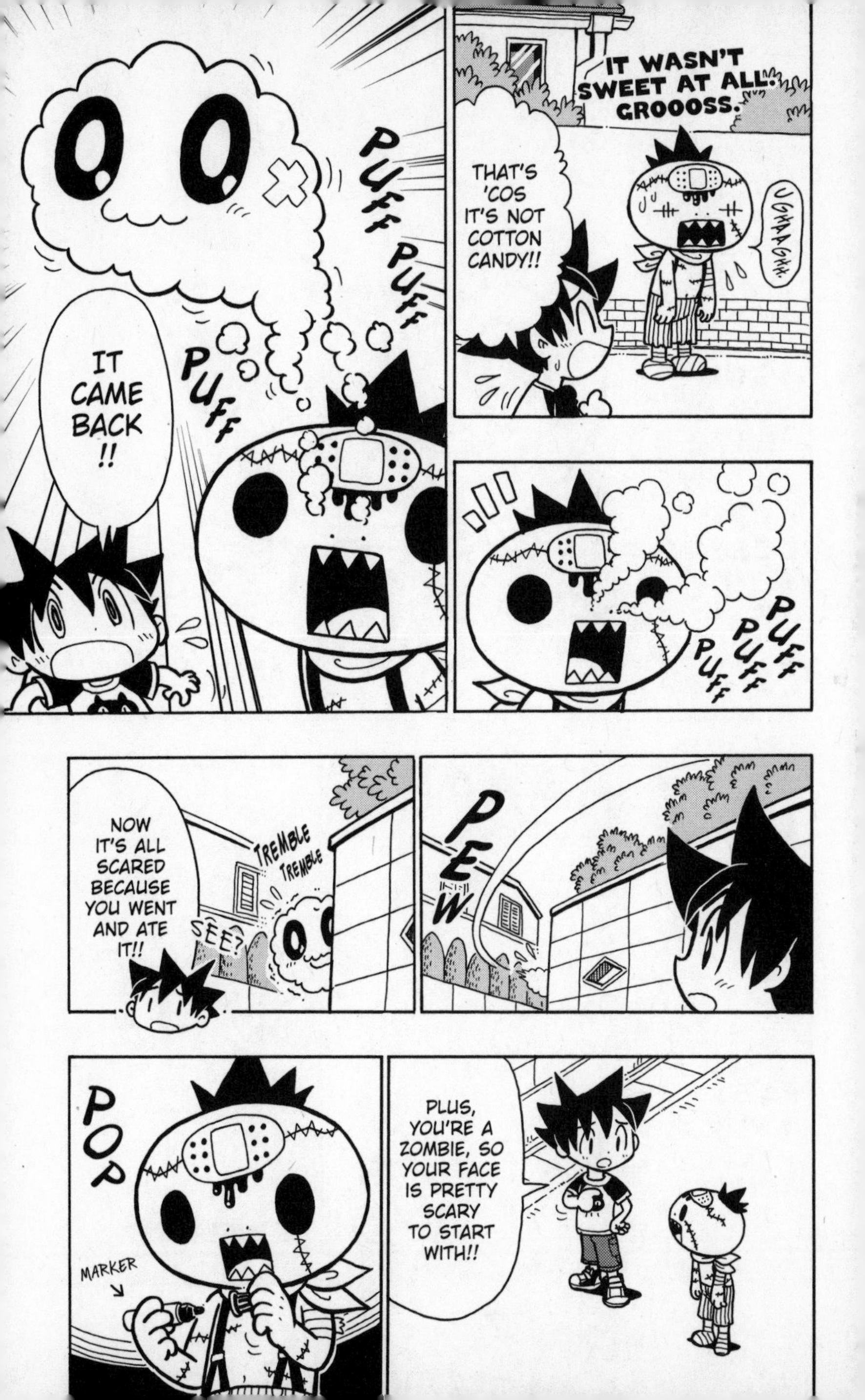

IT WASN'T SWEET AT ALL. GROOOSS.
UGHAAGHH.
THAT'S 'COS IT'S NOT COTTON CANDY!!
PUFF PUFF PUFF
PUFF PUFF
PUFF
IT CAME BACK!!
PEW
TREMBLE TREMBLE
NOW IT'S ALL SCARED BECAUSE YOU WENT AND ATE IT!!
SEE?
PLUS, YOU'RE A ZOMBIE, SO YOUR FACE IS PRETTY SCARY TO START WITH!!
POP
MARKER

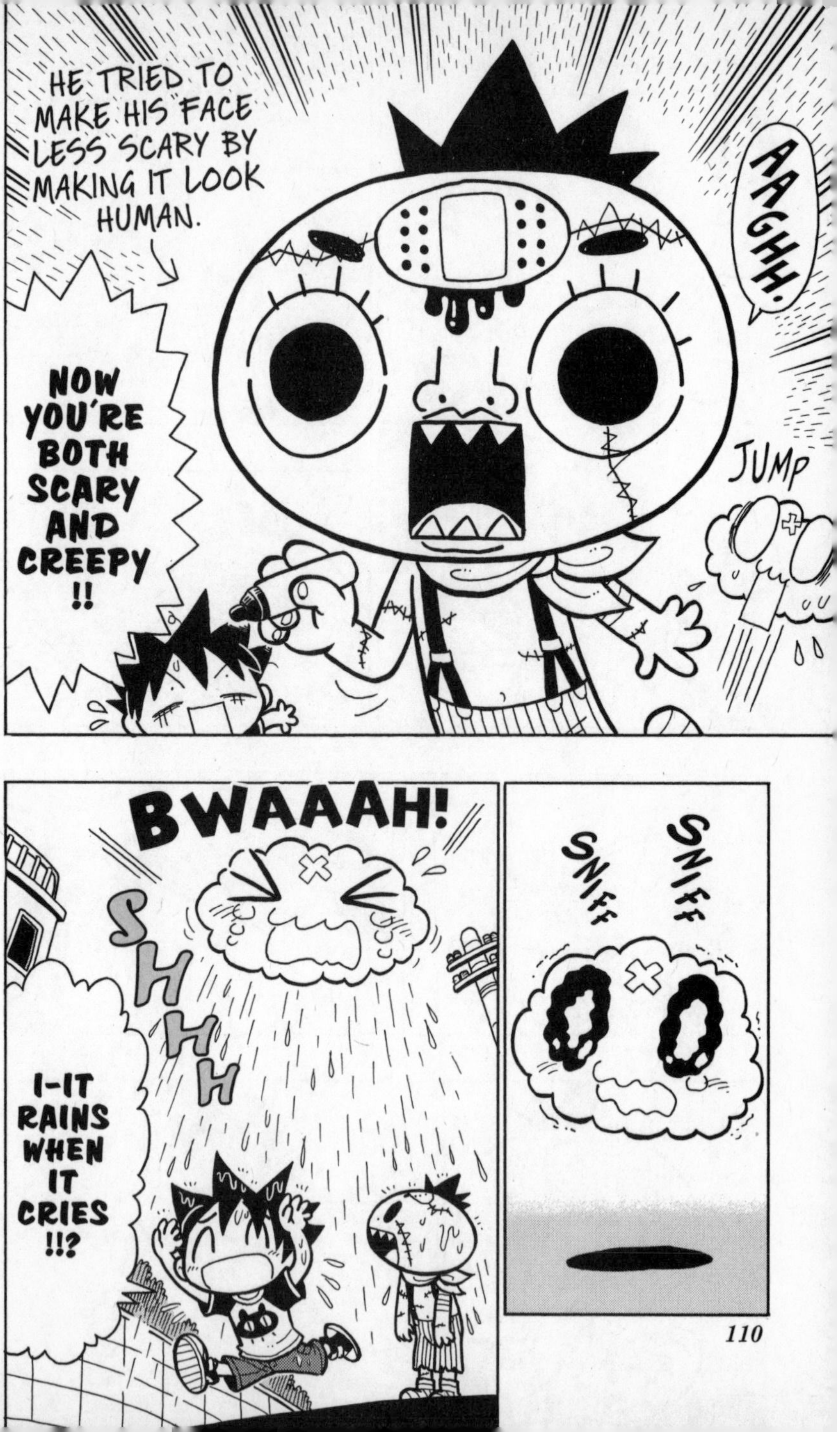
AAGHH.
HE TRIED TO MAKE HIS FACE LESS SCARY BY MAKING IT LOOK HUMAN.
NOW YOU'RE BOTH SCARY AND CREEPY!!
JUMP
SNIFF
SNIFF
BWAAAH!
SHHHH
I-IT RAINS WHEN IT CRIES!!?

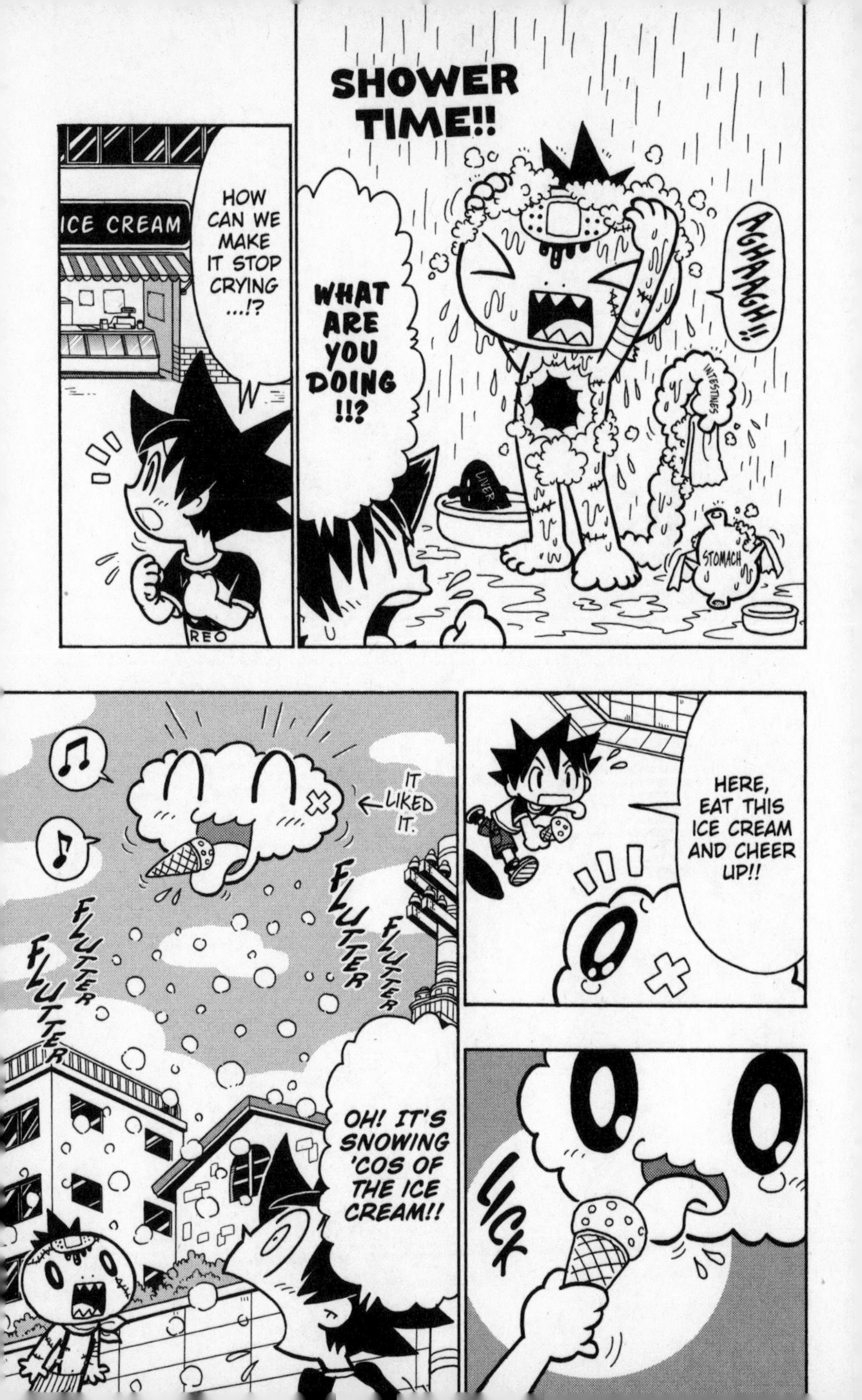
SHOWER TIME!!
AGHAAGH!!
INTESTINES
WHAT ARE YOU DOING!!?
LIVER
STOMACH
ICE CREAM
HOW CAN WE MAKE IT STOP CRYING ...!?
REO
HERE, EAT THIS ICE CREAM AND CHEER UP!!
LICK
IT LIKED IT.
FLUTTER
FLUTTER
FLUTTER
FLUTTER
OH! IT'S SNOWING 'COS OF THE ICE CREAM!!

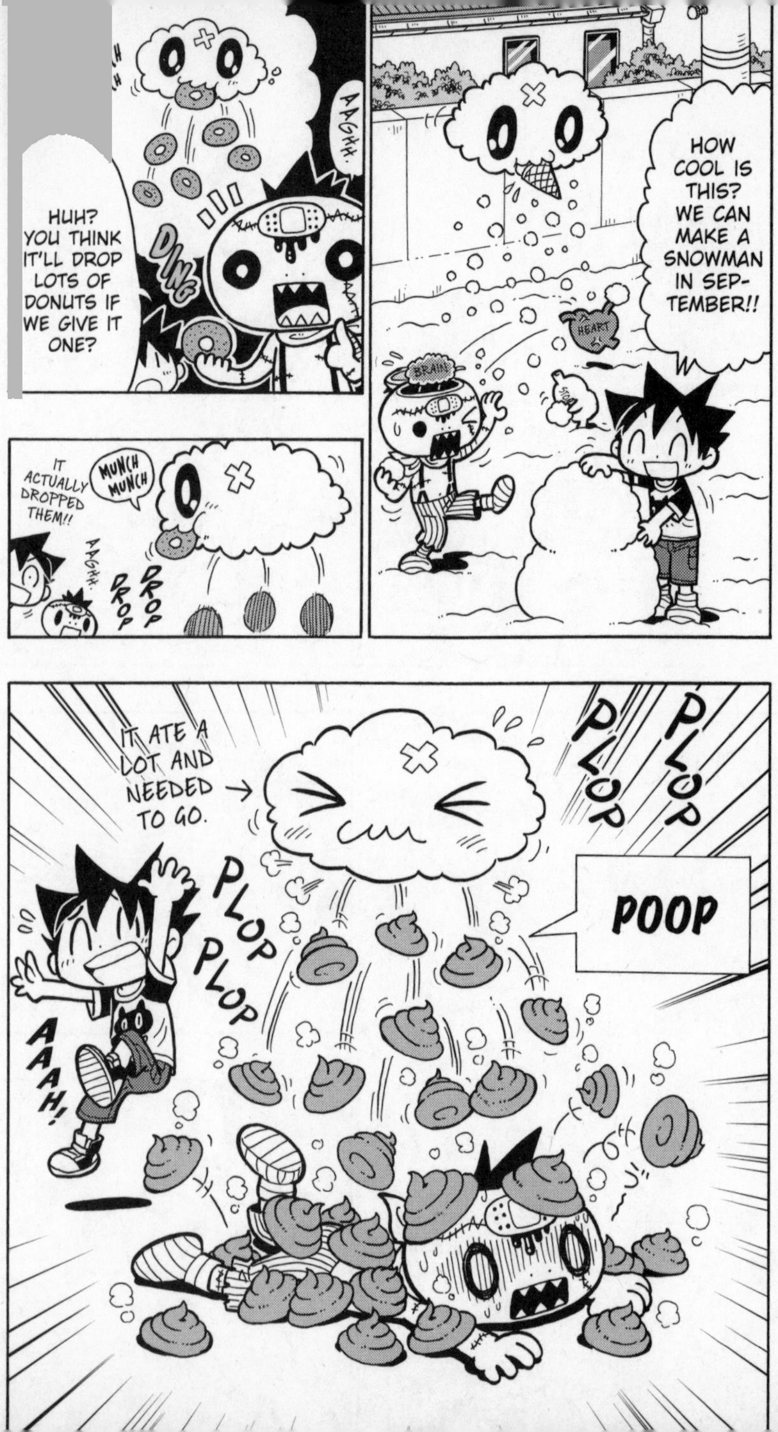
HOW COOL IS THIS? WE CAN MAKE A SNOWMAN IN SEPTEMBER!!
BRAIN
HEART
HUH? YOU THINK IT'LL DROP LOTS OF DONUTS IF WE GIVE IT ONE?
AAGHH.
DING
MUNCH MUNCH
IT ACTUALLY DROPPED THEM!!
AAGHH.
DROP DROP
PLOP PLOP
POOP
IT ATE A LOT AND NEEDED TO GO.
PLOP PLOP
AAAH!

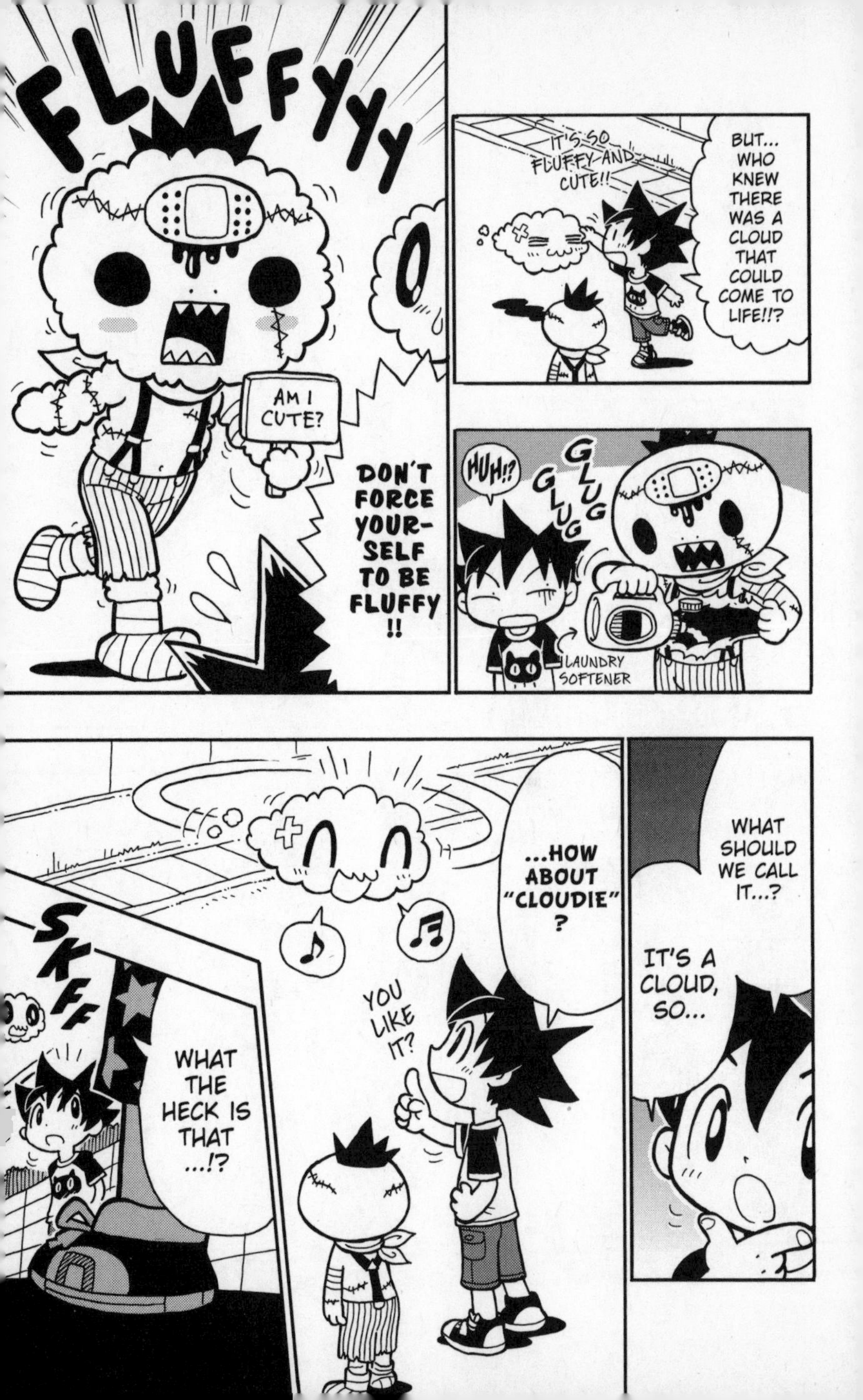
BUT... WHO KNEW THERE WAS A CLOUD THAT COULD COME TO LIFE!!?
IT'S SO FLUFFY AND CUTE!!
HUH!?
GLUG GLUG
LAUNDRY SOFTENER
FLUFFYYY
AM I CUTE?
DON'T FORCE YOUR-SELF TO BE FLUFFY!!
WHAT SHOULD WE CALL IT...?
IT'S A CLOUD, SO...
...HOW ABOUT "CLOUDIE"?
YOU LIKE IT?
SKFF
WHAT THE HECK IS THAT...!?

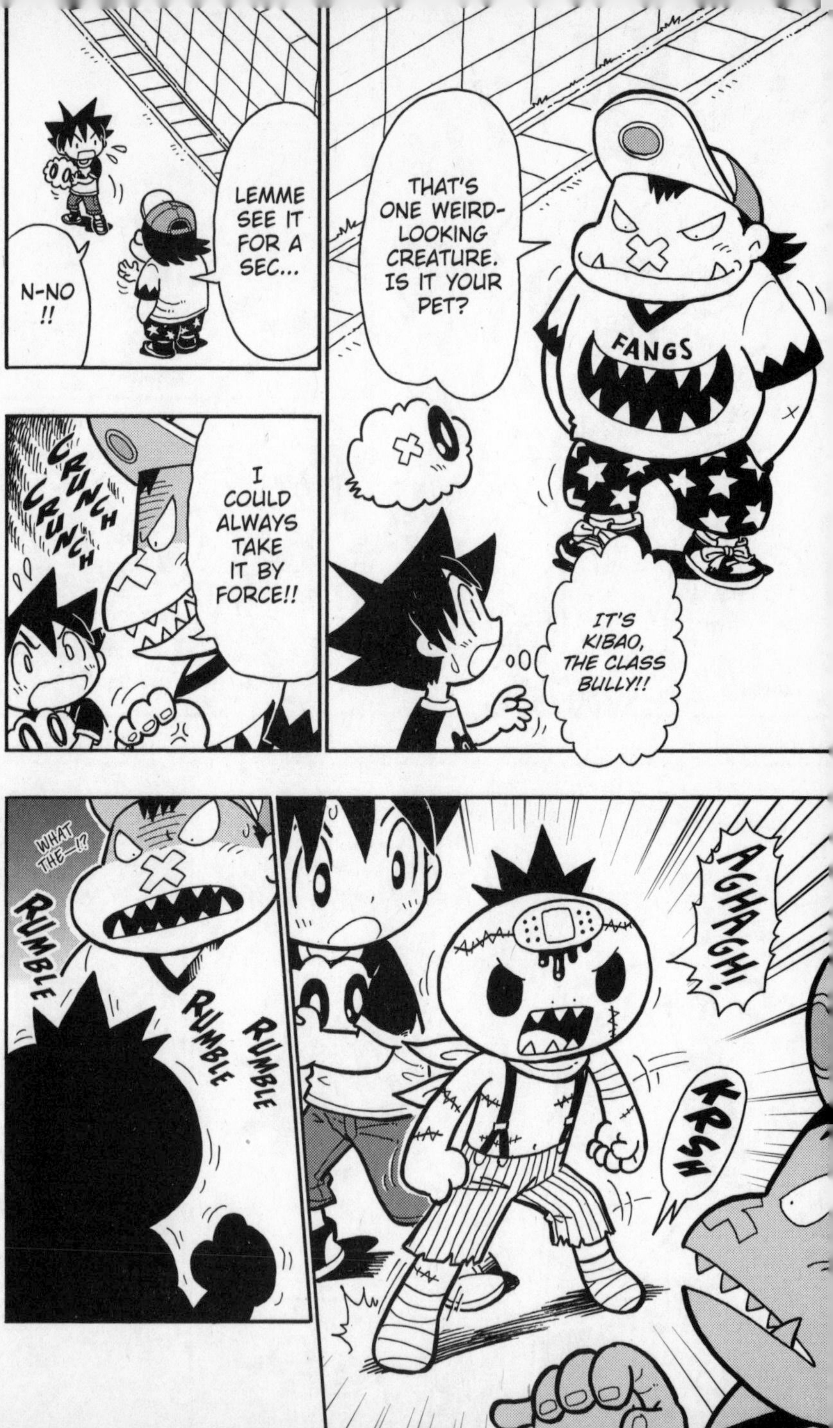
THAT'S ONE WEIRD-LOOKING CREATURE. IS IT YOUR PET?
FANGS
IT'S KIBAO, THE CLASS BULLY!!
LEMME SEE IT FOR A SEC...
N-NO!!
I COULD ALWAYS TAKE IT BY FORCE!!
CRUNCH
CRUNCH
AGHAGH!
KRSH
WHAT THE—!?
RUMBLE
RUMBLE
RUMBLE

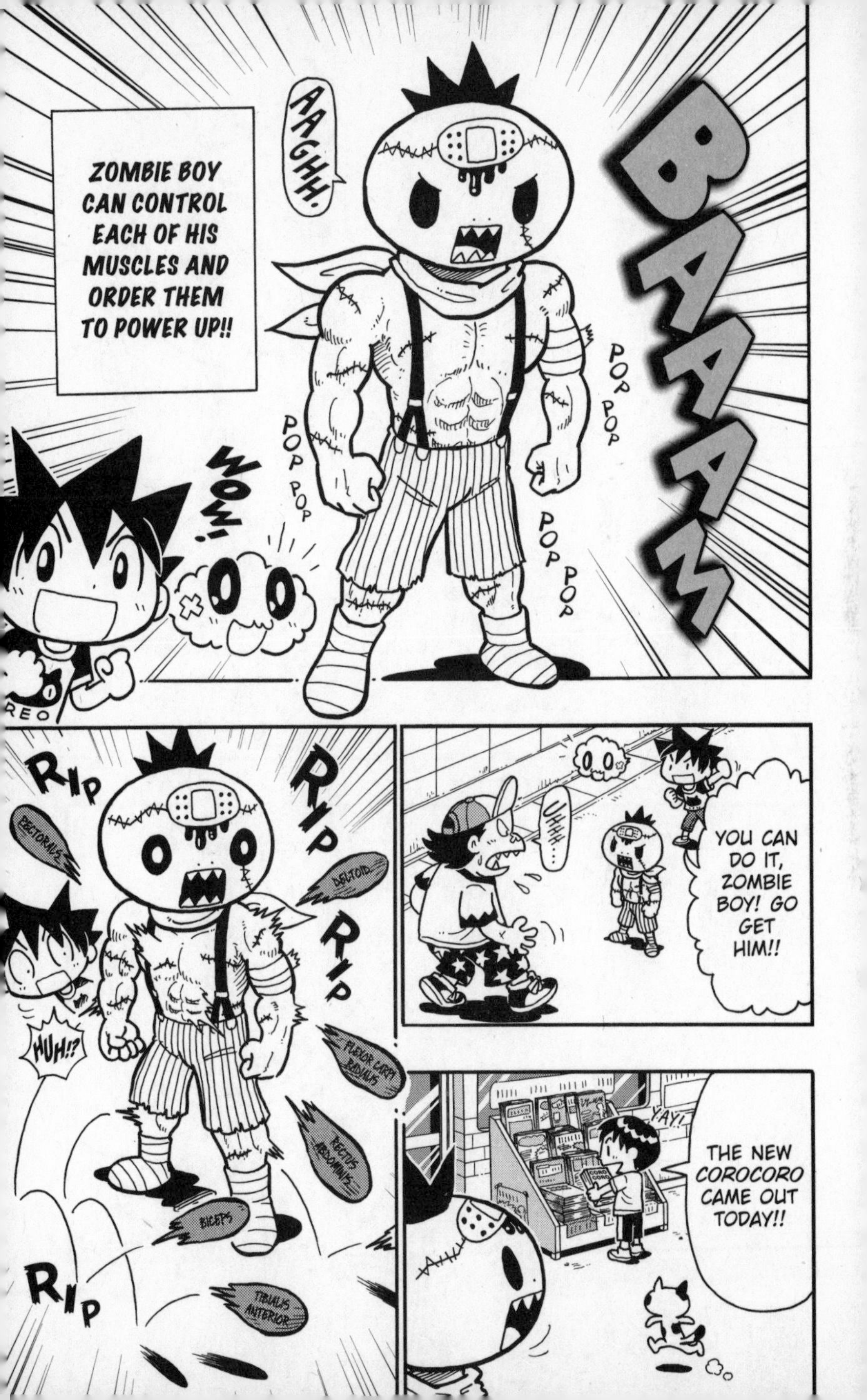
BAAAM
ZOMBIE BOY CAN CONTROL EACH OF HIS MUSCLES AND ORDER THEM TO POWER UP!!
AAGHH.
POP POP
POP POP
POP POP
WOW!
UHHH...
YOU CAN DO IT, ZOMBIE BOY! GO GET HIM!!
THE NEW COROCORO CAME OUT TODAY!!
YAY!
RIP
RIP
PECTORALIS
DELTOID
RIP
HUH!?
FLEXOR CARPI RADIALIS
RECTUS ABDOMINIS
BICEPS
RIP
TIBIALIS ANTERIOR

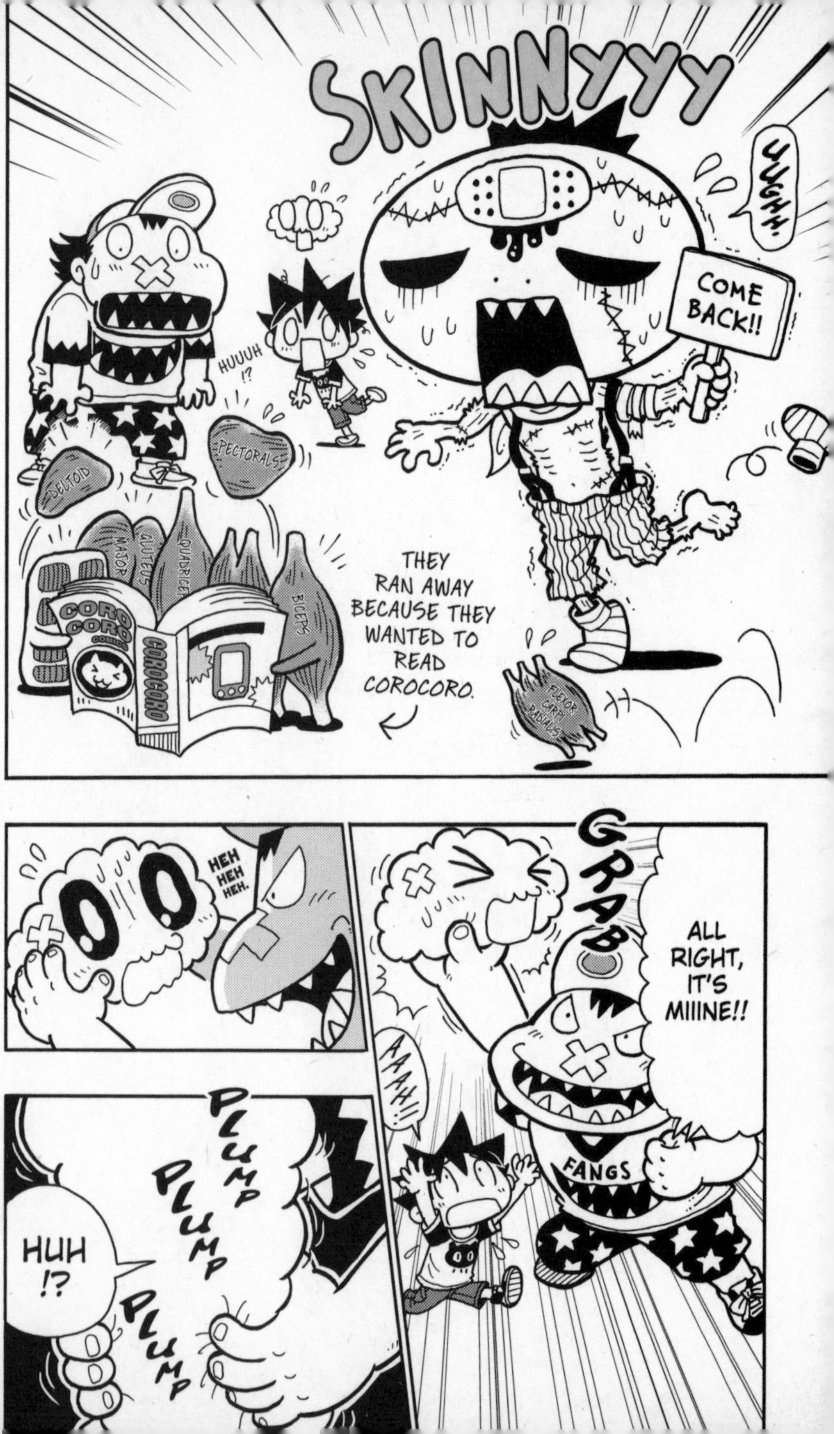

SKINNYYY
UGHHH.
COME BACK!!
HUUUH !?
DELTOID
PECTORALS
GLUTEUS MAJOR
BICEPS
COROCORO COMICS
COROCORO
THEY RAN AWAY BECAUSE THEY WANTED TO READ COROCORO.
GRAB
ALL RIGHT, IT'S MIIINE!!
AAAH
FANGS
HEH HEH HEH.
PLUMP PLUMP PLUMP
HUH !?

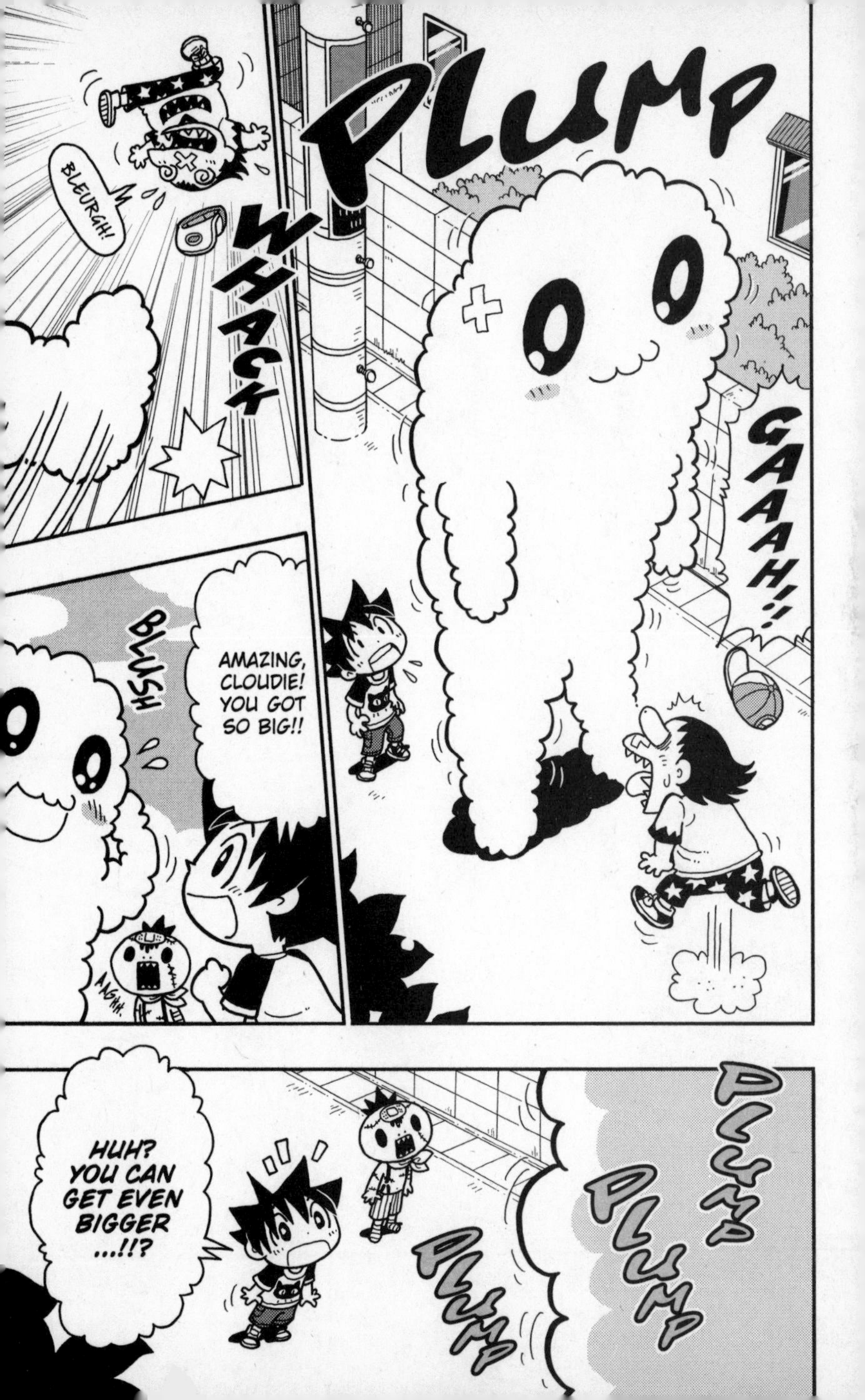
PLUMP
GAAAAH!!
WHACK
BLEURGH!
BLUSH
AMAZING, CLOUDIE! YOU GOT SO BIG!!
ANGHH.
PLUMP
PLUMP
PLUMP
HUH? YOU CAN GET EVEN BIGGER ...!!?

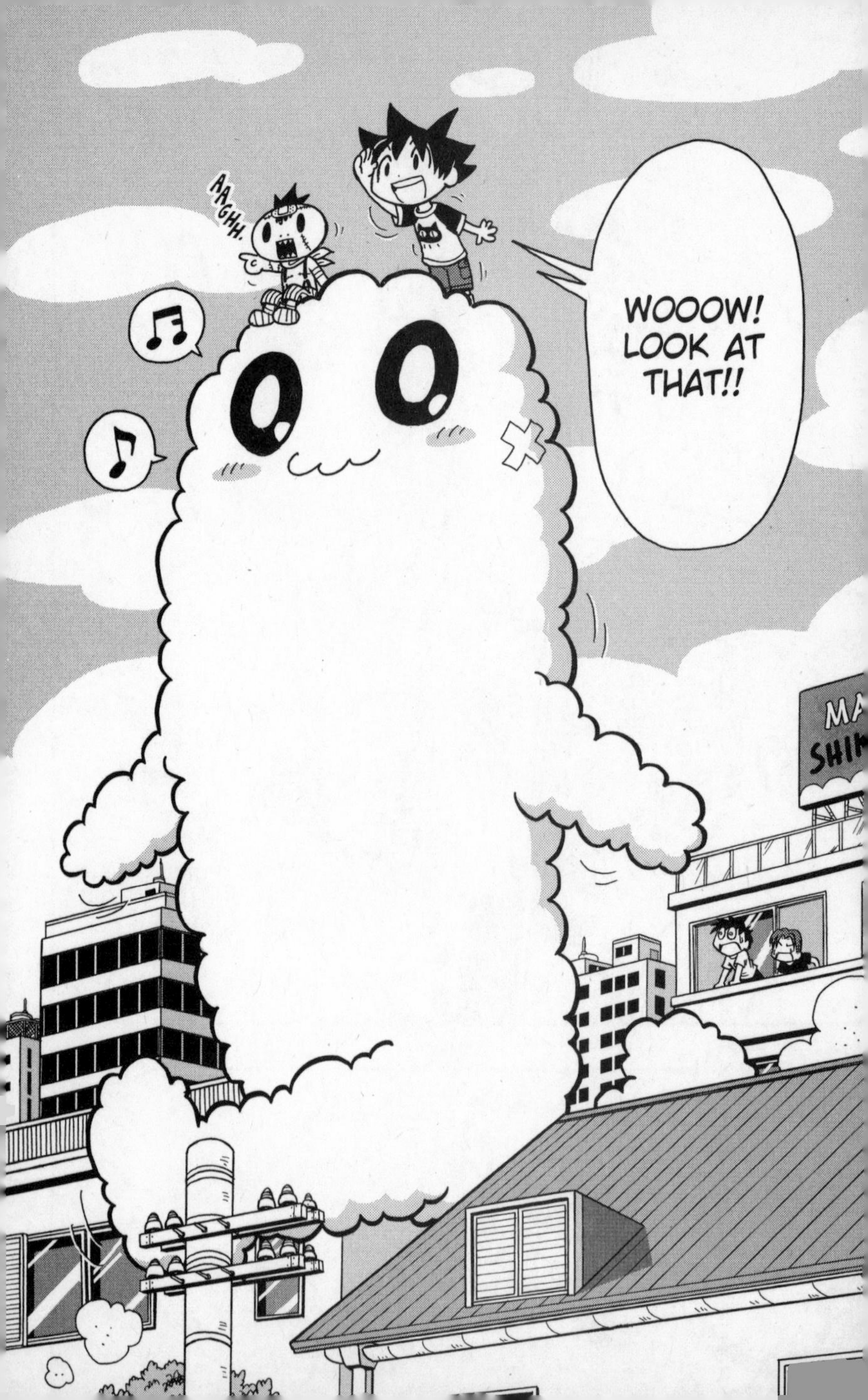
WOOOW! LOOK AT THAT!!
AAGHH.

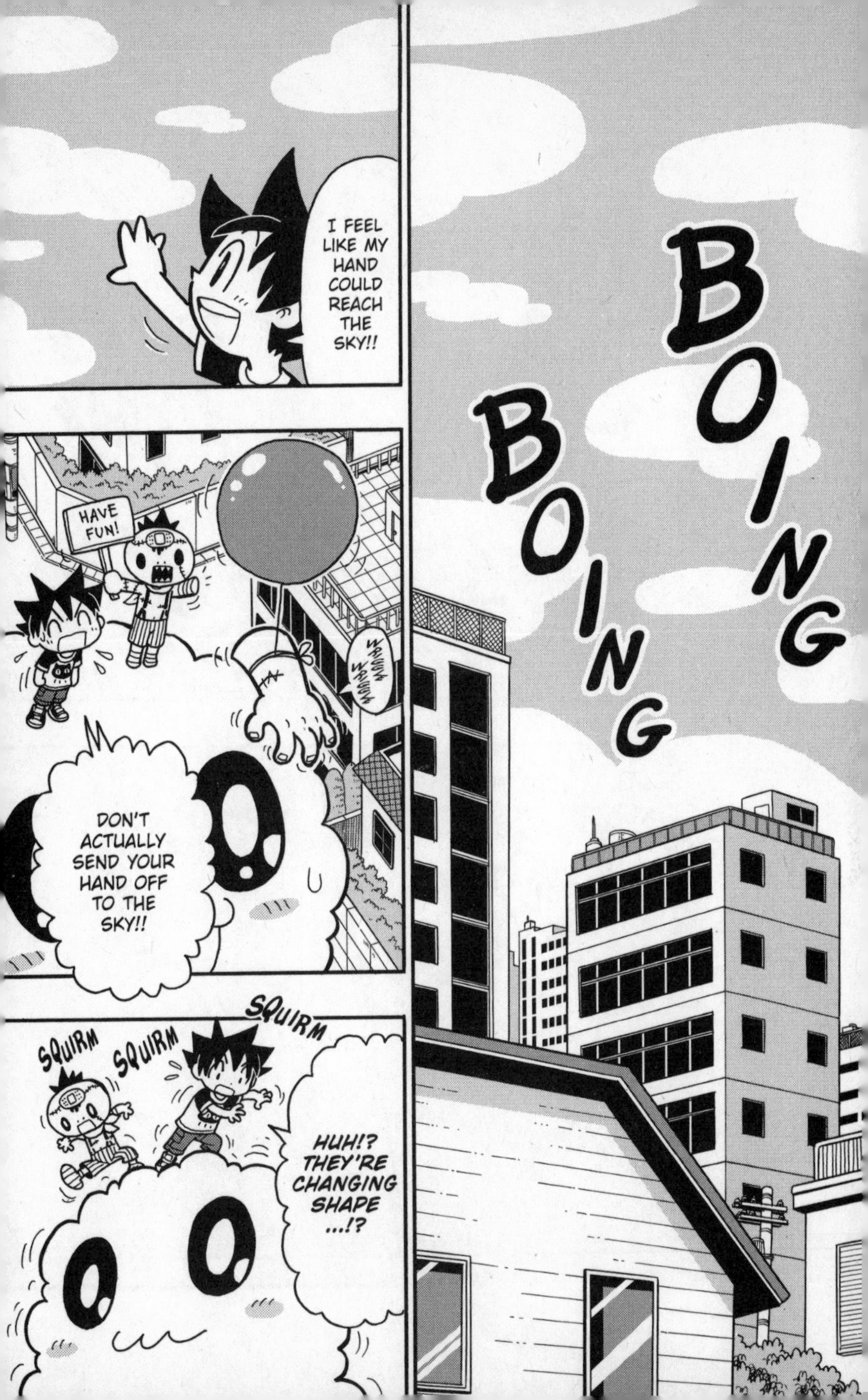
BOING
BOING
I FEEL LIKE MY HAND COULD REACH THE SKY!!
HAVE FUN!
WRIGGLE WRIGGLE
DON'T ACTUALLY SEND YOUR HAND OFF TO THE SKY!!
SQUIRM
SQUIRM
SQUIRM
HUH!? THEY'RE CHANGING SHAPE ...!?

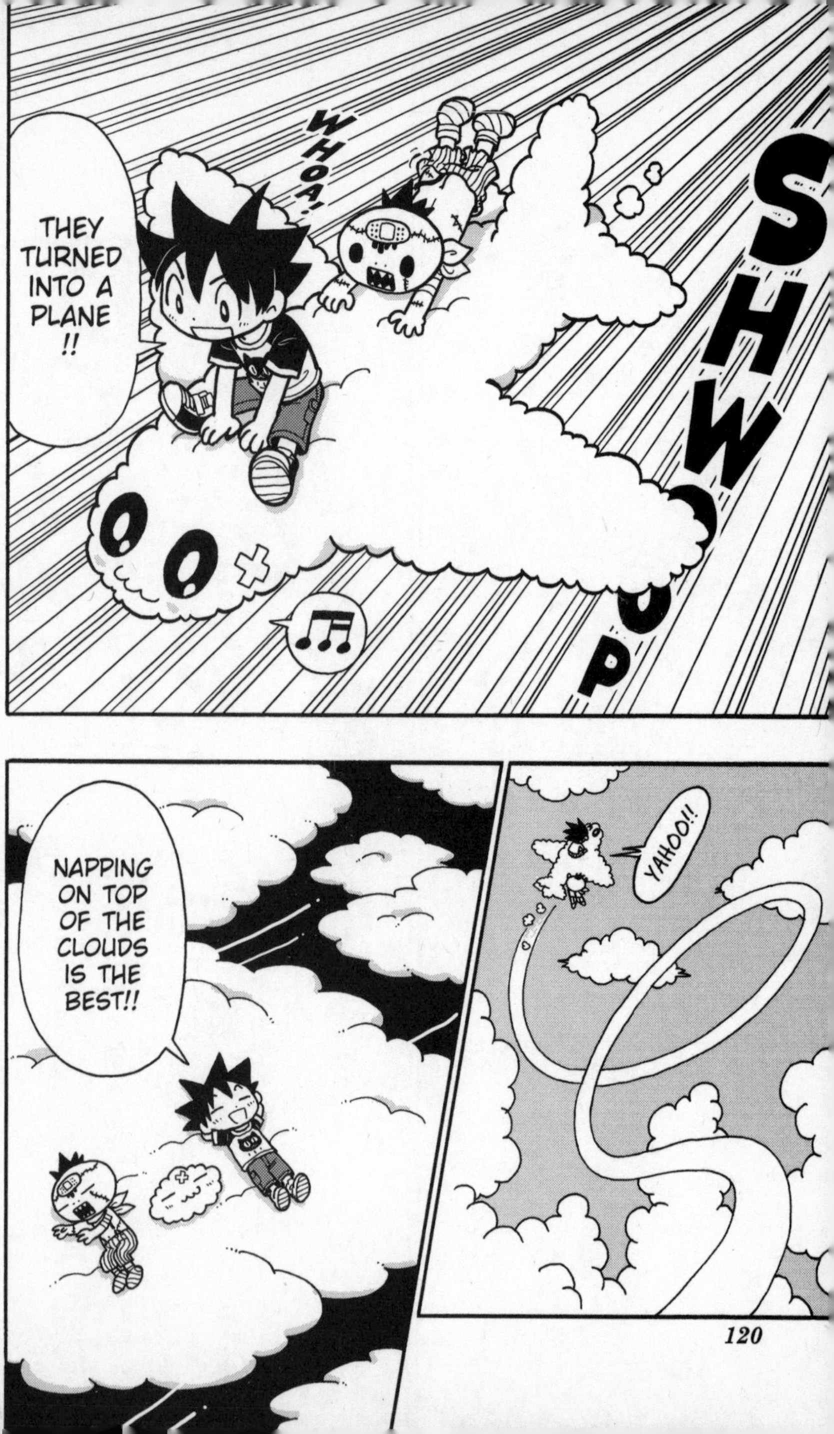
SHWOOP
WHOA!
THEY TURNED INTO A PLANE!!
YAHOO!!
NAPPING ON TOP OF THE CLOUDS IS THE BEST!!

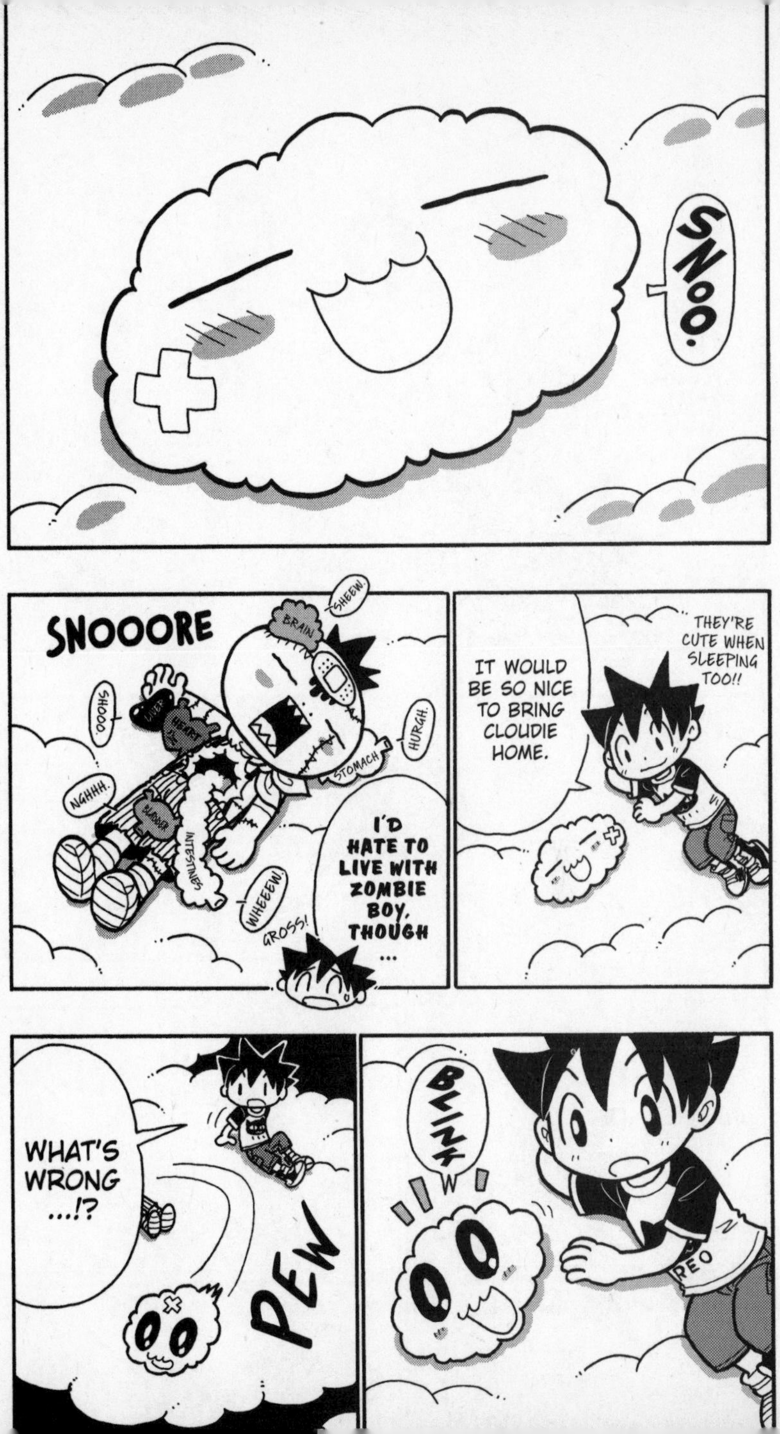
SNOO.
THEY'RE CUTE WHEN SLEEPING TOO!!
IT WOULD BE SO NICE TO BRING CLOUDIE HOME.
SHEEW.
BRAIN
HURGH.
STOMACH
SNOOORE
LIVER
HEART
SHOOO.
NGHHH.
BLADDER
INTESTINES
WHEEEW.
I'D HATE TO LIVE WITH ZOMBIE BOY, THOUGH ...
GROSS!
BLINK
REO
WHAT'S WRONG ...!?
PEW

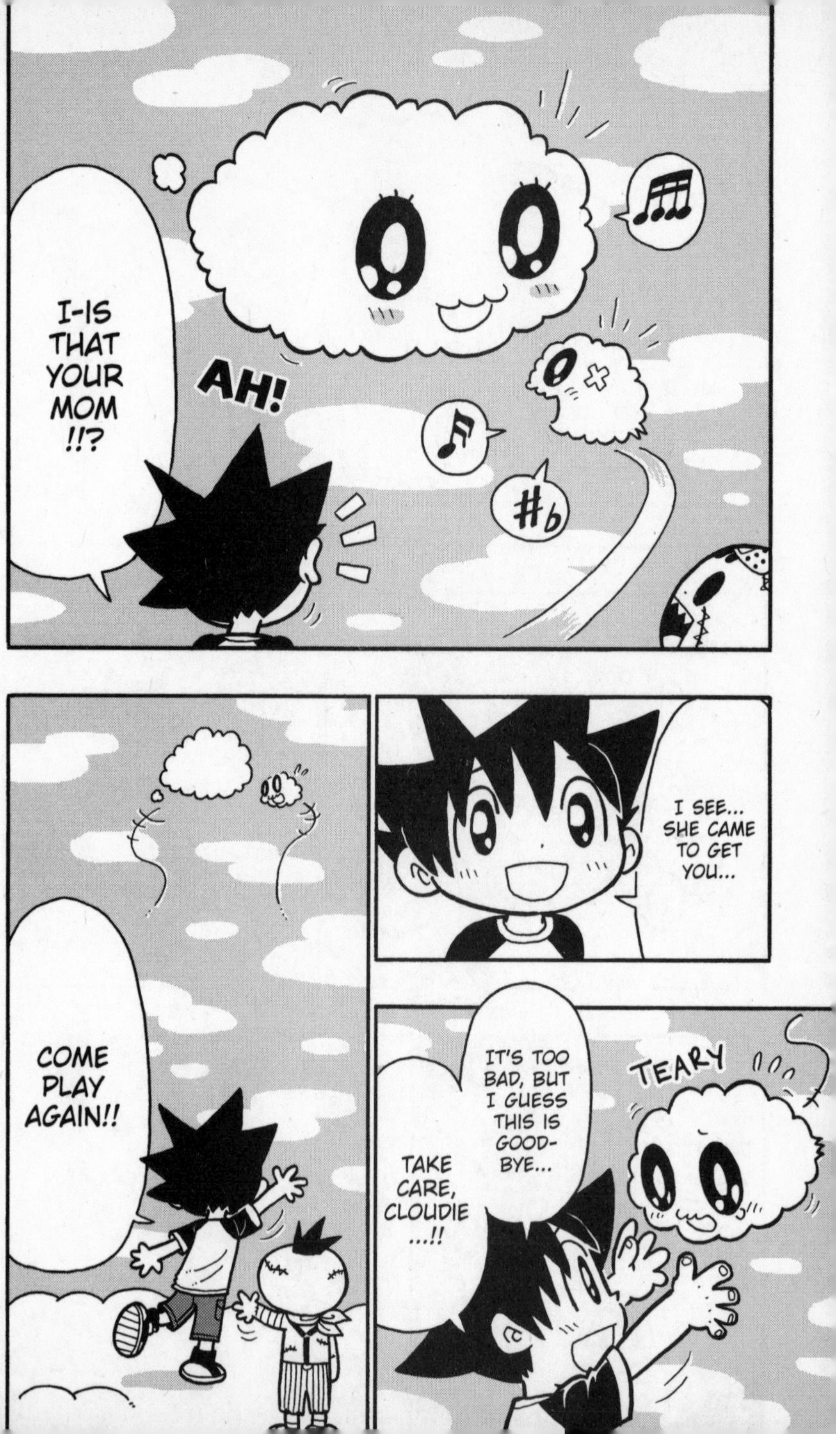
AH!
I-IS THAT YOUR MOM!!?
I SEE... SHE CAME TO GET YOU...
TEARY
IT'S TOO BAD, BUT I GUESS THIS IS GOOD-BYE...
TAKE CARE, CLOUDIE ...!!
COME PLAY AGAIN!!

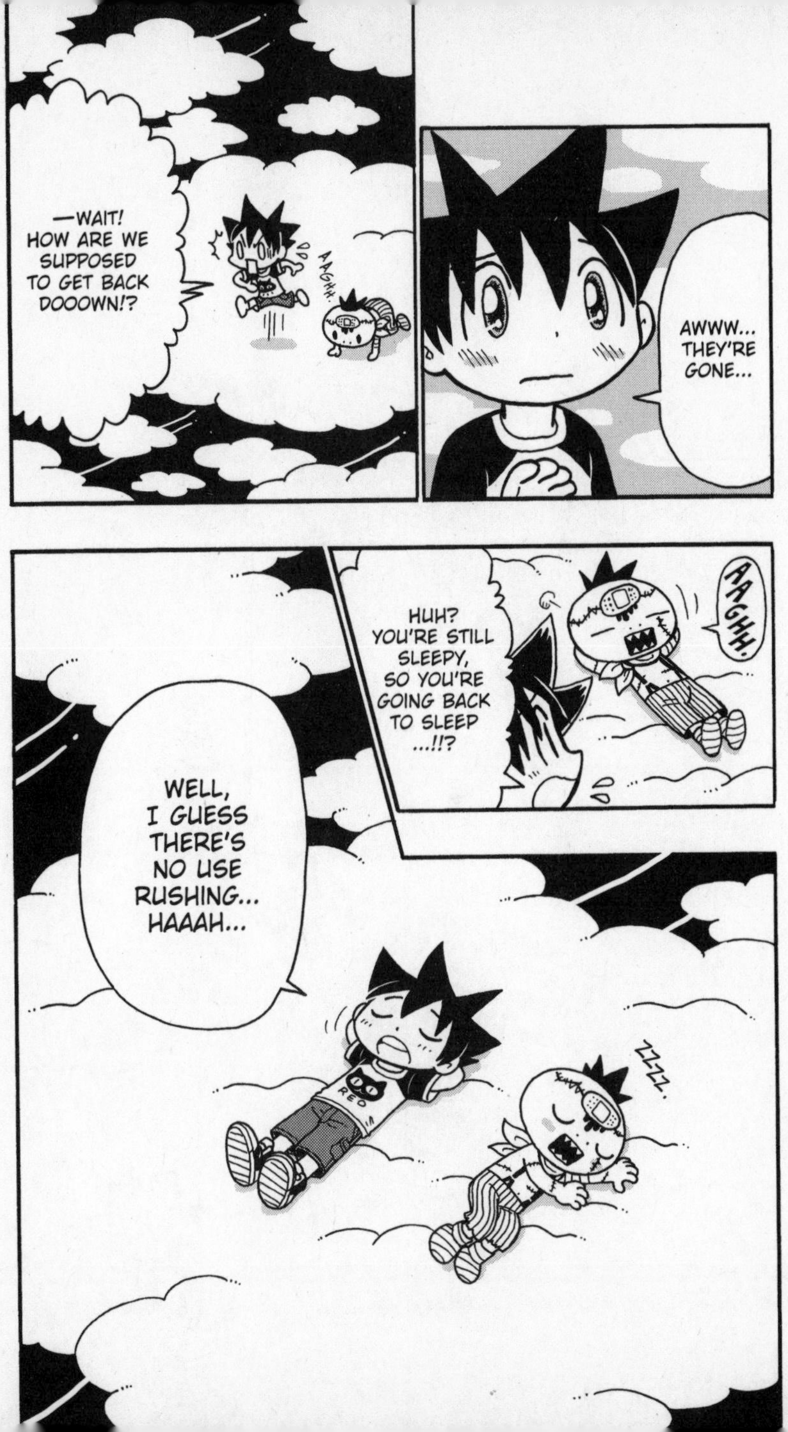
AWWW... THEY'RE GONE...
AAGHH.
—WAIT! HOW ARE WE SUPPOSED TO GET BACK DOOOWN!?
AAGHH.
HUH? YOU'RE STILL SLEEPY, SO YOU'RE GOING BACK TO SLEEP ...!!?
WELL, I GUESS THERE'S NO USE RUSHING... HAAAH...
ZZZZ.
RED

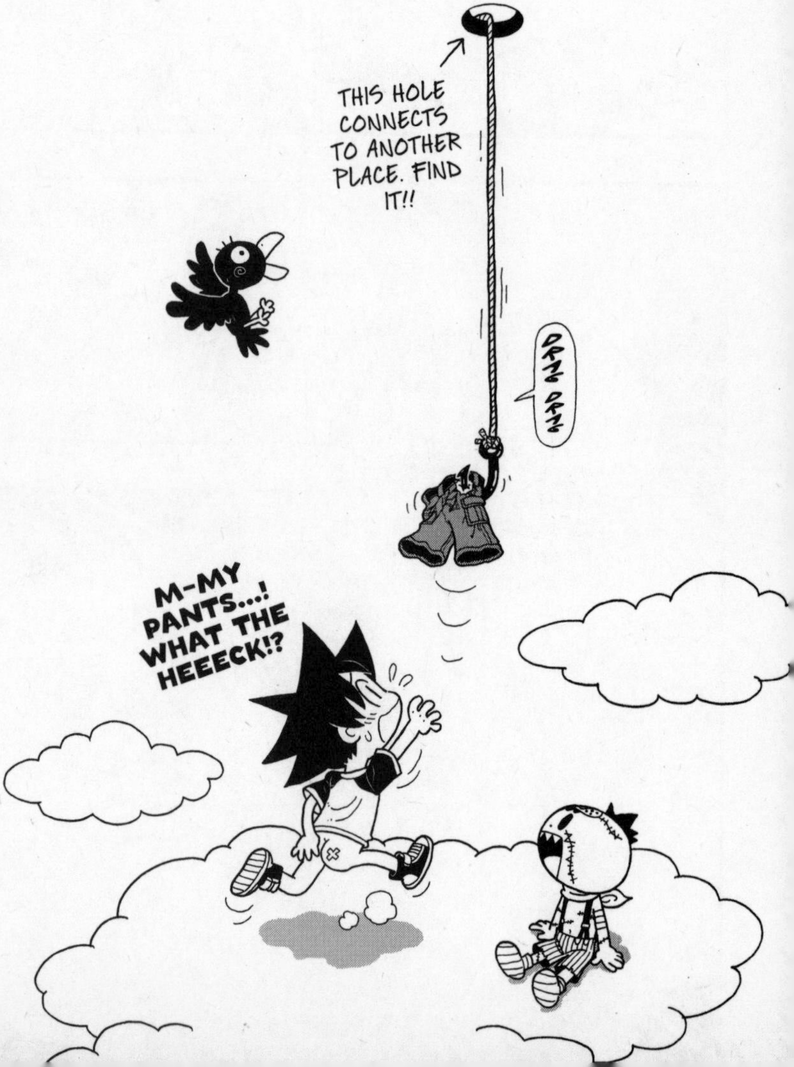
THIS HOLE CONNECTS TO ANOTHER PLACE. FIND IT!!
DRAG DRAG
M-MY PANTS...! WHAT THE HEEECK!?

ZOMBIE BOY TRIEZ TO GET POPULAR!

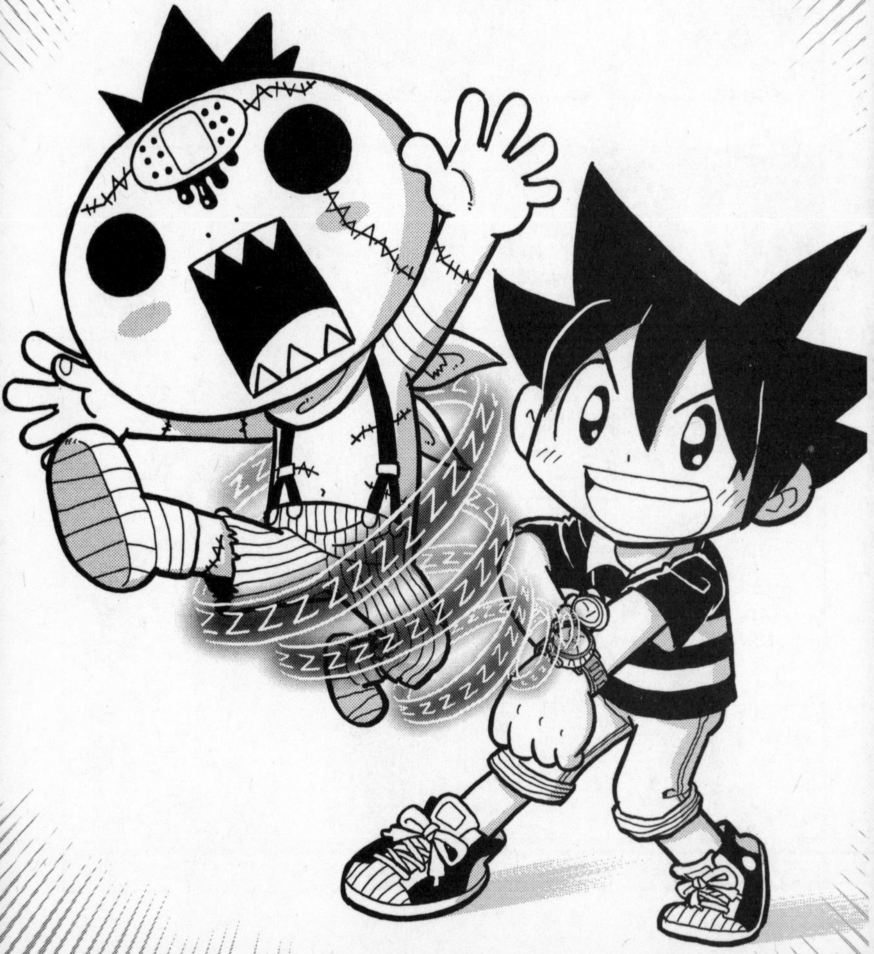

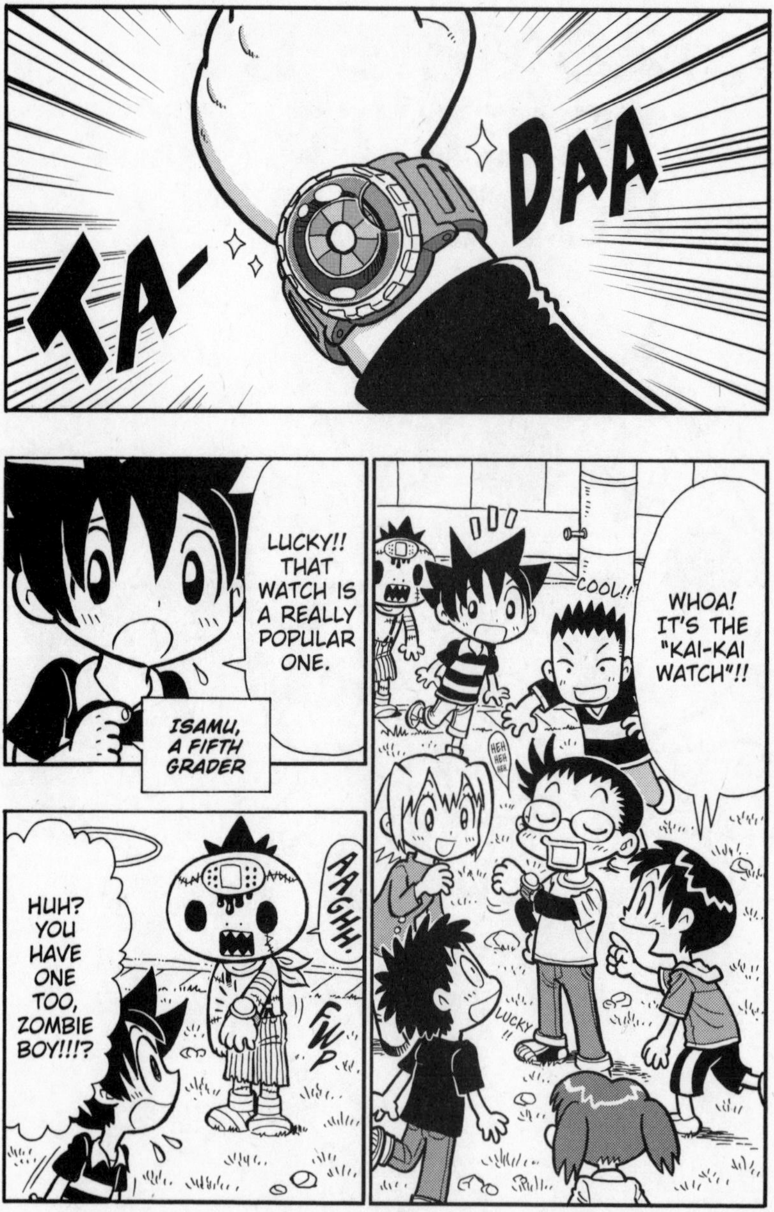
TA-
DAA
WHOA! IT'S THE "KAI-KAI WATCH"!!
COOL!!
HEH HEH HEH
LUCKY!!
LUCKY!! THAT WATCH IS A REALLY POPULAR ONE.
ISAMU, A FIFTH GRADER
HUH? YOU HAVE ONE TOO, ZOMBIE BOY!!!?
AAGHH.
FWP

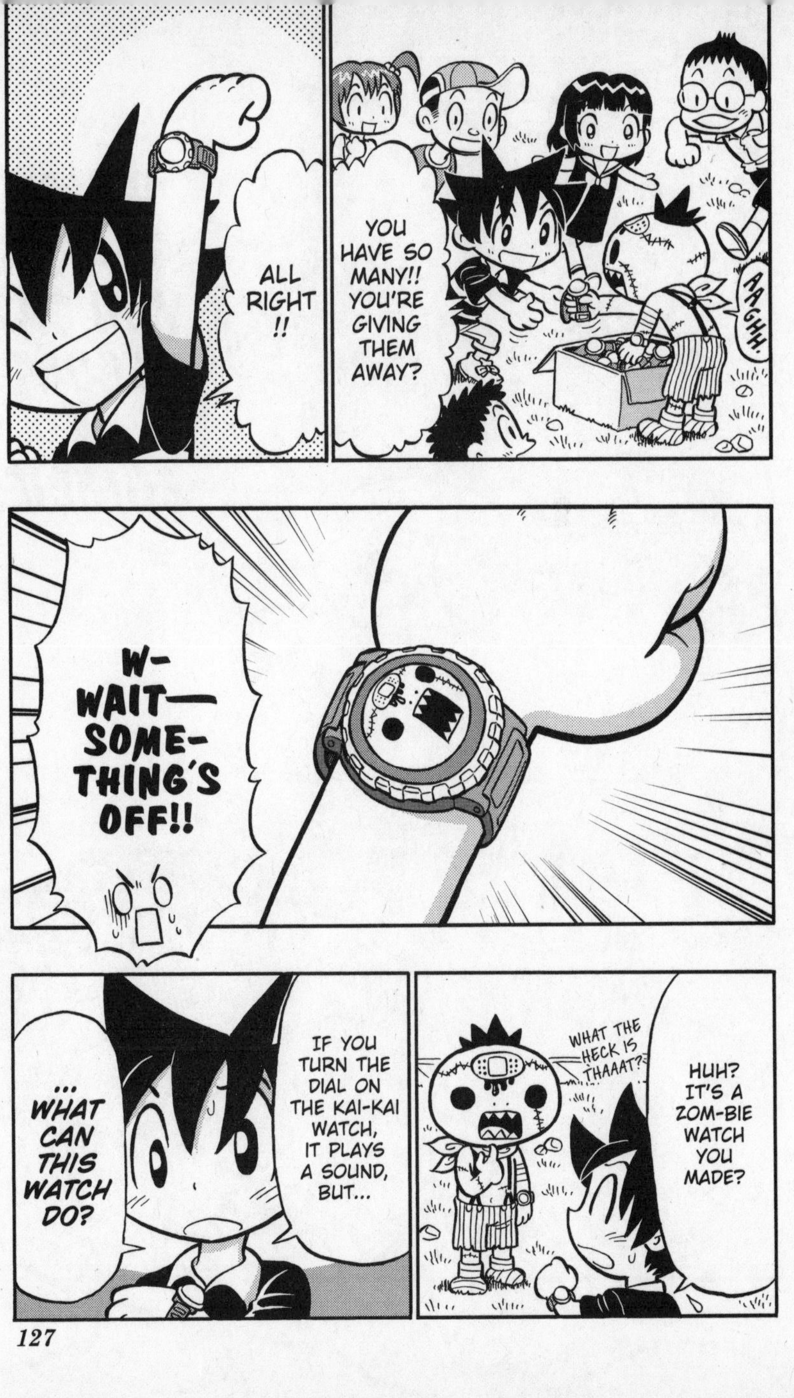
AAAGHH.
YOU HAVE SO MANY!! YOU'RE GIVING THEM AWAY?
ALL RIGHT!!
W-WAIT—SOME-THING'S OFF!!
HUH? IT'S A ZOM-BIE WATCH YOU MADE?
WHAT THE HECK IS THAAAT?
IF YOU TURN THE DIAL ON THE KAI-KAI WATCH, IT PLAYS A SOUND, BUT...
...WHAT CAN THIS WATCH DO?

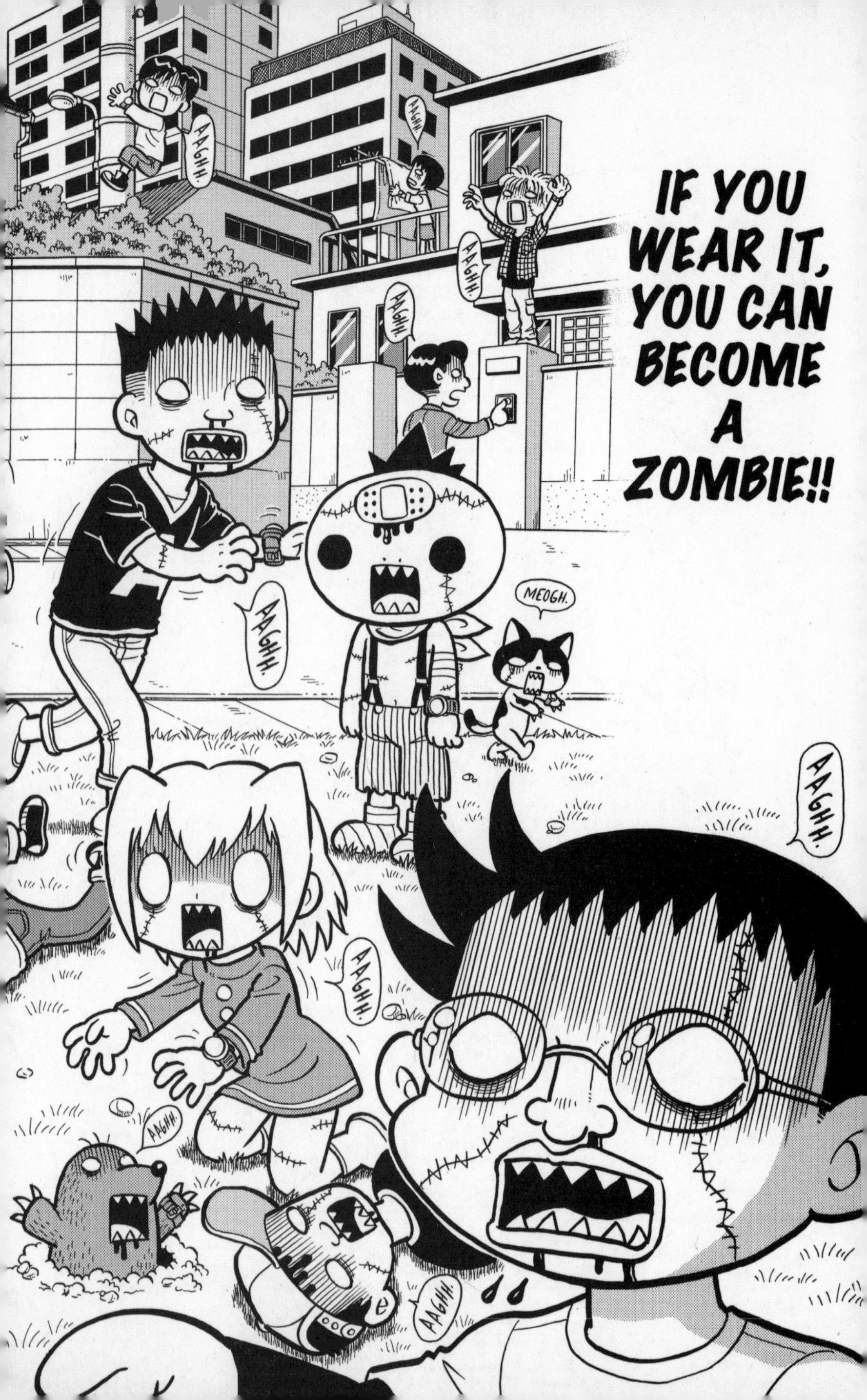
IF YOU WEAR IT, YOU CAN BECOME A ZOMBIE!!
AAGHH.
AAGHH.
AAGHH.
AAGHH.
MEOGH.
AAGHH.
AAGHH.
AAGHH.
AAGHH.
AAGHH.

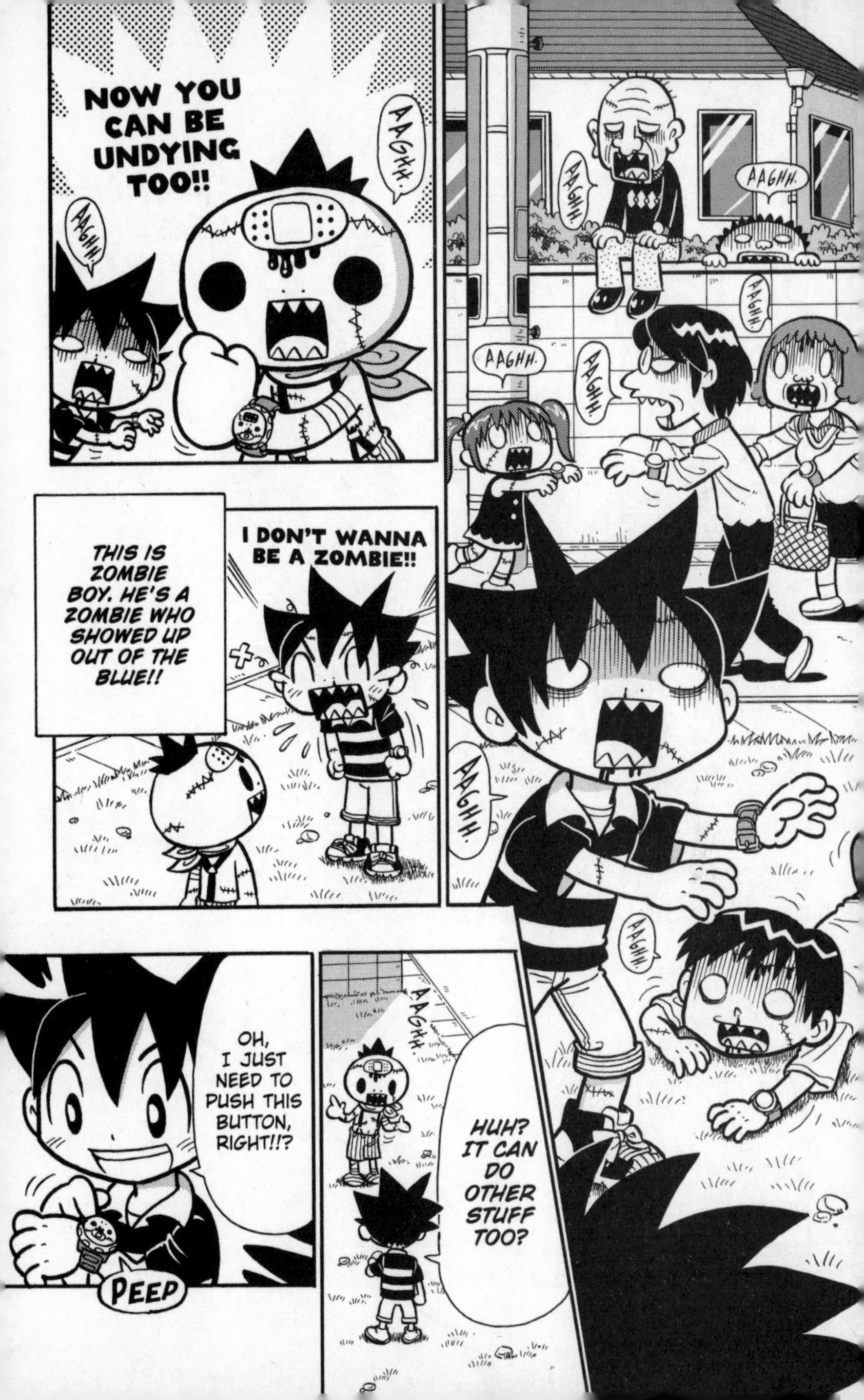
AAGHH.
AAGHH.
AAGHH.
AAGHH.
AAGHH.
AAGHH.
AAGHH.
AAGHH.
NOW YOU CAN BE UNDYING TOO!!
AAGHH.
AAGHH.
I DON'T WANNA BE A ZOMBIE!!
THIS IS ZOMBIE BOY. HE'S A ZOMBIE WHO SHOWED UP OUT OF THE BLUE!!
AAGHH.
HUH? IT CAN DO OTHER STUFF TOO?
OH, I JUST NEED TO PUSH THIS BUTTON, RIGHT!!?
PEEP

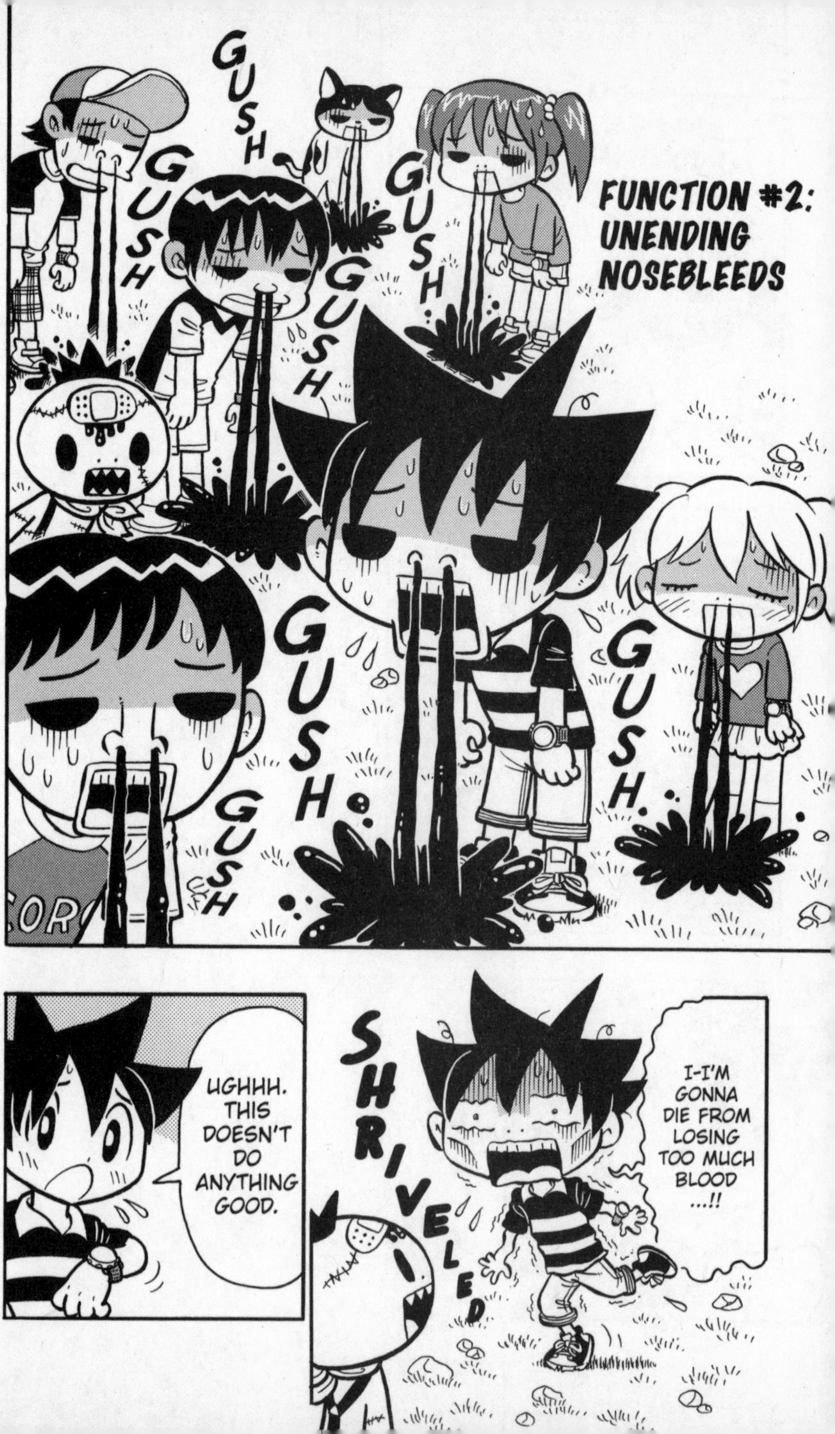
FUNCTION #2: UNENDING NOSEBLEEDS
GUSH
GUSH
GUSH
GUSH
GUSH
GUSH.
GUSH
GUSH
GUSH
I-I'M GONNA DIE FROM LOSING TOO MUCH BLOOD ...!!
SHRIVELED
UGHHH. THIS DOESN'T DO ANYTHING GOOD.

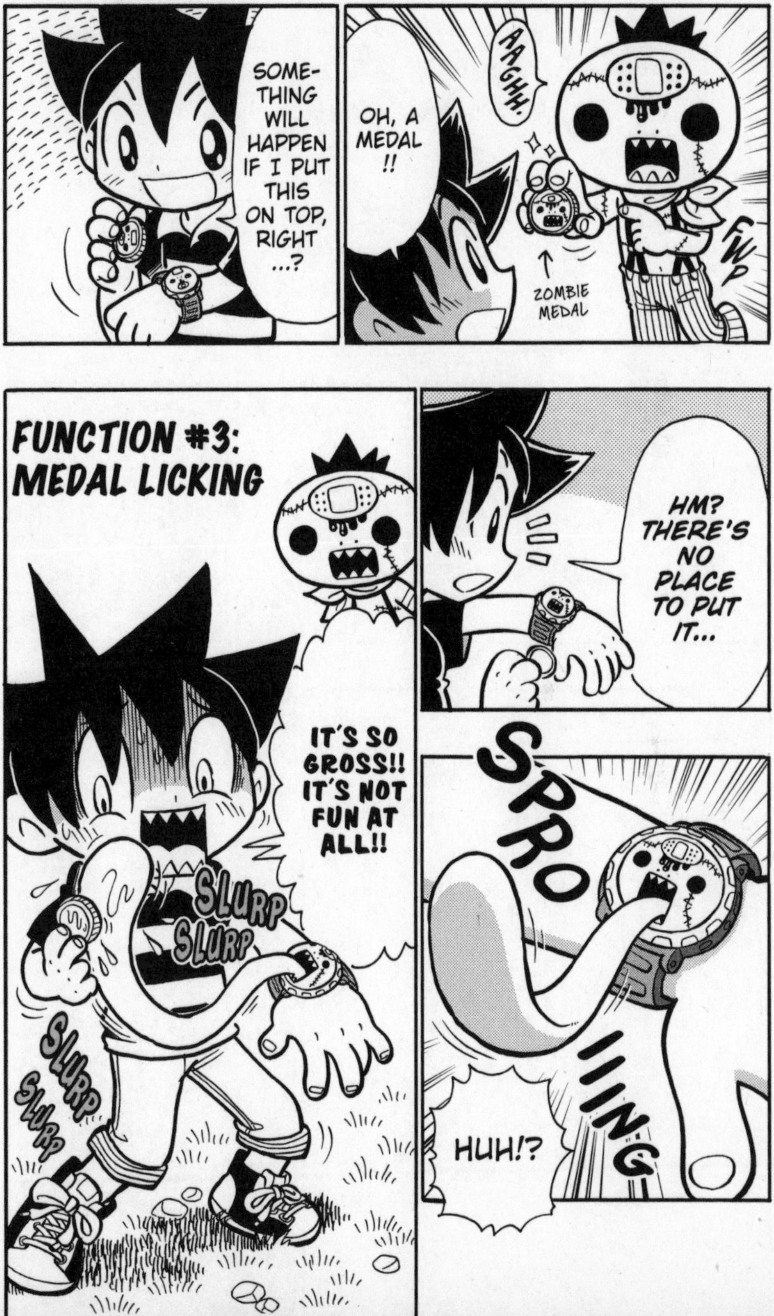
AAGHH.
OH, A MEDAL!!
FWP
ZOMBIE MEDAL
SOMETHING WILL HAPPEN IF I PUT THIS ON TOP, RIGHT...?
HM? THERE'S NO PLACE TO PUT IT...
SPROIIIING
HUH!?
FUNCTION #3: MEDAL LICKING
IT'S SO GROSS!! IT'S NOT FUN AT ALL!!
SLURP SLURP
SLURP SLURP SLURP

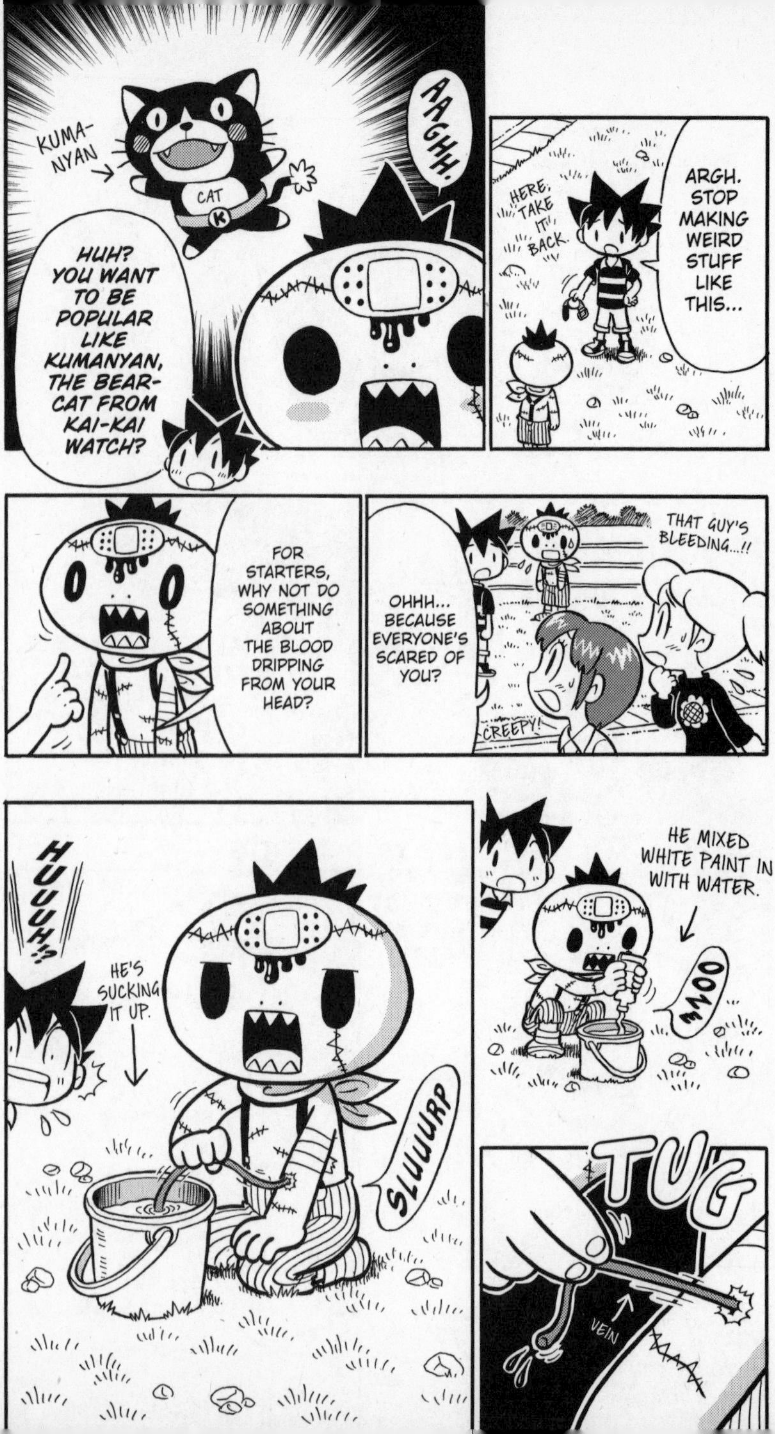
ARGH. STOP MAKING WEIRD STUFF LIKE THIS...
HERE, TAKE IT BACK.
AAGHH.
KUMA-NYAN
CAT
HUH? YOU WANT TO BE POPULAR LIKE KUMANYAN, THE BEAR-CAT FROM KAI-KAI WATCH?
THAT GUY'S BLEEDING...!!
OHHH... BECAUSE EVERYONE'S SCARED OF YOU?
CREEPY!
FOR STARTERS, WHY NOT DO SOMETHING ABOUT THE BLOOD DRIPPING FROM YOUR HEAD?
HE MIXED WHITE PAINT IN WITH WATER.
OOZE
TUG
VEIN
HUUUUH!?
HE'S SUCKING IT UP.
SLUUURP

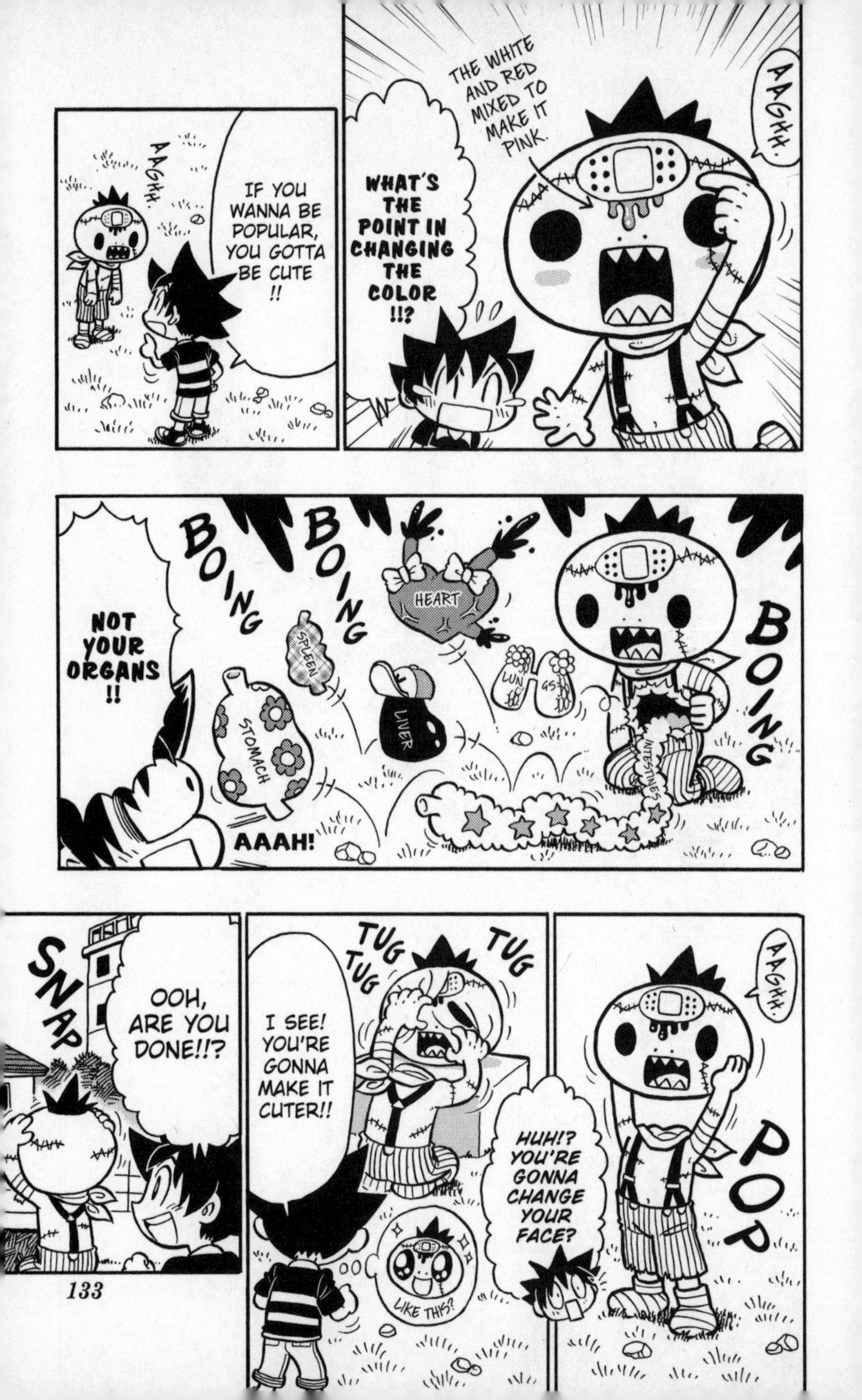
AAGHH.
THE WHITE AND RED MIXED TO MAKE IT PINK.
WHAT'S THE POINT IN CHANGING THE COLOR !!?
AAGHH.
IF YOU WANNA BE POPULAR, YOU GOTTA BE CUTE !!
BOING
HEART
LUNGS
INTESTINES
LIVER
SPLEEN
STOMACH
BOING
BOING
NOT YOUR ORGANS !!
AAAH!
AAGHH.
POP
HUH!? YOU'RE GONNA CHANGE YOUR FACE?
TUG TUG TUG
I SEE! YOU'RE GONNA MAKE IT CUTER!!
LIKE THIS?
SNAP
OOH, ARE YOU DONE!!?

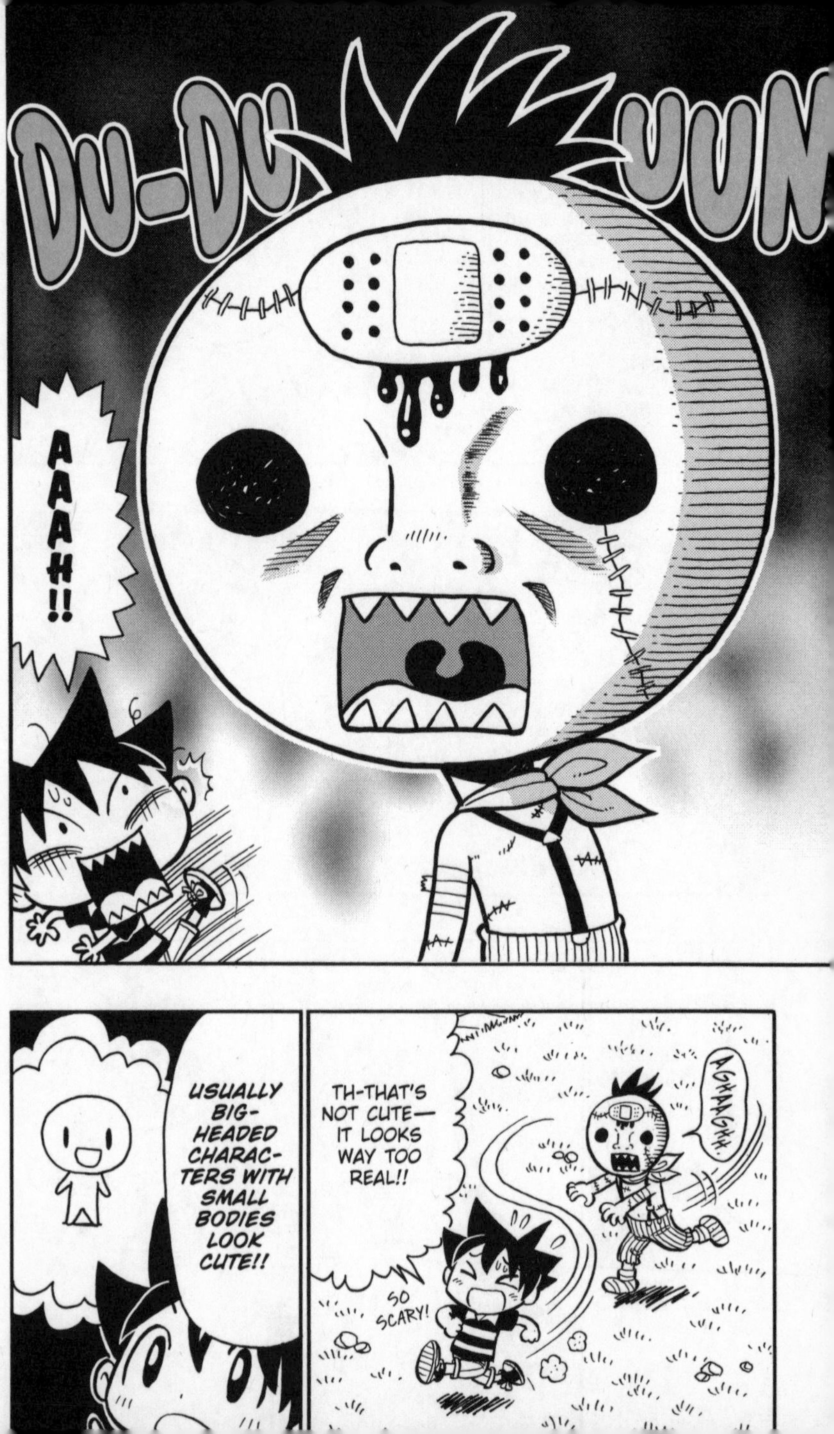
DU-DU-UUN
AAAH!!
AGHAAGHH.
TH-THAT'S NOT CUTE— IT LOOKS WAY TOO REAL!!
SO SCARY!
USUALLY BIG-HEADED CHARACTERS WITH SMALL BODIES LOOK CUTE!!

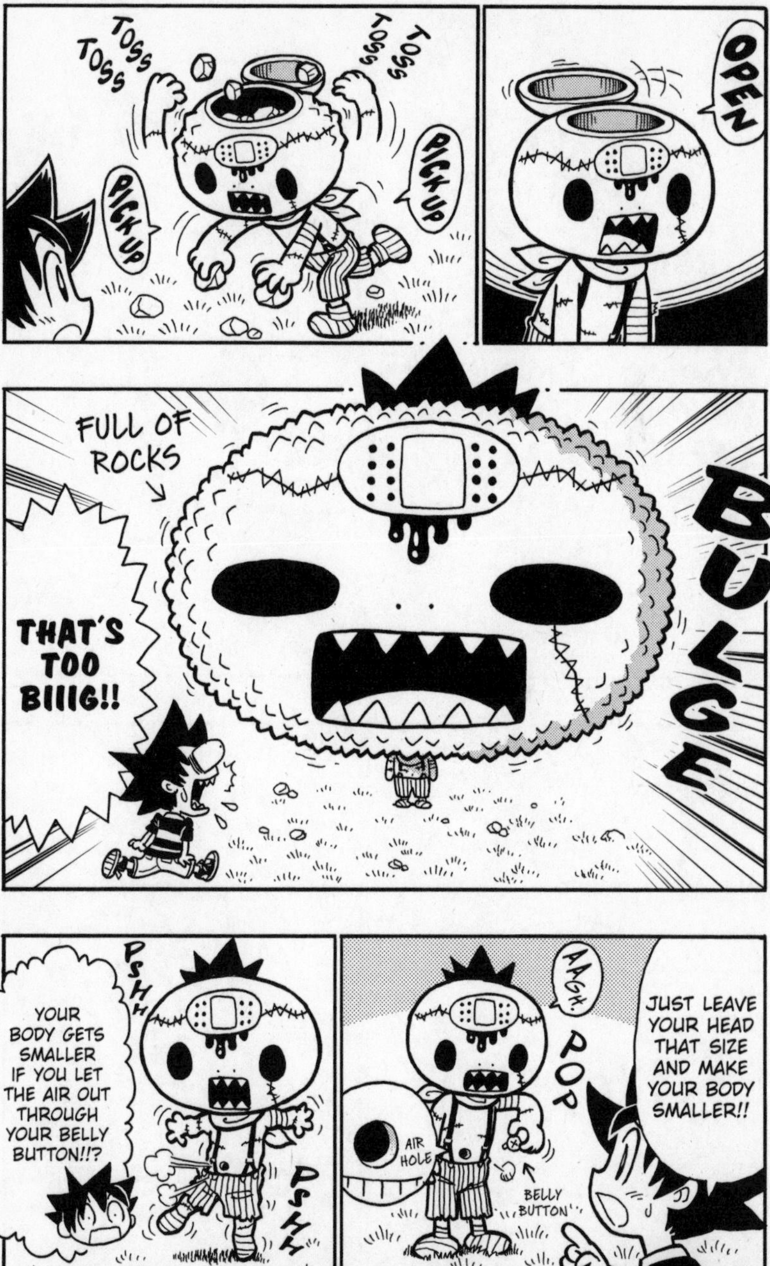
OPEN
TOSS TOSS
PICK UP
TOSS TOSS
PICK UP
BULGE
FULL OF ROCKS
THAT'S TOO BIIIG!!
JUST LEAVE YOUR HEAD THAT SIZE AND MAKE YOUR BODY SMALLER!!
AAGH
POP
AIR HOLE
BELLY BUTTON
PSHH
YOUR BODY GETS SMALLER IF YOU LET THE AIR OUT THROUGH YOUR BELLY BUTTON!!?
PSHH

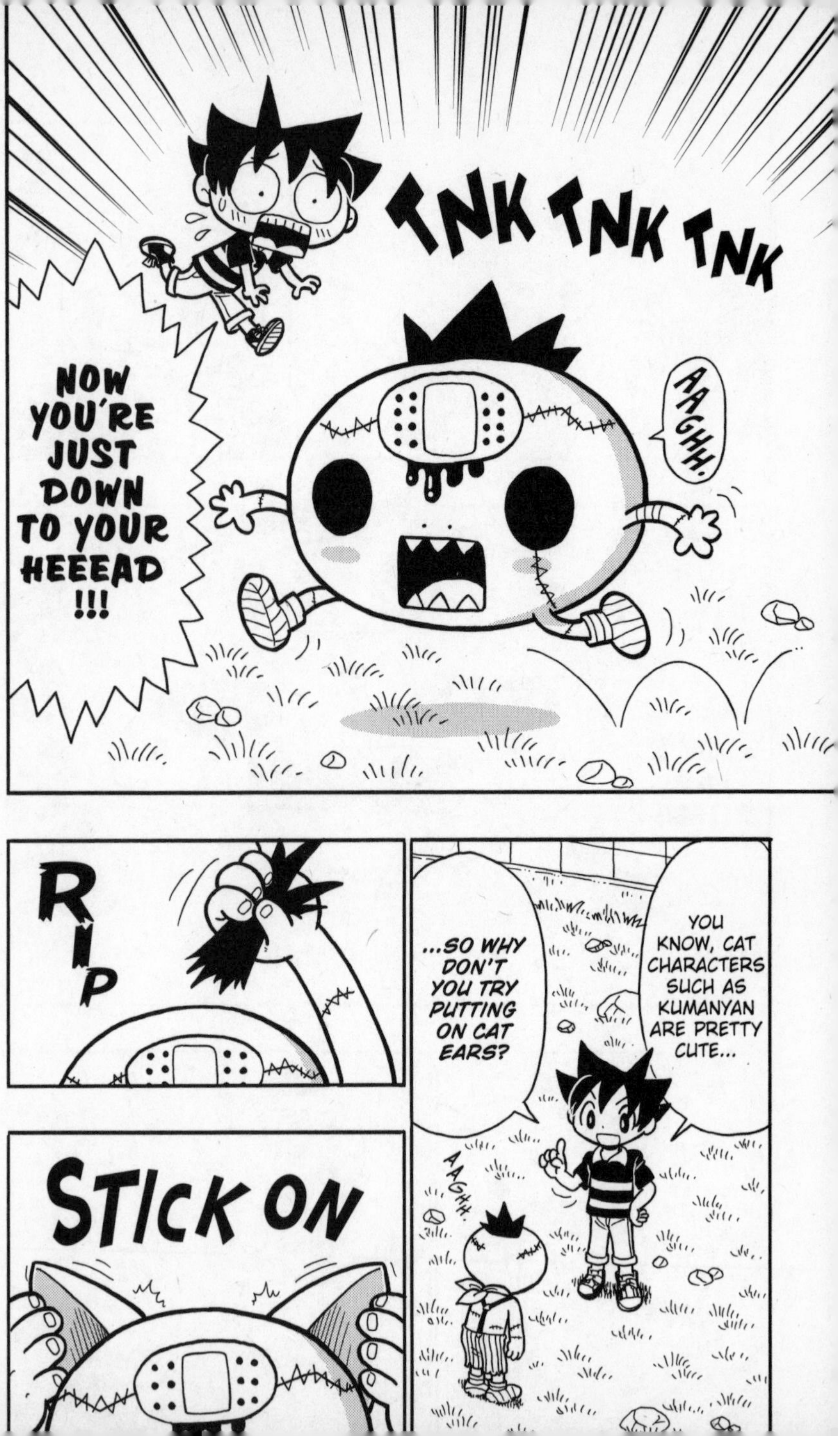
TNK TNK TNK
AAGHH.
NOW YOU'RE JUST DOWN TO YOUR HEEEAD!!!
YOU KNOW, CAT CHARACTERS SUCH AS KUMANYAN ARE PRETTY CUTE...
...SO WHY DON'T YOU TRY PUTTING ON CAT EARS?
AAGHH.
RIP
STICK ON

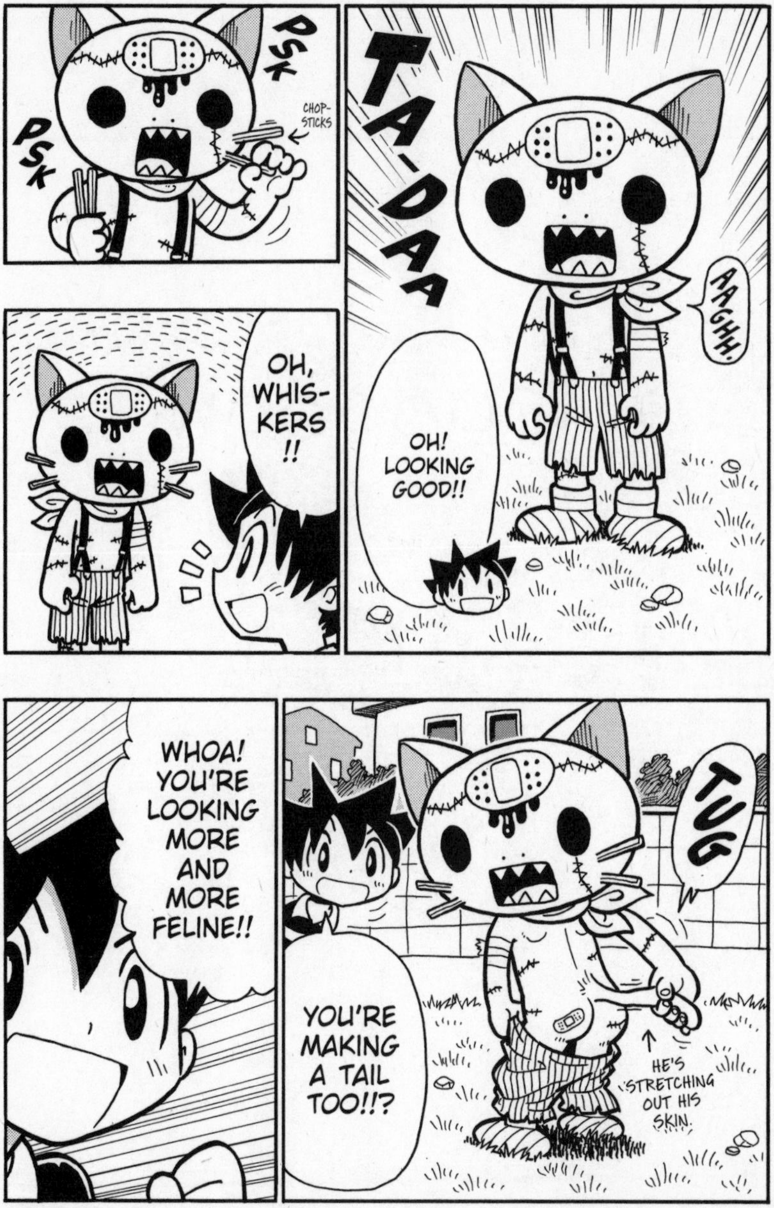
TA-DAA
AAGHH.
OH! LOOKING GOOD!!
PSK
PSK
CHOP-STICKS
OH, WHIS-KERS!!
TUG
YOU'RE MAKING A TAIL TOO!!?
HE'S STRETCHING OUT HIS SKIN.
WHOA! YOU'RE LOOKING MORE AND MORE FELINE!!

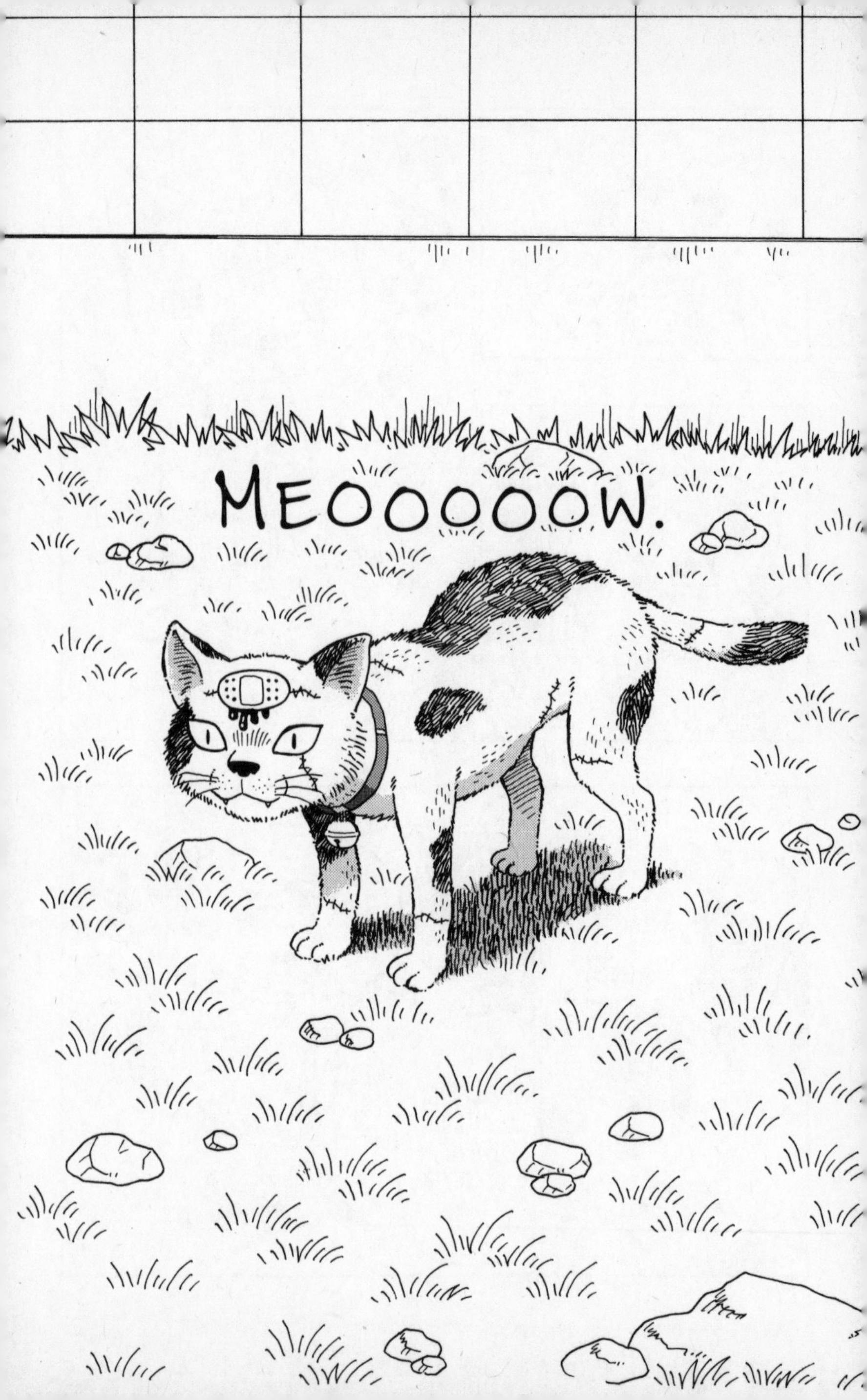
MEOOOOOW.

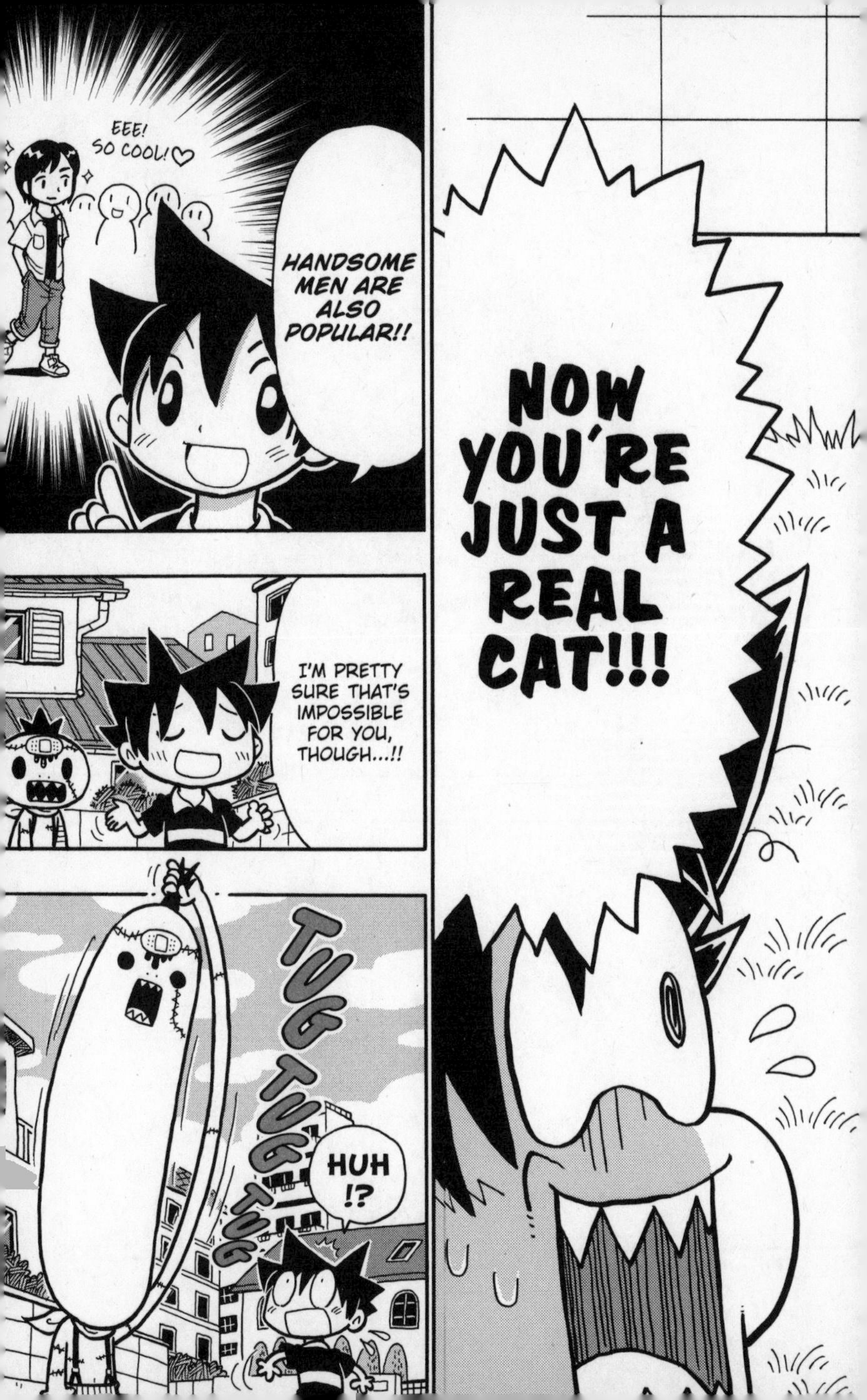
NOW YOU'RE JUST A REAL CAT!!!
HANDSOME MEN ARE ALSO POPULAR!!
EEE! SO COOL! ♡
I'M PRETTY SURE THAT'S IMPOSSIBLE FOR YOU, THOUGH...!!
TUG TUG TUG
HUH !?

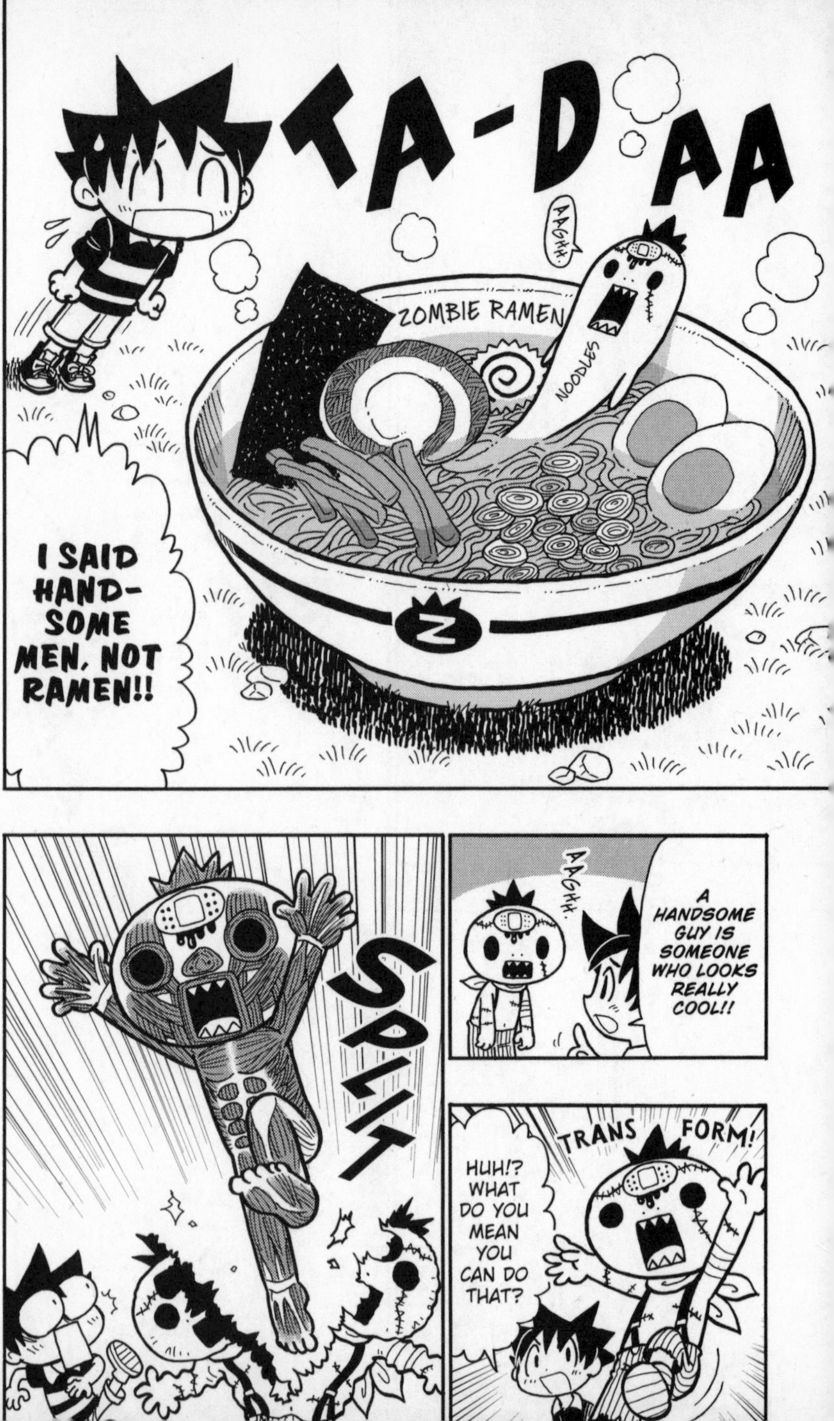
TA-DAA
AAGHH.
ZOMBIE RAMEN
NOODLES
I SAID HAND-SOME MEN, NOT RAMEN!!
AAGHH.
A HANDSOME GUY IS SOMEONE WHO LOOKS REALLY COOL!!
TRANS FORM!
HUH!? WHAT DO YOU MEAN YOU CAN DO THAT?
SPLIT

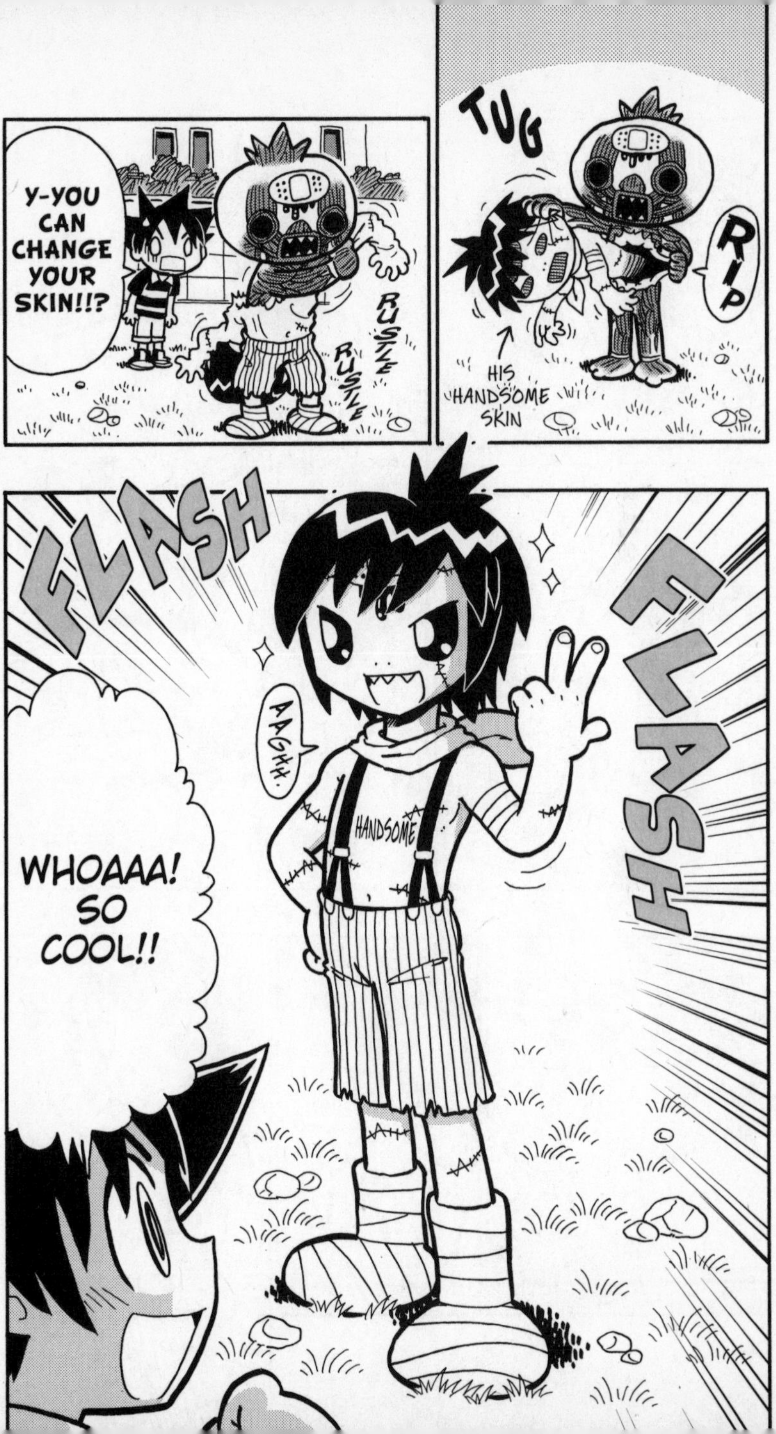
RIP
TUG
HIS HANDSOME SKIN
RUSTLE
RUSTLE
Y-YOU CAN CHANGE YOUR SKIN!!?
FLASH
FLASH
AAGHX.
HANDSOME
WHOAAA! SO COOL!!

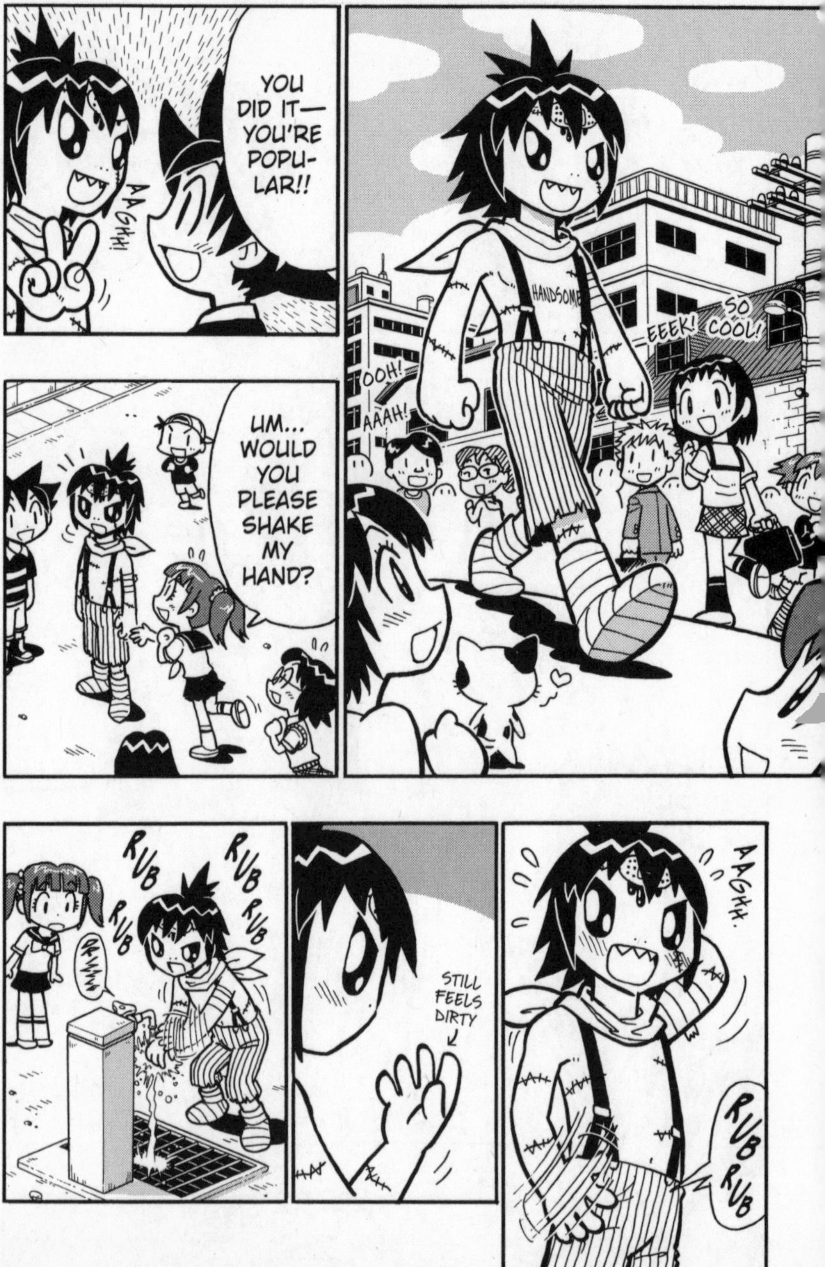
HANDSOME
SO COOL!
EEEK!
OOH!
AAAH!
YOU DID IT—YOU'RE POPULAR!!
AAGHH!
UM... WOULD YOU PLEASE SHAKE MY HAND?
AAGHH.
RUB RUB
STILL FEELS DIRTY
RUB RUB
RUB RUB

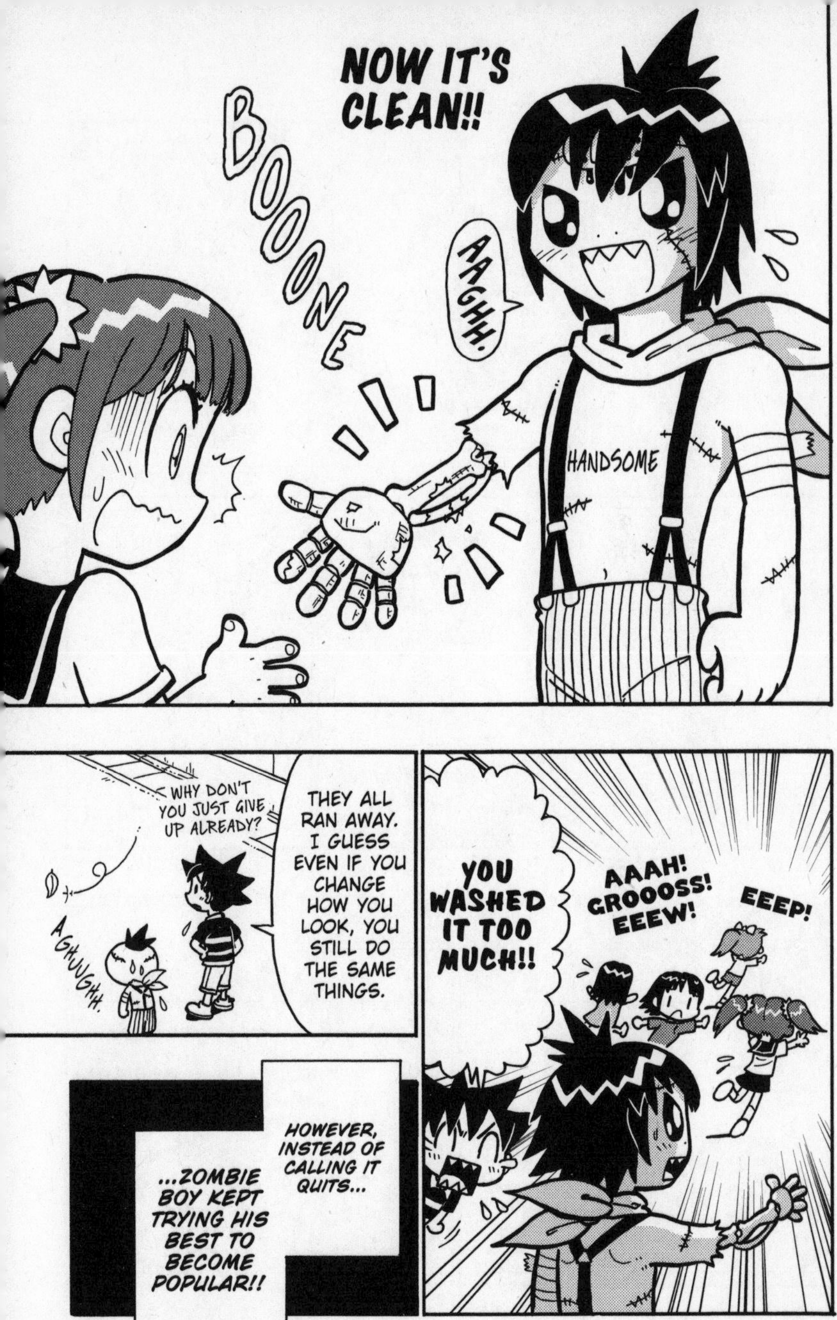
NOW IT'S CLEAN!!
BOOOONE
AAGHH.
HANDSOME
EEEP!
AAAH! GROOOSS! EEEW!
YOU WASHED IT TOO MUCH!!
THEY ALL RAN AWAY. I GUESS EVEN IF YOU CHANGE HOW YOU LOOK, YOU STILL DO THE SAME THINGS.
WHY DON'T YOU JUST GIVE UP ALREADY?
AGHUUGHH.
HOWEVER, INSTEAD OF CALLING IT QUITS...
...ZOMBIE BOY KEPT TRYING HIS BEST TO BECOME POPULAR!!

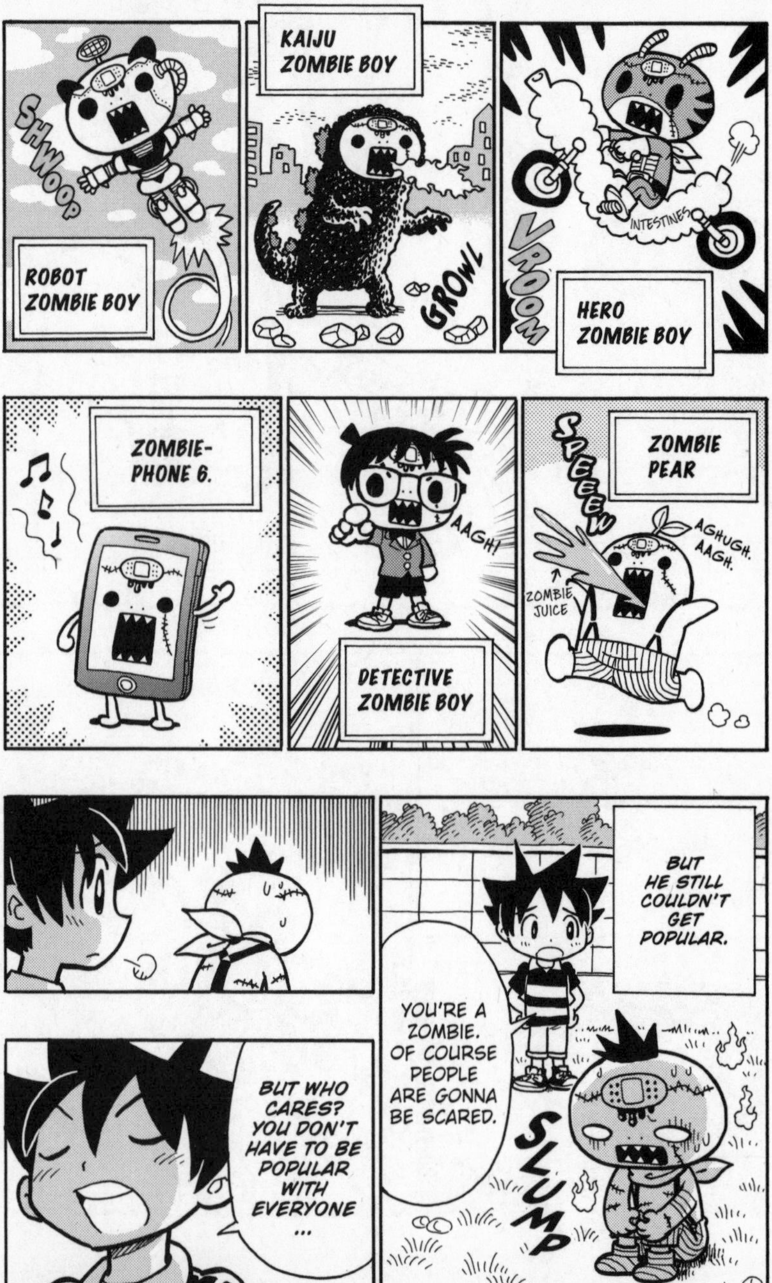
HERO ZOMBIE BOY
VROOM
INTESTINES
KAIJU ZOMBIE BOY
GROWL
ROBOT ZOMBIE BOY
SHWOOP
ZOMBIE PEAR
SPEEEW
AGHUGH. AAGH.
ZOMBIE JUICE
DETECTIVE ZOMBIE BOY
AAGH!
ZOMBIE-PHONE 6.
BUT HE STILL COULDN'T GET POPULAR.
YOU'RE A ZOMBIE. OF COURSE PEOPLE ARE GONNA BE SCARED.
SLUMP
BUT WHO CARES? YOU DON'T HAVE TO BE POPULAR WITH EVERYONE ...

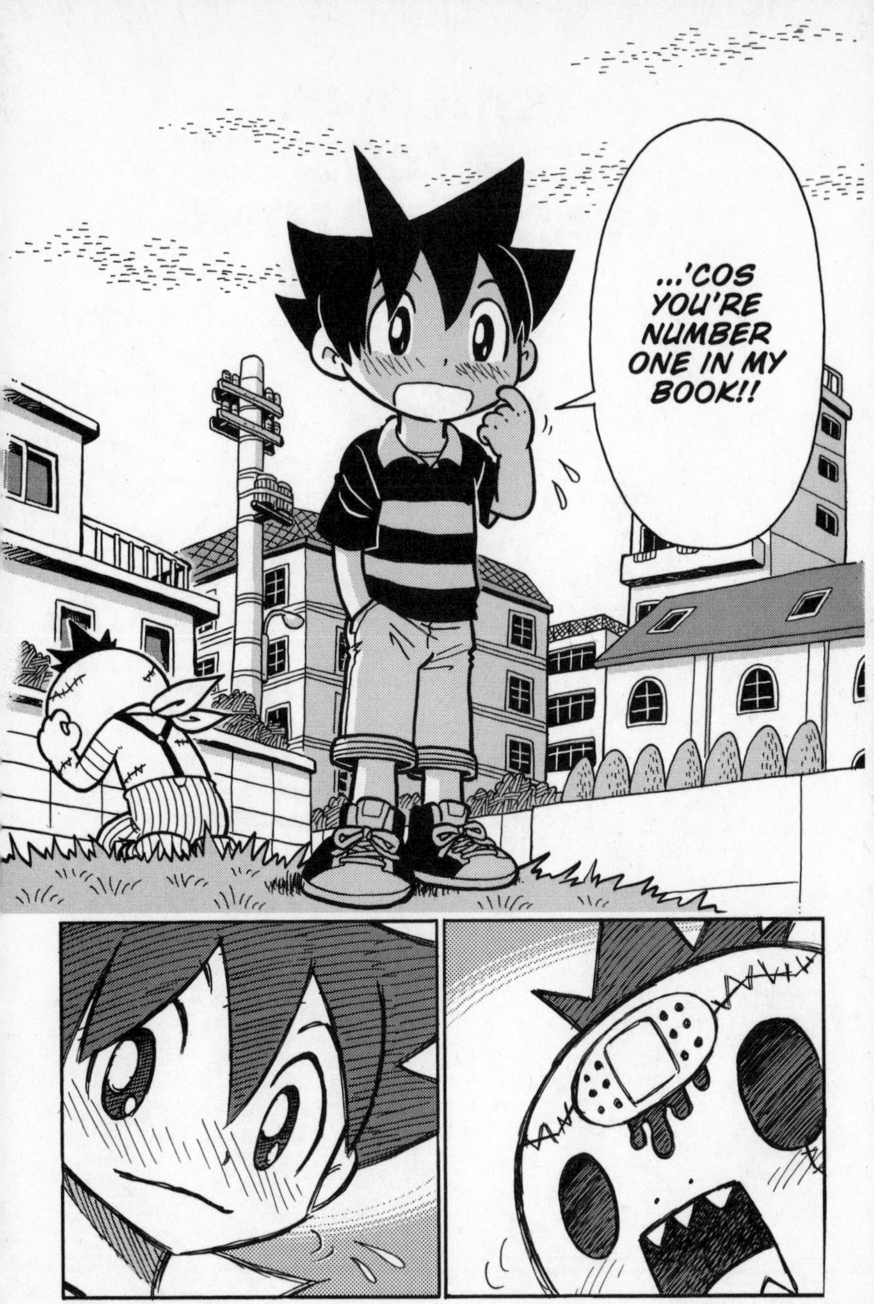
...'COS YOU'RE NUMBER ONE IN MY BOOK!!

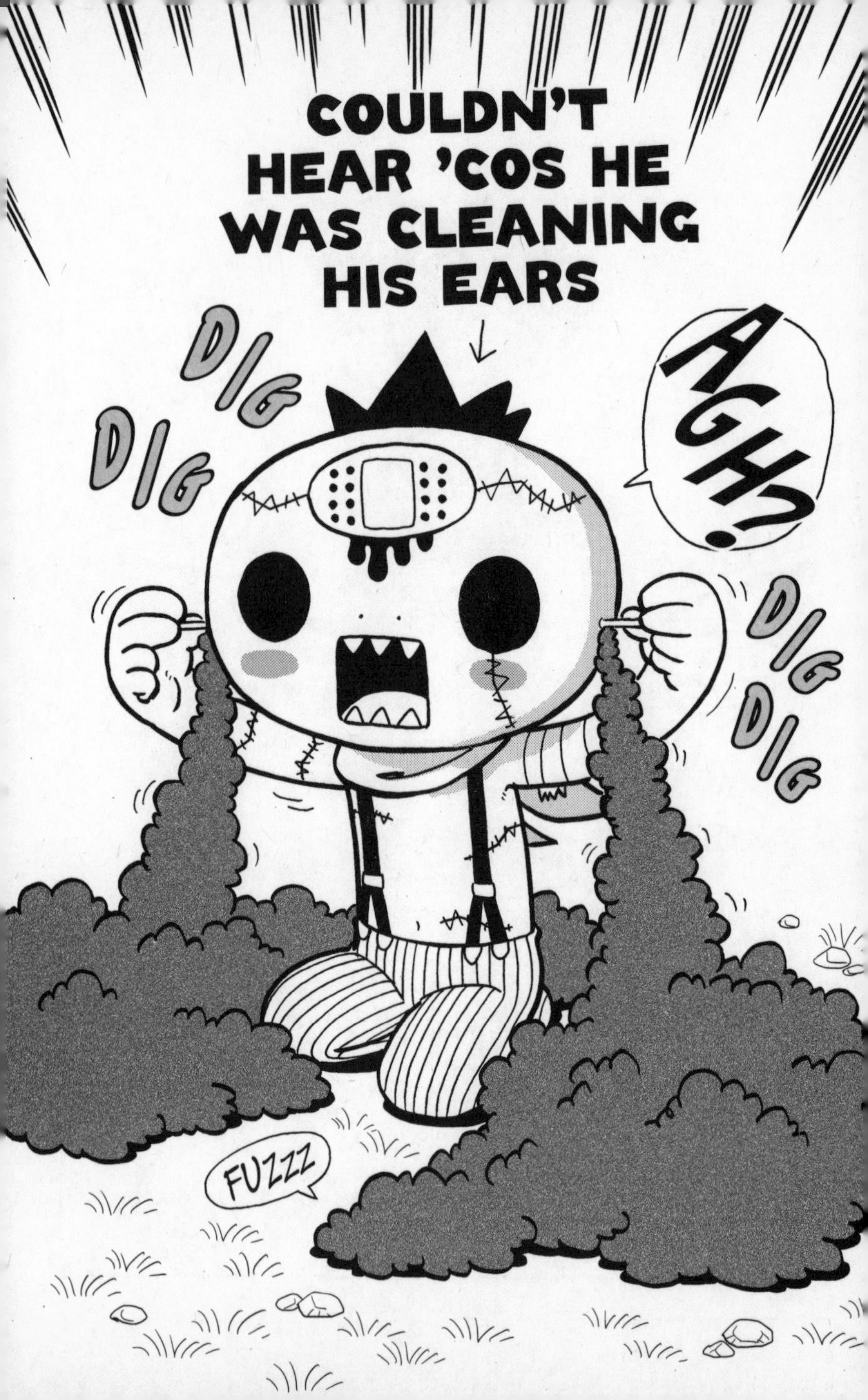

COULDN'T HEAR 'COS HE WAS CLEANING HIS EARS
AGH?!
DIG DIG
DIG DIG
DIG DIG
DIG DIG
FUZZZ

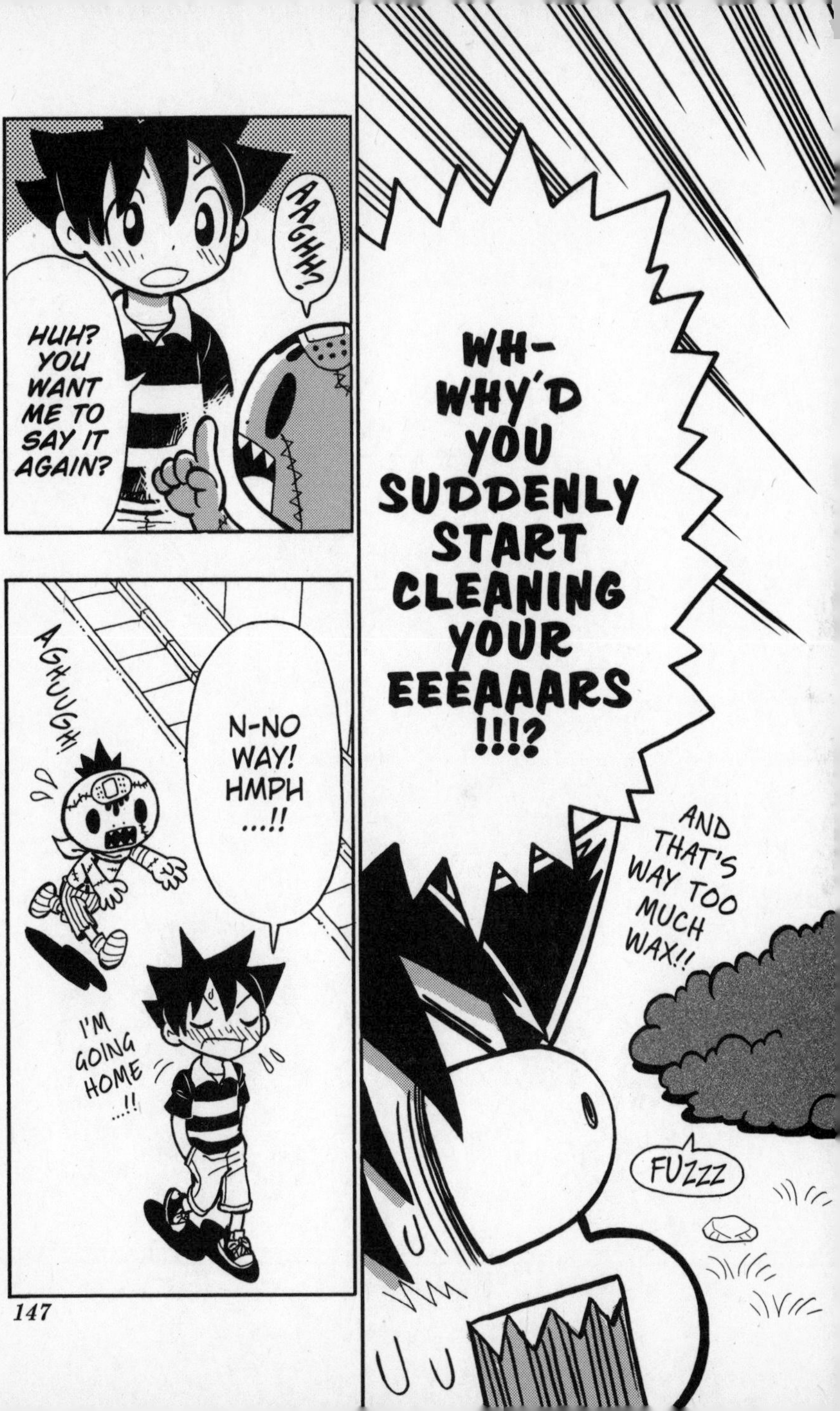
WH- WHY'D YOU SUDDENLY START CLEANING YOUR EEEAAARS !!!?
AND THAT'S WAY TOO MUCH WAX!!
FUZZZ
AAGHH?
HUH? YOU WANT ME TO SAY IT AGAIN?
N-NO WAY! HMPH ...!!
AGHUUGH!
I'M GOING HOME ...!!

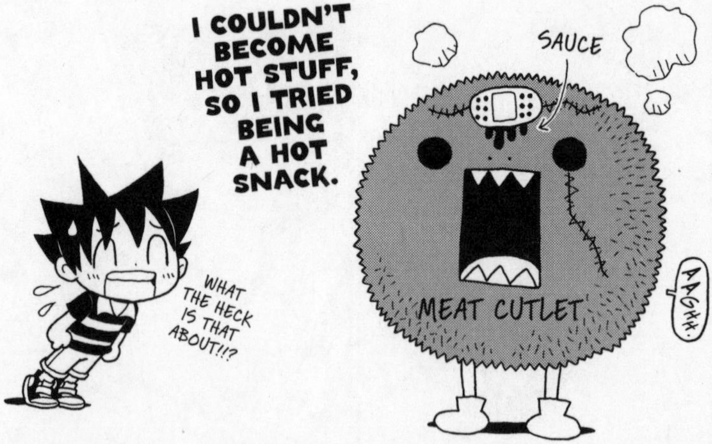
I COULDN'T BECOME HOT STUFF, SO I TRIED BEING A HOT SNACK.
SAUCE
MEAT CUTLET
AAGHH.
WHAT THE HECK IS THAT ABOUT!!?

ZEDUCTION BY DONUT!

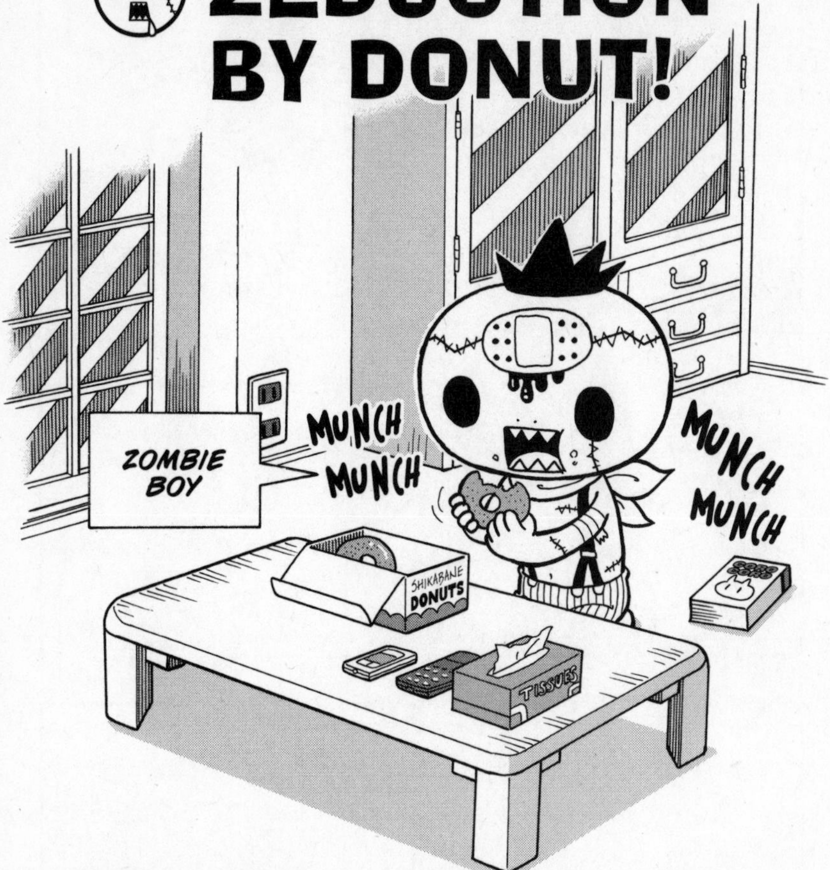

MUNCH MUNCH
MUNCH MUNCH
ZOMBIE BOY
SHIKABANE DONUTS
TISSUES

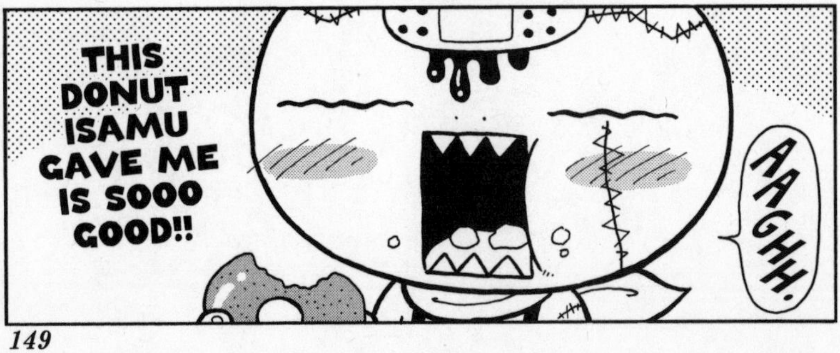

AAGHH.
THIS DONUT ISAMU GAVE ME IS SOOO GOOD!!

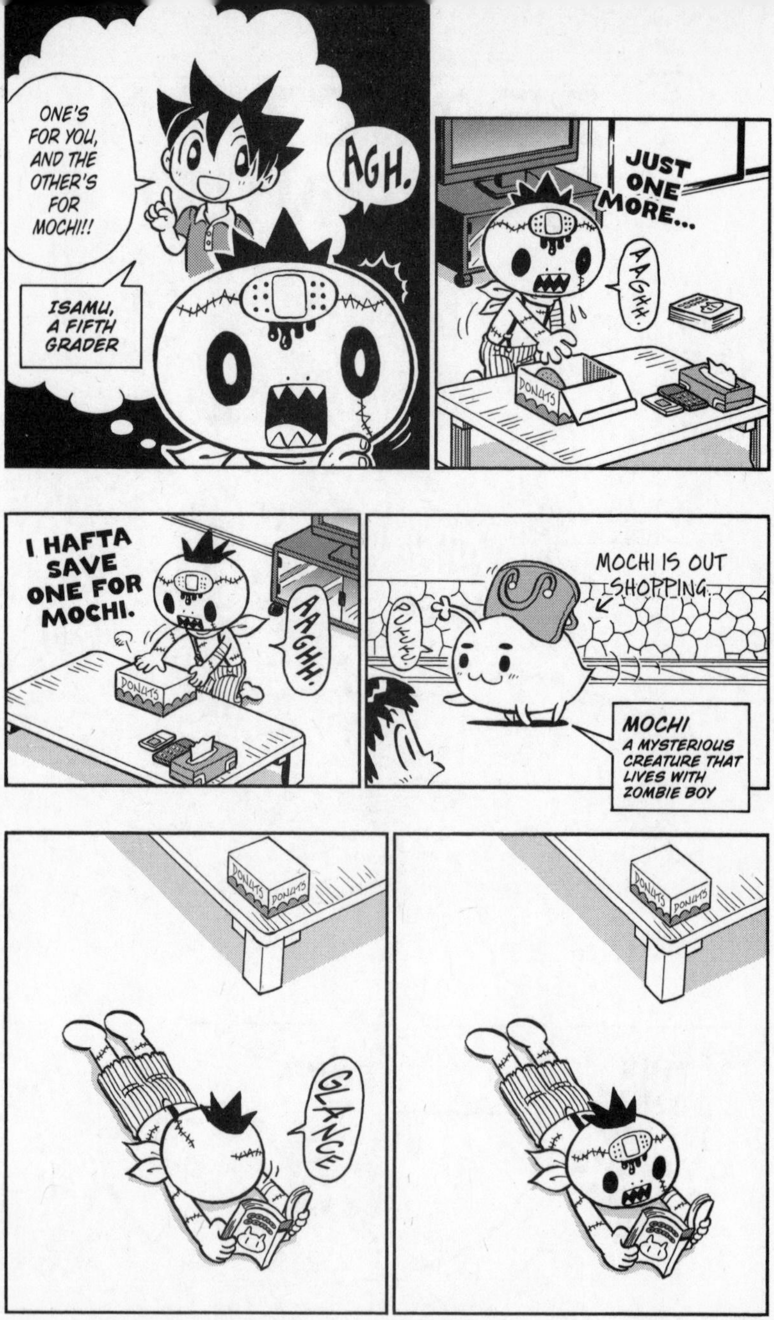
JUST ONE MORE...
AAGHH.
AGH.
ONE'S FOR YOU, AND THE OTHER'S FOR MOCHI!!
ISAMU, A FIFTH GRADER
MOCHI IS OUT SHOPPING.
PUKUKU.
MOCHI
A MYSTERIOUS CREATURE THAT LIVES WITH ZOMBIE BOY
AAGHH.
I HAFTA SAVE ONE FOR MOCHI.
DONUTS
GLANCE

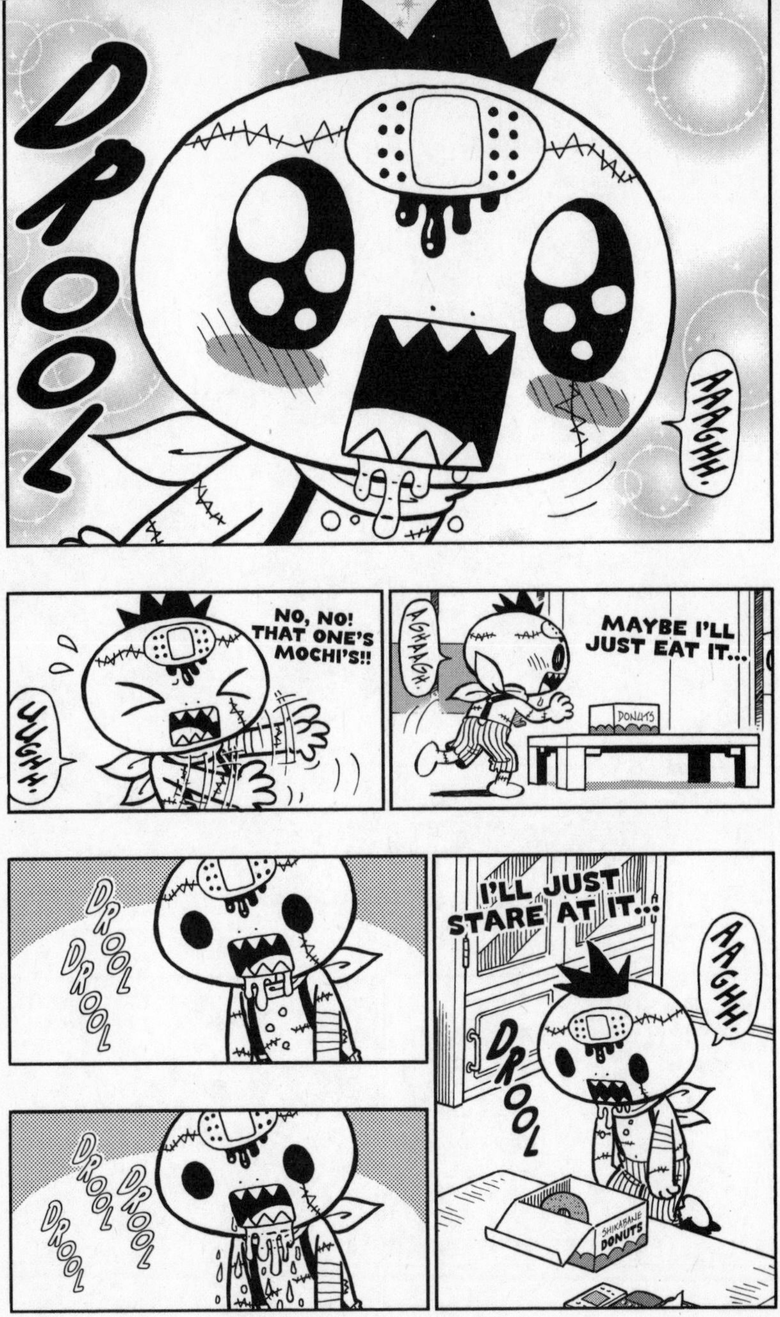
AAAGHH.
DROOL
MAYBE I'LL JUST EAT IT...
AGHAAGH.
NO, NO! THAT ONE'S MOCHI'S!!
UGHH.
I'LL JUST STARE AT IT...
AAGHH.
DROOL
DONUTS
SHIKABANE DONUTS
DROOL DROOL
DROOL DROOL DROOL

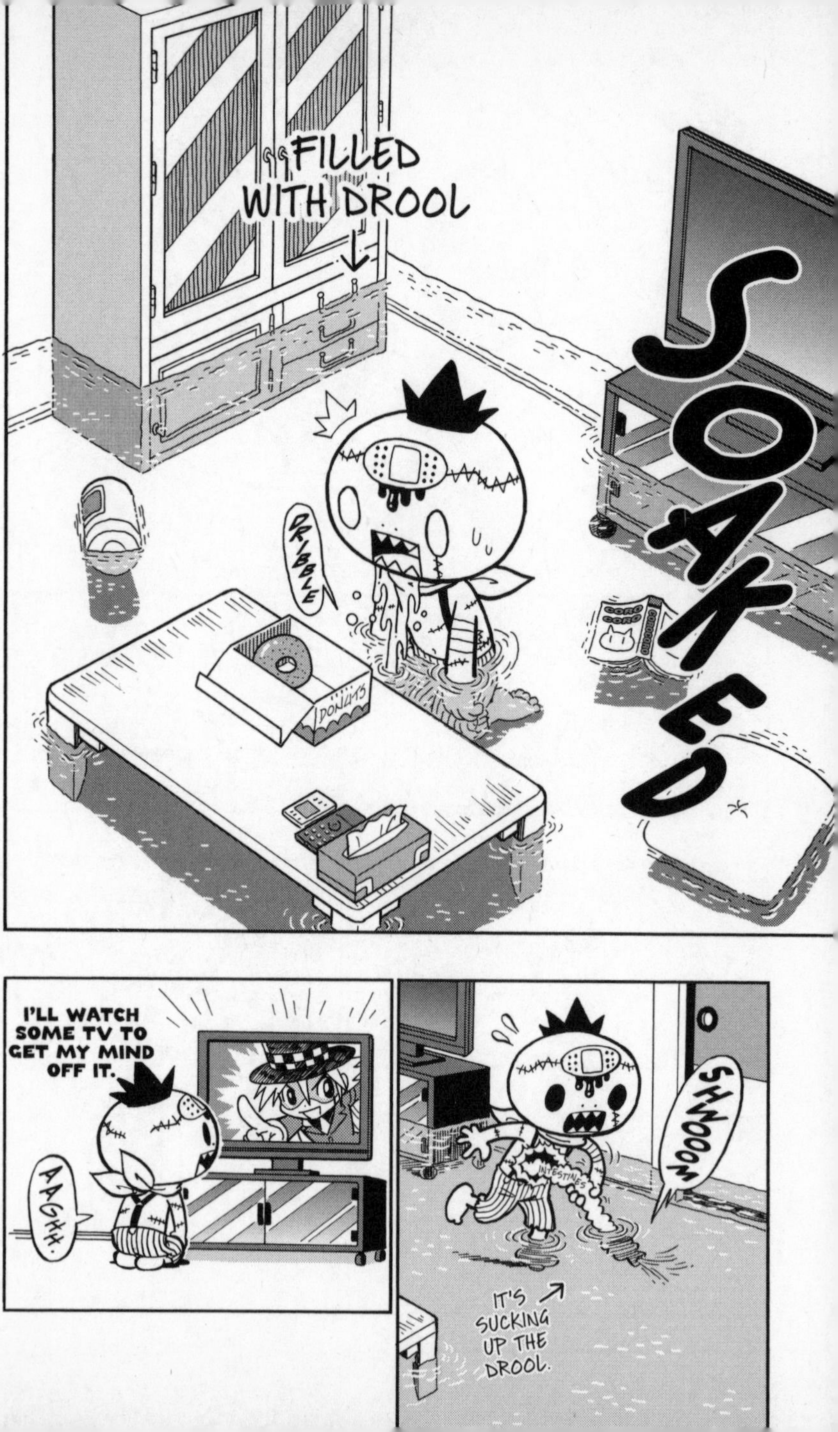
FILLED WITH DROOL
SOAKED
DRIBBLE
DONUTS
SHWOOOM
INTESTINES
IT'S SUCKING UP THE DROOL.
I'LL WATCH SOME TV TO GET MY MIND OFF IT.
AAGHH.

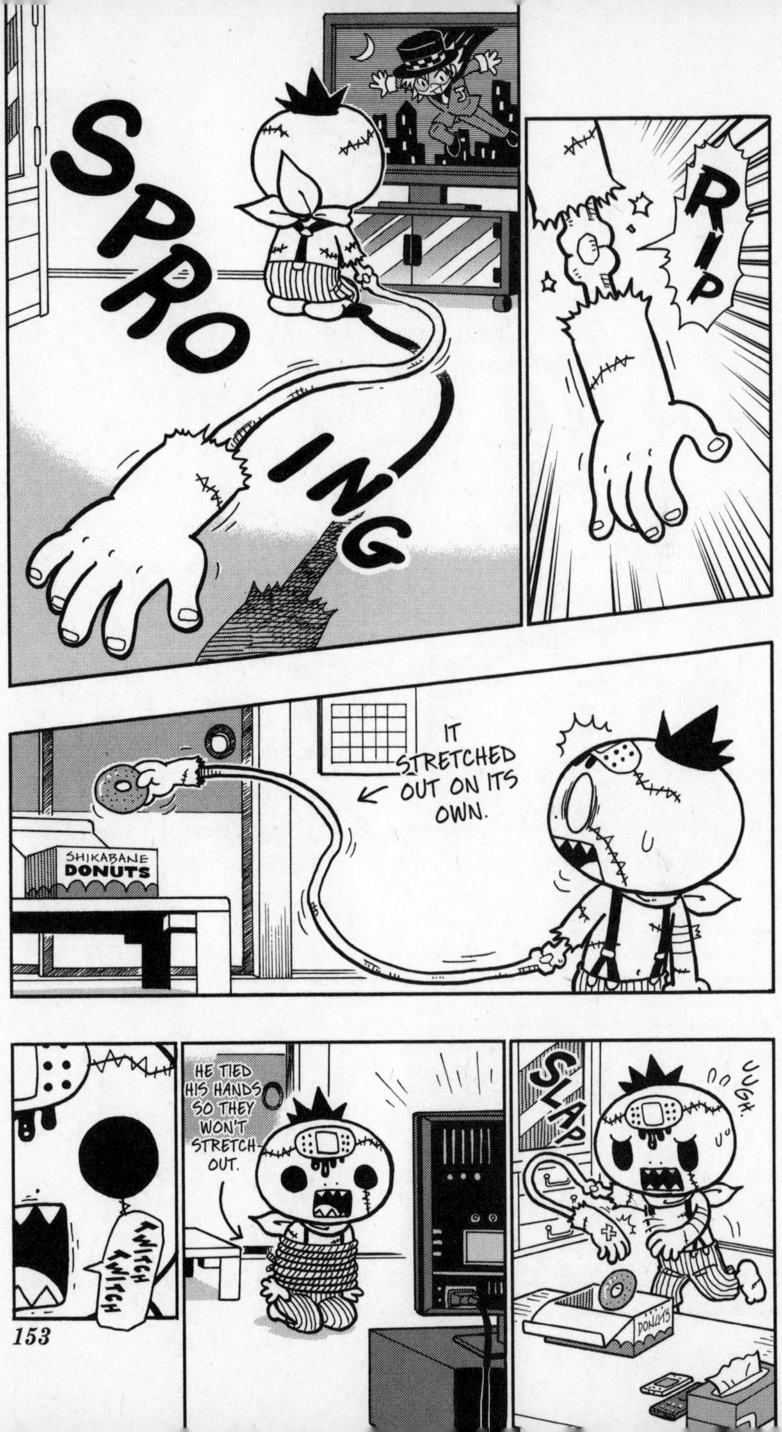
RIP
SPROING
IT STRETCHED OUT ON ITS OWN.
SHIKABANE DONUTS
SLAP
UUGH.
DONUTS
HE TIED HIS HANDS SO THEY WON'T STRETCH-OUT.
TWITCH TWITCH

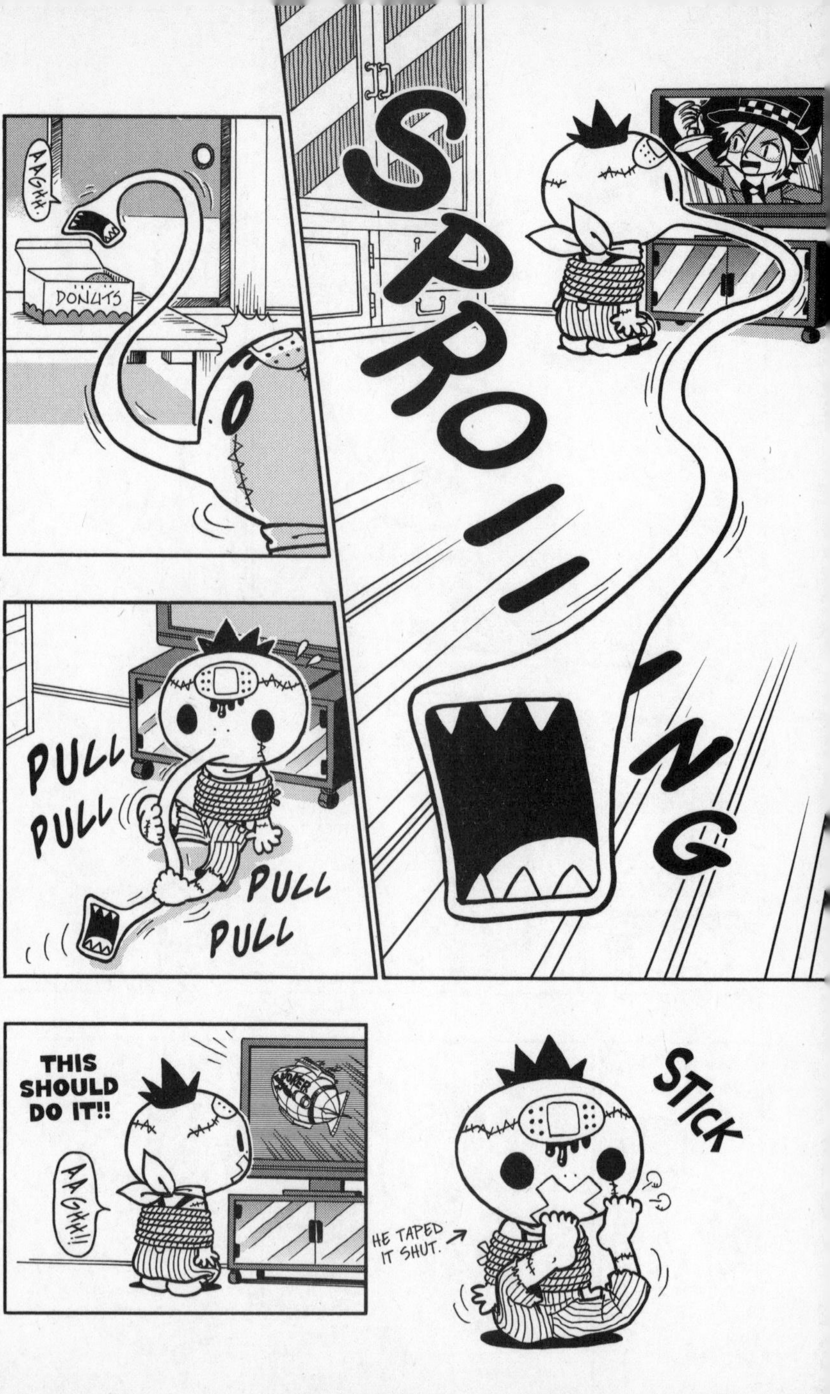
SPROIIIING
AAGHH.
PULL
PULL
PULL
PULL
STICK
HE TAPED IT SHUT.
THIS SHOULD DO IT!!
AAGHH!!

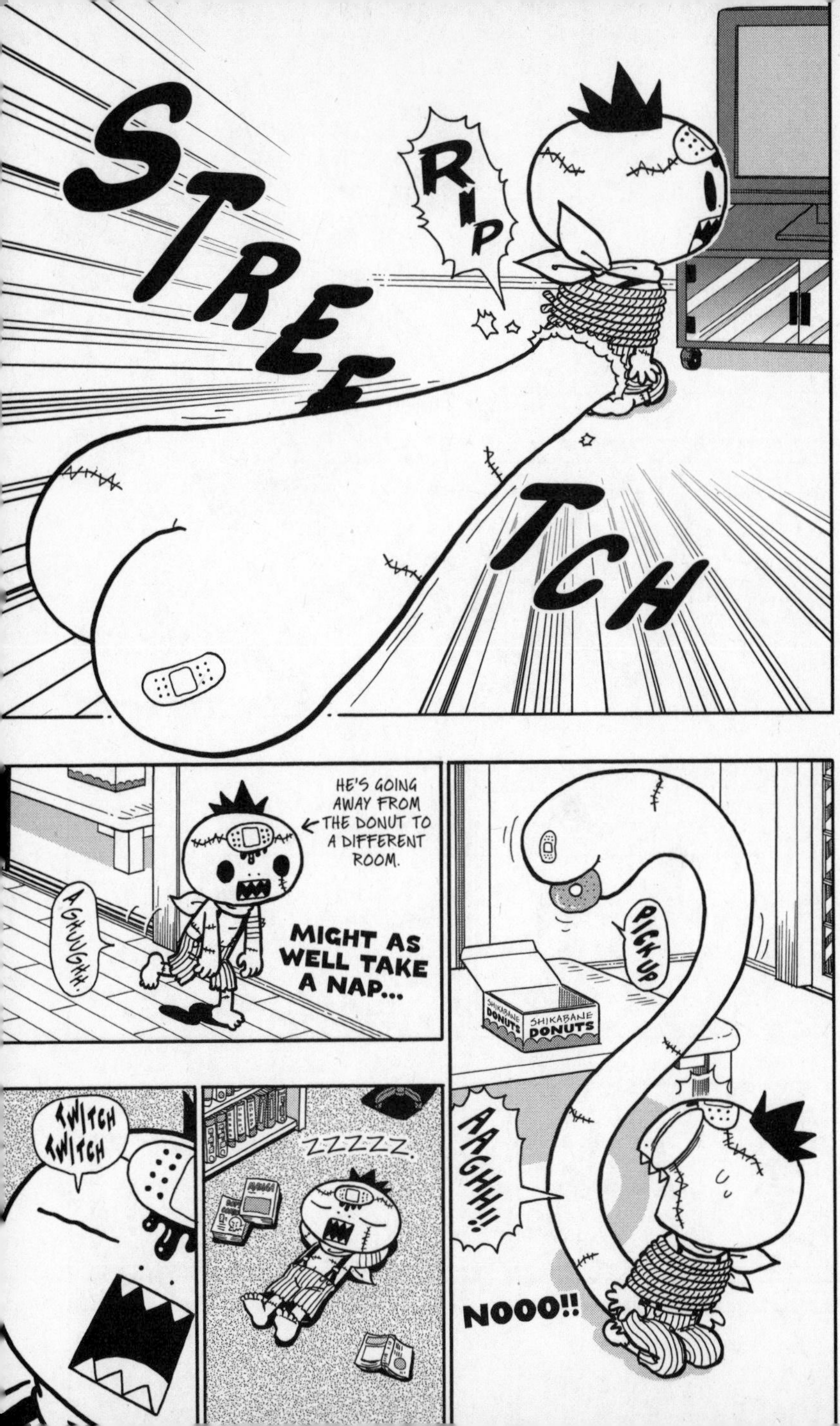
RIP
STREETCH
PICK UP
SHIKABANE DONUTS
SHIKABANE DONUTS
AAGHH!!
NOOO!!
HE'S GOING AWAY FROM THE DONUT TO A DIFFERENT ROOM.
AGHUGHH.
MIGHT AS WELL TAKE A NAP...
ZZZZZ.
TWITCH TWITCH

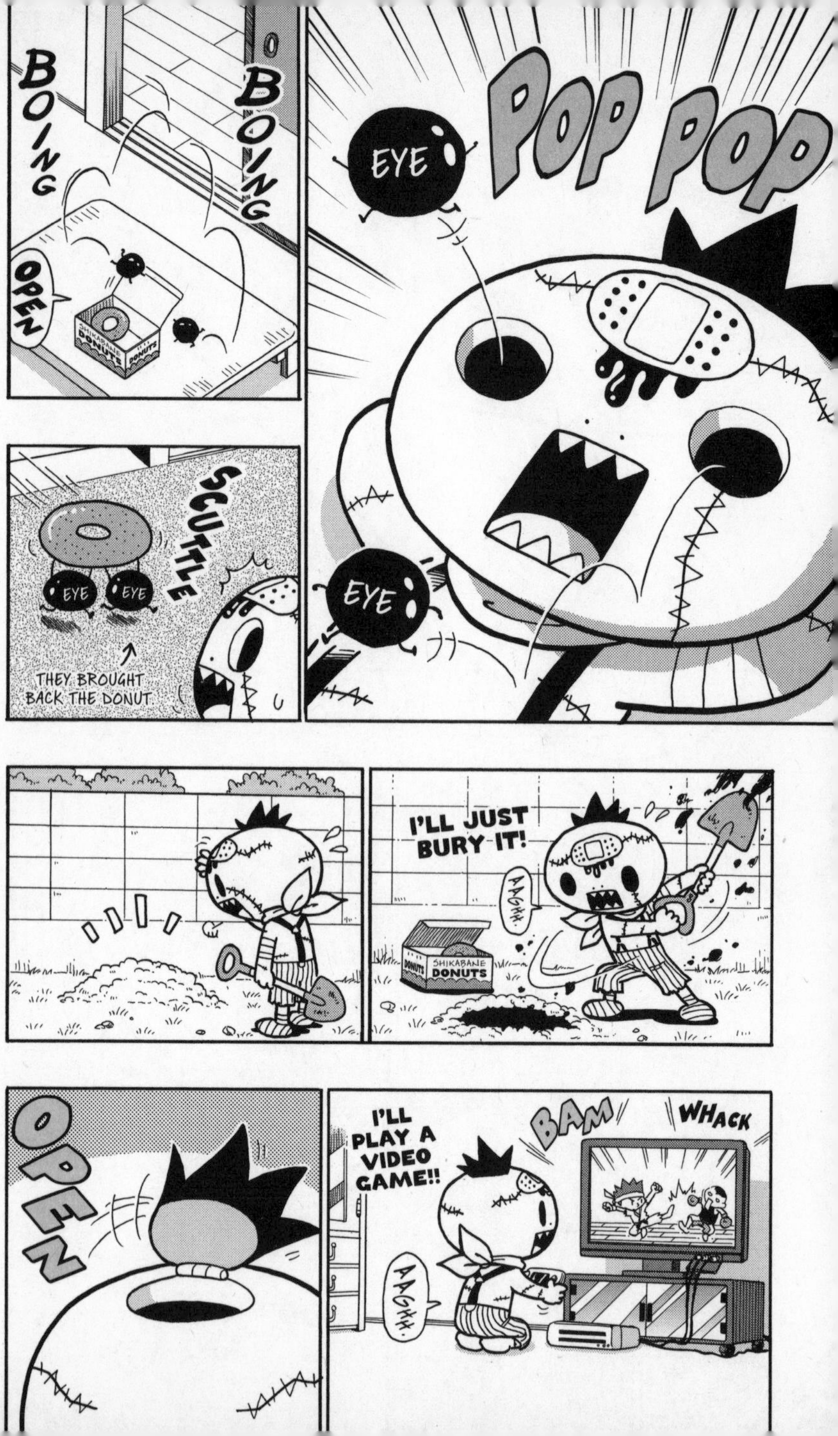
POP POP
EYE
EYE
BOING BOING
OPEN
SHIKABANE DONUTS
DONUTS
SCUTTLE
EYE
EYE
THEY BROUGHT BACK THE DONUT
I'LL JUST BURY IT!
AAGHH.
SHIKABANE DONUTS
DONUTS
BAM
WHACK
I'LL PLAY A VIDEO GAME!!
AAGHH.
OPEN

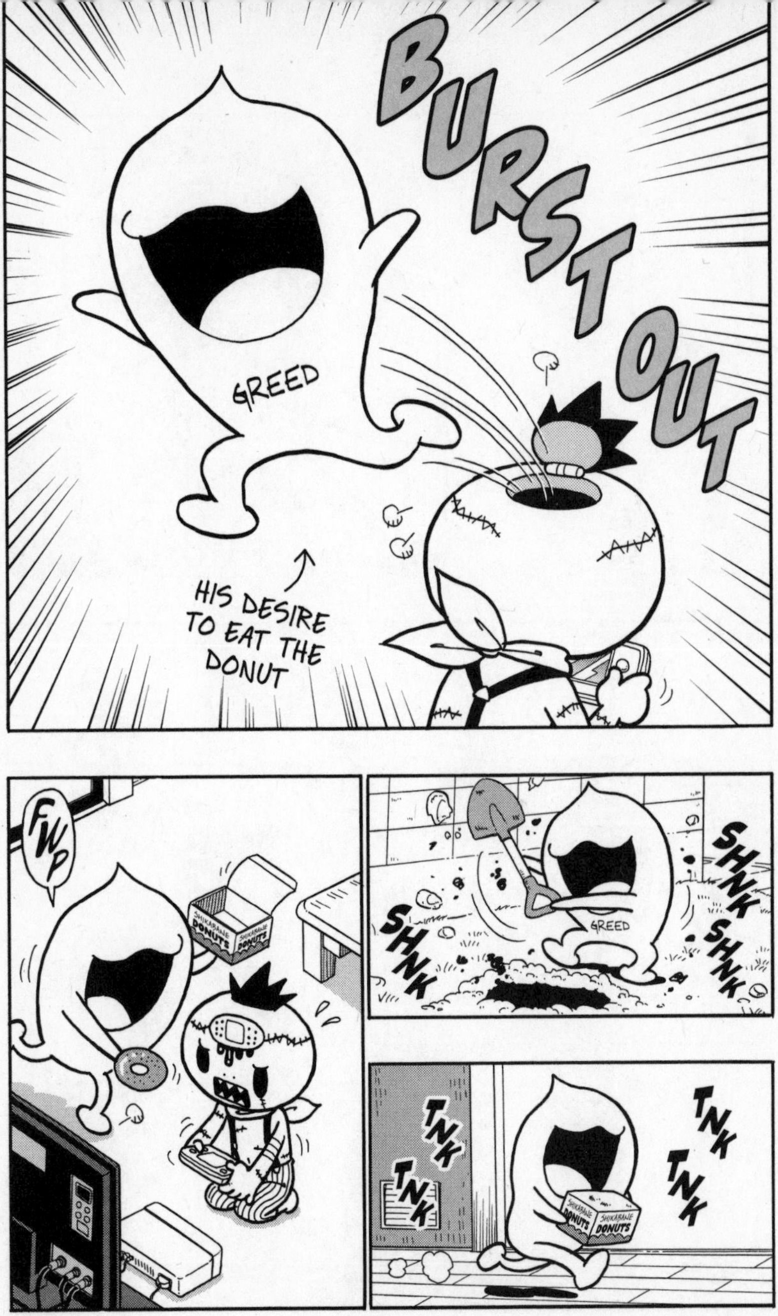
BURST OUT
GREED
HIS DESIRE TO EAT THE DONUT
SHNK SHNK
SHNK SHNK
GREED
TNK TNK
TNK TNK
SHIKABANE DONUTS
FWP
SHIKABANE DONUTS
SHIKABANE DONUTS

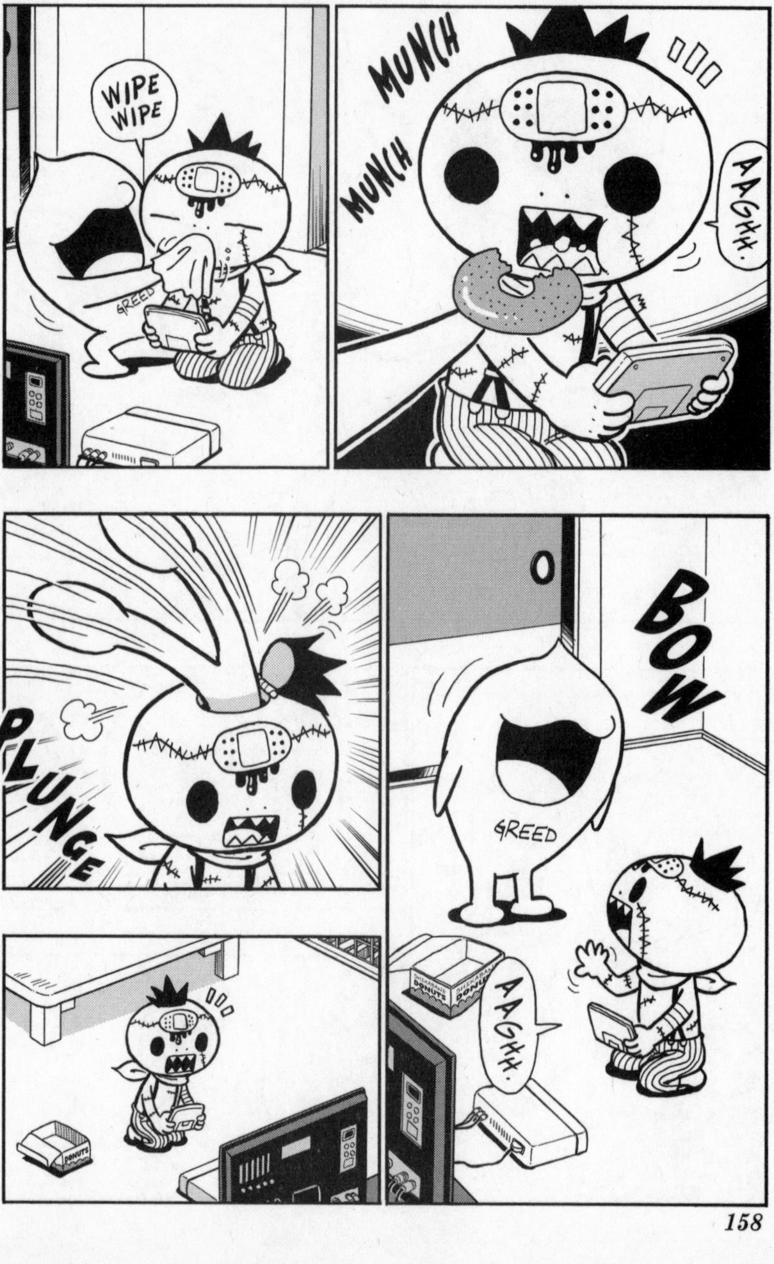
MUNCH
MUNCH
AAGHH.
WIPE WIPE
GREED
BOW
GREED
SHIKABANE DONUTS
AAGHH.
PLUNGE
DONUTS

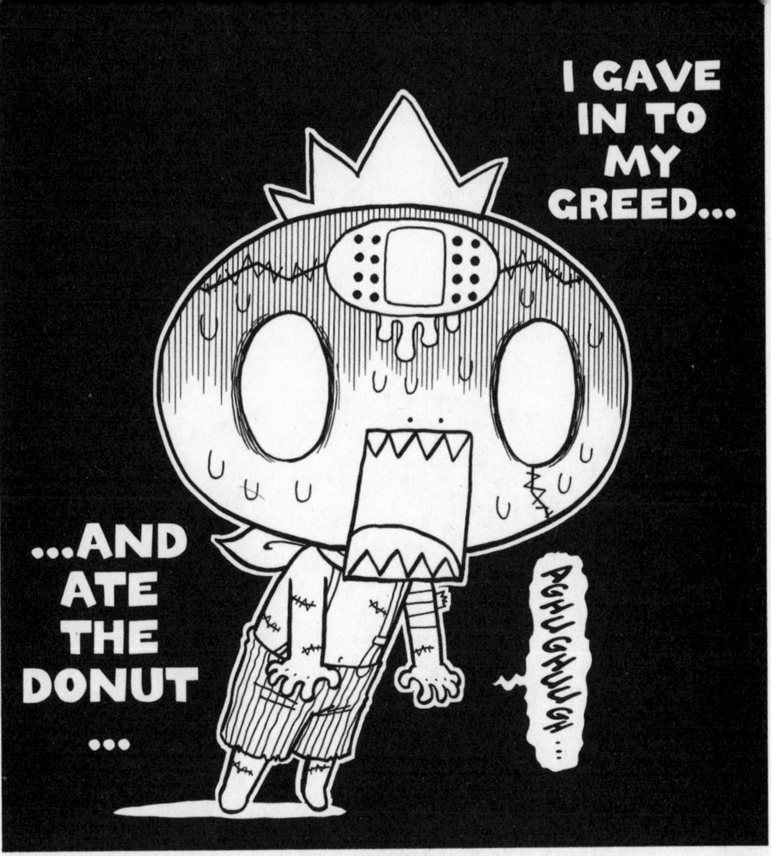
I GAVE IN TO MY GREED...
AGHUGHUUGH...
...AND ATE THE DONUT ...

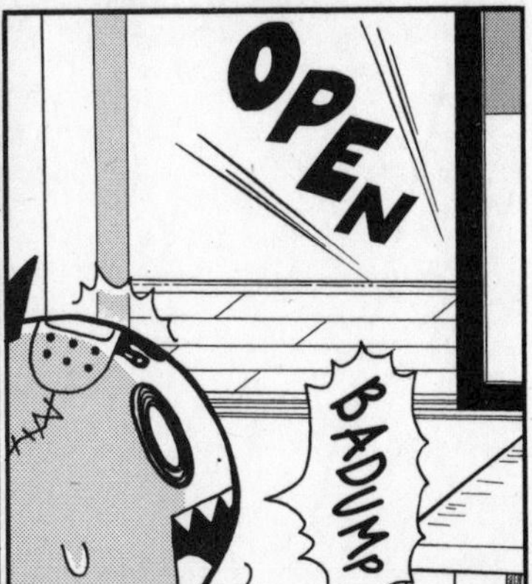
OPEN
BADUMP

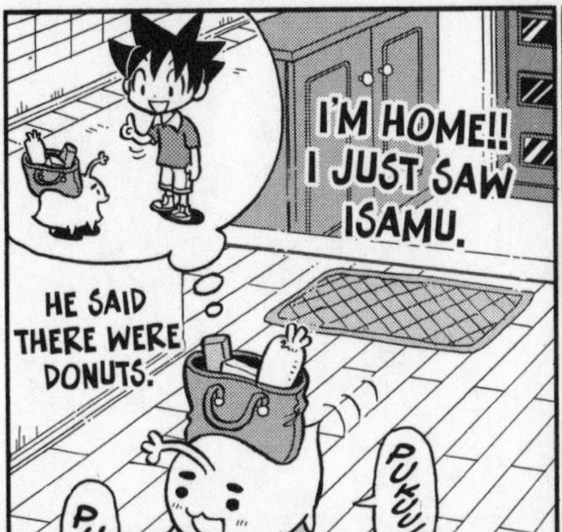
I'M HOME!! I JUST SAW ISAMU.
HE SAID THERE WERE DONUTS.
PUKUU!!
PUU!

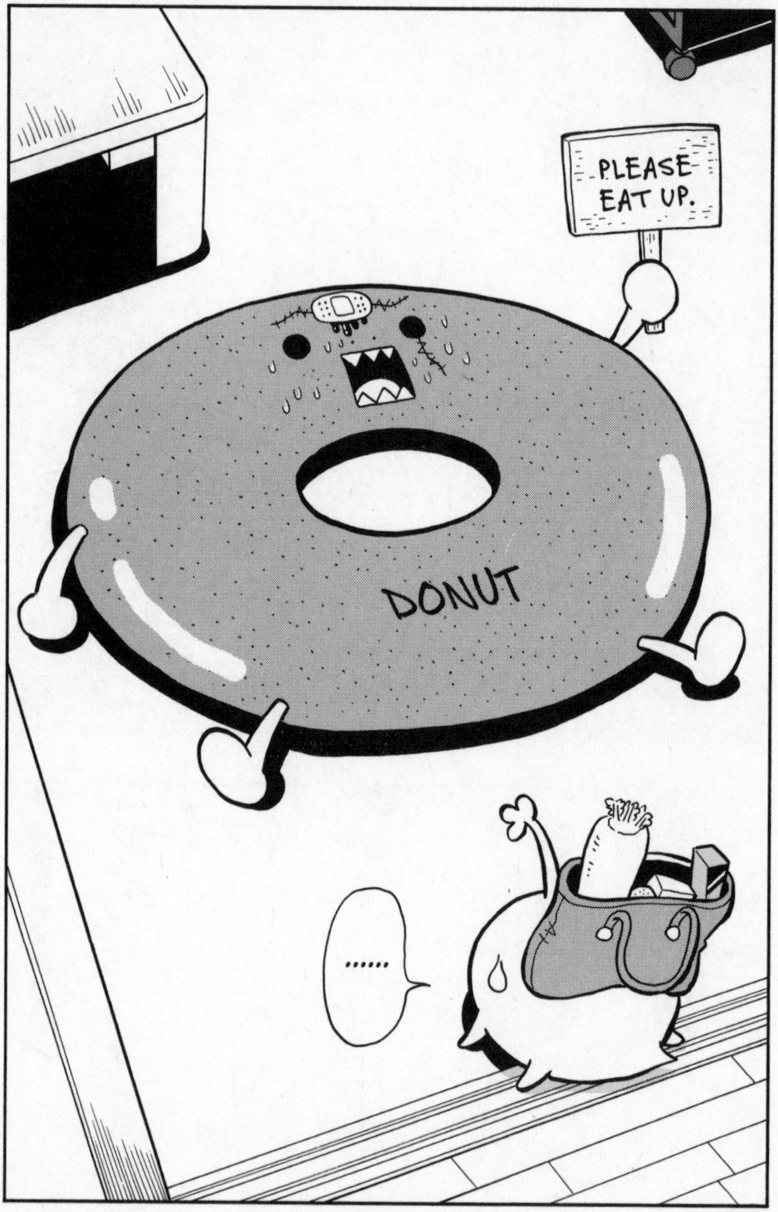
PLEASE EAT UP.
DONUT
......

DONUT

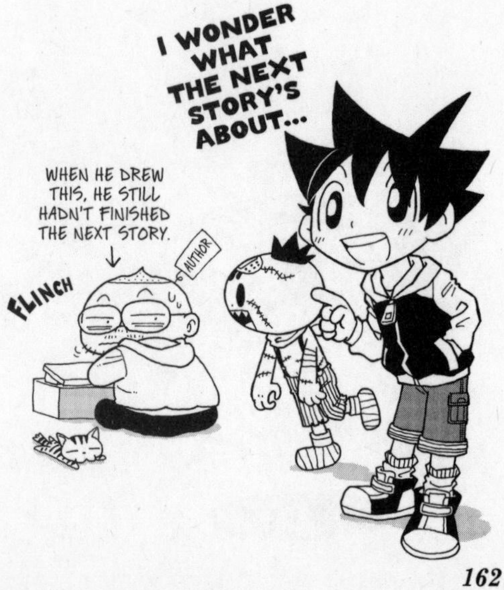
I WONDER WHAT THE NEXT STORY'S ABOUT...
WHEN HE DREW THIS, HE STILL HADN'T FINISHED THE NEXT STORY.
AUTHOR
FLINCH

A ZOMBIE HUNTER SURPRIZE!

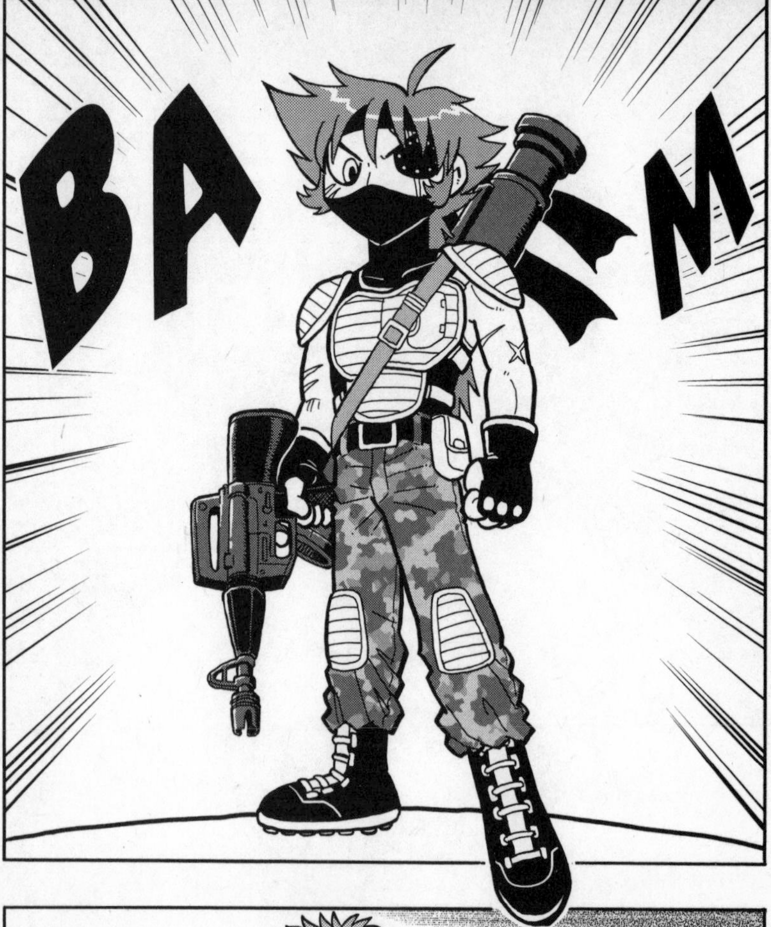
BAM

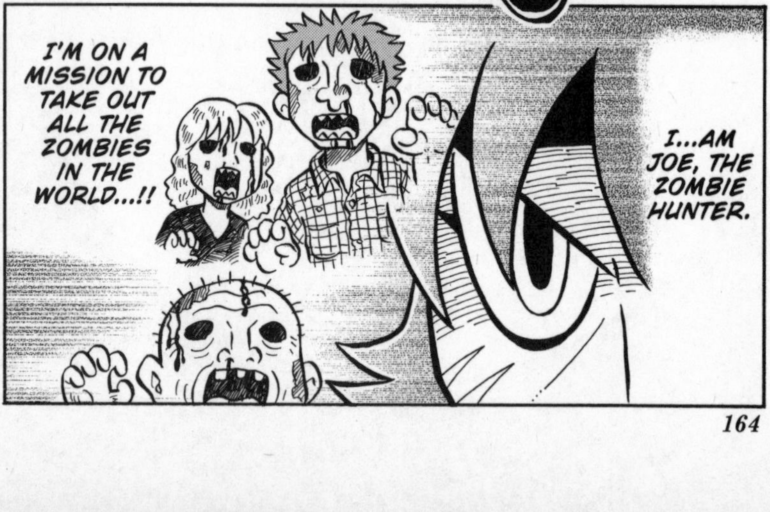
I...AM JOE, THE ZOMBIE HUNTER.
I'M ON A MISSION TO TAKE OUT ALL THE ZOMBIES IN THE WORLD...!!

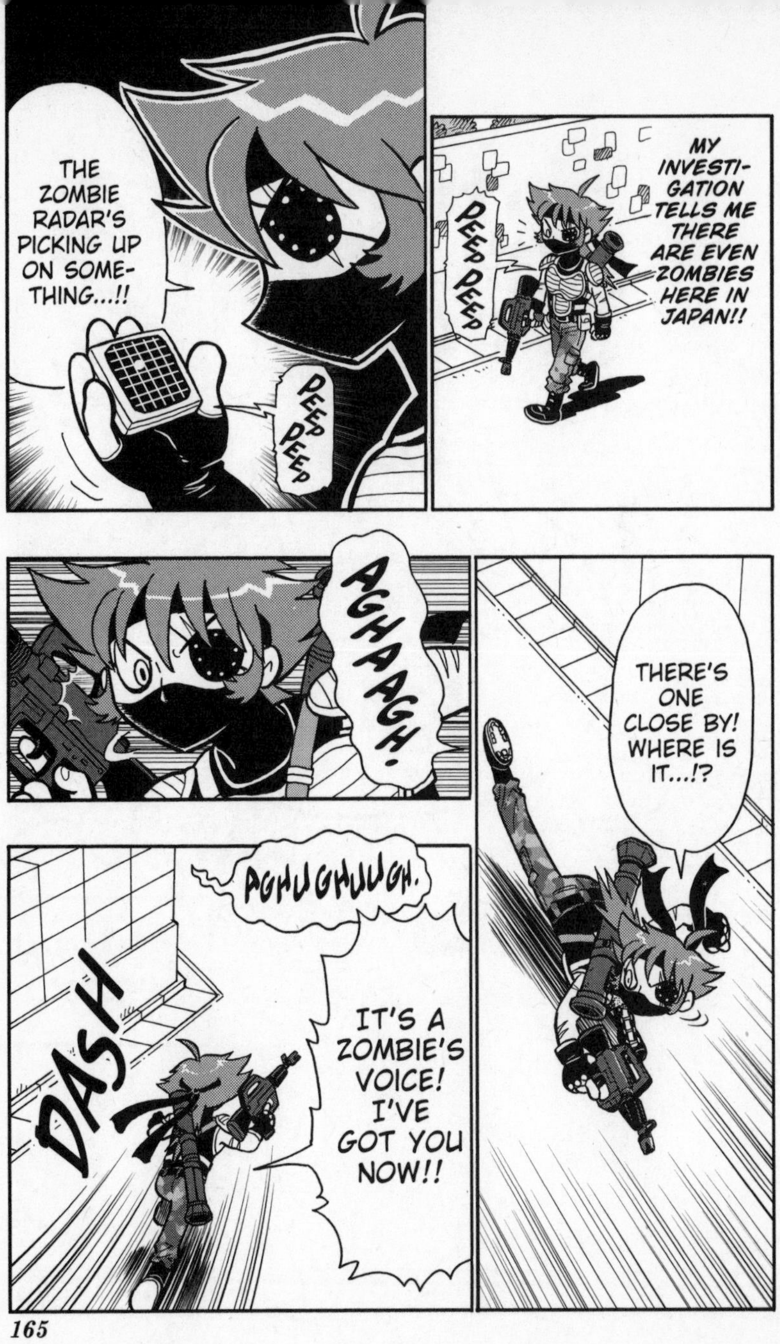
MY INVESTIGATION TELLS ME THERE ARE EVEN ZOMBIES HERE IN JAPAN!!
DEEP DEEP
THE ZOMBIE RADAR'S PICKING UP ON SOMETHING...!!
DEEP DEEP
THERE'S ONE CLOSE BY! WHERE IS IT...!?
AGHAAAGH!
PGHUGHUUGH.
DASH
IT'S A ZOMBIE'S VOICE! I'VE GOT YOU NOW!!

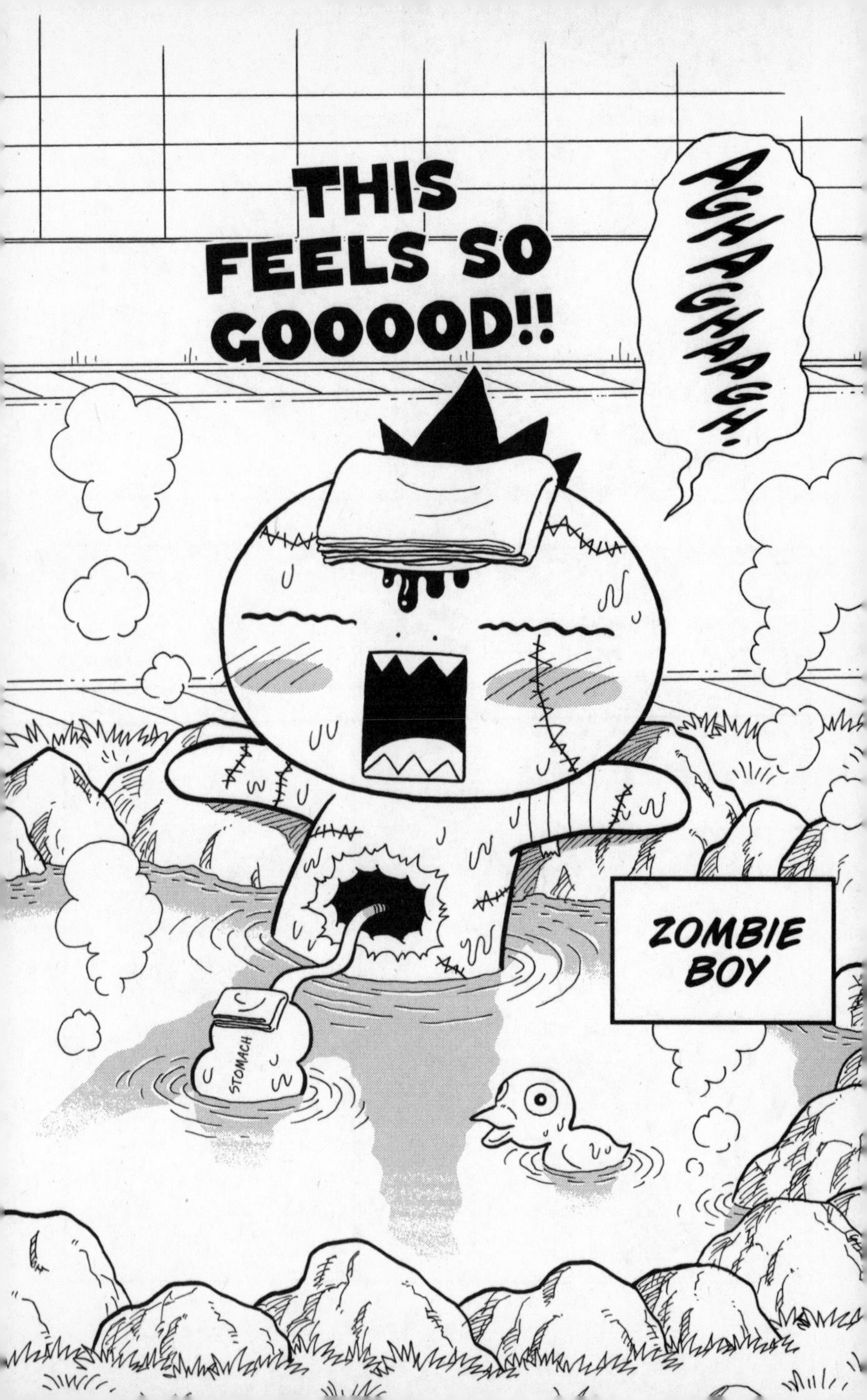
AGHAGHAAGH!
THIS FEELS SO GOOOOD!!
ZOMBIE BOY
STOMACH

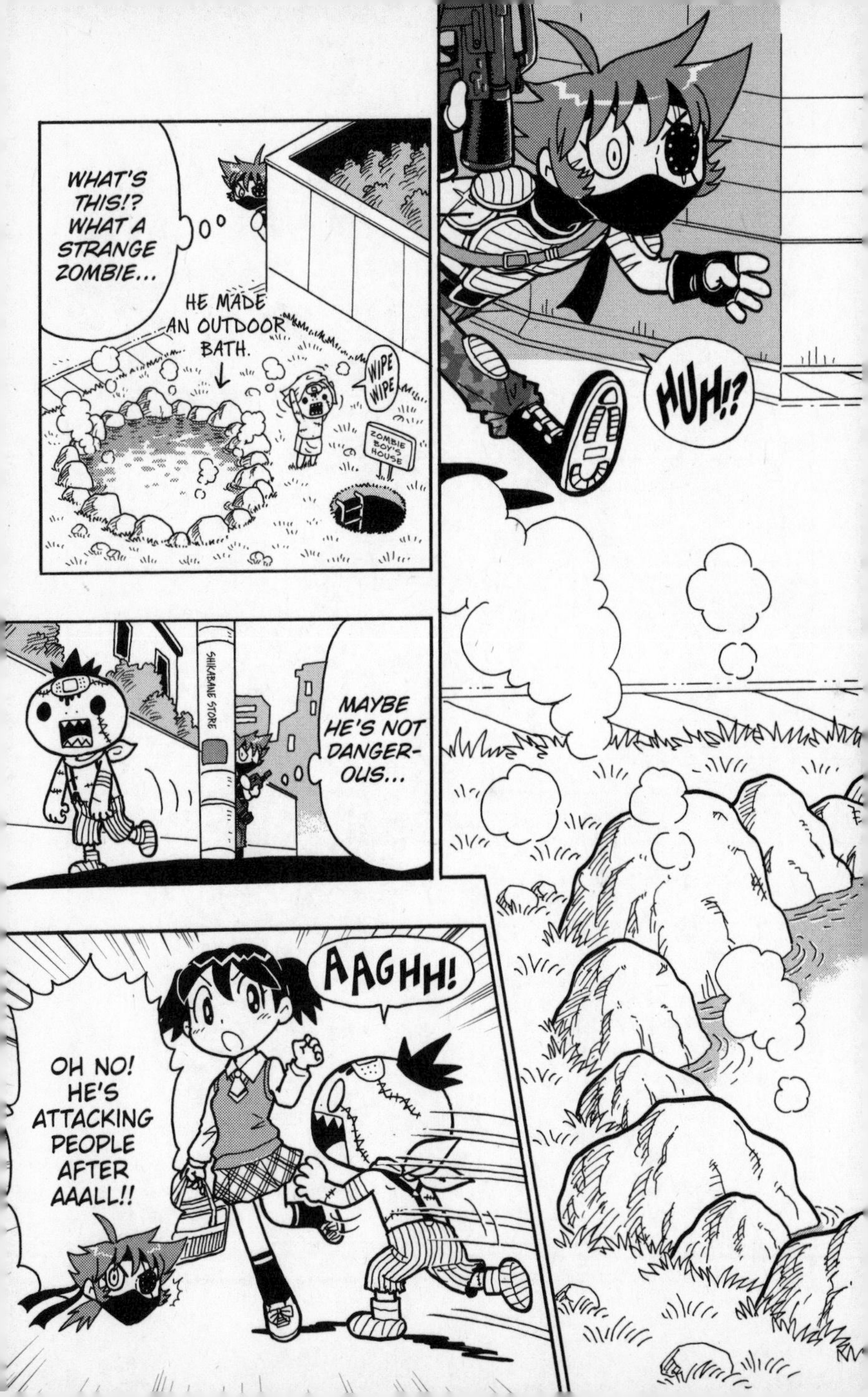
HUH!?
WHAT'S THIS!? WHAT A STRANGE ZOMBIE...
HE MADE AN OUTDOOR BATH.
WIPE WIPE
ZOMBIE BOY'S HOUSE
MAYBE HE'S NOT DANGER-OUS...
SHIKABANE STORE
AAGHH!
OH NO! HE'S ATTACKING PEOPLE AFTER AAALL!!

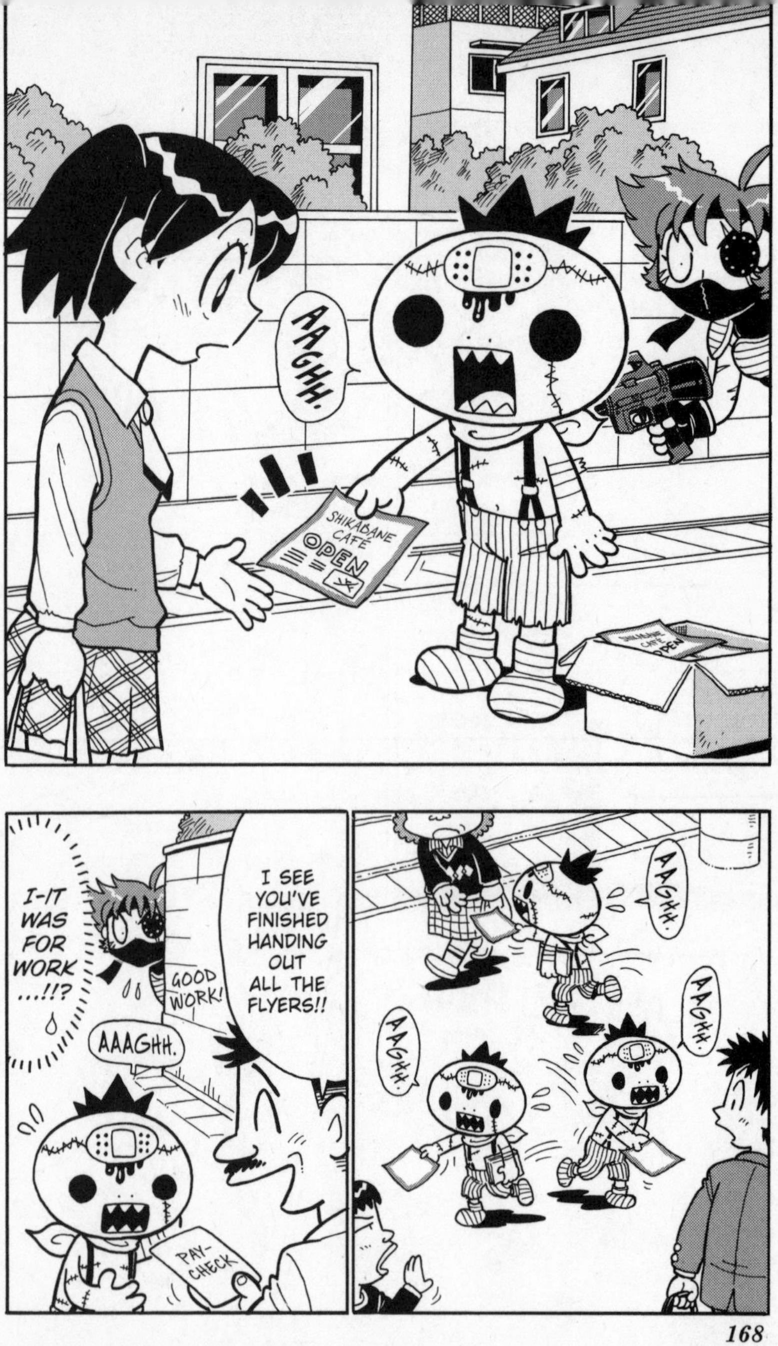
SHIKABANE CAFÉ OPEN
AAGHH.
SHIKABANE CAFE OPEN
AAGHH.
AAGHH.
AAGHH.
I SEE YOU'VE FINISHED HANDING OUT ALL THE FLYERS!!
GOOD WORK!
I-IT WAS FOR WORK ...!!?
AAAGHH.
PAY-CHECK

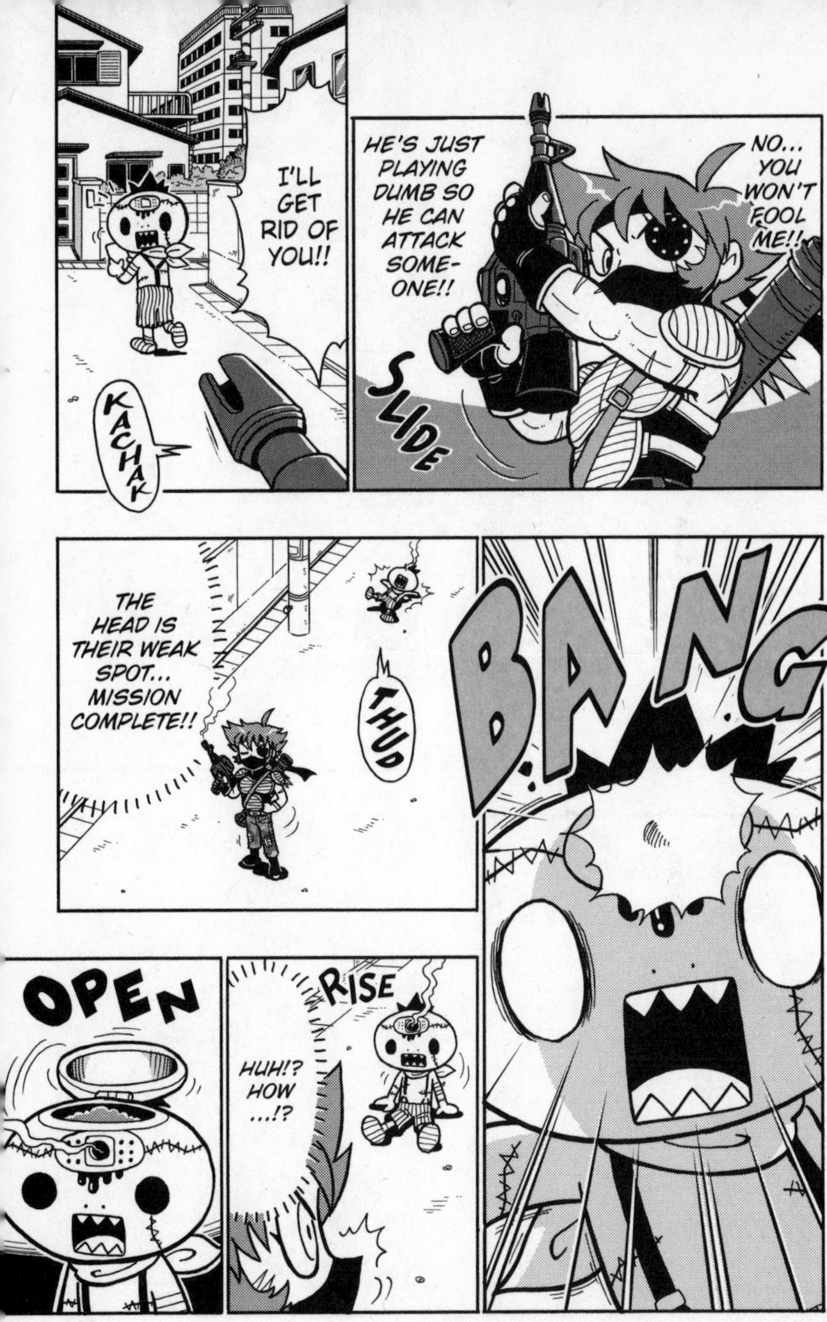
NO... YOU WON'T FOOL ME!!
HE'S JUST PLAYING DUMB SO HE CAN ATTACK SOME-ONE!!
SLIDE
I'LL GET RID OF YOU!!
KACHAK
BANG
THUD
THE HEAD IS THEIR WEAK SPOT... MISSION COMPLETE!!
RISE
HUH!? HOW ...!?
OPEN

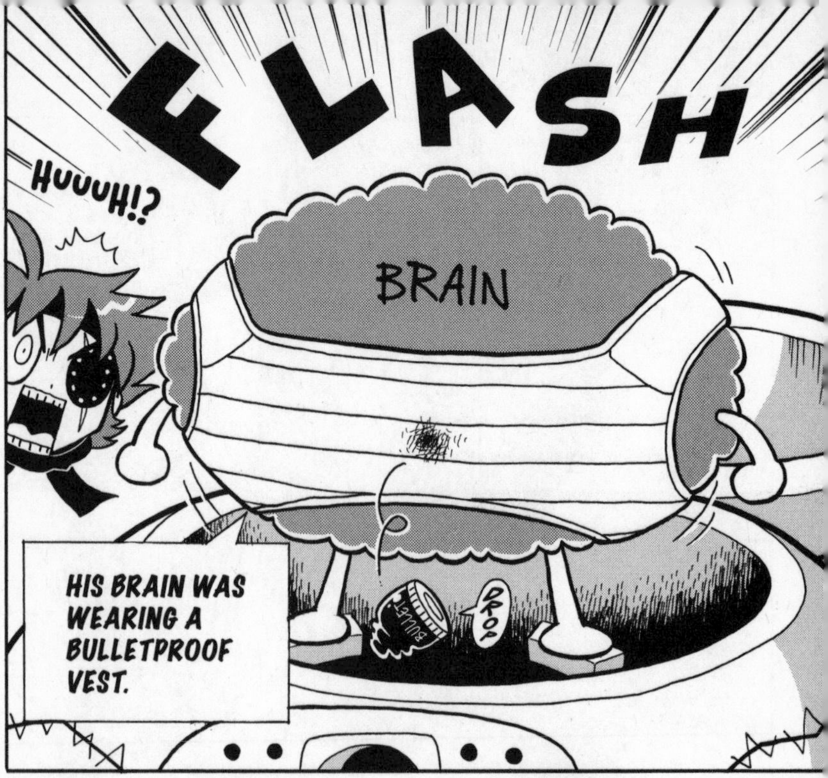
FLASH
HUUUH!?
BRAIN
BULLET
DROP
HIS BRAIN WAS WEARING A BULLETPROOF VEST.

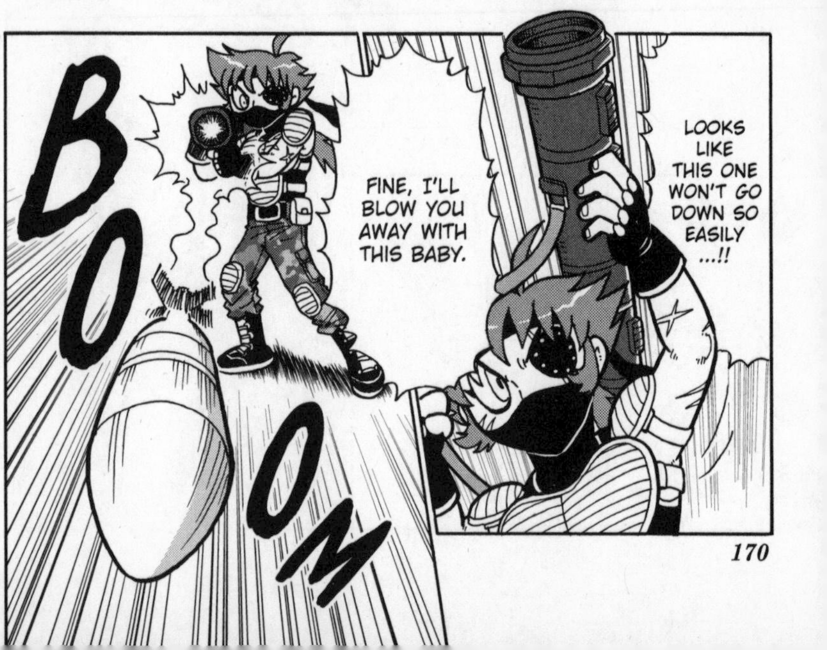
LOOKS LIKE THIS ONE WON'T GO DOWN SO EASILY ...!!
FINE, I'LL BLOW YOU AWAY WITH THIS BABY.
BOOM

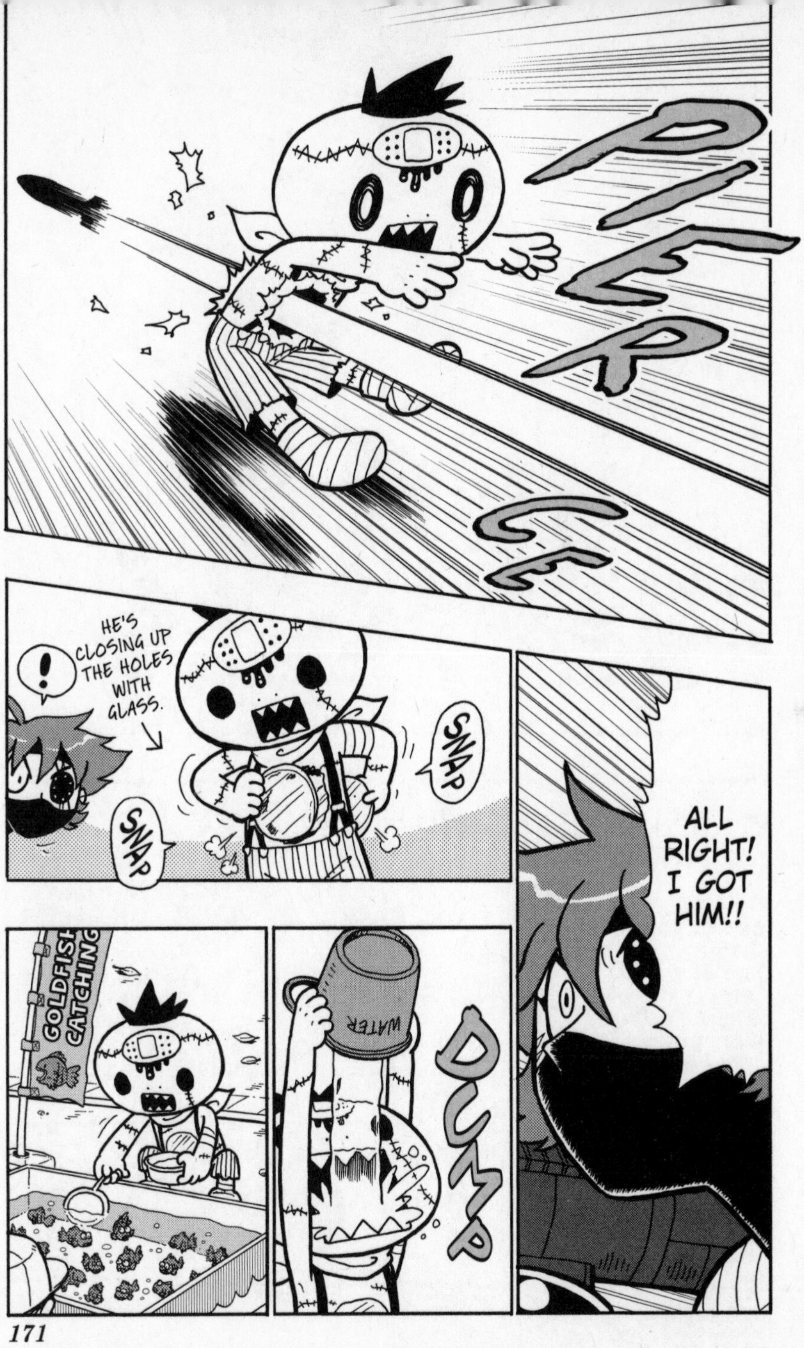
PIERCE
ALL RIGHT! I GOT HIM!!
!
HE'S CLOSING UP THE HOLES WITH GLASS.
SNAP
SNAP
DUMP
WATER
GOLDFISH CATCHING

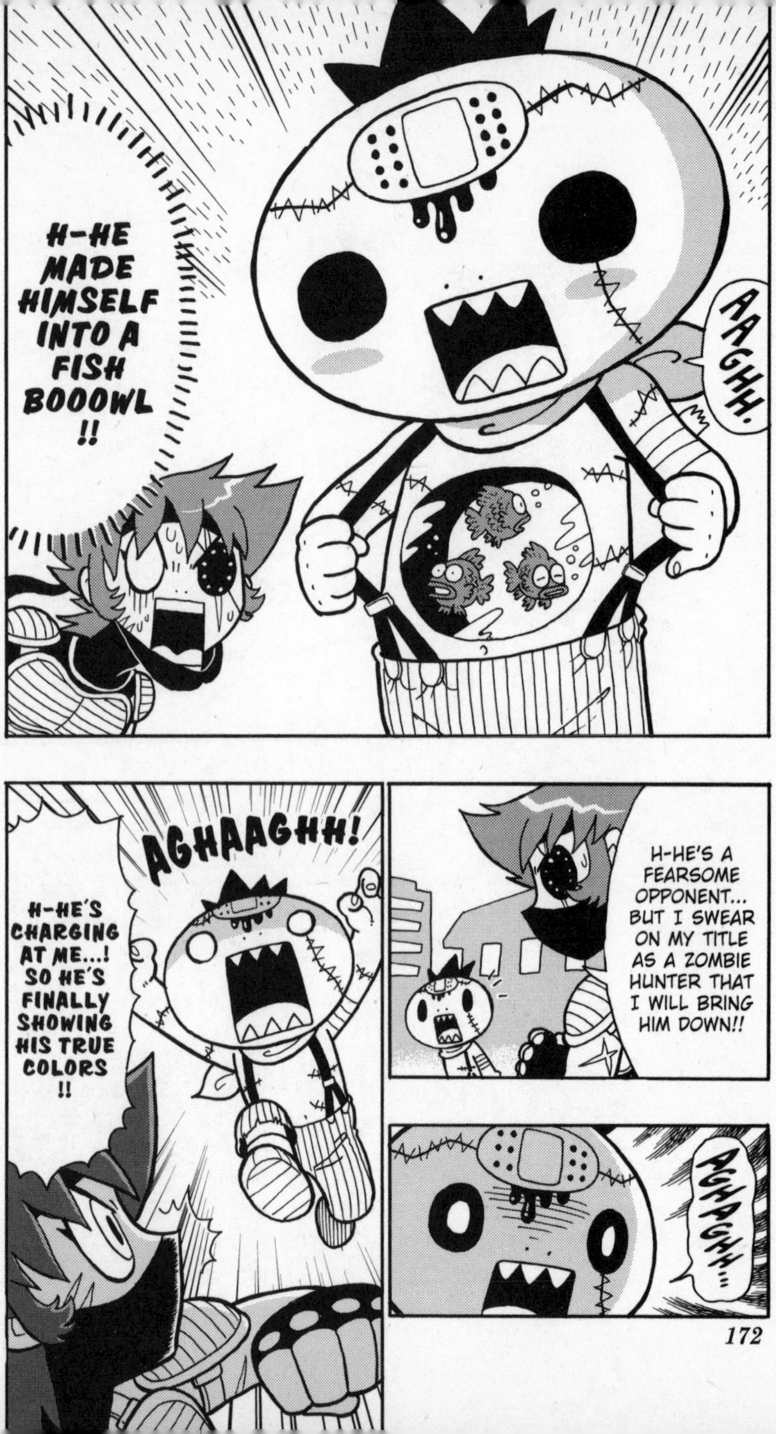
AAGHH.
H-HE MADE HIMSELF INTO A FISH BOOOWL!!
H-HE'S A FEARSOME OPPONENT... BUT I SWEAR ON MY TITLE AS A ZOMBIE HUNTER THAT I WILL BRING HIM DOWN!!
AGHAGHH...
AGHAAGHH!
H-HE'S CHARGING AT ME...! SO HE'S FINALLY SHOWING HIS TRUE COLORS!!

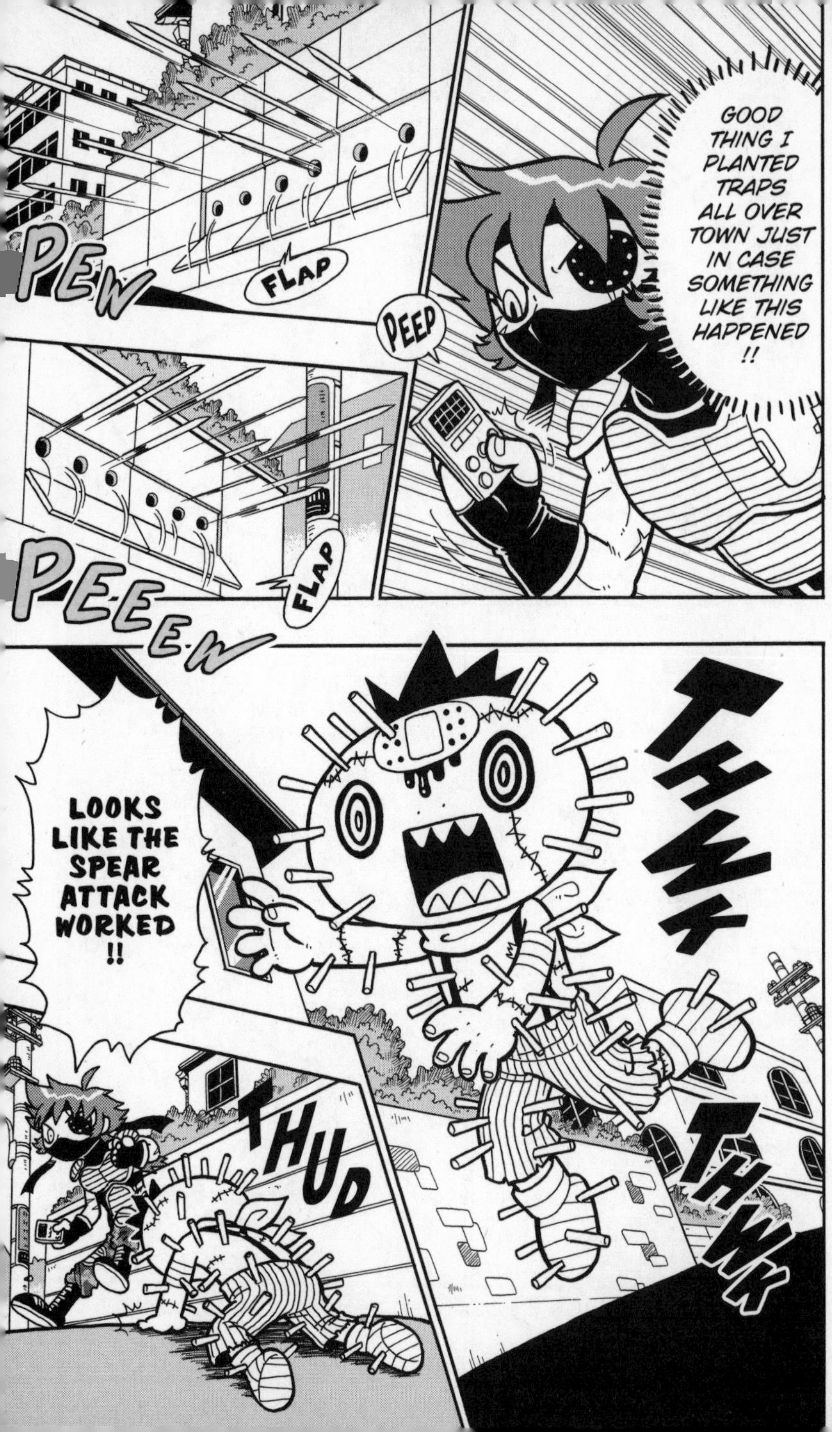
GOOD THING I PLANTED TRAPS ALL OVER TOWN JUST IN CASE SOMETHING LIKE THIS HAPPENED !!
PEEP
PEW
FLAP
PE-E-E-E-W
FLAP
THWK
LOOKS LIKE THE SPEAR ATTACK WORKED !!
THUD
THWK

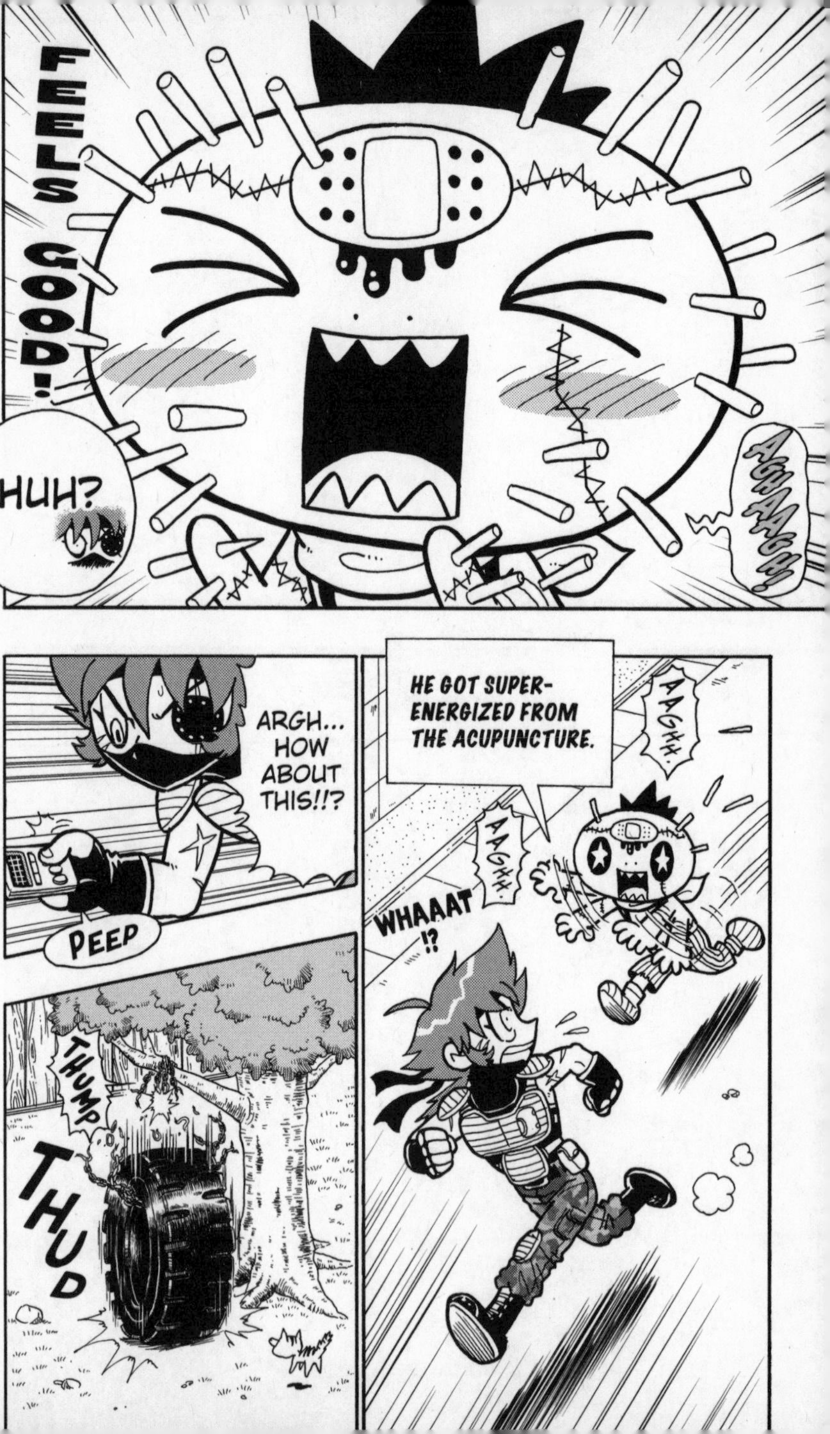
AGHAAAGH!
FEELS GOOD!
HUH?
HE GOT SUPER-ENERGIZED FROM THE ACUPUNCTURE.
AAGHH.
AAGHH.
WHAAAT!?
ARGH... HOW ABOUT THIS!!?
PEEP
THUMP
THUD

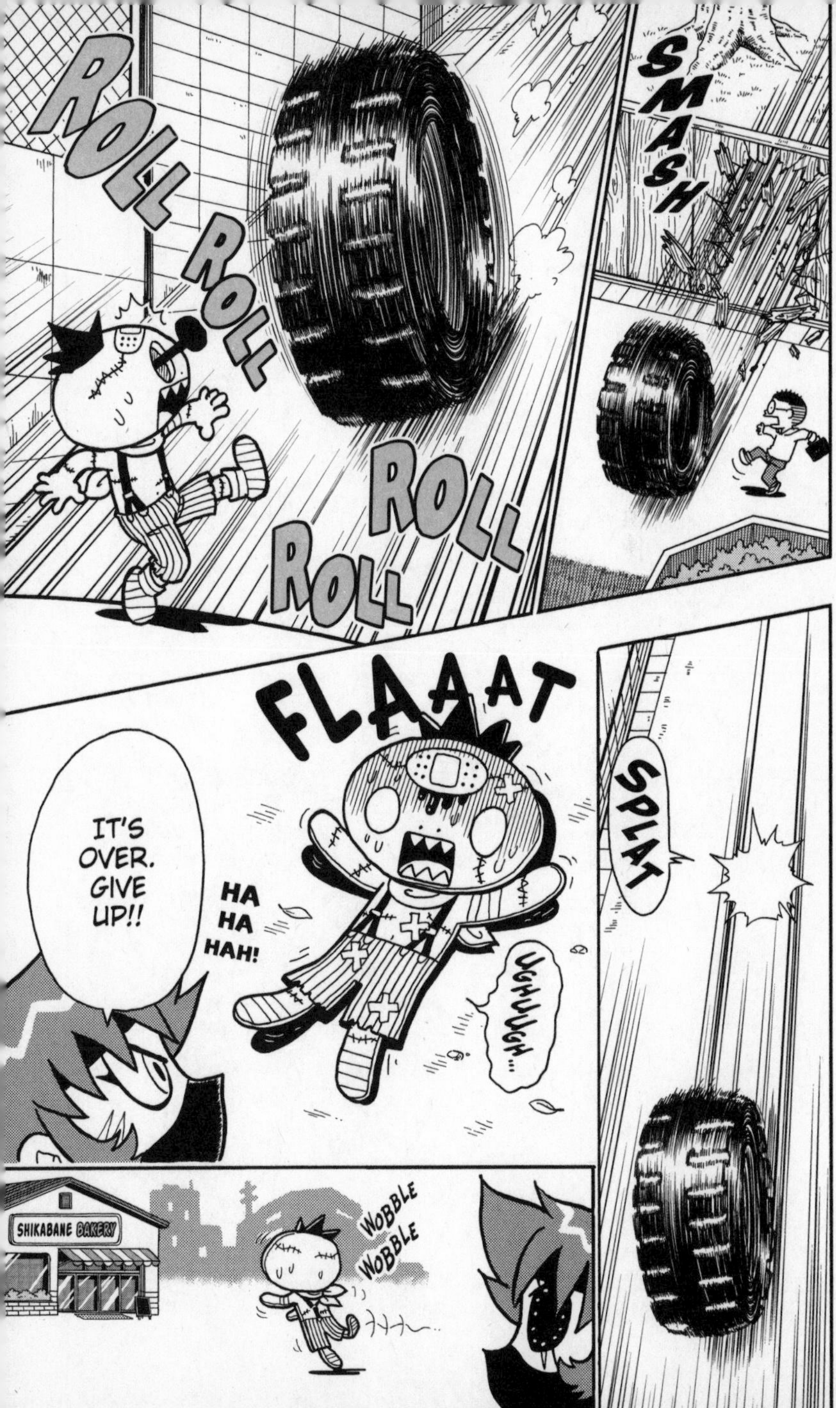
SMASH
ROLL ROLL
ROLL ROLL
SPLAT
FLAAAT
UGHUUGH...
HA HA HAH!
IT'S OVER. GIVE UP!!
WOBBLE WOBBLE
SHIKABANE BAKERY

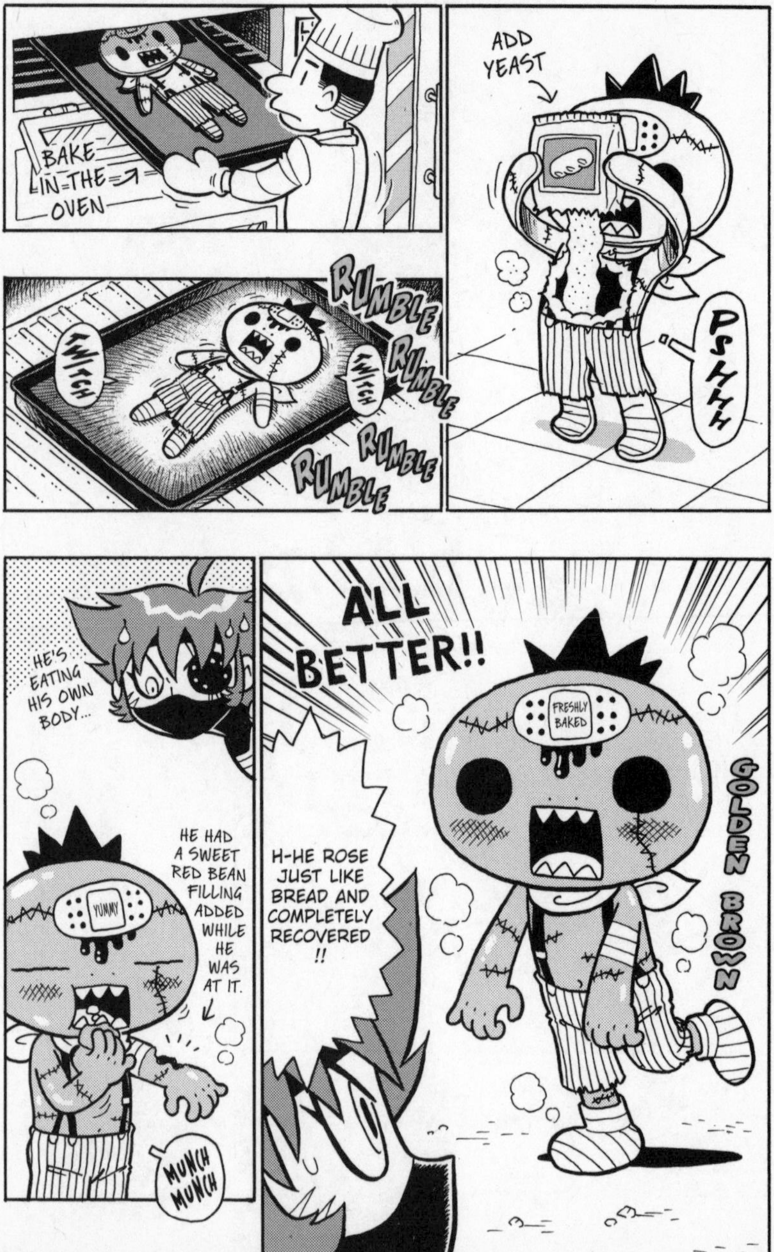
ADD YEAST
PSHHH
BAKE IN THE OVEN
RUMBLE RUMBLE RUMBLE RUMBLE
TWITCH
TWITCH
ALL BETTER!!
FRESHLY BAKED
GOLDEN BROWN
H-HE ROSE JUST LIKE BREAD AND COMPLETELY RECOVERED !!
HE'S EATING HIS OWN BODY...
HE HAD A SWEET RED BEAN FILLING ADDED WHILE HE WAS AT IT.
YUMMY
MUNCH MUNCH

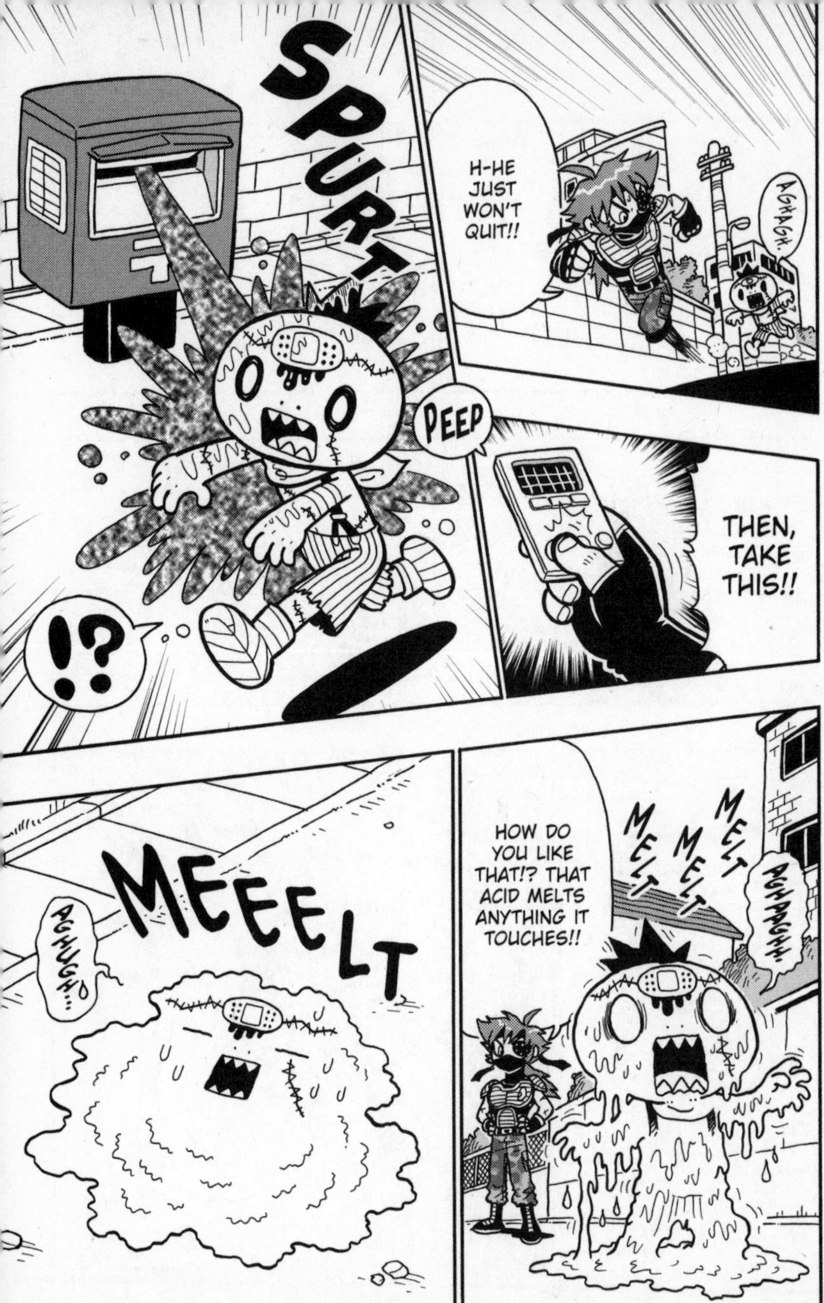

H-HE JUST WON'T QUIT!!
AGHAGH.
THEN, TAKE THIS!!
SPURT
PEEP
!?
HOW DO YOU LIKE THAT!? THAT ACID MELTS ANYTHING IT TOUCHES!!
MELT MELT MELT
AGHAGHH.
MEEELT
AGHUGH...

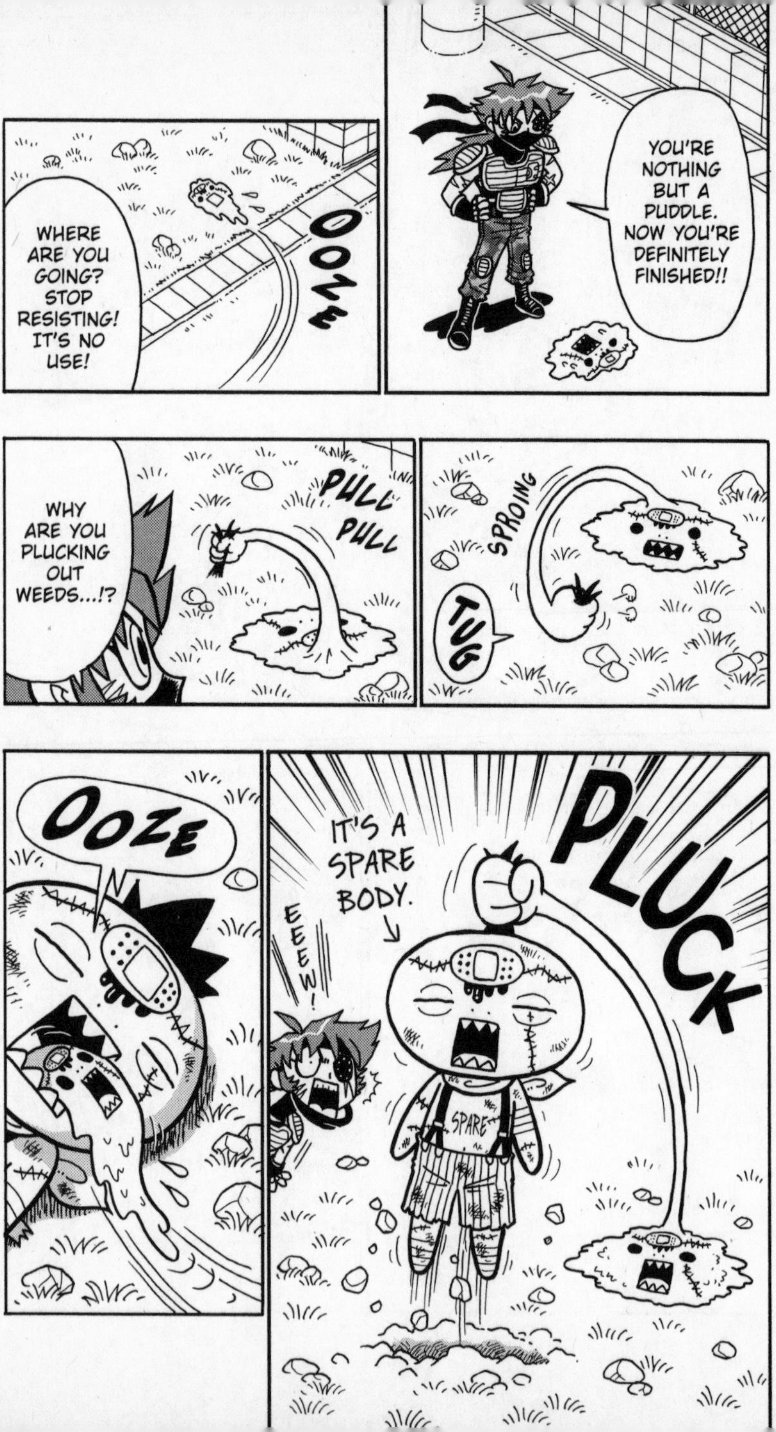
YOU'RE NOTHING BUT A PUDDLE. NOW YOU'RE DEFINITELY FINISHED!!
OOZE
WHERE ARE YOU GOING? STOP RESISTING! IT'S NO USE!
SPROING
TUG
PULL
PULL
WHY ARE YOU PLUCKING OUT WEEDS...!?
PLUCK
IT'S A SPARE BODY.
EEEEW!
SPARE
OOZE

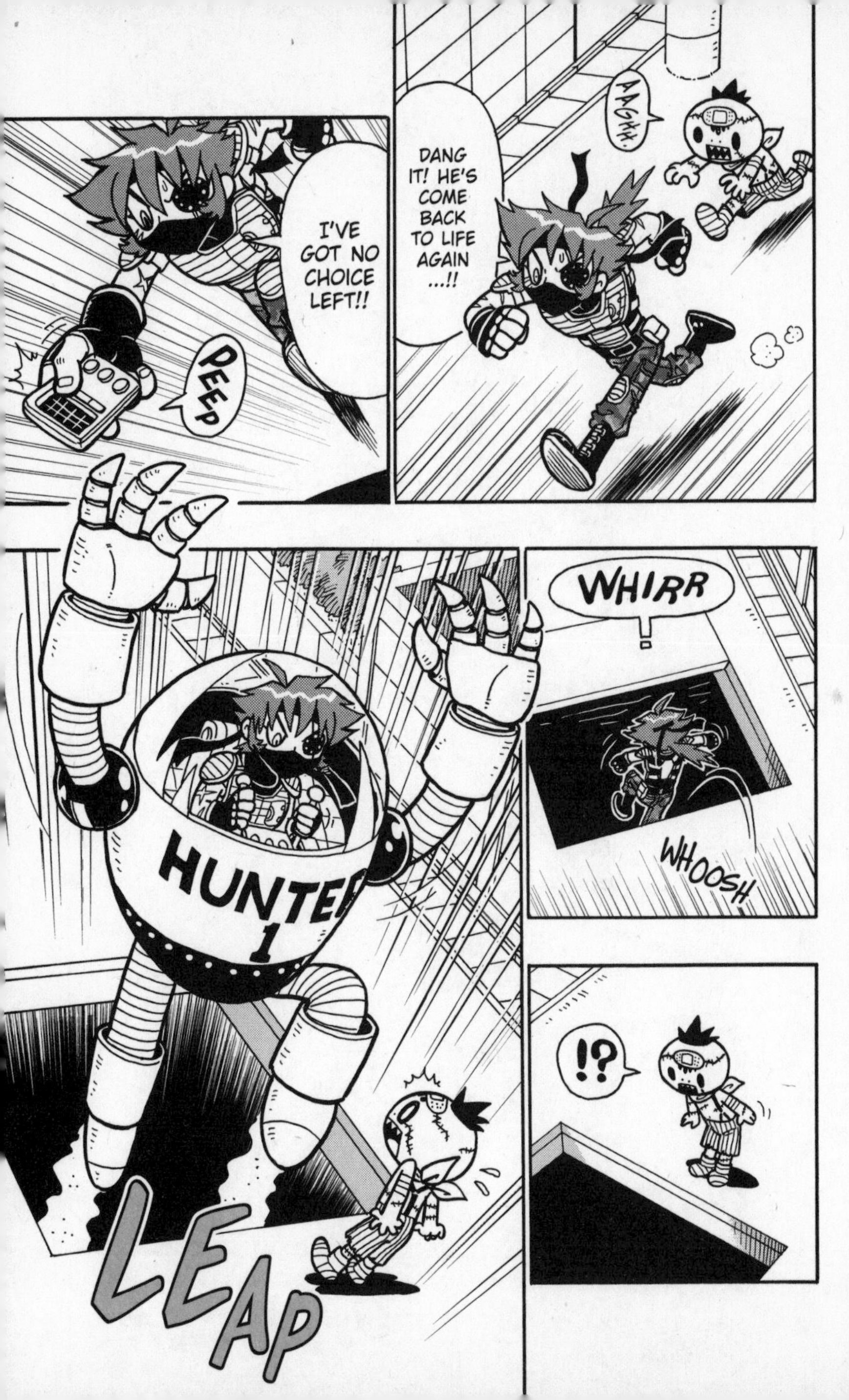
AAGHH
DANG IT! HE'S COME BACK TO LIFE AGAIN ...!!
I'VE GOT NO CHOICE LEFT!!
PEEP
WHIRR
WHOOSH
!?
HUNTER 1
LEAP

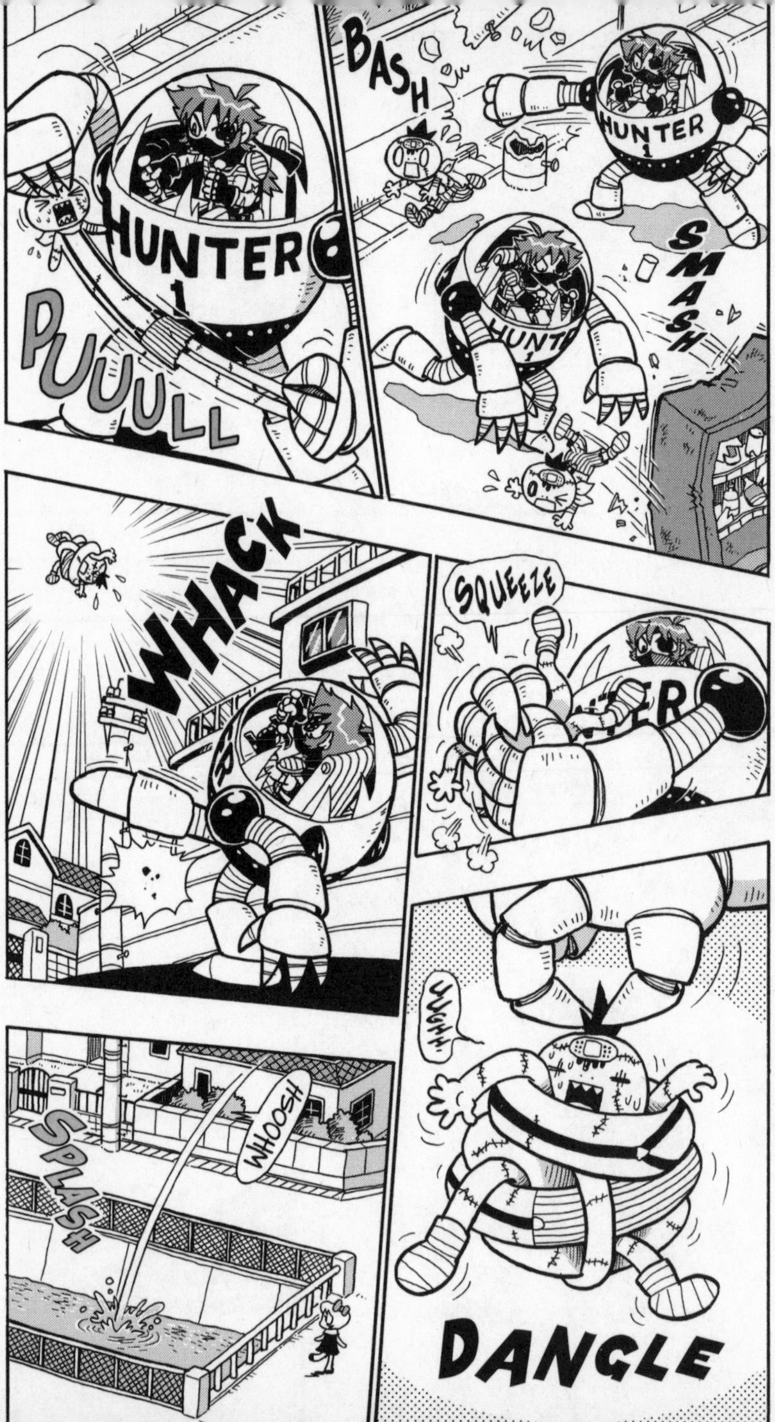
BASH
SMASH
PUUUULL
SQUEEZE
WHACK
UUGHH.
DANGLE
WHOOSH
SPLASH

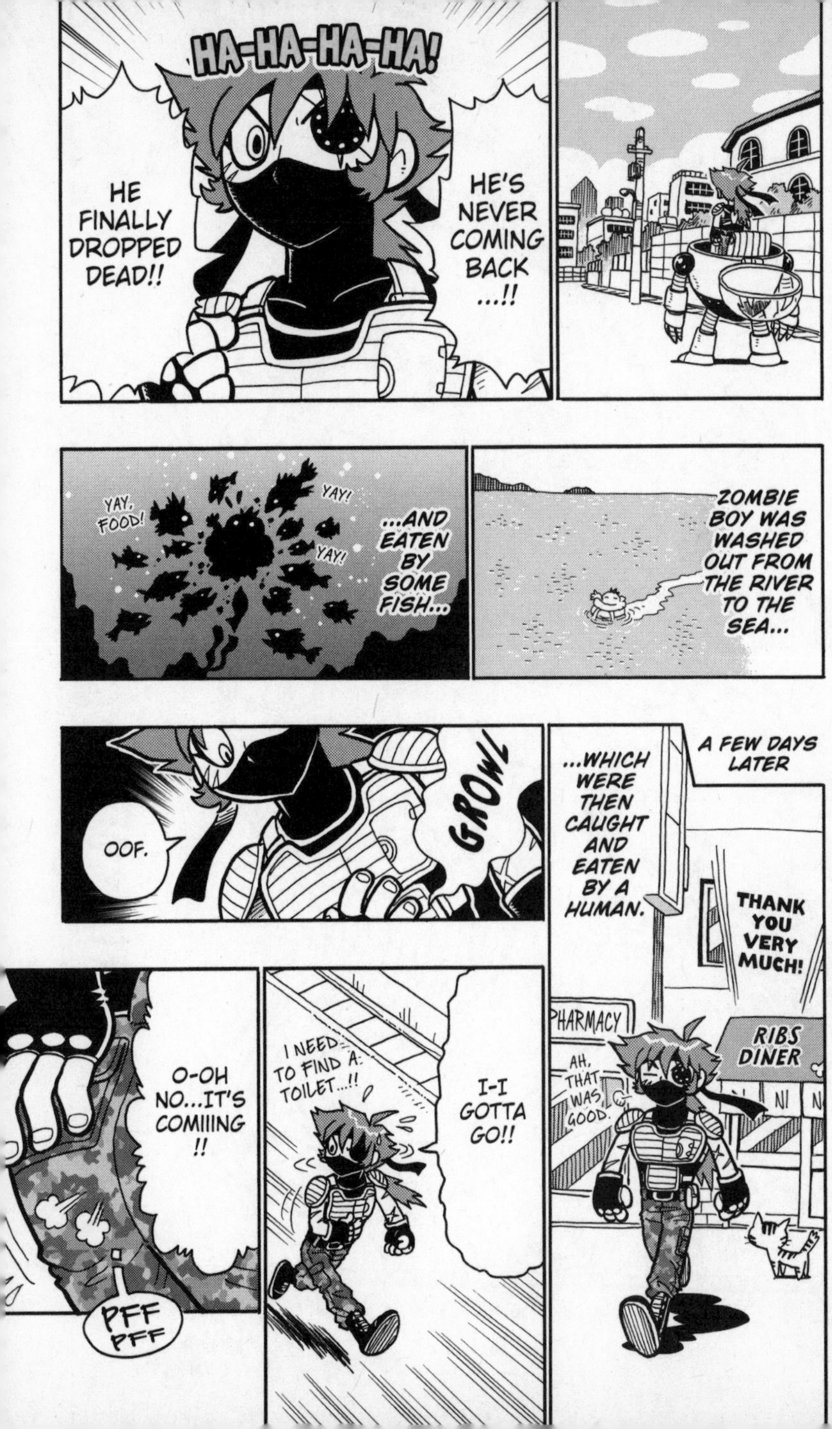
HA-HA-HA-HA!
HE'S NEVER COMING BACK ...!!
HE FINALLY DROPPED DEAD!!
ZOMBIE BOY WAS WASHED OUT FROM THE RIVER TO THE SEA...
...AND EATEN BY SOME FISH...
YAY!
YAY!
YAY, FOOD!
A FEW DAYS LATER
...WHICH WERE THEN CAUGHT AND EATEN BY A HUMAN.
THANK YOU VERY MUCH!
RIBS DINER
PHARMACY
AH, THAT WAS GOOD.
GROWL
OOF.
I-I GOTTA GO!!
I NEED TO FIND A TOILET...!!
O-OH NO...IT'S COMIIING!!
PFF PFF

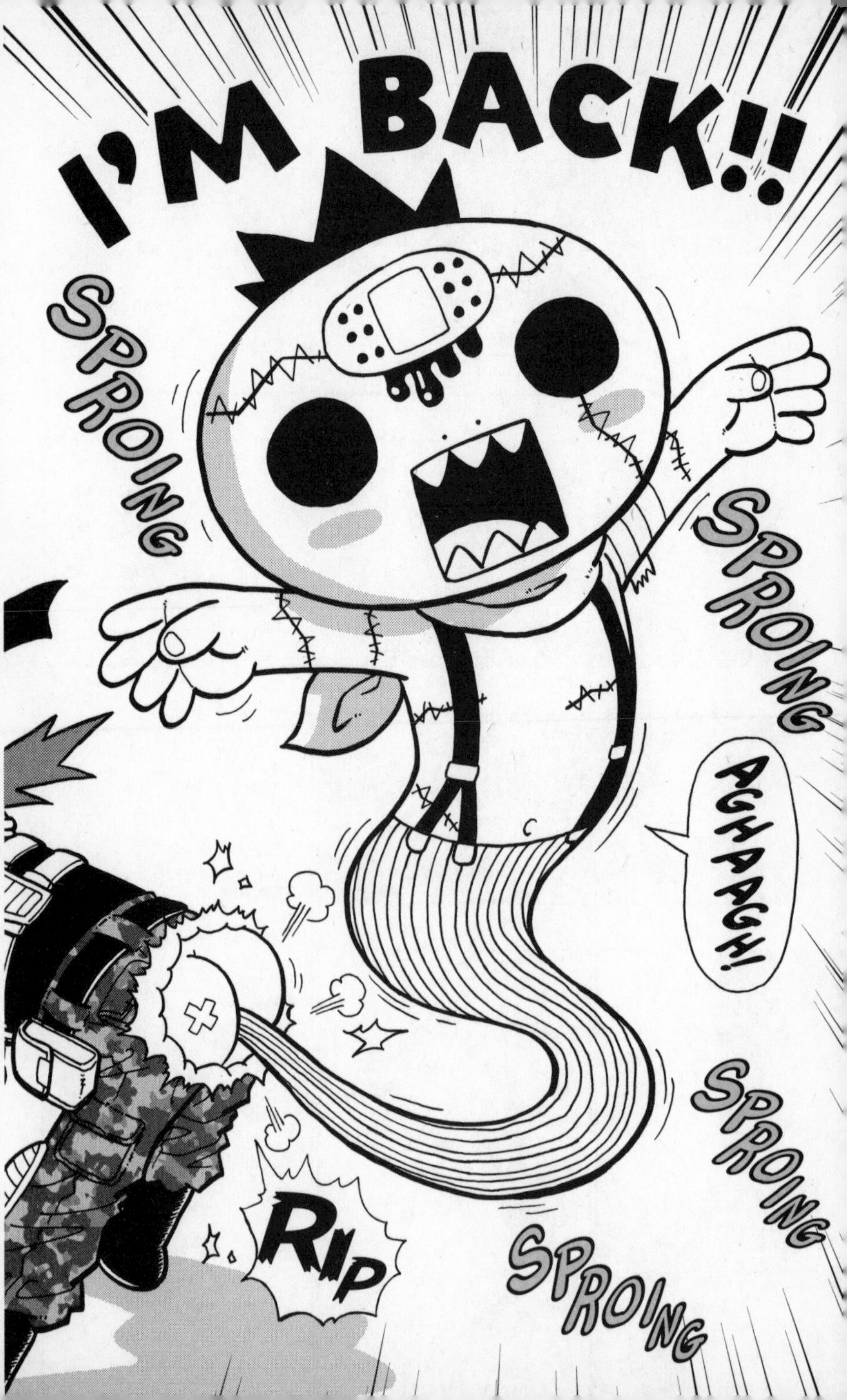
I'M BACK!!
SPROING
SPROING
AGHAAAGH!
SPROING
SPROING
RIP

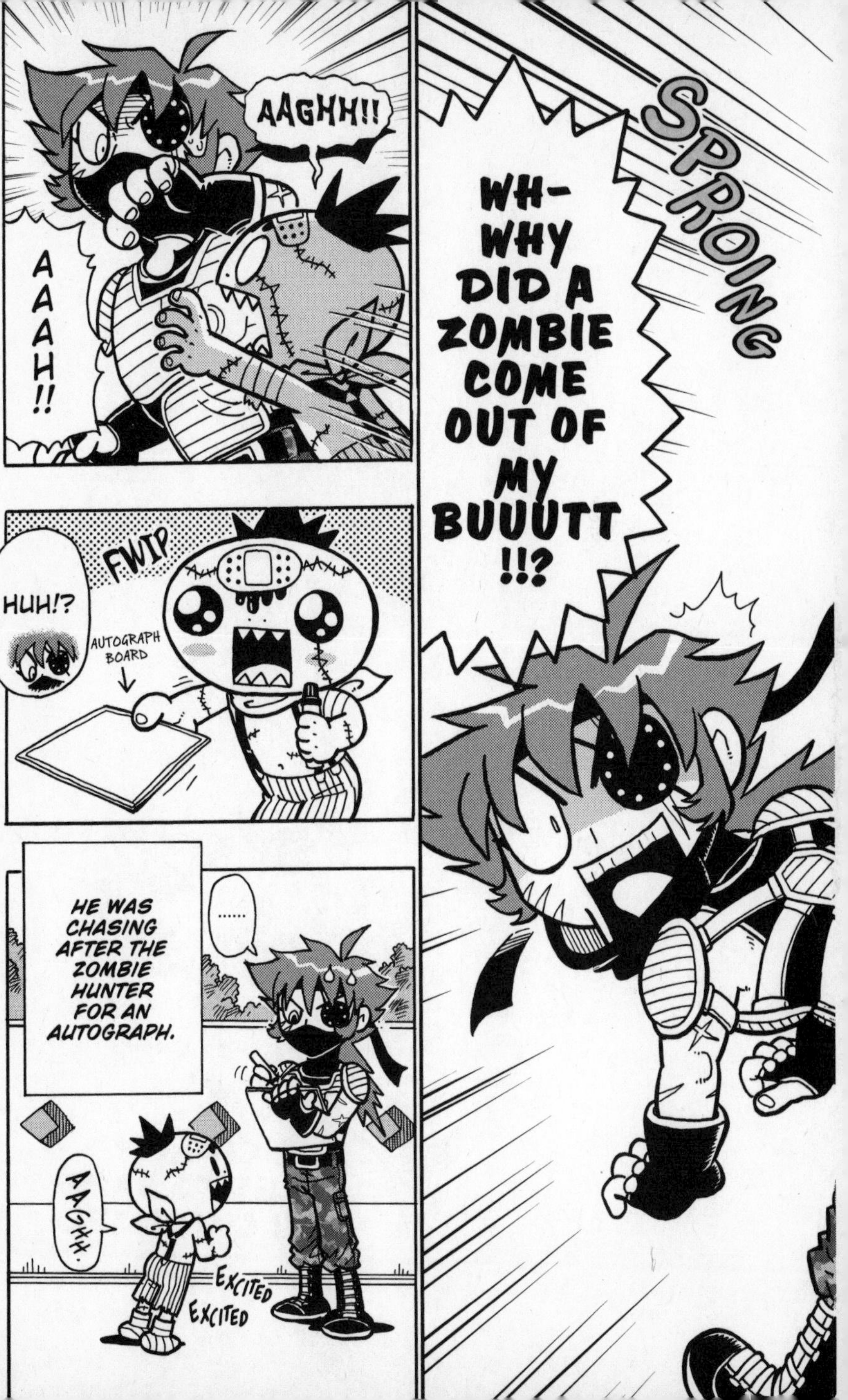
SPROING
WH-WHY DID A ZOMBIE COME OUT OF MY BUUUTT!!?
AAGHH!!
AAAAH!!
FWIP
HUH!?
AUTOGRAPH BOARD
......
HE WAS CHASING AFTER THE ZOMBIE HUNTER FOR AN AUTOGRAPH.
AAGHH.
EXCITED
EXCITED

A SHORT-
SLEEVED SKIN
FOR SUMMER.

Extra FOUR-PANEL ZOMBIE BOY

AAGHH.

ZOMBIE BOY

RAMEN
SLURP SLURP
SLURP SLURP
SLURP SLURP
SLURP SLURP
BUUURP
NOODLES
SPROING SPROING
SPROING SPROING

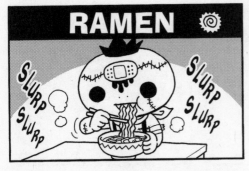

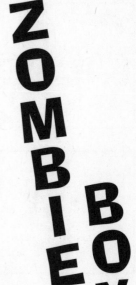

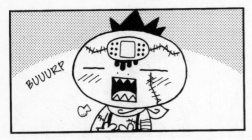

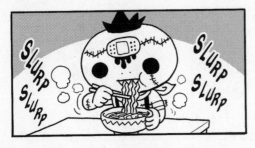

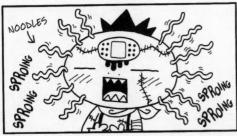

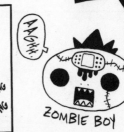

HATS
SQUEAK
SQUEAK
SQUEAK
SQUEAK
SLAP
TUG
AAGHH.
HE STRETCHED OUT HIS SKIN INTO A BRIM.

THUMBTACKS
PRICK
SHAKE
SHAKE
PLOP
THUMBTACK FAIRY
BOW
DASH

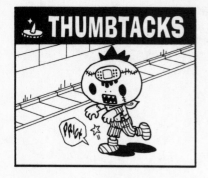

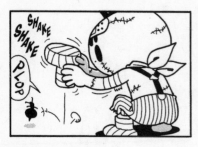

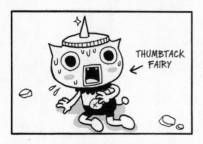

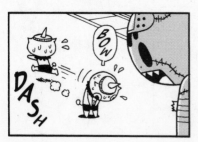

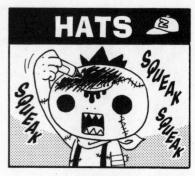

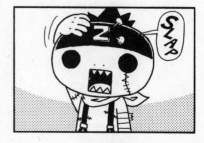

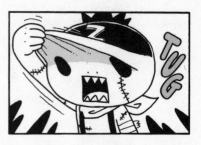

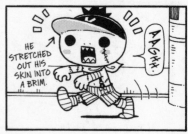

HAIRCUTS

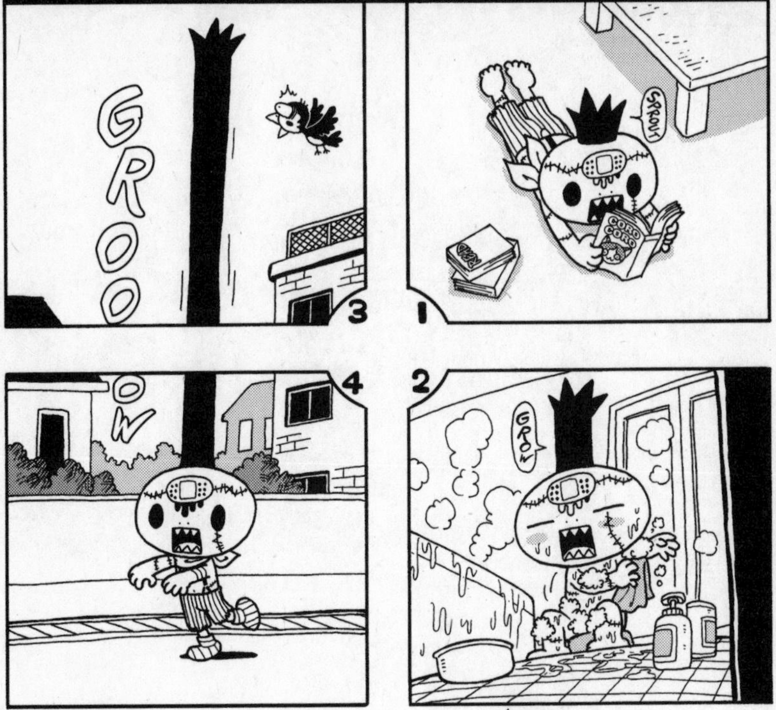
SPROUT
CORO CORO
GROW
GROO
OW

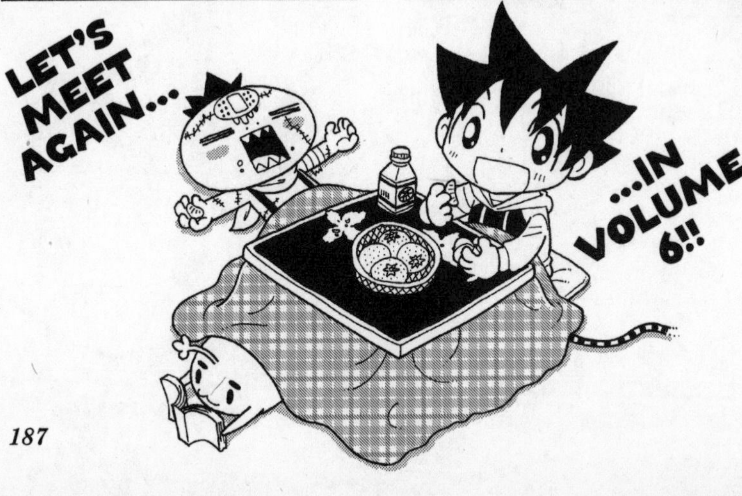
LET'S MEET AGAIN...
...IN VOLUME 6!!

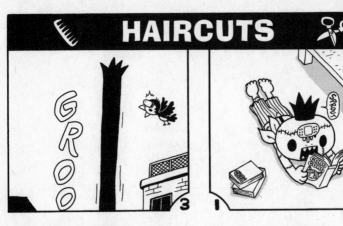

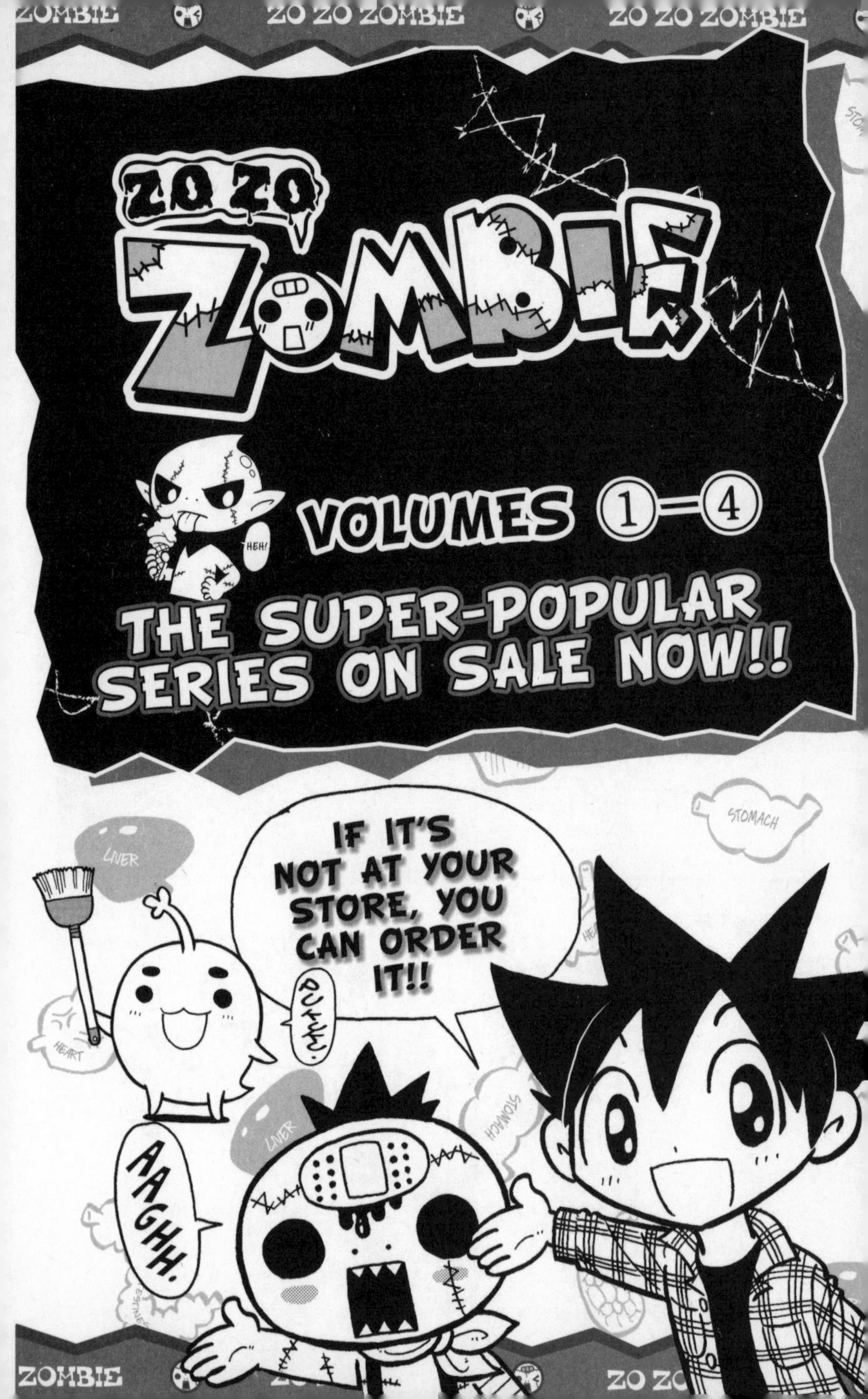
ZO ZO ZOMBIE
ZO ZO ZOMBIE
VOLUMES 1–4
HEH!
THE SUPER-POPULAR SERIES ON SALE NOW!!
STOMACH
LIVER
IF IT'S NOT AT YOUR STORE, YOU CAN ORDER IT!!
HEART
LIVER
STOMACH
AAGHH.

COMICS by MR. NAGATOSHI

VOLUME 1

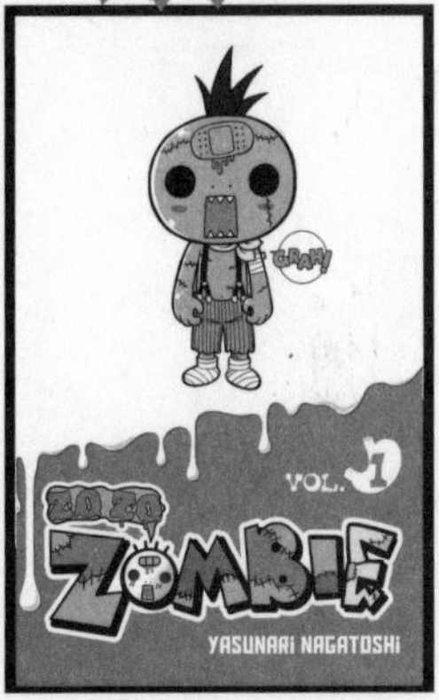
VOL. 1
ZO ZO ZOMBIE
YASUNARI NAGATOSHI

THE FIRST OF ITS KIND! CHECK OUT THE BIRTH OF A SERIES THAT STARS NONE OTHER THAN A ZOMBIE!! THIS UNDYING, ENDEARING LITTLE MONSTER IS STARTING A ZOMBIE BOOM IN JAPAN IN THIS FUN, CUTE GAG COMIC...!!

VOLUME 2

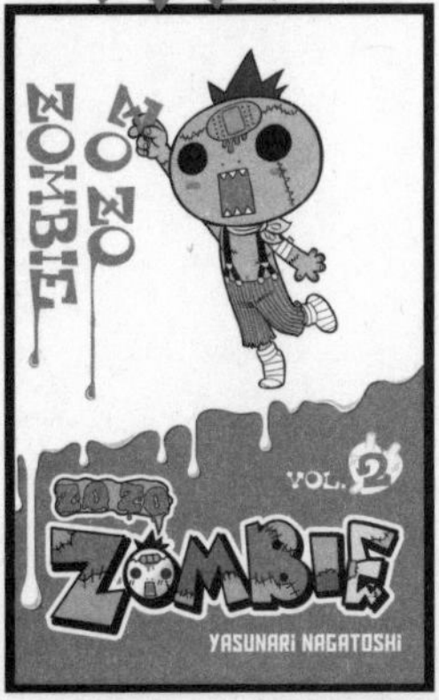
ZO ZO ZOMBIE
VOL. 2
ZO ZO ZOMBIE
YASUNARI NAGATOSHI

HE'S KIND OF GROSS BUT ALSO KIND OF CUTE! THE MORE YOU READ, THE MORE YOU'LL LOVE THIS VOLUME! IT'S FILLED WITH A BUNCH OF EXTRA COMIC STRIPS AND SPECIAL DESIGNS!!

VOLUME 3

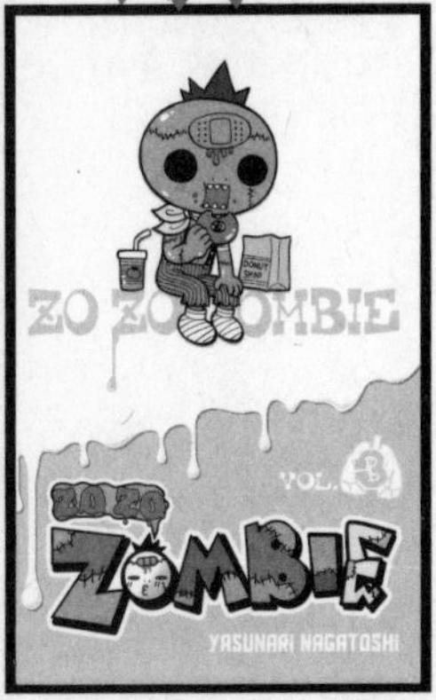
ZO ZO ZOMBIE
VOL. 3
ZO ZO ZOMBIE
YASUNARI NAGATOSHI

ZOMBIE BOY'S LIFE GETS A LITTLE MORE EXCITING WHEN HE MEETS A NEW FRIEND, THE MYSTERIOUS MOCHI!! YOU WON'T BE ABLE TO PUT DOWN THIS THIRD VOLUME, NOW OUT IN PEAK ZOMBIE FORM...!!

VOLUME 4

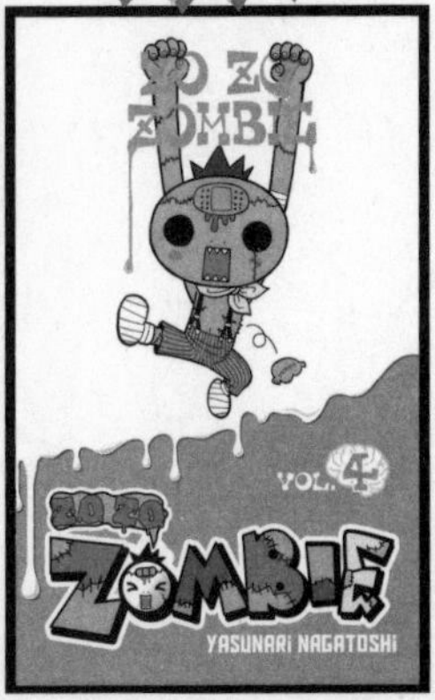
ZO ZO ZOMBIE
VOL. 4
ZO ZO ZOMBIE
YASUNARI NAGATOSHI

GET READY FOR THE DEBUT OF TONS OF NEW SPECIES OF TERRIFYING BUT SUPER-CUTE ZOMBIES!! DON'T MISS THE LAUGHS, THE BATTLES, AND THE DEVELOPMENTS IN ZOMBIE BOY'S LOVE LIFE!!

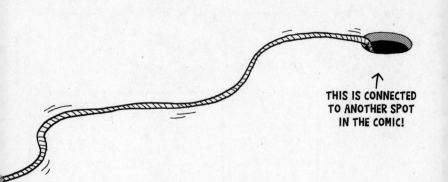

THIS IS CONNECTED
TO ANOTHER SPOT
IN THE COMIC!

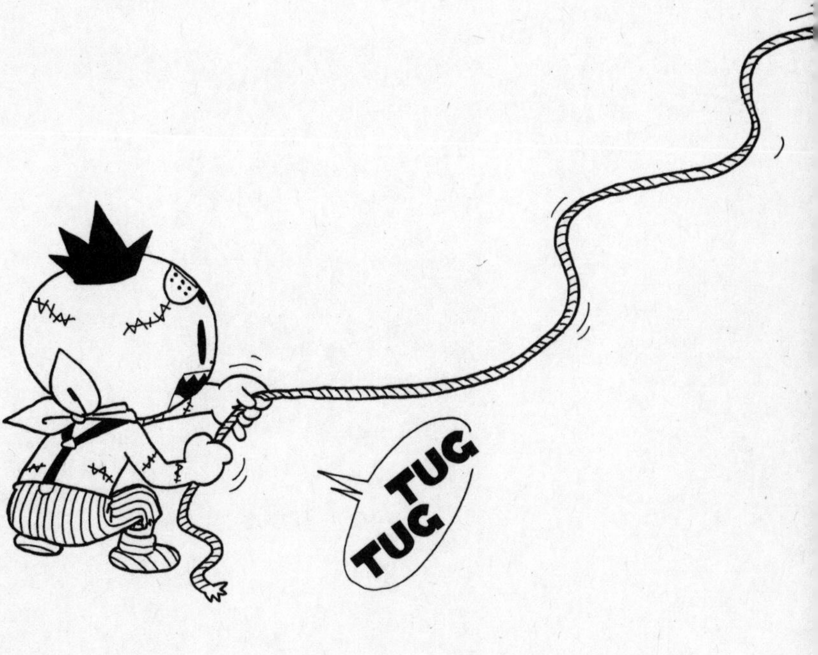
TUG TUG

Keep up with all their adventures in this award-winning series!

Have you met the kids from Berrybrook Middle School yet?

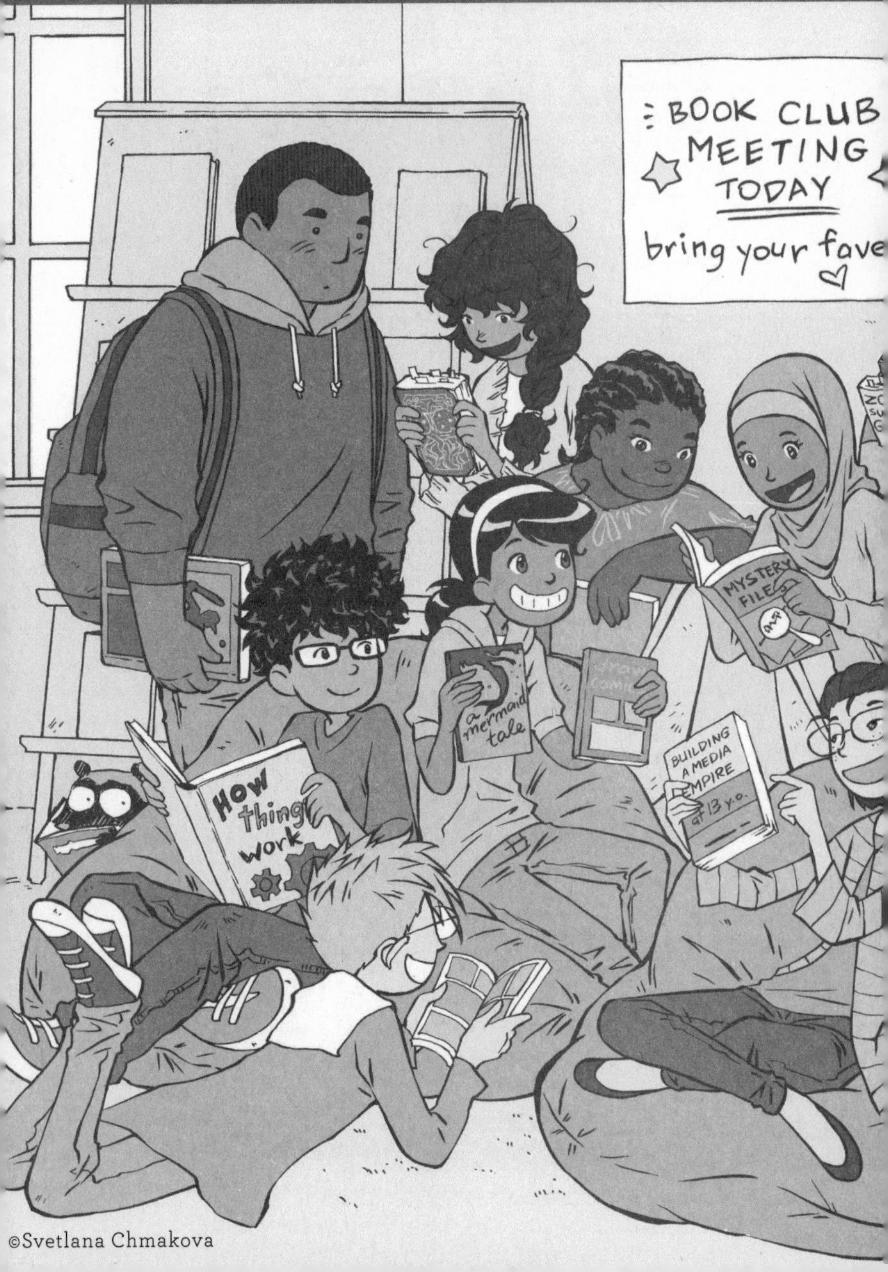
BOOK CLUB
MEETING
TODAY
bring your fave
HOW thing work
a mermaid tale
MYSTERY FILES
BUILDING A MEDIA EMPIRE at 13 y.o.

ZO ZO

ZOMBIE 5

YASUNARI NAGATOSHI

Translation: ALEXANDRA MCCULLOUGH-GARCIA ♣ Lettering: BIANCA PISTILLO

ZOZOZO ZOMBIE-KUN Vol. 5
by Yasunari NAGATOSHI
© 2013 Yasunari NAGATOSHI
All rights reserved.
Original Japanese edition published by SHOGAKUKAN.
English translation rights in the United States of America, Canada, the United
Kingdom, Ireland, Australia and New Zealand arranged with SHOGAKUKAN
through Tuttle-Mori Agency, Inc.

English translation © 2019 by Yen Press, LLC

JY
150 West 30th Street, 19th Floor
New York, NY 10001

Visit us at jyforkids.com ♣ facebook.com/jyforkids
twitter.com/jyforkids ♣ jyforkids.tumblr.com ♣ instagram.com/jyforkids

First JY Edition: November 2019

JY is an imprint of Yen Press, LLC.
The JY name and logo are trademarks of Yen Press, LLC.

Library of Congress Control Number: 2018948323

ISBNs: 978-1-9753-5345-2 (paperback)
978-1-9753-8630-6 (ebook)

10 9 8 7 6 5 4 3 2 1

WOR

Printed in the United States of America